Charlotte Sapori has led a wonderful life, safely tucked in the bosom of her family. Her mother, Irene Adler, is a renowned opera singer, while her father, Lucca Sapori, does important government work that frequently takes him away from them. Charlotte is close to her older brother, Nicco, and they are both doted on by their parents. All is well until her mother receives an unexpected diagnosis which shakes the family to its core.

Knowing herself to be dying, Adler confesses to Charlotte things that have long been kept from her, telling her to find and read her diary. A distressed Lucca Sapori tells his daughter to read his as well. And by the way, Lucca Sapori is not his real name. In fact, she may have heard of him—he is actually the world-famous detective, Sherlock Holmes.

Charlotte finds both diaries and plunges into the hidden world of Irene Adler and Sherlock Holmes as she discovers what brought them together, and how they managed to stay together for thirty years despite having to battle the odds.

Song For Someone

ISBN: 978-1-4874-3688-9
Cover art by Angela Waters

Published by eXtasy Books Inc

Extasy BOOKS

Look for us online at:
www.eXtasybooks.com

To Nicola

Song For Someone Sherlock Holmes and Irene Adler Mysteries 1

By

KD Sherrinford

Lovely to meet you at the [illegible]

Best wishes

K.D. [illegible] X

15/7/2023

Dedication

For my late sister Susan Holman

Acknowledgements

This book is a result of a conversation that started between my daughter Katie Leahy and myself in November 2019, after a visit to the Sherlock Holmes Museum in London.

Song for Someone, has been inspired by the works of Sir Arthur Conan Doyle, featuring characters and ideas recognisable from his original stories.

The novel took an incredible amount of time and effort. This story would not exist without the invaluable contributions of several people.

First, I would like to thank Abigale McIntosh, who read so many versions of this story with immense thoughtfulness, insight, and generosity. I am grateful for her suggestion that I write a Scandal in Bohemia from Irene Adler's POV.

My amazing graces Jayne Leahy and Gayna Dagnell for believing in me, and for the staggering amount of help, encouragement, and support, that went above and beyond the call of friendship.

My husband John, who read all my early drafts, and kept me supplied with endless cups of coffee.

My friends and family, including my son David Leahy, my sister Lesley Williams, and my niece Caroline Holman, for not writing me off as barking mad—although the Jury is still out on that one.

My team of beta readers—Abigale McIntosh, Isabelle Felix, Judith Powell, Lauren Leach, and Melanie Kelly. Thank you for all your inspirational feedback.

My late father Denis O'Doherty, for igniting my passion for

writing.

My innovative English teacher—John James.

The amazing publishing team at Extasy Books. Special thanks to the ever-patient Editor in Chief (EIC) Jay Austin, and Martine Jardin for her fabulous artwork.

Finally, I would like to thank you, the readers. A massive thank you for picking up this book. I hope you enjoy the story.

Prologue: A Very Bohemian Scandal: Irene Adler

It's strange how two words can turn your world upside down.

I had no way of knowing that the witness to my wedding to the lawyer Godfrey Norton would come back to haunt me in years to come. My cousin Estelle once told me that the true love of one's life is the one who catches you unaware and changes you inexplicably.

I was in my late twenties when I moved to London in 1887, having spent the past few years performing as a contralto at La Scala in Milan, and then a term as prima donna with the Imperial Opera of Warsaw. And it was in Warsaw where I first met Wilhelm Gottsreich Sigismond von Ormstein, Grand Duke of Cassel-Feldstein, the hereditary king of Bohemia.

I suppose it all sounds rather grand, given his title, but Wilhelm was a kind, fun-loving man, and a huge fan of the opera. A big man, in every sense of the word, he was a tall, imposing figure—well-built with broad shoulders and a muscular frame, black hair, sparkling brown eyes, and a handlebar moustache. He would often make a grand entrance with his entourage, insisting the cast join him for drinks afterwards. They all adored him, of course. He was thoughtful and generous. So I thought little of it when a bouquet of flowers appeared in my dressing room every night.

A few months after meeting Wilhelm, I was invited and accepted into the elitist fold of La Scala's theatre chorus. My dream had always been to train at the prestigious Opera House. Wilhelm took the news badly. He told me he'd developed feelings for me, and while I had grown very fond of him, I knew I had to follow my dreams. Looking back, enrolling at La Scala was one of the happiest moments of my life. But then I gave it up for the position of prima donna at the Grand Opera House in Warsaw, which was the worst decision of my life.

A few weeks after my arrival in Warsaw, a letter from Wilhelm revealed he had returned to the city upon learning of my new appointment and asked if he could take me to luncheon. I accepted the invitation. In truth I was looking forward to seeing Wilhelm again. I missed his infectious humour and I hoped we could remain friends. We spent a lovely morning together and laughed watching the waiters scurry around, eager to please him. His disposition and exuberant personality were so endearing, always the life and soul of the party. I was always aware he held a torch for me, but I was taken aback when he declared his undying love and his intention to make me his wife. I was speechless, swept away by the excitement of it all until I came to my senses.

"No." I shook my head. "This can't be. Your parents would never allow it."

Wilhelm became animated, insisting he would be king one day and could choose his own bride. Although I was young and naïve, I knew the matter was not that simple. Wilhelm claimed he would speak to his parents, confident they would listen to reason. He pleaded with me to be patient

More than four weeks passed before I received a letter informing me of his failed attempts to win over his parents. His father was so enraged at the absurd prospect that he ordered Wilhelm to propose to Clotide Lothman von Saxe-Meiningen, the second daughter to the king of Scandinavia. There was no apology. Wilhelm even had the audacity to suggest I become his mistress and, to add insult to injury, demanded the return of a photograph he'd had taken of us.

Incensed at the disrespect I'd been shown, I decided to retire from the stage and move to London. They say hell hath no fury like a woman scorned. In an act of foolishness, which I later regretted, I told Wilhelm I intended to send the photograph to Clotide's family should the engagement be announced. This was admittedly scandalous behaviour, but I was young and I and had never experienced rejection. I still remember the feelings of anger, betrayal, and jealousy, as though I'd felt them only yesterday—they were all-consuming.

Wilhelm's response was to send his agents after me. Upon my arrival in London, I was searched at Charing Cross station before my house in St John's Wood was broken into. Wilhelm's pursuit of the photograph was relentless, although I was always one step ahead of him. Before I left Warsaw, I arranged with a friend to post the photograph, which was addressed to my agent in London, secreted in the sleeve of a book. I kept it in a secure hiding place, one I was certain Wilhelm's agents would never find.

It was around this time I went to see my old friend, Sarah Burton, who was performing as Desdemona in Shakespeare's Othello at the Theatre Royal on Drury Lane. After the performance, she invited me to join her and a few friends for dinner at Rules in Covent Garden. And that was where I was introduced to Godfrey Norton. He was a dashing man—tall, dark—and I was instantly taken with him. Godfrey was neither vain nor arrogant, an attentive listener with a talent for putting those around him at ease. I told him about Wilhelm and what had transpired, but that did little to dampen his ardour. On the contrary, Godfrey pursued me relentlessly over the coming weeks. He sent me flowers and frequently escorted me to the theatre and dinner. During the day we enjoyed long leisurely strolls through the park, at which times Godfrey spoke incessantly of his hopes and dreams, his plans for the future—plans which he said included me.

I was, of course, flattered by his attention, but I had no wish to give him any false hopes. I had naively convinced myself I was still in love with Wilhelm, until finally I realised I'd been possessed by a mere girlish infatuation. I didn't really know love at all. In fact, I doubted if it even existed. But Godfrey didn't care. He was certain that given enough time I would learn to love him. After my experience with Wilhelm, I felt vulnerable. It was comforting to have someone on my side, so I gladly accepted his proposal.

Godfrey arranged for a special licence so we could be married right away. Having obtained a licence that was only valid for a few days, Godfrey found a clergyman willing to carry out the ceremony at such short notice. This proved to be an extremely stressful period for both of us. Not only were we desperate to be married, but Godfrey was also attempting to obtain fake identities. We intended to flee London shortly after the wedding to be rid of Wilhelm and his agents for good. The thought of being constantly under surveillance was beginning to take its toll. I even considered returning the photo to Wilhelm, but Godfrey insisted we needed it as leverage in case Wilhelm had second thoughts and decided to come after us.

I still remember the day Godfrey suddenly burst into our drawing-room, pacing up and down like a caged animal, explaining the clergyman had sent him an urgent telegram stating he was unable to perform the wedding ceremony as planned. If we were to be married, it had to be at that hour or not at all.

"We need to get to the church by twelve noon!" Godfrey looked frantically at his watch. The time was now 11:30. "We must travel separately. Wait five minutes, no longer, then follow me!"

I arrived at the church to find Godfrey's cab at the front of the main entrance, the horse sweating profusely. I entered the church to find Godfrey and the clergyman in a heated altercation at the altar. The clergyman explained to Godfrey that he could not marry us without a witness as the marriage would not be legal. Godfrey ran his hand through his hair, a look of profound exasperation upon his face. Suddenly we were disturbed by a cough and noticed an elderly gentleman who had slipped into one of the aisles.

Without hesitation, Godfrey ran over to the man. "Thank God! You'll do, come!"

"What?" cried the man, a startled expression on his face.

"Come, man, come," Godfrey said exasperated. "Or it won't be legal."

Godfrey dragged the poor man towards the altar, where he pledged things he could never have been privy to, but nevertheless, the man proved indispensable in our betrothal. After the ceremony, Godfrey and I thanked the gentleman, and I slipped a sovereign into his hand.

At the church door, Godfrey and I embraced before going our separate ways. Godfrey set off to the Temple, while I returned home. Dusk had already fallen by the time the landau pulled up outside the house. A group of men stood under the streetlamp. They rushed forward to open the door, no doubt in the hope of earning a tip, but one man was pushed roughly aside by another.

A fierce altercation broke out, one which was further agitated by two guardsmen who took sides with the first man. I jumped out of the cab in a desperate attempt to defuse the situation. Finding myself surrounded by a group of angry-looking men, I suddenly felt afraid for my safety, my heart beating nineteen to the dozen. Then out of the corner of my eye I noticed an elderly clergyman enter the throng, forcing his way through the crowd. He nodded and smiled at me reassuringly. But before he could reach me, the man cried out and fell to the ground, blood flowing freely from his face. At his fall, the guardsmen and the other boys panicked and fled the scene. Neighbours gathered around the stricken man. I ran up the steps, fumbling in my bag for the front door key, before turning back.

"Is the poor man hurt?" I asked.

"He's dead!" a voice cried out.

"No, there's life in him," shouted another. "But he'll be gone before you can get him to the hospital."

"He's a brave fellow," said another woman. "They would have had the lady's purse and watch if it hadn't been for him. Ah, he's breathing now."

"He can't lie in the street; may we bring him in, ma'am?" asked another voice.

"Of course, bring him into the sitting room," I said, leading them towards the hallway.

The men followed me through, gently laying the man on the sofa. I brought him a glass of water and a pillow. There was something about his eyes that seemed familiar. They stared at me with a brooding intensity. His index finger caught my hand as I handed him the glass of water, sending a quiver through my body. He sat up on the couch and motioned for me to open the window. I asked Tilly, my housemaid, to do so. The next thing I knew, I heard a cry of fire as thick clouds of smoke engulfed the room, billowing in from the open window.

I ran into the hallway and opened the sliding panel that hid the photograph of Wilhelm and me. I had just laid my hands on it when came a cry of "False alarm!" I quickly returned the photography to its hiding place. Looking around the sitting room, I caught a glimpse of rushing figures, and it was at that moment I realised I had not only been tricked by the celebrated consulting detective Sherlock Holmes, but I had also foolishly given away the hiding place of the picture that Wilhelm was so desperate to possess. I had been warned by friends that if Wilhelm employed an agent he would choose the best, and that man would undoubtedly be Sherlock Holmes, whose address had been given to me.

I went back to the sitting room to find the clergyman had disappeared. I quickly changed into the disguise of a slim youth. My coachman John dropped me off at Baker Street, and it was there I saw Holmes standing under a streetlamp, fumbling in his pocket for his keys, and I caught a final glimpse of those mesmerising grey eyes I had already seen twice that day, albeit in disguise, and at that moment my heart stopped in my chest.

"Goodnight, Mr Holmes," I said, before mingling with the throng of people on the pavement, intending to walk off into the night. But, before I left, I heard Holmes call out to Doctor Watson.

"I've heard that voice before," said Holmes. "Now I wonder who the deuce that could have been."

I smiled to myself as I realised that Irene Adler had got one over on the celebrated detective, and I instinctively knew he would not like that one bit.

Making my way to the Temple, I explained to my shocked husband all that had transpired. We returned to Briony Lodge, quickly packed my clothes and a few personal possessions, including the photo of Wilhelm and me. We knew it was only a matter of time before Holmes would return, possibly with a search warrant and the Metropolitan police. Godfrey had secured our passage to the continent—we would leave from Charing Cross the following afternoon. Dinner that evening was a sombre affair. We stayed with Sarah, who could see I was worried. I felt sick with apprehension. I told her I would not feel safe until Godfrey and I boarded the train at Charing Cross.

"When do you think Holmes will return to the villa?" asked Sarah.

"At first light, I would expect. He will do doubt want to catch me unawares. Why do you ask?"

"Please allow me to help you." She stared at me imploringly.

"Whatever do you mean?"

"Suppose I was to pose as your maid." Sarah laughed at my perplexed expression. "I shall sleep at the villa this evening and be ready for Holmes in full disguise from dawn onwards. What's wrong?" She chuckled. "Don't you think I can pull it off?"

"I don't doubt it for one second. You are one of the finest character actresses of your generation." I shook my head. "But that would be far too risky."

Sarah waved her hand dismissively. "Don't be silly. Consider it a wedding gift." She laid her hand on my arm. "I know you have concerns, but don't you see this way you will have closure? With my photographic memory, well versed in remembering lines, I will be able to narrate to you word for word all that transpires."

"All right, but only if you're sure. I can't begin to thank you for all you've done for Godfrey and me."

"Nonsense." Sarah took my hand in hers. "Do you know I am rather looking forward to meeting the celebrated detective?"

"Rather you than me." I shuddered.

"And what will you call yourself?" Godfrey quizzed.

"Hmm, how about Miss Catherine O'Neill, a colleen from Belfast?" said Sarah in a thick Irish accent.

"Sounds perfect to me." Godfrey laughed.

After breakfast the following morning, Godfrey set off for the last time to the Temple. Before he left, he arranged for our luggage to be collected later that afternoon. All I needed to do was turn up at Charing Cross to meet my husband. I waited impatiently for Sarah to return. In truth, I was far more concerned about the sequence of events that would have taken place at Serpentine Avenue than our escape to the Continent. So, you can imagine my relief when I heard the sound of a carriage pull up outside the front door at 11 o'clock and saw my friend's smiling face beaming at me as she jumped down from the landau and ran up the front steps towards me.

I threw my arms around my friend, hugging her tightly. "Thank God you're back! I have been so worried. Do you think Holmes suspected anything?"

Sarah shook her head. "I'm sorry I'm late. I wanted to make sure I wasn't being followed. And to answer your question, Nene, no, I doubt he suspected a thing. He wasn't the least bit interested in me." Sarah insisted on pouring us a cup of fresh coffee before she continued to update me on the events of the morning. "I need to concentrate. I have no wish to fluff my lines." She laughed.

Sarah told me she'd been scrubbing the front steps when a carriage pulled up outside Briony Lodge at approximately 8:30. "Well, you know how I am such a stickler for detail." Sarah chuckled, continuing her narrative with a theatrical flair. "Holmes, Watson, and Wilhelm Ormstein all jumped out of the brougham and were duly greeted with a sardonic smile by yours truly.

"Top of the morning to you gentlemen," I said, staring straight at the celebrated detective. "Mr Sherlock Holmes, I believe?"

"I am Mr Holmes," he replied, although rather ungraciously. He looked at me with a rather puzzled and questioning gaze.

"Indeed," I said. "My mistress told me you were likely to call. She left earlier this morning with her husband by the five-fifteen train from Charing Cross, headed for the Continent." Well, you could have knocked Holmes down with a feather. His face was white as putty, as if he'd seen a ghost.

"Do you mean that she has left England?" He stared at me in amazement

"Never to return," I said.

And then Wilhelm Ormstein chipped in, with his strongly marked German accent. God, he was an imposing sight. He must be six feet four in his stockinged feet. "And the papers?" Ormstein quizzed. "Then all is lost!"

"We shall see," said Holmes before rudely barging past me and rushing into the drawing-room, quickly followed by Ormstein, Doctor Watson, and yours truly. The men were shocked to discover the room in disarray, furniture scattered in every direction as if it had been hurriedly ransacked, which of course it had. It was like a scene from a French farce. Holmes rushed to the bell pull, tore back the small sliding shutter. Pulled out a photograph and the letter you had addressed to him, Nene. He was mortified to discover the photograph was not of you and Wilhelm Ormstein, but instead the one you had replaced it with—Irene Alder in full evening dress at La Scala. My god, how I wished I had a camera. The look on his face was priceless, one of utter amazement. I don't know how I managed to keep my composure. Holmes tore open the envelope and, much to my amusement, all three men read the letter together, with the same look of astonishment on their faces.

The letter read in this way:

My dear Mr Sherlock Holmes You really did it very well. You took me in completely. Until after the alarm of fire, I had no suspicion. But then I found out how I betrayed myself and I began to think. I had been warned against you months ago. I had been told that if the King employed an agent, it would certainly be you, and your address had been given to me. Yet with all this, you made me reveal what you wanted to know. Even after becoming suspicious, I found it hard to think evil of such a dear, kind old clergyman. But you know, I had been trained as an actress myself. Male costumes are nothing new to me. I often take advantage of the freedom they give. I sent John the coachman to watch you, ran upstairs, got into my walking clothes as I call them, and came down just as you departed. Well, I followed you to your door and made sure that I was really an object of interest to the celebrated Mr Sherlock Holmes. I rather imprudently wished you a good night, then I went to see my husband at the Temple. We both thought the best resource was flight when pursued by so formidable an opponent. So you will find the nest empty when you call tomorrow. As to the photograph, your client may rest in peace. I love and am loved by a better man than he. The King may do what he will without hindrance from one whom he has cruelly wronged. I keep it only to safeguard myself and preserve a weapon that will always secure me from any steps he might take in the future. I leave a photograph which he might care to possess, and I remain my dear Mr Sherlock Holmes, very truly yours, Irene Norton nee Adler.

"What, oh, what a woman!" cried Ormstein after all three had read your letter. "Did I not tell you how quick and resolute she was? Would she not have made an admirable Queen? Is it not a pity that she was not on my level?" Wilhelm addressed Holmes with a searching gaze.

"From what I have seen of the young lady, she seems indeed to be on a very different level to your Majesty," said Holmes dryly, fixing Ormstein with a cold stare. "I am sorry that I have not been able to bring your Majesty's business to a more successful conclusion."

"On the contrary, my dear sir," cried Ormstein, grinning like a Cheshire cat. "Nothing could be more successful. I know that her word is inviolate. The photograph is now as safe as if it had been thrown into the fire!"

"I am glad to hear your Majesty say so."

"I am immensely indebted to you. Pray tell me in what way I can reward you. This ring?" He slipped an emerald snake ring from his finger, holding it out towards the celebrated detective in his open palm.

Holmes shook his head. "Your Majesty has something that I should value even more highly."

"You have but to name it," said Ormstein.

"This photograph."

We all stared at him in amazement.

"Irene's photograph?" cried Ormstein. "Certainly, if you wish it."

"I thank your Majesty," said Holmes. "Then there is no more to be done in the matter. I have the honour to wish you a very good morning." Holmes bowed, picked up the photograph and letter before abruptly turning away, completely ignoring the hand that Ormstein held out to him. And then Holmes and Doctor Watson left the building as quickly as they came in, without as much as a by-your-leave for little old me, oh well. No one takes much notice of a domestic servant, and that's the shame of it.'"

I stared at Sarah incredulously. "I am so glad you were there, Sarah. I don't think I would believe one word of that story if it had been narrated by anyone else. But why would Holmes ask for my photograph in return for Wilhelm's ring? If Sherlock Holmes wanted my photography, he needed only to request a copy from La Scala. That would cost him a few pounds at most. It doesn't make any sense. Holmes has never struck me as the sentimental type."

"Who knows what's in a man's heart?" Sarah shrugged. "I gave up on men long ago. But I think you're missing the point, my dear. He clearly wanted the photograph you had chosen, the one you laid your hands on."

"Well, I guess we will never know, as it is unlikely I will ever see him again." I sighed.

Some months later a friend of mine told me that Holmes used to make merry regarding the cleverness of women, but Watson said he had not heard him do so since our encounter. And when Holmes spoke of me or referred to my photograph, which held pride of place on his mantlepiece at Baker Street, it was always without exception under the honourable title of *The Woman*, which was probably the finest compliment of my life.

Another seven years would pass before our paths would cross again and I came to realise how strongly his presence would feature in my life. Our next encounter would be the start of an intense and profoundly meaningful relationship that would endure for over thirty years.

CHAPTER ONE: CHARLOTTE SAPORI

Some people, like my mother, believe in fate, while others, like my father, adopt respectful scepticism. However, I am confident the following events would not have taken place if it wasn't for the murder of Godfrey Jones, my mother's first husband.

My mother, the acclaimed contralto, Irene Adler, known as Nene to those closest to her, was the most beautiful woman I ever knew. My brother Nicco and I attribute our success in life to the moral altruism and academic education we received from Nene and our beloved father, Lucca Sapori.

My brother and I were cared for by our Aunt Estelle whenever our parents were away. We adored Estelle. She treated us like her own children, especially Nicco. She had a real soft spot for him—who wouldn't? He was a striking boy—tall, slim, with blazing blue eyes, and darkly handsome. We were all thrilled when he won a scholarship to Harvard Medical School in Boston, Massachusetts, graduating as a paediatric surgeon with the highest honours. My mother wept tears of joy throughout the graduation ceremony, much to the embarrassment of my father and me. We should have expected it. My mother could get sentimental over burnt toast.

Nicco had accepted a position at the Children's Hospital Boston, working under the inaugural Chief of Surgery, Dr Harvey Cushing. Our parents were, of course, delighted, as was I. We were all incredibly proud of Nicco and his many accomplishments. My brother showed an avid interest in music and philosophy in his early years. He now had a glittering career ahead of him. Helping other people, especially children, had been his primary vocation in life from an early age.

Born in the UK to an English mother and an Anglo-Italian father, our father fostered our love of Britain and many happy childhood memories. The country is such a beautiful place—one that will always hold a special place in our hearts, from the architecture to the beautiful landscapes and countryside.

In addition to our main family home, Red Oaks, a sprawling colonial townhouse in Trenton, New Jersey, our parents owned a ten-acre farm on the beautiful Sussex Downs. My mother, brother, and I would make the 6-day transatlantic crossing from New York to Liverpool on The Majestic during the holidays. We regularly visited Ash Tree Farm, which was our favourite place because my brother and I were allowed so much freedom. We would run down to Arundel every morning and swim with the tide in the Arun River. Mother called it "Down the shore." Well, she was from New Jersey. We rode our ponies in the afternoons and had picnics by the river, sometimes with our father when he was at home. He would sometimes take us down to the Three Tunnes Inn for an early supper. Those were such beautiful memories.

Father was routinely away for weeks, sometimes months, at a time. He travelled extensively, working for the British government. A position he rarely spoke of to anyone. Consequently, there was always an air of mystery and speculation regarding his profession for my brother and me. Nicco was adamant Father was a spy. I wasn't as convinced. My father showed no interest in politics, although he was certainly clever enough. His knowledge of the law and sciences was phenomenal. So, my brother and I became adept at standing beneath the stairwell, listening to the clandestine conversations behind the closed doors of our parents' chambers, which was thrilling, yet terrifying at the same time. But, of course, father was far too clever for us. He soon realised what we were up to, so we received a stern dressing down and a look that would have curdled cream. We never tried that again.

When my parents grew older, they spent most of their time at the farm. My mother rode her beloved horse Shadow, a magnificent black Friesian, a gift from my father from the first Christmas they spent at the farm. We would find her in the wildflower meadow if she were not with Shadow. My father teased Mother that she loved her horse more than him, but I knew better. My mother loved Shadow and adored her children, but my father . . . well, he was on a completely different level. As for father, he worshipped the ground Nene walked on. After more than thirty years together, his eyes still lit up when she walked into the room. I once asked my mother for her love advice on how to find the right man. She told me it was far better to be alone than with the wrong person and never to marry anyone unless they could convince you that they couldn't live without you. Well, that's easier said than done. Hence why I'm still single. Mind you, I have always been fussy. Mother knew that I was looking for a man like my father, with values, strength, integrity, and intelligence.

Every man I met, of course, fell short of my unrealistic expectations. Mother would look at me and sigh.

"Charlotte, value your independence and build a life worth living before you consider getting married. When I first met your father, I didn't like him all that much. But, as I got to know him, a friendship developed that blossomed into a love affair. So never give up. Love will find you when you least expect it. And when that day arrives, life may never be the same again."

Mother's moral code was never to be afraid, never be jealous. Jealousy, in her opinion, was a complete waste of time and energy. So, I asked her how she and my father kept their relationship fresh. Mom told me the secret of any successful relationship is to work at it, work at it every day.

I laughed and said, "even if you are with someone you adore?"

"Especially then," she said.

How ironic that our farm, where my parents spent so many happy hours, was where my mother would have been on the day she died had she not travelled to Trenton to celebrate my Aunt Estelle's seventieth birthday. We had all been invited to a social gathering to mark the occasion. In the end, only my mother and I attended, my brother being unable to take time off work. My father was recovering from a nasty chest infection. His doctor advised him not to travel, reminding him he was no spring chicken at seventy-three. Despite my father's protestations, my mother agreed with the doctor, insisting he recuperate at the farm until she returned. My parents had no way of knowing that would be the last time they ever saw each other.

Chapter Two: Charlotte Sapori

My mind often drifts back to the events leading up to my mother's death—the day she died remains indelibly imprinted on my memory. I still recall the silk print dress she wore on that ill-fated day. Our housemaid Stella found Mother collapsed in the drawing-room and called for an ambulance. My mind was racing as I travelled with her to All Souls Hospital. I was sobbing and shaking uncontrollably as I held her hand in mine. The consultant said it had been a mild attack. He was hopeful she would fully recover. I was allowed to stay with my mother in a private room where she slept for some time. I was gently braiding her hair when she opened her beautiful violet eyes. Even in a hospital nightgown, she looked as beautiful as ever. Age had not yet withered her features, although she appeared a little paler than usual.

Smiling at me, she squeezed my hand. "Charlotte, why don't you go home and get some rest?"

"Mother, you are the one who needs the rest. You're always putting others first."

"Well, if you won't go home, my darling girl, come and sit here with me for a moment. There are events in my past that you are not yet aware of, things that I need to tell you." She paused. "I don't want you to worry. Death does not exist to me. But please bear in mind the events that transpired were primarily to protect you and your brother. Always remember that."

I squeezed her hand. She was starting to worry me. "It's all right. It was only a mild attack. The doctors said that with plenty of rest there was no reason why you won't make a full recovery."

My mother sighed, gesturing to the locker beside her bed. She asked me to pass her bag. I handed it to her and watched as she unfastened the clasp and took out a silver key.

"Well, Charlotte Grace, you are right, of course. I am still exhausted. I need to sleep right now. I want you to return to the house and have dinner with your Aunt Estelle. Please send her my heartfelt love. This is the key to my bedside cabinet. You'll find my journal there. When the time was right, your father and I planned to tell you and Nicco the whole story. But, Charlotte, before you read it, pour yourself a glass of wine, sit back on my bed, and make yourself comfortable."

I raised my eyebrows, looking at her curiously as she held my hand in hers.

"I know you have questions, Charlotte. Your father told you to question everything and not take anything at face value. He gave you good advice. We raised you to have an open mind. Trust me, my darling girl, you will need it. Everything you will want to know is in my journal. The madness that was my life began in the City of London in February 1893, the day my first husband, Godfrey Norton, was found brutally murdered."

The nurse entered the room with a jug of fresh water and my mother's medication. Then the consultant arrived to check her pulse and heart rate.

Finally, he turned to me, gently placing his hand on my shoulder. "Your mother needs to rest now, Miss Sapori. You may come back in the morning. We have your number at home. We will call you if there is any change in her condition."

Mother lay back on her pillow and sighed. "My dearest Charlotte, when you speak to your father, please tell him that I love him and that he's not to worry. It's all thanks to him that I finally reached it."

I shook my head. "Reached what, mother?"

"My hill of Calvary. Your father will understand. I wish I'd met him years earlier. I wish it had always been him."

I looked at her anxiously. She sounded delirious. My parents had been together for over thirty years. This did not make any sense. I presumed it to be the medication talking.

Mother closed her eyes, whispering something I couldn't quite make out that sounded like, "I can go now."

I shook my head. I must have misheard her. She was telling me that *I* could go now. I kissed her on the cheek and whispered, "I love you, sleep well."

I put the key into my bag and returned to the house. To this day, I have no memory of leaving the hospital or getting a cab home. I joined Estelle for dinner later that evening. Although we hardly ate a thing, I managed to convince her that Mother would be fine. Then I made my excuses and phoned my brother to update him on Mother's progress.

Nicco was pleased with our mother's prognosis, having already called the hospital to check up on her. He promised he would be on the first train out of Boston the following morning. I then phoned my father at our farm on the beautiful Sussex Downs. He seemed relieved to hear from me, although I could sense the anxiety in his voice. I explained what the doctors had said and told him not to worry and that mother would recover. He didn't sound at all convinced, although he perked up a little when I mentioned that Nicco would be travelling from Boston the following day. I asked how he was only to hear him complain that the doctor was useless and the medication he'd been prescribed wasn't working.

However, Father admitted he felt a little better after indulging in whiskey, honey, and soda water. I laughed at his response. My father had never been a good patient. Fortunately, he was rarely ill. He had a strong constitution, far more robust than most.

"Charlotte, you have no idea how good it is to hear your voice,"

"Please try to get some sleep," I replied. "I promise I will call you back in the morning. Oh, I nearly forgot, Mother asked me to send you her love. She said not to worry, that you helped her reach it, her hill of Calvary, whatever that means."

My father gasped. "Have you read it yet?"

"No, not yet. Mother asked me to read her journal this evening." I frowned. "Wait a minute! How on earth could you possibly know?"

My father paused before he answered. I could feel the tension in his voice. "Charlotte, I could do with a drink right now. I will speak to you again tomorrow. Be sure to tell your mother that I love her. I would give anything in the world to be with her right now."

"I think she knows that."

"Tell her anyway. I wish you a good night, Charlotte. If you need anything, call me. It doesn't matter what time; promise you will do that?"

"Yes, sir, of course. I will be sure to do so."

I retired to Mother's bedroom just as she had asked. I sat on her bed for a while, staring at the key, sipping from my glass of red wine. Opening the locker, I took out the journal, making myself comfortable on the four-poster bed. Opening the thick black book which contained her memoir, I smiled at the introduction, which was dedicated to Nicco and me. I began to read Mother's words from the brown-tinted pages bearing the unmistakable patina of age. My heart stopped in my mouth as I digested her first sentence. The tears began to flow, realising with a start that mother had only asked me to read her journal because she thought she was dying. The thought completely broke my heart. My grandparents, Alfred and Marianne, had died prematurely due to heart problems.

I sat on the bed sobbing uncontrollably. I called the hospital only to be told Mother was sleeping peacefully and there was no cause for alarm. I asked if I could come back to see her, and they said not until the following morning. Due to the lateness of the hour, they didn't want the other patients to be disturbed. Feeling reassured, I sat back down on the bed and read her journal:

Hello, my darlings Nicco and Charlotte.

Well, I guess if you have found this, I am either dead or deranged. As you can see, I have kept a private journal. It was never intended for publication, but I would like you both to read it. I want you to know that any decisions your father and I made regarding your future were to protect you, our precious children.

It was a tremendous privilege to be your mother. It was one of the best things that ever happened to me, the other was meeting your father. I cherished every single moment I have spent with you all. I send you both my heartfelt love. You are intelligent, beautiful, wonderful human beings – clever, considerate, and kind.

When growing up, my Nicco, the sagacious scholar, you were a forty-year-old trapped in a child's body, but now, a responsible young man with an exceptional level of intelligence. And then my lovely Charlotte, who Lucca describes as a revolver. Sharp as a tack, fearless, and curious, she can at times be all dramatic, much to the disdain of her long-suffering father.

I laughed out loud at that. It was true that my father would go out of his way to avoid meaningless interaction. I was aware that I often drove him to distraction, especially when I was younger and demanded that he read to me. Literature, novels, and children's stories had little or no appeal to him, but he would begrudgingly read to me if I asked. Then, shaking his head, he would roll his eyes and say, "Not *Alice in Wonderland* again, Charlotte!" Finally, he would add extra excitement to the text and always stop at a cliff-hanger.

My beautiful Charlotte, who is funny, sharp-witted, and kind, always believe in yourself. Be anything in the world you want to be, and if I have sung my last song by the time you read this narrative, then so be it. I have seen my own mortality many times. Although I briefly crossed over to the other side, there was nothing to fear from what I could see.

The sun will continue to set. Despite everything, the world will still turn even when we are not in it. I will not lie to you – grief is a long-lasting pain, the price we pay for loving someone. Love of the highest mark. I do not think it ever goes away entirely. But the overwhelming sadness does get easier with time. We can only hope to live on in the memories of those who loved us. And when we lose someone, we shouldn't wallow in all of the misery. Instead, we should think of all the love and beauty that person has left behind.

I turned over the page and gasped at the introduction.

London 13th February 1893

The day that would change everything and turn my world upside down began when my husband, Godfrey Jones, was found brutally murdered.

I turned over the page just as the phone began to ring. I answered it with some trepidation thinking the worst, that it was the hospital. I was surprised to hear my father's voice instead, especially so soon after our last conversation.

"Charlotte, I'm sorry to disturb you at this late hour. But you deserve to know the whole truth. I, too, kept a record of our time together, your mother and me. When you feel ready, I want you to go to my study and open the safe. The code is your mother's date of birth. My chronicles are in there. I wish I could be with you to explain everything. But before you read our narratives, there is something else I need to tell you." He paused for a moment. "I am not who you think I am."

"Whatever do you mean?" I cried.

"My name is Sherlock Holmes. You may have heard of me."

CHAPTER THREE: CHARLOTTE SAPORI

I was up and dressed when Estelle knocked on my bedroom door the following morning. I had hardly slept, struggling to digest my parents' extraordinary story, annoyed with myself when Sherlock Holmes finally ended the call. I was barely able to speak during our conversation. There were so many unanswered questions. Was Nicco also the offspring of the celebrated detective? And if so, then who was Lucca Sapori? Where did he fit into the equation? This didn't make any sense. From what little I knew of Sherlock Holmes, he was an eccentric solitary figure, a confirmed bachelor. He lived alone at his flat at Baker Street, his only companions his housekeeper, and his friend and colleague Doctor John Watson. I only knew this because my brother was an avid fan. He read all of Doctor Watson's chronicles, outlining Holmes's most famous cases. My god, how could I tell my brother he was most likely the son of the celebrated detective he hero-worshipped. I decided not to say anything for now, not until I had garnered more information. I figured I had some investigating of my own to do.

When Estelle and I arrived at the hospital, we entered mother's room and were shocked to discover the bed was empty. The nurse ran over to speak to us.

"We have been trying to contact you," she said. "Your mother suffered a stroke half an hour ago. She's in the operating theatre." The nurse squeezed my hand. "The stroke was massive so prepare yourself for the worst."

Estelle and I were escorted to the waiting room, someone

brought us coffee, and we sat in stunned silence for over two hours, so grief-stricken, we could barely speak. Eventually the consultant entered the room, shaking his head.

"I am so sorry, Miss Sapori. We did everything we could, but the stroke caused too much damage, and we couldn't save her."

Estelle and I collapsed into each other's arms, sobbing uncontrollably.

"May we see her?" I asked.

The doctor nodded. "Yes, of course. Please give us time to prepare."

We were eventually ushered into a side room next to the hospital mortuary where my beautiful mother lay on a bed in the stillness of death. She looked so serene and peaceful. I kissed her on the cheek and held her hand, her body still warm.

"I wish you'd told me," I whispered.

"Told you what?" quizzed Estelle, staring at her through her tears.

"It doesn't matter," I said. "In the grand scheme of things, it doesn't matter at all."

We sat with mother for an hour before slipping into the hospital chapel to light a candle to help guide my mother on her final journey to the afterlife which she believed in so strongly. We eventually returned home. I was heartbroken. Not only had I lost my beloved mother, but the person I had known as my father had disappeared from my life. As far as I was concerned, I had lost both my parents within hours of each other. I never felt so alone in my life. I wanted answers, and I was determined I would find them.

It was the end of August before we could finally travel to Fiesole, Florence, where my father's friends Ludo and Violetta Esperito lived, with their son Francesco. Their daughter Ava, a celebrated soprano, arrived earlier from Milan with her husband Javier, and Robert and Sophia Moon. Since a first-year student at La Scala, Sophia had been my mother's best friend. The quartet of friends travelled together by train to help celebrate the life of a remarkable woman.

Ludo and Violetta had very kindly invited us to stay with them for a few days until my mother's memorial service. Father was, by this time, feeling much better. Although he had been too ill to attend Nene's funeral in Trenton, he was determined not to miss the memorial service. So, despite his doctor's reservations, he travelled over by train from London.

Nicco and I slept in the barn conversion where our parents first stayed together over thirty years ago. Every night after dinner, we sat with father on the patio, celebrating Mother's life with a toast of whisky or wine, with either Beethoven or Wagner playing in the background. We came to regard those evenings as sacrosanct.

Ava and Sophia opened the memorial service with an outstanding rendition of Nene's favourite hymn, "Amazing Grace." Then the priest read psalm 42. Afterwards my father recited "When You Are Old" by William Butler Yeats. There wasn't a dry eye in the church after that. Finally, Sophia delivered a beautiful and touching eulogy, speaking eloquently about Nene and how much she meant to her as a friend. She recalled when they went out to dinner during their first year at La Scala. A young gentleman approached their table, he was barely nineteen. He introduced himself to Sophia and told her she was one of the finest opera singers he had ever heard. Sophia thanked him profusely, thrilled that someone had recognised her talent. Unfortunately, Sophia's joy was short-lived.

After a few minutes, the man tentatively approached Sophia with a puzzled expression on his face. "I am so sorry. I've mistaken you for someone else. I thought you were Irene Adler."

After that humiliating experience, Sophia was, of course, mortified. And as for Nene, she couldn't stop laughing. The tale certainly got a chuckle from the congregation. Even the priest laughed. That young man was Arturo Toscanini, destined to be a lifelong friend and now principal conductor of the New York Philharmonic Orchestra in New York.

Sophia addressed the congregation with good grace and a faint smile. She nodded before continuing with her narrative:

"That young man was right, of course. Who could ever forget that remarkable talent? Nene was my oldest and dearest friend. I'll never forget the first time we met on registration day at La Scala. I walked into the room, and she stared at me, this girl with her magnificent violet eyes. I gazed up at her statuesque figure, lustrous auburn hair, beautiful, flawless porcelain skin, and high cheekbones. This girl, who adored Beethoven and Stephen Foster, smiled at me as if I were a close friend she hadn't seen for years. We made a connection that day that never left us—we became inseparable. Nene's life was, of course, later consumed with the deep abiding love she had for her family. Although mainly for her beloved husband Lucca and her two exceptional children, Nicco and Charlotte. She had great pride in her profession and captivated everyone around her. She was a fearless, fabulous force of nature with an inimitable voice. Richard Strauss once said that the human voice was the most beautiful instrument. I do believe that Nene was living proof of that testament. The combination of her personality, beauty, courage, and sheer emotional power all contributed to making her the brilliantly skilled contralto and performer she came to be. Nene was the best friend anyone could ever hope for, and I know I speak for everyone who has come here today to honour her memory. We will miss her beyond words. The loveliest light has gone out."

Sophia looked upwards, smiling through silent tears. "I

love you, Nene. It was so special to have known you as a friend. May you rest in peace until we meet again."

CHAPTER FOUR: CHARLOTTE SAPORI

After the memorial service, we returned to Le Sole for the wake. We scattered Mother's ashes in the beautiful tranquil garden behind the barn. And. what an afternoon it was. Francesco and Ludo planted a rose bush as a lasting, living memorial to Mother's memory. There was a moment of silence in which everyone was lost in an ocean of grief. The thought that the rest of the world could carry on with dazzling grace when she was no longer with us seemed wrong.

We drank copious amounts of wine and whisky. We played music on the gramophone, raising a toast to the iconic Irene Adler—opera singer, friend, philanthropist, mother, and wife. I closed my eyes, basking in the afternoon sun, wondering what it must have been like thirty-two years ago when my parents first arrived in Fiesole.

Later that afternoon, Nicco, Javier, and I performed one of my mother's favourite modern-day compositions," Careless Love Blues." The bright young things from the roaring twenties were doing a new dance called the Charleston. They dominated the newspapers with outrageous fashions and indulgent lifestyles, loosening morals and sexual inhibitions. But, of course, my father took a dim view of all of it, much to my mother's amusement. She was far more liberally minded in such matters and always made a point of championing those of her sex vilified by men.

Mother and Nicco were huge fans of an artist who became known as the father of jazz, Buddy Bolden. They adored Buddy Bolden's Blues, such as "Funky Butt." My brother was a talented singer, blessed with a fine baritone voice. He also played several musical instruments, including the pianoforte, cello, and violin. Nicco would have made a fine musician if he had not become a doctor. He and Mother had tried in vain to get father interested in jazz. Nicco explained to my bemused father that people didn't realise they wanted jazz until they heard it for the first time. Father would have none of it, describing jazz as insolent noise, preferring to listen to his beloved German composers Wagner and Beethoven.

There was a piano in the drawing-room. One evening my father asked me to play for him. First Schubert, then one of my mother's compositions, a piece she wrote during a weekend in Harrogate the Christmas before she died.

I have fond memories of that time. Mother had spent most of the last three decades fundraising for underprivileged children. Then, finally, she became a patron of Doctor Barnardo's. They said her philanthropic spirit and generosity had made an enormous difference in the lives of so many children. Father had intended to accompany her to a fundraiser and Christmas carol concert in Harrogate. But unfortunately, the day before they were due to travel, he was called away to work in Lewisham on what he described as a pressing matter. He asked if I would take his place, explaining that he had booked a spa hotel, The Black Swan, as a surprise.

On the 10th of December, Mother and I set off from Kings Cross on our train journey to Harrogate. A bitterly cold east wind blew as we boarded the train and settled into the first-class carriage father had Insisted on booking. And I'm so glad he did. Not because I'm a snob, far from it. But because the train was full of commuters snuggling close together and children pressing their faces against the windows as they travelled home for the festive season.

We were due to arrive in Harrogate just after three o'clock, but there was a delay on the line. When we reached York station, we learned that a Yorkshire terrier had fallen between the train and the platform gap, forcing us to wait for the conductor to arrive. He finally managed to free the dog, to the delight of the commuters waiting on the platform. The porter reunited the dog with its owner, an elderly lady in a mink coat. We were pleased the dog was safe, but it meant we didn't arrive at our hotel until five o'clock. This barely gave us time to change and organise a hansom to take us to the theatre. We had no time for dinner.

Mother was naturally magnificent. She walked onto the stage of that delightful theatre, dressed in a striking peacock blue gown, to rapturous applause. She sang the opening Christmas carol, "O Holy Night" (also known as "Cantique De Noel"), accompanied by the Harrogate male voice choir.

Seeing the reaction from the audience, I gasped and thought *My God, I am actually in the presence of an icon.* My dazzling, wonderful mother had lost none of her captivating aurae despite her advanced years. Now there I sat, floored yet again by this incredible woman.

At the concert's end, a diminutive elderly lady dressed in a black silk dress and hat presented mother with an award for children's services. Then we hailed a cab and returned to our hotel. We were relieved to find the dining room still open as we hadn't eaten since breakfast. By the time we finished dinner, the dining room was almost empty save for a lady sitting on her own at an adjoining table, nursing a cup of tea. She was wearing a black sparkling evening dress, so we assumed she must have come from the dance, as the band was still in full swing next door at the Palm Court. Mother introduced herself, inviting the lady to come and join us for drinks. The lady smiled. She recognised the great Irene Adler. She told us she was quite a fan of the opera, Wagner being one of her favourite composers. The lady came over to join us and introduced herself as Nancy Tresser. Nancy was in her late thirties with dark wavy hair swept off her face, deep-set dark eyes with well-defined brows, full lips, and a rather aquiline nose. I remember she was tall. Nancy declined Nene's offer of wine, explaining she was teetotal, so Mother ordered coffee for us and a pot of Earl Grey for Nancy.

We spoke at length until the subject eventually came around to music and composers. Mother said she had attempted to write a few of her own compositions over the years. Nancy appeared intrigued and asked if Nene would play a little for her. She gestured towards the grand piano in the lounge. Nancy and I stood around the piano as Mother began to play melancholy music.

Appreciating the beautiful melody, which flowed with ease, I looked at my mother with a raised eyebrow. "But how on earth do you even begin to write a song?"

Mother laughed. "Well, I begin with a few chords and find a melody." She ran her fingers over the keyboard effortlessly, playing the first few bars of "Where My Love Lies Dreaming."

"Do you think this will catch on?" she asked, laughing softly at my puzzled expression. "My dear Charlotte. I long ago resigned myself to the fact that I will never emulate Beethoven or the great Stephen Foster. I should stick to singing."

We retired to the dining room and our conversation continued. Nancy told us her mother had recently passed away. She was staying in the hotel on her own. We noticed she wore a wedding band, although she never explained why she was alone, and we felt it inappropriate to ask. Eventually Nancy made her excuses and retired for the night, politely declining Mother's offer to join us for dinner the following evening. I remember thinking how fortunate I was to be part of a family that loved me unconditionally and would do anything for me. The thought of my parents parting ways made me shudder.

The following morning after breakfast, Mother and I went into town for a little Christmas shopping. I bought candy, fudge, and some toffee for Nicco from Farrah's Olde Sweet Shop, presented in a gorgeous blue-and-silver tin. Then I picked up a box of my father's favourite Cuban cigars from the tobacconist. Our next stop was Louis Cope's emporium on Parliament Street, famous for its bespoke off-the-peg haute couture. Queen Mary was said to be a customer.

Mother bought me a delightful dress of silk Canton crepe in contrasting tones of red-and-black with metallic thread, along with a pair of black patent leather pumps and two pairs of grey silk stockings. She then chose a Poiret sheen coat for herself in grey, delicate and soft, to which she added an aristocratic air of elegance when she tried it on. Departing from the store two hours later, we had afternoon tea at Betty's before returning to the hotel, where we spent the rest of the afternoon relaxing in the spa.

After we arrived home on Tuesday afternoon and read the newspapers, Mother and I were shocked to discover we had been in the company of Agatha Christie. She was reported missing several days earlier and checked into the hotel under the assumed name of her husband's mistress. Again, Mother and I were stunned. We just prayed that things would work out for her. Agatha Christie would, of course, become a prolific author. I had already read her first three novels: *The Mysterious Affair at Styles, The Murder on The Links* and *The Murder of Roger Ackroyd,* much to my father's bemusement.

I have vivid memories of my mother rehearsing the song she composed that Christmas. She made me promise I would play it for Father if anything happened to her. The melody reminded her of a time in her life when she was estranged from my father, when they thought they would never see each other again. It was entitled "Emergence."

I smiled nervously at my father. "This was a dedication to you from my mother. She asked if I would play it for you."

Father looked at me curiously. A flicker of a smile

appeared on his face as he nodded his approval. I began to play. The haunting melody moved my father to tears. That was the first and only time I'd ever seen him cry. Father was stoic by nature, and like most men of his time and generation, crying did not come easily to him. But being in the barn wasn't only a poignant reminder of my father's return to the place that had offered him and my mother sanctuary all those years ago. This was also where they had fallen in love. After I finished, I sat with my father on the patio. Taking his hand in mine, I kissed him on the cheek.

He smiled back at me through his tears.

"Charlotte, when you were sitting there, playing that beautiful melody, it took my breath away. You looked just like her, your mother. You may take that as a compliment, young lady. Your mother was the most beautiful woman I have ever laid eyes on."

I stared at him curiously. "I read your journals, yours and Mother's. The hill of Calvary she spoke of, the night before she died, that was a secret code between the two of you, wasn't it? It was her way of letting you know what was about to happen?"

Father nodded. "We need to talk, Charlotte. I know you have questions, and you deserve answers, but not tonight. I am exhausted. Tomorrow after dinner, we shall talk then. I promise I will tell you everything you need to know."

Chapter Five: The Death of Godfrey Norton: Irene Adler

London 13th February 1893

It was a chilly, grey February morning, the kind of day that made people yearn for spring. The early morning fog was beginning to rise as Polly Hawkins disembarked from the omnibus that terminated at Ludgate Hill. Polly shivered as she fastened the top button of her mute black long coat, wrapping her scarf tightly around her neck and pulling her black felt hat firmly down over her ears to protect her from the icy north wind and to prepare her for the eight-minute walk to Fleet Street. Walking briskly through the temple, she passed the snow-covered dome of St. Paul's cathedral hovering in the background. Polly turned into Fleet Street, home of the infamous Ye Olde Cheshire Cheese Tavern, a favoured watering hole of the solicitors and lawyers who resided in the Temple. The tavern had been rebuilt shortly after the great fire of London in 1666. It was steeped in history and said to have been frequented by numerous literary figures, including Charles Dickens, Samuel Johnson, Alfred Tennyson, and Mark Twain.

Not yet seven o'clock, Fleet Street was already alive with activity as hansom cabs and broughams trotted down the straw-covered street. The hustle and bustle added an air of anticipation. Domestic servants thronged the road, walking or cycling their way to work. Men in dark suits and bowler hats went about their business. Chimney sweeps, crossing sweepers, tavern owners, and shop vendors called out to each other as they prepared to open.

Polly walked past several solicitors' offices before finally reaching Gibbs, Robinson and Starkie Solicitors, Commissioners for Oaths, and Notary Public. She ran up the front steps, admiring the smartly painted black front door with gleaming brass door knocker and plaques nestling beneath the bell pull, each bearing the names and qualifications of its partners and associates. Polly smiled with pride at the gleaming brass. Scrubbing the steps and polishing the brasses was her responsibility, a job she carried out meticulously every morning. Removing a glove, she held onto the railings as she fumbled in her bag for the front door key.

The clock of Saint Dunstan's church was chiming seven. Polly noticed the front door was ajar. Mr Jones must have come in early again, which was not unusual. That was one of his little peculiarities. Hanging up her hat, scarf, coat, and bag in the scullery, Polly walked into the kitchen. She filled the kettle and removed two mugs and a tea caddy from the overhead cupboard as she expected her friend, Daisy Moffatt, to join her shortly. She wished Daisy would hurry as it was her turn to fetch the milk. Daisy was a fellow domestic servant responsible for cleaning the first floor of the building. Late again, Daisy had recently confided to Polly that she'd been having problems at home with her husband, Ted. Daisy suspected he was carrying on with another woman. Polly put on her white mop cap, carefully pushing the loose strands of flaming red hair underneath. Tying a white apron around her long black cotton dress, she checked her reflection in the kitchen mirror. A slim, diminutive girl of twenty years stared back at her with a pale, freckled face and round animated blue eyes. She removed a coal scuttle from the cupboard under the stairs in the hallway. She was just about to go back into the kitchen when she heard the distinct sound of raised voices coming from Mr Jones' office. Polly sighed. She'd have to wait to clean the grate in his room and set the fire, which would set her back. Shaking her head, she tutted, deciding to clean the grate in the kitchen instead. Polly considered asking Mr Jones if he wanted a cup of tea then thought better of it. First of all, there was no fresh milk, and second, Mr Jones had a client with him. He never liked to be disturbed whilst he was working. Besides, she was sure he would ring the bell if he wanted anything. He knew she came in at seven o'clock, regular as clockwork.

"Polly put the kettle on!" he would shout out to her, laughing at his own joke.

Other mornings she would be lucky to get a grunt out of him. The raised voices continued. Polly stood motionless, unsure what to do. She was not expecting the other lawyers to arrive before luncheon. Michael Turner was usually first on the scene after Mr Jones. In his mid-twenties, Turner was the youngest of the solicitors. Mr Gibbs had been dead for quite some time. The senior partners, Mr Starkie and Mr Robinson, both had cases at the Old Bailey that morning.

Polly strained her ears, trying to make out what they were saying. The second man appeared to be doing most of the talking. Polly picked out the odd curse from the muffled voices. She raised her eyebrows, recognising some of the words from her nights spent as a barmaid at the King's Head public house, her second job. She and her fiancé, Jack Taylor, were saving up to get married. Jack didn't like Polly working at the King's Head, but they needed the money, and the extra work would be worth it in the end. Jack had reluctantly agreed, although he insisted on meeting Polly at the end of her shift and walking her home. Jack was a good man. Just turned twenty-five, he worked long, hard hours as an apprentice butcher at Smithfield Market.

For a moment, the voices went quiet. And then a blood-curdling scream erupted through the air. Polly stood in the corridor, petrified, unable to move. Mr Jones' office door swung open. She could see a man running towards her, his face blacker than any thunderstorm. The man appeared shocked to see Polly. He glared at her with furrowed brow, cursing under his breath. A blood-stained knife glinted in his right hand. Polly could hear her heart hammering in her chest. The man hesitated, his cold, blue eyes boring into her. Polly noticed a scar running down from his ear to his cheekbone and realised that she recognised him from the King's Head. He was Wild Bill Palmer, the leader of the notorious Tooley street gang, rumoured to be a former henchman of the late professor Moriarty. Splashes of blood dotted his shirt. She closed her eyes. A sensation of wetness trickled down her legs as she waited for him to stab her. Polly's thoughts turned to Jack and his comely, freckled face. She began to cry. Large, salty tears ran down her cheeks. She could smell the man's breath on her face, the stench of stale beer, tobacco, and brandy. She felt the cold blade of the knife on her neck. She was shaking uncontrollably, speaking to the man in a hoarse whisper, barely recognising her own voice.

"Please, don't hurt me, Mister. I'm expecting a little 'un." The man hesitated for a moment before roughly knocking her to the floor.

She fell onto her side, winded from the fall. She lay on the ground for several minutes and struggled to catch her breath. Then came the unmistakable sound of the front door slamming. Breathing a sigh of relief, Polly almost laughed. Who would have thought that the weight she put on over Christmas would save her life? Jack would gently tease her about her weight gain. "Who ate all the mince pies?" he would mock before she whacked him over the head with a newspaper. Not that he minded. Polly wasn't an unhealthy weight by any stretch of the imagination, and Jack preferred more curves on a woman.

Polly stood up slowly, holding onto the wall, her legs shaking, her black laced boots scuffing along the floor. She tentatively tiptoed towards Mr Jones' office. A deathly silence had fallen, apart from the clock ticking in the hallway. Her heart was pounding, almost in sync with the clock. She pushed the door. It opened slowly, creaking upon its hinges. Polly glanced around the office, which was in a state of wild disarray, books, papers, and files littered across the floor. The safe was half open, pictures hung off the walls. The Chesterfield settee had been pushed over on its side, its cushions slashed.

Her eyes darted towards Mr Jones' desk. What she saw cut her to the quick. Mr Jones' lifeless body lay sprawled in a twisted heap over the desk, his eyes wide open in a terrible fixed stare. His once crisp white shirt was now crimson, blood dripping off the desk onto the carpet below. Polly ran out of the office as fast as her legs would carry her. Once on the street, she screamed hysterically. A man standing on the pavement grabbed her tightly by the shoulders. Polly closed her eyes, thinking the worst, that the intruder had returned. The man spoke to her softly, gently releasing his grip. Polly recognised the crystal-cut, well-modulated voice. She opened her lids, crying out with utter relief. She had fallen straight into the arms of Michael Turner. Polly told me of the above shocking events when I visited her at her home in Islington, three days after Godfrey's murder.

Chapter Six: February 1893: Irene Adler

I shall never forget the events of that ill-fated day. When I heard the doorbell ring, I was alone in the dining room at my home, Laburnum Villa, located in sedate Kensington Square. Our housemaid Bertha entered the room a few minutes later to advise me that Inspector Lestrade from the Metropolitan police was asking to see me.

Entering the parlour with some trepidation, I found the inspector and his sergeant waiting for me, an expression of the utmost gravity on their faces. The inspector showed me his badge before asking me to take a seat.

"Mrs Jones," said Lestrade in a booming voice. "I'm afraid there's no easy way to say this, but we have found a body this morning which we believe to be that of your husband, Godfrey Lucien Jones. He was found dead at his place of employment. We have reason to believe that foul play was involved. Fortunately, we do have an eyewitness who was at the crime scene. They have been able to give us a detailed description of the perpetrator. A murder enquiry is underway, and we believe we are close to finding him, Mrs Jones. Very close indeed."

I stared hard at Lestrade, fighting back the tears. I could hear the inspector's words ringing in my ears. He sounded as though he were speaking from inside a tunnel. "But why would anyone want to kill my husband? What reason would they have to murder him?"

"I don't know, Mrs Jones," said Lestrade. "But we will get to the truth of the matter, I assure you. We will know more after the autopsy report. The only thing I can tell you right now is that your husband was assaulted. My sergeant and I would like to extend our condolences."

Lestrade hesitated for a moment. "We appreciate this must be a challenging time, but we need somebody to identify your husband's body. Would you be willing to take a look? We could ask one of the partners at the firm if you don't feel up to it."

I shook my head. "No, I will do it, Inspector. I don't want you to bother Godfrey's work colleagues, that wouldn't be fair. Godfrey's parents are both dead. He has no siblings. I'm his wife, it's down to me." I took a deep breath. How I wished my beloved father Alfred was there to console and comfort me. He was expected to arrive in London on Saturday. I could hardly wait to see him.

We set off to the mortuary. When the mortician pulled back the sheet from Godfrey's face, I gasped. I stared in horror at the translucent alabaster skin and blue pallor of his lips and face. His eyes were closed, but there was no doubt this was Godfrey. I was utterly traumatised by Godfrey's death. Although things had not been good between us, and I was about to leave him, I would never have wished him dead. Lestrade smiled at me gently.

"I'm much obliged for your assistance, Mrs Jones. My sergeant will take you home now. We will keep you updated on any fresh developments."

Sergeant Green summoned a carriage and escorted me back to Kensington. I immediately retired to my bedroom. Sitting on the bed, I cried unceasingly. Godfrey's senseless death had left me completely shattered and totally unprepared for the intensity of my feelings. My husband had been a complicated man—cold, mean-spirited, a bully and a sadist. How often had I prayed for him to disappear from my life? And now, he was gone? The guilt ate away at me. After crying myself into a troubled sleep, my mind drifted back to the events that transpired on that fateful August night five months earlier. However, it felt as though it had only been yesterday when the perception of my world changed forever. Every night in my dreams, I relived each excruciating moment.

Late evening, I was disturbed by the sound of the bedroom door opening with a savage abruptness. I turned my head to find Godfrey standing in the opening, staring at me grimly. My blood ran cold. I had become accustomed to living in constant fear of the dark scowl that appeared on his face with the slightest provocation, the violent threats, and coarse sneers I endured daily. Godfrey's altered mood and mental state was a result of his heavy drinking and opium addiction.

"Nene," said Godfrey. "I need five hundred pounds to pay off a gambling debt. I must have this money now or I won't be able to show my face in front of Mounsey again."

"Well, surely that can't be a bad thing!" I retorted.

Godfrey's scowl turned into a bitter smile. "I must have the money now. I am about to enter a winning streak. Muscroft fancies his horse in the first at Newmarket tomorrow. Don't you see? When it wins, I'll be back in the game!"

"You wouldn't recognise a winning streak if it fell in front of you, Godfrey. How dare you speak to me in this way? I am your wife, although you seldom treat me as such. Tell me what exactly am I to you?"

"A spoiled rich bitch with a pretty face," Godfrey bellowed. A deep scowl marred his once handsome features. "I cannot remember the last time I asked you for money."

"Godfrey, this is the second time this month you have asked me. I can't keep doing this."

His face flushed with rage, Godfrey raised his fist, smacking me hard across the face. With a sickening thud I fell onto the bed, striking my head against the bedpost. Godfrey cried out in anguish—he must have realised he'd gone too far. He reached out his hand to help me up, but I recoiled at his touch. The last thing I wanted was for him to come anywhere near me. Not surprisingly, Godfrey became offended, as if he had any right to be so. He slapped me again before climbing onto the bed. His features contorted into a spasm of vengeful hatred and pain. He bound a dressing gown cord around my neck and squeezed tightly. I tried, in vain, to push him away. That proved impossible for Godfrey was far too strong. I could feel his hot sour breath on my face as his lecherous lips ravaged my unresponsive mouth, wincing in pain as he forced himself inside me.

"Come on, Nene," he sneered. "I love it when you fight back a little. I know you like it rough!" I felt another painful sting across my face as Godfrey smacked me again.

I felt something prodding at my flesh. I instinctively tried to get away from the knife, but I couldn't move. Godfrey was pressing down on top of me. My whole body trembled as he slowly traced the blade over my naked body, nicking me just under my left breast. I turned away from him. Godfrey grabbed my hair and turned my head round to face him. There was to be no avoiding his gaze. He thrust into me even harder, the pain excruciating.

"Do you realise how much I sacrificed for you, moving away from London, just as my career was taking off?" he screamed. "Have you any idea how difficult it has been for me to climb back to the top of my profession? I hate having to ask my own wife for help, makes me feel inadequate." He punctuated his words by thrusting into me even harder.

"You are worthless. You are nothing!" he bellowed.

Godfrey rolled over on the bed when he'd finished, immediately falling into a deep sleep, snoring like a pig. I dragged myself out of bed and staggered into the bathroom and recoiled in horror upon seeing my reflection in the mirror. My cheeks flamed scarlet, livid bruises covered my face and body. I had a black eye where Godfrey had punched me. Blood gushed from my nose and mouth. Inspecting the wound under my left breast, I dabbed it with alcohol before covering it with a clean bandage. I consumed painkillers and brandy, which did little to dull the pain. I lay in the bath for hours, broken and humiliated, scrubbing my body until it was red. I felt as though I would never be clean again.

The following day I confronted Godfrey at breakfast. He looked at me sheepishly, the bruises on my face a painful reminder of the shocking abuse he had inflicted the night before. I greeted Godfrey with a cold stare before throwing an envelope onto the table.

"I want you to know Godfrey that this is the last money you will ever receive from me. I will no longer support your depraved lifestyle. From this evening onwards, you will sleep in your own room. I don't want you to touch me ever again. Do you understand?"

"And if I refuse? What will you do?" He sneered.

"I will kill you!"

Godfrey stared at me hard. Something in the way I had spoken to him, the hard glint in my eyes, appeared to have unnerved him. He shrugged and laughed as he picked up the envelope from the table and walked out of the room.

A few months later, during a routine visit to my Doctor, I was discovered to be pregnant. I decided to leave Godfrey for good. I could not allow my child to be brought up in a toxic environment. I wrote a long letter to my father, Alfred Adler, in Trenton, New Jersey. My father was a widower, recently retired as a history, economics, and constitutional law professor at Rutgers University. I informed my father that I intended to leave Godfrey. However, I decided not to tell Godfrey or my father about the child.

My father's response was immediate. He messaged to say he'd booked his passage on the SS Berlin with American Line. He would depart the following Wednesday and disembark in Southampton ten days later.

When the hansom cab pulled up outside my house in Kensington on Saturday morning, my father had no idea that Godfrey was dead. He stepped out of the cab, a tall, clean-shaven distinguished-looking man, just over six feet tall. He was dressed in a light linen suit with a watch chain on his vest. His striking blue eyes were concealed behind half-moon glasses. I fell straight into my bemused father's arms, hugging him tightly, crying out with relief. During dinner that evening, I gently relayed all that had transpired with Godfrey and my subsequent pregnancy.

The coroner had released Godfrey's body. My father took over all the arrangements. He visited Holliwells, the undertakers, to organise Godfrey's funeral, a quiet, sombre affair. Only my father, three of Godfrey's work colleagues, and a couple of the domestic servants attended the church service and the interment at Brompton Cemetery. The day was cold, drizzly and grey. I shivered as Godfrey's coffin was lowered into the ground and my father threw a handful of soil over the coffin. I could not cry, I felt numb. When my father and I returned home, we were shocked to discover that the house had been broken into, the back gate swinging off its hinges. The servants arrived ahead of us. Having disturbed the burglars, they had already alarmed the police. Father and I searched the house. We were relieved to discover that nothing of value appeared to be missing.

Later that evening, Father and I dined together. I had little appetite, feeling exhausted and unwell. Excusing myself, I kissed my father, bidding him goodnight before retiring to my bedroom, where I fell into a deep sleep. I felt a sharp pain in my side. Then I noticed blood on the bedclothes. Dragging myself to the bathroom, I stared at the blood flowing down my legs. I had gone into premature labour. I cried out in anguish. The midwife was called. A small dark-haired Irish woman, Attracta Sweeney, swiftly arrived. She delivered my child, a girl. She only lived for twenty minutes, her lungs too weak to support her. Attracta wrapped the baby in a towel and gently placed her in my arms. A single, gut-wrenching howl escaped from my lips as she took her last breath. A heavy silence engulfed the room for quite some time. Attracta never left my side, holding onto me as I collapsed into her arms, sobbing uncontrollably.

Smiling at me sympathetically, Attracta spoke. "I lost a child too. My son. His name was Connor. They won't issue a birth certificate, but they can't stop you from naming your daughter. What will you call her?"

"Rosemary Blue," I said. "Rosemary, after my favourite flowers and for remembrance."

"Take your time," Attracta said. "When you're ready, we can wash and dress her and take a photograph if you wish." I thanked Attracta then glanced down at my baby girl and kissed her gently on the forehead.

My child was so perfect she looked as though she was sleeping. When Attracta finally left, I stared at the ceiling. Life felt cold, meaningless and cruel. My father made arrangements with the undertakers for Rosemary's funeral. After the service, he arranged to see a specialist at a private clinic on Harley Street where I was admitted as a patient. After a thorough internal examination and minor operation, the specialist arranged a meeting at his surgery to discuss his findings. My father and I found ourselves sitting opposite the eminent gynaecologist, Doctor Patrick Conlon, a tall, imposing-looking man with black hair and a handlebar moustache.

"Mrs Jones," he started. "The loss of your child under such tragic circumstances has unfortunately caused complications known as intrauterine adhesions. There is currently no clear evidence or method to prevent adverse pregnancy outcomes. However, medicine continues to progress. The first case was only published last year by Heinrich Fritsch, who I understand is making remarkable progress. We were able to remove some of the adhesions, although there is no guarantee that these adhesions will not reappear in the future. Unfortunately, this condition has seriously diminished your chances of conception or of carrying a child to full term in the unlikely event that you were to become pregnant should you choose to marry again. I am sorry I don't have better news for you."

My father stood. Smiling grimly, he shook hands with Dr Conlan. "Thank you, Doctor. We appreciate your frankness."

The doctor smiled at me sadly. "Do you have any questions?" he asked.

I shook my head. "No, thank you, Doctor. Not unless you can pause time." His expression was grim.

"Right." I sighed. "I know you've done everything you can for me. I would like to thank you for that. I don't need help. I need bad things to stop happening to me. I'm afraid that even you with all your learned knowledge and medical qualifications are unable to do anything about that."

At dinner that evening, my father begged me to return to the States with him. After everything that had transpired, I took little persuading. Father visited the house agents and instructed them to find a suitable tenant before booking our passage. When we boarded the *Berlin* on Saturday morning, Father and I stood on the deck watching until Southampton had disappeared entirely from view. I was delighted in the knowledge that we were, at last, leaving England. I was determined to never set foot in London again.

Chapter Seven: Irene Adler

Ten days later, our carriage arrived at our family home, a sprawling colonial townhouse in Trenton, New Jersey named Red Oaks. My cousin Estelle Conlin greeted us warmly as well as her three young children—Isabella, Mia, and Noah. Estelle, a widow, was an attractive woman in her late thirties, slim-built with dark brown hair and hazel eyes, a sweet-loving woman from whom I inherited my predilection for reading. Before her marriage, Estelle trained as a nurse, skills that proved indispensable to my father and me. In addition to looking after Alfred, Estelle oversaw the running of the house, managed the domestic servants and adopted the position of the primary housekeeper with considerable efficiency.

Depressed and tormented by the harrowing events in London, I found adapting to family life challenging. I was, at times, plagued by voices, memories, and flashbacks. I spent hours alone in my bedroom staring at the walls, trying to come to terms with the tragic events from my past. I refused to go downstairs or speak to anyone despite Estelle's best efforts. Instead, I took my meals in my room to avoid unnecessary interaction. Reading and listening to classical music were my only distractions as I struggled with an ever-increasing sense of self-isolation.

Gravely concerned for my well-being, my father arranged private counselling sessions with the renowned psychologist Harvey Walpole. But much to Father's dismay, I dug in my heels and stubbornly refused to go.

After a lengthy discussion with my father late one afternoon, Estelle entered my bedroom. Sitting on the bed, she stared at me intently. "So, what is the plan? Do you intend to kill yourself, Nene?"

At my startled expression, Estelle continued. "What on earth is going on? You hardly touch your food, you refuse to speak to anyone, and you have not left this room for three days. Your father is going out of his mind with worry!"

"I am sorry, Estelle. I don't even know who I am anymore. Do you think I'm going mad?"

Estelle spoke to me softly as she gently stroked my hair. "You are not going mad, Nene. On the contrary, you are half-crazed with grief. You have suffered the unspeakable agony of losing your newly born daughter, watched her die in front of you. I cannot imagine what that must have felt like."

"That's what I can't get past," I said. "It's my fault she's dead. Don't you see that Rosemary would still be alive if I had left Godfrey earlier? Instead, every night in my dreams, I see her not as a baby but as the little girl she would have become. So what can it all mean? What is the point of me?"

"It's not your fault you married a monster. You must stop blaming yourself. You need help." Estelle took me by the shoulders. "Listen to me, young lady, you will attend the counselling sessions your father has arranged for you, and I will come with you. I understand you feel broken by the past, but don't you see, my darling girl? Talking about it to a trained professional like Walpole can help you with the tools you need to feel better. Your first session is tomorrow morning at eleven o'clock. I will call to collect you at ten. Promise me you will be ready?"

"All right, Estelle." I nodded in resignation. "I will do it for you and Father. But you must promise me you will not leave my side, not for one moment."

Estelle shook her head, taking my hand in hers. "I promise

I will be with you, Nene, every step of the way. I will do everything in my power to help make you feel better again." I didn't have the heart to tell Estelle that you cannot save someone who doesn't want to be saved.

The following day just after ten o'clock, my father, Estelle, and I embarked on our journey to the New Jersey State Hospital. A trip that was to be one of many. At first, I found the treatment horribly invasive, having to relive the harrowing experiences time after time. Walpole's diagnosis was extreme melancholy after the death of my child. I was suffering from an acute episode of postpartum psychosis.

With the help of the lithium prescribed for me on a short-term basis, my depression slowly began to lift. Estelle ensured I got plenty of the fresh air and exercise Walpole recommended. Every morning after breakfast, weather permitting, Estelle and the children would accompany me to Trenton's oldest park, Cadwalader, situated close to our home in Parkside. We explored the Trenton city museum and the deer park, enjoying leisurely strolls around the stream and lake. When we arrived home, I kept my mind occupied by reading poetry, conversing with my father and Estelle, or playing music on the gramophone. I also spent many happy hours interacting with Estelle's children, playing games, singing, and reading. Estelle and Father told me they would often stand at the bottom of the stairwell listening to the constant chatter and laughter. The children had clearly played a big part in restoring my well-being.

As the year wore on, my spirits revived. Encouraged by my father and Estelle, I took on work as a private tutor. By the beginning of March 1895, I became restless. After much contemplation, I decided to take some time out and travel to Europe. Travelling has always been one of my great passions.

Later that evening, I informed my father and Estelle of my plans. I explained that thanks to Walpole and the children, I felt ready to face the world again. My first port of call would be Milan. How I longed to meet up with my old friends from La Scala. Performing at the prestigious opera house had been one of the happiest periods of my life.

During dinner, I read out a letter that arrived earlier that day from my close friend Sophia Stephanato, a talented mezzo-soprano. Sophia conveyed exciting news—she and Robert Moon, the musical director at La Scala, were engaged. The letter included an invitation to join them for a celebratory dinner on Tuesday, the 26th of March. Naturally I was thrilled to hear of my friend's engagement. I immediately wrote back to Sophia, congratulating her and accepting the kind invitation. My father was delighted to see how much Sophia's letter had brightened my mood. He immediately scheduled my travel arrangements and subsequent passage to Milan.

Chapter Eight: Irene Adler

The boat docked at the Port of Genoa on Sunday, the 24th of March. From there, I took a carriage to the Hotel Carlotta. I felt excited at the prospect of seeing my friends again and attending the opening night of Mascagni's latest Opera, "Silvano."

The following morning, before changing into a blue satin and brown cut velvet striped gown, I had an early breakfast. I made my way through the hotel lobby and at once saw my friend Sophia seated on a chaise lounge. I stared at Sophia for a moment. Such a beautiful, charming woman, dressed with simple elegance in a printed silk creme dress with a matching bonnet enhancing her slender frame, her long glossy black hair worn in an elaborate chignon. When she noticed me, her beautiful face broke into a wide grin. I remembered with fondness our first encounter. Seldom do you meet a person for the first time and find them bright, sharp-witted, and singularly free from grandeur, a winning combination in any person. Such was the case when I first met Sophia at La Scala, where we shared rooms. After that, Sophia became a significant part of my life and was still, to this day, my closest confidante.

We greeted each other with a warm embrace. Holding onto each other tightly produced a raised eyebrow or two from the waiters. When we finally sat, the waiter poured us a cup of fresh coffee, both of us dismissing the cream and sugar. Sophia beamed at me. "I am so thrilled that you are here, Nene. La Scala has just not been the same without you. How are you, my love? I have been so worried about you."

"I'm fine," I said. "I'm all the better for seeing you, Sophia. I am thrilled that you and Robert are engaged. Please let me see your ring."

Sophia removed her glove. I took her left hand in mine, inspecting the ring, a Tiffany diamond with three sapphire side stones. "It's beautiful." I gasped. "Like you, my dear. You know you are a lucky girl, Sophia, and Robert is a very fortunate man!"

"Do you think?"

"I know so. You need to keep reminding him. How is he?"

"Robert, you will be pleased to hear, is in rude health. He is looking forward to seeing you. He is also excited at the prospect of meeting up with his old roommate from university. He will be joining us for the opera and the engagement supper. I don't know much about him except that he's a doctor and has a practice in London." Sophia gave me a knowing smile. "There is, of course, someone else who has missed you almost as much as Robert and I have."

I raised my eyebrows, breaking into a wide grin. "Ah, Arturo! How is he? Does he know I'm here?"

"No, you asked me not to say anything. And, let me tell you, it has not been easy keeping your visit a secret."

"Thank you, Sophia. I wanted to surprise him, that's all. What time is the rehearsal?"

Sophia glanced up at the clock in the hotel lounge. "In one hour. We have enough time to finish our coffee."

Before long we were sitting snugly in our carriage. And, with a crack of the coachman's whip, we set off on our journey to La Scala. Ten minutes later, the hansom arrived at The Teatro alla Scala. I disembarked from the carriage, staring up at the imposing building on the open plaza. This was a sight that never failed to impress me. I was aware that many people considered the facade of the building to be a little too underwhelming. Its arrangement of neoclassical motifs didn't quite capture the grandeur that many people associated with a grand opera house. The interior, however, was another matter entirely. I glanced around the main square, the Piazza del Duomo, smiling at the familiar sight of the pigeons cooing and grunting, the tourists feeding them bird food from the little bags purchased from the street vendors. I had come home.

Sophia and I slipped into the side entrance. The rehearsal was about to start. We found Arturo and Rodolfo Ferrari, the guest conductor for "Sylvano," together in the orchestra pit in deep consultation. Arturo Toscanini was a dapper man around five foot ten with dark brown wavy hair, light deep-set eyes, and a carefully waxed moustache. He always dressed smartly, even for informal occasions, and this morning was no exception. He wore a three-piece grey wool suit and a black bow tie. His manner was, as I remembered, quick and alert. Sophia and I listened intently as Arturo addressed the orchestra.

"Right, gentlemen, I hope you all stayed in last night and practised your parts?" The orchestra nodded in agreement. "Perfetto! Then we shall begin. Let's start from the top." Arturo picked up his baton, and the rehearsal started.

After a few minutes, Arturo waved his wand. "Can't you read? Mascagni's score demands *conamore,* yet you play like old married men. God tells me what the music sounds like, but you stand in my way. The score requires you to be in one orchestra. Play like it! "Arturo waved his baton at the first cellist. "Where are you today, Henrique? Please read the music and play it precisely as the score demands. Gentlemen, I cannot think of a better way to spend a Monday evening than playing in this magnificent theatre. We are all so fortunate, are we not?" The orchestra nodded again in agreement. Arturo picked up his baton again. "Right, gentlemen. Let's start again from the top."

We stifled a laugh as we listened to Arturo in action. I whispered to Sophia. "God, how I have missed that man." The rest of the rehearsal appeared to go well.

Arturo laid down his baton, addressing the orchestra once again. "After I die, I will be coming back to earth as the doorkeeper of a bordello, and I won't let any of you in. Especially John Claude!" Arturo pointed his baton at the pianist. The orchestra burst into laughter. Arturo then addressed Ferrari, a medium-built Italian in his early thirties with dark, languorous eyes Although he wore a white open-necked shirt, black trousers, and a soft cap, he nevertheless portrayed an air of distinction.

"If you want to impress the critics, my friend, then don't play too loud, too soft, too fast, or too slow," said Arturo.

Ferrari nodded in agreement. "This is true." More spontaneous laughter erupted from the orchestra. This was a lovely moment, but Sophia and I were aware Arturo was renowned for his ear for orchestral detail, intensity, sonority, and his eidetic memory.

Ferrari shook hands with Arturo, thanking everybody. Arturo once again addressed the orchestra. "Well done, gentlemen, you have indeed redeemed yourselves. Ferrari and I look forward to seeing you back here this evening. Don't be late! *Non fare tardi!*" Arturo waved his baton, dismissing them.

Sophia and I waited for the orchestra to disband before making our way up the steps into the theatre. Still in the orchestra pit, Arturo looked up in amazement at this interruption. Running over to me, he embraced me warmly, beaming. "*Bentornato,* we all missed you so much, especially me!" He laughed, kissing me on both cheeks.

"I have missed everyone," I said. "I have missed everything, even your pointed insults, Arturo."

Arturo slid his right arm into mine and the other through Sophia's. "Come, ladies, let's go in for drinks. La Scala must celebrate the long-awaited return of the iconic Irene Adler!"

We entered the theatre bar and partook of a glass of Madeira. I looked around the bar as the door opened and a tall, dark-haired man walked in. He wore a grey flannel suit and a Panama hat and beamed when he saw me. I immediately recognised the black wavy hair and the large expressive brown eyes of Robert Moon. A tall, slim, handsome man followed behind Robert. This was John Claude Pierre, La Scala's resident pianist. As elegant as ever, John Claude wore a white shirt and a pearl grey suit, complimenting his dark brown hair, penetrating brown eyes, and tanned complexion. I warmly embraced both men before we sat.

The group conversation and indistinct chatter continued for some time. Eventually, Robert leaned towards me and whispered in my ear. "My dear Nene. Would you consider making a guest appearance for us this evening? One song would suffice. It has been too long." Robert gazed at me imploringly.

Sophia, overhearing the conversation, glared at her fiancé indignantly. "Robert, please leave the poor girl alone. Nene is our guest this evening, not some impromptu performer!"

"I'm so sorry, Robert," I said. "But I don't feel up to performing in public. I'm afraid I'm a little out of touch." Arturo looked at me.

"Nonsense, Nene! Someone of your stature? Come on, you will be fine, and the audience will be thrilled."

"All right, Arturo," I said resignedly. "I have no wish to argue with you. Only the one song, though. And it must be one of my choosing. Something I am familiar with."

Despite Sophia's protestations, Robert couldn't conceal his delight. He ordered champagne to toast my return, kissed Sophia and me on the cheek before dashing off to speak to the front of the house. Sophia confided in me that the box office had so far sold three-quarters of the available tickets for the opera. Still, Robert told her once the general public was aware of my impromptu performance, those remaining tickets would sell like hotcakes, such was my prevalence at La Scala.

After we finished our champagne, John Claude accompanied Sophia and me to the theatre for a quick run-through of the song we had performed many times together. Schubert's *Der Tod und das Mädchen*—Death of a Maiden. Sung in German, just singer and piano, Arturo always said it ideally suited my beautiful contralto voice.

After the rehearsal, we slipped into the wardrobe department where we met Madame Emily, a small, elegant-looking woman, her large brown eyes bright behind horn-rimmed glasses. She wore a loose-fitting black silk dress belted at the hip. She laughed with delight upon seeing me.

"How lovely to see you again, my dear. We are all so thrilled that you are performing for us this evening. Come let's see what we can find for you."

We rifled through the racks of gowns until we all agreed on a stunning pale blue silk evening dress with a low-cut neckline. The dress was a perfect fit. Madame Emily said it complimented my figure. "It's beautiful, Nene," Sophia gasped. "It brings out the diva in you."

I nodded to Madame Emily. "This is perfect. Thank you so much."

Sophia slipped back into the theatre to meet up with Robert. As it was such a lovely day, I decided to walk back to the hotel to take in some fresh air, slipping into the Galleria Vittorio Emanuele 11 shopping arcade, where I purchased a pair of silver shoes for my performance later that evening. Strolling through the arcade, I had a distinct feeling I was being watched. I could feel a presence walking closely behind me in every shop I entered. But every time I looked around, the shadow disappeared from view. Finally, I walked briskly out of the mall, deciding to take a hansom for the remainder of my journey. I stared anxiously out of the cab window to see if it was being followed, then breathed a sigh of relief when the indistinct figure disappeared from view.

Twilight had fallen when I arrived safely back at the hotel and noticed a man walking in the opposite direction on the other side of the road. He was tall and slim, wearing an Ulster and a flat cap. I watched him for a moment, walking briskly with a cane, until he turned a corner and disappeared from view. There was something vaguely familiar about the way he carried himself, his overall deportment—then I realised with a start that he reminded me of Sherlock Holmes. Entering my hotel room, I sat on the bed, sipping from a glass of water. The boat journey had taken more out of me than I first believed—my mind was playing tricks. *Adler, you are losing the plot.* Why on earth would Sherlock Holmes be in Milan? I decided to take an aspirin and a much-needed siesta to be refreshed for the performance later that evening. I had no way of knowing that Sherlock Holmes and Doctor Watson were in Milan on business. My path was destined to cross once more with the consulting detective.

Chapter Nine: Sherlock Holmes

Watson and I arrived in Milan on Sunday afternoon the 24th of March, as I was expected to attend the court of Milan the following morning to give evidence at the Rossini trial, at the Polizia di Stato's request, most notably my old acquaintance Inspector Romano.

Watson had agreed to accompany me upon discovering his old roommate from university days, Robert Moon, had become engaged to Miss Sophia Stephanato, a talented soprano mezzo by all accounts. On Tuesday evening there would be a celebration dinner to mark the occasion to which Watson and a guest had been cordially invited. I have never been much of a fan of social events, finding the banter on such occasions pointless and irrelevant. However, as Watson had kindly agreed to accompany me to Milan, I could hardly decline the invitation. I hoped it wasn't going to be one of those dreadful tedious affairs, plundering new depths of banality.

When Watson pointed out that Moon was the music director at La Scala and, as a special consideration, had reserved tickets for us in a private box for Pietro Mascagni's latest Opera, I gladly fell in with Watson's plans. Indeed, I told Watson I was very much looking forward to it.

An hour before the performance, a carriage came to collect us from our hotel, the *Guilea*. Watson and I arrived at La Scala at precisely seven o'clock, both suitably dressed for the occasion in black tailcoats, cummerbunds, white shirts, black ties, and top hats. We were greeted effusively at the main entrance by Watson's friend Robert Moon, an agreeable young man, before being ushered on a private tour of the theatre and the Museo Tratelle alla Scala, containing a collection of paintings, drafts, statues, costumes, and opera history. Our excursion culminated with complimentary drinks in the green room.

After escorting us to our private box, Moon handed us a programme. "We hope you enjoy the Opera, gentlemen," said Moon. "We shall look forward to seeing you in the green room for refreshments." Then Moon dashed off to consult with Toscanini, Rodolfo, and the Teatro alla Scala, giving Watson and me no time to ask the identity of the guest performer.

Ferrari picked up his baton. Adele Stehle stepped onto the stage to perform Mathilde's opening aria. The first act of Silvano had begun. Watson glanced over to me, nodding his approval. He seemed pleased to find me, his friend, in such an agreeable mood, my smiling face and impassive eyes no doubt sharply contrasting with Holmes the all-knowing detective.

At the end of the two-act opera, Toscanini appeared on the main stage, immaculately dressed in a three-piece black suit with a black bow tie. "Ladies and gentlemen, we hope you enjoyed the opera this evening. We now have a little treat for you. It is my absolute pleasure to introduce you to a good friend of La Scala. Performing the difficult piece Franz Schubert's *Der Tod und das Mädchen*, accompanied by our resident pianist, the prestigiously talented Jean Claude Pierre, ladies and gentlemen, please show your appreciation and welcome to the stage the estimable Miss Irene Adler!"

I was astounded as Irene Adler glided onto the stage, resplendent, oozing elegance to whistles and cheers. She smiled at the audience, gave the pianist a silent nod, and the piece began.

Watson and I looked at each other in astonishment. We'd read in the papers that the train carrying Miss Adler and her husband to the Continent, seven years earlier, had crashed outside Paris, killing everyone on board. Watson was saddened to hear of her demise, although I had my reservations. Still, it was pleasing to know she was still alive.

Then, finally, I contorted my face into a comical but good-natured expression and said quietly, "Watson, this is quite an extraordinary event."

Halfway through the piece, Watson glanced over at me to see my head swaying unashamedly to the music. There was even a tear in my eye as Irene Adler utterly commanded the stage. Her power and vulnerability splendidly entwined as she reached the third and thrilling finale of death's song in D major. I continued to stare in awe at the bold, quick-witted, and intriguing American. She was different from any woman I had met before, free from the old world of stuffy Victorian conventions, and therefore able to set unconventional standards, something I had always admired about her. Staring at her graceful form on the stage, I took in the glossy dark auburn hair, the smouldering violet eyes, the lightly made-up face.

The end of the song drew a thunderous reaction from the audience, who shot to their feet. Irene Adler looked up anxiously at the *loggiona*, but there was no need for concern. They were roaring in delight at her chilling performance. She beamed at them and said, "Thank you, I felt it too." She spoke in her New Jersey accent, which was, I remembered, unmistakable, well-modulated and pleasing to the ear. The accent had a profound effect upon me, quickening my pulse, and I could feel heat rise to my cheeks. Waves of love flooded in from across the crowd, along with cheering, whistling, and several *bravos*. Toscanini walked onto the stage to present Miss Adler with a large bouquet. She kissed him on both cheeks, taking a bow before leaving the auditorium. She returned for a final curtain call a few minutes later, receiving a standing ovation, more chanting and clapping.

Watson and I were amongst the many guests enjoying refreshments and hospitality in the green room. Watson conversed with Moon while I was on the opposite side of the room, with Mascagni and Toscanini. I shook hands with Mascagni, a well-built Italian in his early thirties, with deep-set brown eyes and a shock of wavy black hair.

"I have always held your work in high regard," I said. "I must say I found your latest opera to be rather a technical accomplishment after your earlier success with Cavalleria Rusticana."

"That is quite the compliment, Mr Holmes. Thank you," said Mascagni.

"You are right, of course. Silvano has been a challenge. Although I fear we may have been upstaged this evening by Miss Adler's spectacular performance." Mascagni chuckled, gesturing to a young lady standing beside him. "Mr Holmes, please allow me to introduce you to my wife and manager, Lina."

I bowed and shook hands with Lina Mascagni, a petite, dark-haired young lady with an engaging manner. We spoke until Mascagni and his wife apologised. Their carriage awaited to take them back to their hotel to attend a celebration dinner. After bidding them goodnight, Toscanini and I continued our conversation.

"Well, Toscanini, pray tell me, what were your thoughts of the opera?" I asked.

"I must say that I rather enjoyed it, Mr Holmes. But, for me, Silvano just lacks the fast-moving thrills and spills of Rusticana. Although I freely admit there is merit in its music."

"Yes, I agree with you," I replied. "Although I will say this for Mascagni, his music is never overly worried or prepared. I find that rather refreshing." Finally, I offered Toscanini a cigarette. He politely declined, pointing to his glass.

"I have only one bad habit, Mr Holmes. Well, maybe two. I smoked my first cigarette and had my first kiss on the same day. Ever since then, I have wasted no more time on tobacco." I threw back my head and laughed. Toscanini stared at me curiously. "Tell me, Mr Holmes, your thoughts on Miss Adler's performance this evening."

I waited for the length of a breath before replying. "I thoroughly enjoyed Miss Adler's spectacular performance. I met the young lady several years ago in London, albeit ambiguously, although I was not then aware of the full extent of her extraordinary talent."

"She is indeed magnificent," agreed Toscanini. "Irene's dedication to her craft is remarkable. When that young lady is on the stage, it is almost impossible to look at anyone else. Irene is an old friend of mine, although there was never any romance between us. We know each other too well." He chuckled. "We were, of course, both extremely proud and privileged to be chosen to perform in the world premiere of Giuseppe Verdi's Otello, which the great man conducted himself, here in this very theatre. I played the second cello at the time Irene joined the chorus. After our first performance, I was thrilled beyond words when Verdi asked to meet the man who played the second cello. They were good days, Mr Holmes."

I turned around at the unexpected mention of my name from another quarter, stunned to discover Irene Adler, dressed in a gown of gold and cream colours in deep conversation with Watson and Moon. Breaking off in mid-conversation with Toscanini. I strolled over to them. A quick blush passed across Irene Adler's face as I cast my eye over her.

"Good evening, Miss Adler." I extended my hand and smiled at her warmly. "It is indeed a pleasure and an honour to meet you again."

I was aware I was standing in front of one of the finest

contraltos, a prestigious talent. Without any warning, Miss Adler appeared to experience a syncope—her eyes glazed over, her whole body swayed as though she would faint. Then, with a valiant effort, she managed to steady herself. Watson quickly found a chair. Irene Adler sat, her gloved hands folded on her lap. Watson offered smelling salts and a glass of water while I ordered the waiter to bring a dash of brandy. After a few moments, Miss Adler had recovered. She looked up at me and I laid a glass of brandy within her reach.

"Pray, do keep up your strength with this little reviver. I don't usually have this effect on young ladies, I can assure you."

Toscanini and Moon rushed over to Miss Adler. She told them all was well and not to fuss, she was just a little overwrought from the long journey. Although I suspected it had something to do with seeing me alive after all these years. Then the strangest thing happened. She regained her composure, took a sip from her glass before standing up and extending her hand to Watson.

"It's a pleasure to make your acquaintance, Dr Watson."

"Likewise, Miss Adler. And I must say your performance this evening was transcendent."

"Thank you, Dr Watson. I'm very flattered. I appreciate your comments." She turned her attention back to me, fixing me with those wonderful eyes as though looking into my very soul. "You had me at quite a disadvantage, Mr Holmes. You have already met me twice, while I have merely been introduced to your alter egos."

"I feel honoured that you remember me, Miss Adler."

"You're rather hard to forget, Mr Holmes."

"Ah, yes, the scandal in Bohemia. Well, that was quite some time ago. I long ago deduced you were the injured party in the matter. Please let me assure you that there will be no repercussions from me or anyone else. As far as I'm concerned, the case is closed. Ancient history."

"Thank you, Mr Holmes, I appreciate your candour." She smiled at me.

"I'm afraid Mascagni and his entourage have already left for the evening, a prior engagement apparently," I said.

"Well, that's a shame," she replied. "Although I must say that, given a choice, I much prefer dealing with dead composers than detectives. One does not tend to run into them at functions!"

I chuckled as my gaze darted around the green room. "Is Mr Norton not with you this evening?" I asked, staring at the third finger of her left hand, which was ringless.

She shook her head. "I'm afraid that my husband is no longer with us, Mr Holmes. Godfrey was murdered in London nearly two years ago. The police identified the perpetrator as William Palmer. But, despite my husband's employers putting up a substantial reward, he has yet to be apprehended."

"Ah, Wild Bill," I muttered before composing myself. "Please accept my sincere condolences for your loss, Miss Adler. I read about the case in the papers, although I was abroad at the time. I noticed that the police identified the deceased as Godfrey Jones?" I looked at her questioningly.

She nodded. "That's because we changed our surname by deed poll, very quietly and without any fuss, before returning from the Continent. We didn't want anyone to become curious about us. We needed to avoid any unnecessary attention from the King of Bohemia and, of course, from yourself, Mr Holmes. However, at the time, we were under the misconception that you had passed away. I have to say you look pretty good for a dead man." She flashed me a coy smile. "I am sorry you had such a fruitless journey when you came to my house to recover the photograph of Ormstein and me, but I am pleased you liked the alternative."

I stared at her in disbelief. "How could you have known?"

"My good friend, Sarah Burton. She's an accomplished actress, you may have heard of her. She posed as my maid and told me everything that transpired."

"Everything?"

"Yes, everything, Mr Holmes." She laughed.

"Ah, of course, now it all makes sense. The maid who told me you left for the Continent at five-fifteen from Charing Cross?"

"Yes, I'm sorry about that, but I had to find a way to put you and Ormstein off the scent. Instead, Godfrey and I travelled the following day using fake identities. And after hearing what happened to those poor people, I'm so glad we did."

"I understand your position," I said. "Tell me, what brings you back to Milan?"

"I returned to the States with my father shortly after Godfrey's death. There was nothing to keep me in London. After a while, I became restless and decided to travel to Europe. Milan was first on my list as it holds so many happy memories. It was also good to reconnect with my old friends."

"Where do you plan to travel next?" I asked.

"Rome is next on my list, then Florence. I love the experience of travelling. It's one of my great passions. So tell me, what brings you and Dr Watson to Milan?"

"Watson and I had some business to attend to earlier today. I stood as a material witness at the court of Milan in the Rossini trial. Thanks to the evidence I provided, we received a guilty verdict on the indictment, the only possible outcome as far as I was concerned."

"I didn't realise your occupation involved such extensive travel, Mr Holmes."

"Crime and punishment are symptomatic of our time. My life is usually preoccupied with one or the other." I smiled at her. "Watson and I decided to stay on for a few more days, and I'm so glad we did." I glanced around the room. "This beautiful theatre is where my musical idol Paganini made his debut. Then, of course, your impromptu performance this evening, which I must say was indeed a welcome distraction. You have quite a talent, Miss Adler."

"Thank you, Mr Holmes, you are very kind."

"I have been in conversation with your good friend Toscanini. He has a very high opinion of your talent, and rightly so."

"Dear Arturo. He is indeed a good friend and generous in his comments. He is quite simply a genius, and well known for his eidetic memory, not unlike yourself, Mr Holmes. Did you know that before joining La Scala, Arturo was touring South America with an opera company as a chorus master? The singers were not happy with the conductor and went on strike. The musicians eventually persuaded Arturo to take up the baton. He conducted a two-and-a-half-hour opera from memory, although he was only nineteen at the time. I'm afraid that my talent pales into insignificance compared to his."

"Well, yes, he is indeed a remarkable man," I said. "But please don't diminish your exceptional accomplishments, Miss Adler, you do yourself a terrible disservice."

"My accomplishments may be far less than you imagine, Mr Holmes. However, I have been extremely fortunate in my career." She flashed me a wry smile.

"I fear you gravely underestimate your achievements, Miss Adler. I had deduced that you are a musician. There is quite a humility about your face which bears all the characteristics of one who plays the piano—your smooth, elegant hands, the long delicate fingers."

She looked at me curiously, arching an eyebrow. "Tell me, Mr Holmes, you intrigue me. Is there anything else you've noticed about me?"

"I can see that you have lost weight since our last encounter."

She stared at me in disbelief.

"Other than what you had already told me, I know very little about you apart from the fact you are the only woman who has ever outwitted me."

"Well, I can't argue with that. That was such a long time ago, Mr Holmes."

"I must say that the acoustics in this theatre are excellent," I said. "I much prefer German music to French or Italian. I find it introspective, and I have a particular penchant for Wagner."

"Wagner?" She laughed, shaking her head. "Another Wilhelm, and yet another terrible man. As for Paganini, the celebrated virtuoso, you're right, of course. The great man did make his debut here in November 1813. That appearance was said to have launched Paganini's career. He never looked back afterwards. He was from Genoa, if my memory serves me correctly."

"He was," I said, impressed with her knowledge. "You know, Miss Adler, mediocrity knows nothing higher than itself while prodigious talent like yours and your friend Toscanini's instantly recognise genius."

"Well, thank you." She flashed me an enigmatic smile. "I will take that as a compliment. Tell me, do you and Dr Watson plan to attend Robert and Sophia's engagement dinner tomorrow evening? Sophia is one of my oldest and dearest friends."

"Yes indeed." I replied. "We have it on good authority that the drinks and company will all be exemplary, and of that, I have no doubts."

"Splendid!" said Miss Adler. "You really must forgive me now, Mr Holmes. I'm fatigued from my long journey and the excitement of the evening. I must return to my hotel and prepare myself for tomorrow evening."

"Yes, of course. Please allow me to escort you to a carriage."

"That is very gracious of you." Miss Adler bade her friends a good evening, allowing me to escort her into the foyer, where I beckoned for the porter to send for a carriage.

After a few minutes, the carriage arrived. I unfastened the half door. "Allow me," I said, helping Miss Adler inside. "You know, you really should reconsider Wagner. He represents the all-important things."

"I will give it some consideration, Mr Holmes. I have Ashkenazi Jewish ancestry on my paternal side. Wagner was, after all, an anti-Semite, although I must say that Lohengrin is one of my favourite operas."

I nodded, gazing at her intently. "Watson and I very much look forward to seeing you tomorrow evening. I do believe that our time in Milan has invigorated Watson. He is a widower, you know. His wife Mary died only last year."

"I am sorry to hear that, Mr Holmes. I know from personal experience that to lose someone you love is the worst pain."

I nodded, pausing as though deep in thought, her eyes transfixing me with their searching glance. "I am a bachelor. Just in case you were wondering."

"I wasn't, Mr Holmes, but thank you for enlightening me. I am undoubtedly better informed."

I stared at her with amused surprise. "Just before you entered the green room this evening, your friend Toscanini was speaking to me of your speciality in opera. Sadly we never got a chance to finish the conversation. But pray, humour an old man as you fill me with curiosity. What is it?"

"My speciality is Wagner, Mr Holmes."

I stared at her, astounded. She met my gaze.

"According to Arturo Toscanini, I am an admirable interpreter of Wagnerian roles."

She laughed. "Just because I don't admire Wagner as a

person doesn't mean I cannot appreciate his music. Wagner had talent all right. He was never afraid to celebrate his innate creativity. But being blessed with a prestigious talent like Wagner is a rare thing indeed, one that does not discriminate. You cannot own it or buy it; it is a God-given gift."

I nodded. "I will bid you a good night then, Miss Adler. May I say, it's been a pleasure to meet you again."

"Likewise, Mr Holmes. I shall look forward to seeing you and Dr Watson tomorrow evening." She drew up her kid-gloved hands, waving to me out of the cab window.

I waved an arm in salutation, watching as the coachman brought down the reins on the horse's flanks and the carriage slowly moved away before disappearing from view. There was a spring in my step as I entered the busy throng of the green room, where Watson awaited me with a welcome glass of champagne.

The following morning, Watson and I breakfasted at our hotel. First, I ordered fresh rashers with eggs, coffee, and toast. Then, I picked up the open newspaper from the table and cast my eye over it. First there was a small review of *Silvano* within the inner pages of the publication. Then under a series of flaming headlines, the newspaper displayed a picture and critique of Irene Adler's performance.

I smiled in amusement, taking a theatrical relish in reading it out to Watson. *Irene Adler remains as ever the most talented contralto of her generation. We marvel at the expressive range of her voice and the emotional intelligence and power of her interpretation.* I tossed the paper over to Watson, who scanned the review with a dry chuckle.

"Well, Miss Adler has undoubtedly made quite an impression. But, good god, Holmes, I didn't realise until last night just how damned talented she was. I wonder if she intends to stay on in Milan. La Scala would be mad to let go of such a prize."

"From what the young lady told me last night, I believe she

intends to travel around Europe before making a definitive decision regarding her future. But you will be able to ask her yourself this evening, Watson. You must be aware that she is a good friend of Miss Stephanotis, as they shared rooms years ago, not unlike you and Moon."

"Indeed, Holmes, come to think of it, Moon did mention something last night I'd forgotten with all the excitement. What a small world we live in."

I chuckled as I poured us out a cup of coffee. "Eat a hearty breakfast, Watson. It would appear we are going to have quite a day ahead of us."

Chapter Ten: Irene Adler

Later the following evening, a soiree of guests attended the Hotel Victorie, where a drinks reception was underway in the large reception hallway. An orchestra played music taken from Mozart's most significant works. Holmes handed me a flute of champagne off the tray of a passing waiter.

"I have observed the seating plan and must say that it is indeed an honour to be sat next to you at dinner. I hope that does not prove too tedious for you, Miss Adler?"

"Not at all, Mr Holmes. On the contrary, I have found your conversation to be most entertaining so far."

Holmes's gaze darted around the room, which was filling up with guests in formal evening wear.

"I am hardly a fan of such occasions. But I believe we are to be in stellar company this evening."

"I hope you don't feel too awkward, Mr Holmes?"

"I'm far too successful to feel awkward."

We entered the dining room, taking our seats. Candlelit tables adorned the room, covered with crisp white tablecloths, glistening under ornate chandeliers.

Each place had a card bearing the guest's name, a menu printed in Italian that was decorated with silver vignettes, and a glass of Salento wine as an aperitif.

Robert Moon's mother Christine sat between Sophia and me, a slim diminutive woman. Her pink flushed cheeks were tinged with rouge, and her dark brown hair sprinkled grey fell in light curls on either cheek.

"Miss Adler, please forgive me for interrupting your

conversation with Sophia. But I wonder if you would be kind enough to escort me to the powder room? I am a little unsteady on my feet these days"—she gestured to her cane—"one of the many pitfalls of old age, I'm afraid."

I smiled at her. "Yes, of course. Sophia and I will be happy to accompany you."

Sophia and I escorted Christine to the restroom. On the way back to the table, Christine stopped for a moment, placing her hand on my sleeve. "Miss Adler, I hope you don't find me too impertinent, but I wondered if you would be kind enough to humour an older woman and allow me to switch seats. Also, I would love the opportunity to speak confidentially to Mr Holmes. I am such an ardent admirer of his work. I have read all of Dr Watson's chronicles. I hope you don't find that too much of an imposition?"

"Yes, of course. I did not realise you were such a fan. I'm sure Mr Holmes will raise no objections. In fact, that will allow me to speak to Sophia more freely."

"Thank you, Miss Adler," said Christine Moon, her face breaking into a wide grin. "You have made an old woman very happy." We returned to the dining table. The swap appeared to have gone unnoticed.

Holmes was in deep conversation with Doctor Watson and Arturo as the waiters cleared away the main course. The wine glasses were refilled with Chianti by the sommelier. Arturo, fortified with wine, was in full flow, entertaining Watson and Holmes. I could not resist eavesdropping on their conversation as Arturo narrated his favourite anecdote.

"After conducting a concert in a small town, I once received the following note from a farmer who attended the performance. Dear Sir, I wish to inform you that the man who played the long thing he pulled in and out only did so during brief periods when you were looking at him."

Watson and Holmes roared with laughter. Watson refilled

Arturo's glass. "My wife Mary was quite a fan of the Waltz King, Johann Strauss. The Blue Danube was her personal favourite. That song brought out the romantic in her."

"Yes indeed, Dr Watson," said Arturo. "Did you know that Strauss was inspired to write that waltz after reading the poem *Beck* by Karl Isidor? Each Stanza of that poem ends with the line *by the Danube, beautiful blue Danube*."

"I know little about the romantic waltz," said Holmes. "But I am familiar with the poem. Although one could hardly describe the Danube as blue."

In astonishment, Watson stared at Holmes and Arturo, shaking his head in good humour. Arturo held up his glass. "Gentlemen, to Strauss, the composer, I take off my hat. To Strauss the man, I put it back on again!" They laughed.

"I have always had a great appreciation for the German composers. Beethoven and Wagner in particular," said Holmes.

"Gentlemen," interrupted Arturo. "I believe the first movement of Beethoven's third, the great Eroica symphony, to be one of the most critical milestones in classical music."

"Yes, I agree," said Holmes. "That was indeed Beethoven's magnum opus."

"Did you know, Mr Holmes, that the Eroica symphony was originally a tribute to Napoleon?" Arturo once again raised his glass. "So to some, it *is* Napoleon. To some, it is Alexander the Great. While to others it is a philosophical struggle, to me, it is always allegro con brio."

The men raised their glasses. "A toast to allegro con brio!"

"Beethoven was fascinated by Napoleon," Arturo rejoined. "He considered himself his musical equal. They were, of course, both geniuses of their time. Beethoven intended to dedicate the Eroica to Napoleon. But when Napoleon crowned himself Emperor. Beethoven tore up the dedication page. Then he changed his mind, declaring, *Now he will trample on all the rights of man.*

"Napoleon was indeed a great leader," Holmes agreed. "He made a significant impact on the course of history with his uncanny knack for evaluating his enemies and finding the best way to defeat them. He would have made a remarkable detective. Napoleon said, *There are two powers in the world, the sword and the mind. In the long run, the sword is always beaten by the mind.* I feel quite an infinity with both men. I understand Beethoven remained a bachelor all of his life."

"Yes, Holmes, I quite see the similarities," said Watson.

"Beethoven may never have married, but he enjoyed women's company," said Arturo. "He had a penchant for married women. But sadly, the Maestro was unlucky in love, forcing him to frequent the city's many brothels. But you know his music doesn't belong in a court or a palace. He wrote for the people. You don't need to have an intimate knowledge of Beethoven's repertoire to enjoy his music, to feel the majesty, the greatness, of his talent. You ask Miss Adler if you don't believe me. She is quite the fan."

Holmes turned to his right to speak to me and looked surprised to discover Christine Moon sat beside him. He glanced over to me, raising an eyebrow.

I shrugged, grinning back at him. "You have quite an admirer," I whispered, gesturing towards Christine Moon. Holmes nodded he understood. He smiled at me, making polite small talk with Christine Moon, which appeared to satisfy her curiosity, before re-joining his conversation with Watson and Arturo.

Sophia and I were speaking of the engagement and the forthcoming wedding. "Have you set a date yet?" I quizzed.

"We have yet to agree on a date," said Sophia. "We were thinking late July. I asked my sister Ornella to be a bridesmaid, but unfortunately, she couldn't be here with us this evening. She is about to appear on stage in Warsaw."

'Oh, that's a shame, I have fond memories of your sister

from when we shared rooms together'

"Here's an essential question for you, Nene," said Sophia, a solemn expression appearing on her lovely face. "Would you do me the honour of being my matron of honour?"

"Yes!" I shrieked. "I would be delighted. Let me know the time and place and I promise I will be there to help with all the arrangements." I leaned over to kiss Sophia on the cheek, overcome with emotion.

"Nene, you will never guess who I received a letter from this morning."

"Who?"

"Katia Leahz."

I stared at Sophia. "The lovely Katia from Ukraine?"

Sophia nodded. "Katia read about the engagement in the newspapers. She wished to convey her congratulations at the earliest opportunity. She's engaged herself to the renowned surgeon Lars Feldstein."

"Well, her fiancé would hardly be a hospital porter, would he?" I quipped.

Sophia and I remembered Katia with fondness. The three of us shared a house when we were first-year students. Shared may have been a mild exaggeration. Katia was rarely at home. A year older than Sophia and me, Katia was tall, slim and elegant with fantastic waist-length wavy red hair, alabaster skin, and ice blue eyes. I recalled Katia always had long tapering pink fingernails and beautiful couture clothes. She attracted an army of ardent admirers but would only consider dinner invitations from the most affluent men, the start of every new dalliance recorded in ecstatic detail in her diary. Katia became engaged twice during that first year. On each occasion she ended the relationship, returned the gold rings but retained the stones and used the services of a jeweller. As naive first-year students, Sophia and I were fascinated by the outrageous stories she told us. We would sit up together until the small hours, arguing about life and love, getting a little tipsy on wine and Russian vodka. Our eyes would brighten with wonder as Katia offered her earthy and emancipated views on sex and relationships, speaking to us in her thick east European accent.

"Darlings, always remember it is just as easy to love a rich man as a poor man. I would never consider having an orgasm, darling, not until the man has paid for dinner. That would be entirely out of the question. Always remember, if men wish to sample the milk, they must first purchase the cow." Her advice to two impressionable girls was to drink copious amounts of champagne, always smile, and never tire of desire. In her opinion, sexual abandonment was a wonderfully liberating experience. Katia lived a luxurious lifestyle, a bon viveur, partial to expensive face creams, French restaurants, fine linen, and spa hotels. If she were about to order her last meal, Katia would ask for a wine list.

"Well, Nene, what about your friend Mr Holmes? What is the likelihood of a little romance between the two of you?" In a particularly naughty mood, Sophia couldn't help but tease me. "Do you not find him rather handsome? He's nice and tall, and he's got great legs. That's if you don't mind that intense introspective aura and those eyes that appear to look straight through you." Sophia stared knowingly at me, whispering confidentiality, "Nene, you know what they say about raw-boned men—they make the best lovers. Luckily for you, he's still a brooding bachelor."

"Well, I wondered who had the bright idea to seat me next to Mr Holmes. I should have known it was you. Subtlety was never your strong point. I'm sorry to disappoint you, Sophia, but embarking on a relationship with a narcissist megalomaniac is hardly priority. Admittedly he is handsome, but I doubt Mr Holmes is capable of loving anyone as much as he loves himself."

"Please forgive me," said Sophia. "I have been insensitive, especially after everything you endured with Godfrey. But you cannot retreat to your fantasy world just because fate has dealt you a terrible hand. There are plenty of interesting people out there in the world. You must be brave enough to look."

"Sophia, you of all people are aware that I don't actively seek notoriety or the limelight. I met Godfrey after a friend persuaded me to go to a dinner party, and we all know how that ended. No, not for me. I am through with romance."

Sophia took me by the hand. "One day you will see him. The one right for you. When the time comes, you will know."

"If you say so." I rolled my eyes. "I love your optimism." I glanced across at Holmes, who had just turned round to speak to Christine. His all-seeing penetrating eyes noticed me staring back at him. Our eyes fixed on each other. I quickly turned my head away, resuming my conversation with Sophia.

Christine was feeling unwell. She complained to Sophia and me that her mouth felt dry. I passed her a glass of water from the table. "Is there anything else I can get for you?" I asked. I noticed Christine's cheeks were flushed and blood red, her pupils dilated.

"The wine is very bitter." Her voice trailed off.

Watson and Holmes were still in deep conversation and banter with Arturo. Finally, they turned around after being disturbed by my cry as Christine collapsed. Watson immediately dashed over to her side. He took her pulse then checked her temperature and said both were high. He checked her heartbeat, which he said was racing rapidly. We all looked on anxiously as Holmes removed a napkin from the table and picked up Christine Moon's glass, carefully pouring the contents into an empty one before pressing the glass to his nose. As an expert on poisons, Holmes said he was shocked to discover the unmistakable floral scent. The tell-tale signs were all there. He pointed to the sediment of the shiny blackberries of the plant mashed into a pulp.

Holmes glanced over to Watson. "Atropa Belladonna has poisoned this woman."

Holmes quickly took control of the situation and ordered the hotel manager to lock all the windows and doors. No one was allowed to leave or enter the hotel except Roberto, the kitchen porter, whom Holmes sent out to fetch the police and summon the ambulance. Meanwhile Doctor Watson picked up a dessert spoon from the dining table and pressed it firmly into the back of Christine Moon's mouth. She began to retch. The hotel manager, Lucco Risso, brought in a bowl and a jug of warm water from the kitchen. Holmes passed Watson a salt cellar and a mustard pot from the dining table. Watson emptied the contents into the warm water, stirred the concoction with the spoon and then slowly began to pour the solution down Christine Moon's throat attempting to neutralise and dilute the toxins. Christine Moon retched again. Despite the less than appetising scenes, Doctor Watson was doing everything in his power to save her life.

The horse-drawn ambulance arrived to take Christine Moon to the Santa Maria Nuova Hospital accompanied by her son Robert as well as Sophia. My friend told me the doctors carried out a thorough examination and immediately started treatment. We later discovered that the toxicology report confirmed belladonna had indeed poisoned Christine Moon. However, thanks to the swift actions of Doctor Watson and Sherlock Holmes, Christine Moon was expected to fully recover.

Meanwhile Inspectors Romano and the Polizia arrived at the hotel. Romano, a medium-sized thick- set Italian, shook hands with Holmes before casting his dark eyes over the crime scene. Holmes later told me that he and Romano interviewed the remaining dinner guests before entering the kitchen to question the staff. Nicole had informed him that the sommelier, Peter Blythe, had absconded. Moreover, she gave an accurate physical description of Blythe, which matched that of William Palmer.

Holmes quietly took me aside. I was shocked to see him so grim-faced. He explained that he expected Blythe had posed incognito and was in all probability the fugitive William Palmer. "Miss Adler, you must follow my instructions exactly. Your life may well depend upon your compliance. It gives me no pleasure to inform you that you were, in fact, the intended victim of the poisoner. And I fear that you are now in mortal danger."

"Me?"

"Yes, it would appear so. I have spoken to Inspector Romano, and he would like to post a man in uniform outside your bedroom door. As a precaution, you understand?"

"If you feel it is entirely necessary, and if it will set your mind at rest, then I will, of course, comply. You obviously have friends in very high places, Mr Holmes, to go to all this trouble for me."

"The Inspector and I go way back," said Holmes. "Romano owes me a favour. I must go now, as I have much to do. I will come back to see you later. We are going to search Blythe's house. Romano's constables are checking the ports and the railway stations as we speak. No stone will be left unturned, I assure you."

Later that evening, Holmes returned to my hotel, where he found me still a little shaken from my ordeal. He explained how he, Romano, and Doctor Watson had searched Blythe's lodgings, but to no avail as he was long gone. Romano's constables, in the meantime, were still busy checking the ports and stations. Holmes ordered brandy, which he handed to me, speaking to me gently, in soothing tones. "I'm afraid travelling is going to be out of the question, for now, Miss Adler. If your intention was to return to the States, then I would not recommend that either. Certainly not at this moment in time."

"Why ever not, Mr Holmes?"

"Because you will not be safe until Palmer is apprehended. Embarking on either journey would be risky. Although we have alerted all the ports, the peril would still be far too great. I must make it crystal clear to you that you are in danger. To pretend otherwise would indeed be a cruel deception."

"I appreciate your candour, Mr Holmes. Thank you."

"I would like to offer you my services, at least until Palmer is apprehended. If you refuse, I cannot predict what will happen, but if you allow it, I can give you my undivided attention. I am asking you to trust me. Miss Adler. Will you?"

"Thank you, Mr Holmes," I said, staring at him pointedly. "But why would you do that? Why put yourself at risk?"

"Because I can, Miss Adler. And because I consider it a moral imperative. If you treat me as a confidante, you will find that I will justify that trust. I am hardly a wholehearted admirer of womankind. I have found most women I have come across to be inscrutable, but I can see that you are on quite a different level to any other woman before you."

"Thank you, Mr Holmes. I feel happier now you have offered to represent me. If you are certain it would not be too much of an imposition then yes, it would be a privilege to accept your services. Hopefully it won't be too long before this man is apprehended. Will Doctor Watson be joining us?"

Holmes shook his head. "I'm afraid not. Watson is travelling back to London tomorrow. Unfortunately, his locum is due to go on annual leave shortly, and Watson has several urgent cases to attend to at his surgery. However, he has very kindly agreed to lend me his revolver. Let me assure you I will do everything in my power to bring Palmer to justice.

Your anxiety will soon, I hope, be alleviated."

"Thank you, Mr Holmes. My father will be more than happy to pay your fee and any expenses we may incur."

"Then you may write to your father. First, to advise him that you are in safe hands and secondly that he may be at liberty to defray any expenses at a time to suit. Then suppose you let me have his address. I would like to write to him myself to put his mind at rest."

I removed a notepad from my handbag and scribbled down my father's address, which I passed to Holmes. He said he was in awe of my tenacity and bravery.

Chapter Eleven: Irene Adler

At first light I was showered and dressed. Holmes settled my hotel bill, advising the concierge his imaginary nephew, Horatio, would arrive later in the day to take over Watson's room. We then joined Watson for breakfast. Holmes handed the good doctor two letters, one addressed to Lestrade and the other to his brother Mycroft, happy that Watson would have them couriered to their respective recipients as soon as he arrived in London.

Later that morning, Watson, Holmes, and I arrived at Milano Centrale. Watson and I boarded the train to London.

We sat opposite one another in our first-class carriage. Sensing my anxiety, Watson tried to reassure me, patting my hand soothingly. "If you work with Holmes and support him, he will not let you down, my dear. You may trust him with your life,"

"I sincerely hope it doesn't come to that," I replied.

Watson put his hand on my arm, his face a mask of concern. Leaning forward in his seat, Watson whispered in my ear, "There are things you need to be aware of before you venture on this journey with Holmes."

He warned me of Holme's Bohemian habits, his brooding intensity, and his challenging demeanour. But at the same time, Watson assured me that I couldn't wish for a better protector.

"Thank you," I said, squeezing his hand. "You have been most informative. But I don't want you to worry, I have been dealing with difficult men for most of my adult life. It could be worse." I laughed. "It's not as though Holmes and I are married. In fact, Perish the thought."

Little did I know those words would come back to haunt me.

I left the train at Pavia disguised as a slim youth. I wore an Ulster, my hair tied up and concealed under a soft cap. I returned to the hotel as fast as the hansom could bring me. Upon checking into my room, I changed into a light blue dress and applied a little makeup before joining Holmes for dinner next door in his private suite, accessed via a communicating door.

Chapter Twelve: Sherlock Holmes

After supper, Irene Adler and I returned to the sitting room.

Motioning to the sofa, I sat across from her on a hard-backed easy chair. "I beg you to tell me anything that comes to mind that may help this case."

She nodded. "I would ask that you be patient, Mr Holmes. My narrative may at times be a little shaky, especially after all that has transpired."

Irene Adler spoke to me of her late husband's mental health issues, his opium addiction, and the trauma she endured after the burglary. I listened to her narrative with patience and scarcely an interruption up to that point.

"Did the burglars take anything of value?" I quizzed.

"I had a small casket where I kept my costume jewellery. It had been forced open, its contents discarded on the floor, although nothing was missing. The police found it all very strange. But unfortunately, they were unable to apprehend the perpetrators."

"There appears to be something of great value and importance to the perpetrators which has so far eluded them. However, after revealing your identity at La Scala, they now seem to have become focused on you, Miss Adler. Do you have an idea what they may have been looking for?"

She shook her head. "I have no idea. Mr Holmes. Godfrey did become involved with some questionable types, I know that. But whatever he was hiding could not have been worth dying for, surely. And why would this Palmer want to kill me? I am nothing to this man!" She paused for a moment. "I remember a man calling to see Godfrey at our home in Kensington. I only saw him from a distance, but I remember he had a distinctive scar on his left cheek, just here." She touched her own cheek and shuddered.

"He looked a nasty piece of work."

"Yes indeed. Palmer is one of the most dangerous men in England, and also the main suspect in a jewellery heist that took place over two years ago in Belgravia. The victim of the crime was the renowned jeweller Andrew Muscroft. There was little doubt that Palmer was the main protagonist. But, unfortunately, the police were unable to pin anything on him. Ronald Pickering and Ernest Sarti, two other gang members, were subsequently caught and arrested. They refused to give Palmer up. They said there is honour amongst thieves. Most likely they were afraid of what Palmer would do to them once released from Pentonville."

"I remember Andrew Muscroft. He was one of Godfrey's clients. Godfrey told me they met at Newmarket Downs."

"Yes, indeed. On the day of the heist, the Muscrofts were enjoying a day out on Newmarket Heath. Their horse Flickering won the Bunbury Cup by half a length."

"Yes. I remember Godfrey was there that day. He received a formal hospitality invitation."

"The Muscrofts and your husband were all there to cheer the horse on. How ironic that Muscrofts' house in Belgravia was under siege at the fall of the flag. The perpetrators were aware the family would be away that day and they would only have a couple of elderly servants to confront. They tied them up and thrust chloroform rags into their mouths. It would appear that your late husband and Palmer had some involvement with the missing carbuncle, the precious Alexandria diamond from Russia. The police never recovered the stone, for which a substantial reward was offered. It was fortunate for Andrew Muscroft that the London Insurance Company, who put up the reward, honoured his claim. Of course your husband had a first-rate alibi, having been invited by Muscroft to the races. Who would suspect him, a respectable lawyer, of being an accomplice? I know for certain it was the carbuncle they were after. Your husband's murder linked one event to the other, you see. I daresay they planned to wait until the coast was clear and then take the stone abroad to have it cut into pieces, which would make it easier to sell. I am a methodical man, Miss Adler, as you will no doubt discover during our journey together."

"I see that you are as meticulous in your line of work as I am in mine, Mr Holmes. I realise Godfrey was a lot of things, but I would not have had him down as a thief."

"Palmer was more than likely blackmailing your husband. And something went wrong. Whatever occurred between them, the stone is still missing and worth a Queen's ransom. It would appear that Palmer is under the impression that you either had the diamond or are privy to its whereabouts. He will not sleep easy at night until he has it. He disappeared after your husband's murder. No doubt hiding within the darker recesses of the criminal underworld, furthermore. Your appearance at La Scala has drawn him out, and I'm afraid that you are his intended target. But take heart, Miss Adler. Palmer may think he's clever, but he is no criminal mastermind."

"Godfrey never discussed anything with me, I can assure you. I certainly know nothing of any precious stone. I wear little jewellery, Mr Holmes, and mainly only paste when performing. Amongst my most treasured possessions is the broach I was presented with at La Scala before I took up the position of prima donna in Warsaw, and my late mother's wedding ring, which I wear on my right hand. Neither of these items holds great monetary value, but they have precious sentimental value. Jewellery and diamonds—life's trappings—are of little interest to me. If Godfrey became involved in a jewellery heist, it was certainly not for my benefit."

"Your innocence was never in doubt to me, Miss Adler. As far as I am concerned, your word is inviolate. Palmer is a complex character. He once was a skilled draughtsman and earned an honest living. He has already been in jail for assaulting a man over a game of cards because he bit off his ear. Hence his nickname Wild Bill Palmer." I smiled at her gently. "Palmer was known for frequenting a notorious opium den in Whitechapel. If your husband accompanied him there, as I suspect he did, he would have become putty in Palmer's hands. Men like Palmer are adept at exploiting weak links. But you must not fear. We will put matters right."

"Mr Holmes, I'm neither afraid nor hysterical and not usually prone to fainting." She smiled softly. "I can handle whatever there is to come, but you are right, of course. There are things from my past that you need to know. They are memories that continue to haunt me."

I leaned forward in my chair with a look of the utmost curiosity.

"You have my full attention, Miss Adler. Pray, please continue, and give me all the facts. You have my word that your narrative will go no farther than these four walls."

She took a deep breath, lowering her eyes, speaking almost in a whisper. "Godfrey inveigled his way into my affections at a time when I was vulnerable. Of course, I adored him, but I was not in love with him."

"From what I can remember, Norton was a rather handsome devil?"

"He was a devil, all right. And you're right, he was handsome. But it wasn't his looks that attracted me to Godfrey—I liked him. I found him charismatic and interesting."

"Wilhelm Orenstein told me much the same thing when he discovered you were married. He said she could not love him. Those were his exact words. I'm sorry to interrupt you, pray do continue. You have my full attention."

"Well, Wilhelm got that right at least." she scoffed. "Godfrey offered me the comfort I needed at the time. However, it turned out to be cold comfort in the end. I told Godfrey I wasn't in love with him. I felt I owed him that. He said he didn't care. He was certain I would eventually learn to love him. He told me I should always remember that the most important thing in a successful marriage was stability, which I thought was an odd thing to say at the time. Anyway, I married him, as you are aware, Mr Holmes." She stared at me pointedly.

I returned her gaze with an amused expression. "You knew!" I exclaimed.

"Oh, not at first, Mr Holmes, but later when I followed you to Baker Street and rather impudently wished you goodnight. I saw your face under the streetlamp. Your eyes gave it away, those windows to the soul. Anyway, I digress. Things were good between Godfrey and me until we returned to London, and that's when his behaviour began to change. That caused our marriage to unravel. Godfrey drank a great deal of brandy, he smoked incessantly, and not just tobacco." She smiled ruefully. "My husband was predisposed to fits of anger. He functioned perfectly well during the day, as his intellect was never affected. However, when Godfrey had drunk whiskey and taken opium in the evenings, he became a monster. Once he lifted me off the floor by my throat and I truly believed he would kill me that night. And I embraced the thought of it. Since that time, I have held no fear of dying. I finally plucked up the courage to tell Godfrey I intended to leave him. He broke down completely. He admitted he had mistreated me, and he had been unfaithful. I was already aware that he had other women."

She shook her head. "I appear to have acquired quite a skill for choosing habitual philanderers. Godfrey would not allow me to leave him. He didn't want everything to come out, you see, or for his employers to discover what he was. To the outside world, Godfrey was a man of class and position. Moreover, he expected to become a partner in the law firm within the year. He needed me to maintain that facade. I realised our marriage was just a cover for his profanities." She paused for a moment, taking a deep breath. "And then, I'm afraid, things got very bleak. After I threatened to leave him again, Godfrey attacked me, but this time it was much worse. He forced himself upon me. I was less than nothing to him."

Irene Adler paused for a moment. She swallowed hard, looking me in the eyes. Her pain was palpable to see. Her narrative had stunned me into raised eyebrows silence. I rose from my chair and poured a glass of water from the pitcher, handing it to her without saying a word. She sipped from the glass before continuing her conversation.

"Godfrey told me the only way I would get out of our marriage would be in a coffin."

I glanced over at her. She was deathly pale. "But did you have no one to confide in?"

"I didn't see the point in burdening other people, fearful that I would put them at risk. I have no relatives in England. Thanks to Godfrey, I had lost contact with my friends. I only had my father, and I did *not* want to burden him as he is not in good health."

I sat back in my chair, my head sunk in my hands. "He subjected you to an unimaginable life of terror. I can't even imagine how harrowing it must have been for you."

"The situation became so bad that suicide crossed my mind. That wasn't a cry for help, I just wanted it to be over. I considered all the ways to do it. Then I discovered I was with child and that changed everything. I wanted my child to live in a happy environment, without hate or negativity, so what did I do? I decided to leave Godfrey for good and return to New Jersey. I wrote to my father. He arranged to come to London to help me move. I knew if I stayed any longer, I would die. That was such a low point in my life, Mr Holmes."

"That was incredibly brave of you. It is when we are pushed to our limit that we realise what we are capable of."

"I discovered an inner strength I never knew I had. Then I found out Palmer murdered my husband two days before my father arrived in London. I remember Inspector Lestrade calling round to the house in Kensington to inform me. The first thing I felt was relief. Then I came back from the morgue and broke down completely. Even after everything that transpired between us, my husband did not deserve to die in that way. I lost my child on the day of Godfrey's funeral. My daughter was born silent, Mr Holmes. She fought so hard to make it into the world. Unfortunately, she only lived for a short time, too tiny to be viable. But before she passed away, she opened her eyes for a moment, and they were the most vivid, beautiful blue eyes. All I have left of her is a photograph and a lock of her hair. I called her Rosemary Blue—Rosemary for remembrance. There's an unimaginable grief that comes over you when someone you love dies before your eyes and you're too powerless to stop it. But at least Rosemary is at peace now and she lives on in my heart. I assume you don't have any children, Mr Holmes?"

"Sadly, not Miss Adler. I never married."

"Then forgive me, but I don't see how you can understand what I went through, and I hope to God that you never do. I later discovered I had a medical condition. The chances of my conceiving again are negligible. After I learned that, I was barely functional."

I sat back in my chair, my head sunk into a cushion. I half

opened my eyes and glanced over at her. "Miss Adler, the harrowing ordeals you have endured at the hands of your late husband, the shocking abuse, the sadness and loss of a precious child . . . you have shown remarkable courage under great adversity."

"The depression that followed was the most profound and darkest period of my life. I felt an emptiness that has never left me."

"You must have despised your husband."

"No, I didn't despise him. That is such a strong word. I would never allow bitterness to overshadow my life, but sadness, well, that's another thing entirely. No, I don't hate anyone Mr Holmes, not even Godfrey. Although I'm still shocked and saddened by what he became, I have forgiven him. In many ways, Godfrey was as much a victim as I was, tortured by his demons. When our lives on earth are over, and all our worldly cares are through, all our petty disagreements and our unwillingness to forgive others will come back to haunt us. They will become maggots that devour our very souls."

"Time can be a great healer," I said.

"In my experience, time does not heal, it merely accommodates." She met my gaze. "I want to thank you, Mr Holmes, for listening to my narrative. It is good to have the opinion of someone I admire and respect. But I don't want you to think of me as an object of pity. I am hardly Tess of the d'Urbervilles. I may no longer be able to hold my daughter, but she is with me every day." She brushed away the tears that sentiment had evoked, staring at me hard.

"Tell me, Mr Holmes, what do you see when you look at me?"

"I see someone who is lost in a grief that engulfs you like a shroud." I smiled at her sympathetically. "I find it outrageous that you have been the victim of another person's controlling behaviour. Bruises heal. It's the psychological damage that endures. We will see this through together. Of that, I have no doubt."

I knew we needed to take the road least travelled to escape Palmer's cronies. I wiped a tear from my eye, contemplating for a moment. Irene Adler's narrative had touched me deeply. I took a sip of whiskey from my glass before refilling Irene Adler's wine glass. We sat in quiet reflection for a while, barely speaking.

"This is a dreadful business, Miss Adler. Rest assured I will be making vigorous enquiries with the assistance of Watson, Inspector Lestrade, and my brother Mycroft. I have asked them to garner specific data. When this is at hand, I will have a clearer picture of what we are dealing with, but unfortunately, this may take some time. In the meantime, I need to get you to a safe house, somewhere quiet and unassuming. We shall be staying with my dear friends, the Espiritos, in Florence at a secluded farm. That is the place I first stayed after my confrontation with Professor Moriarty at the Reichenbach Falls. It is, in my opinion, the safest place to take you now. I have messaged ahead, telling them to expect us tomorrow. We will use a separate barn conversion, away from the main house. There are a handful of domestic servants. However, I'm afraid there will be no lady's maid. You will have to dress on your own for the foreseeable future. We will, after all, be residing on a working farm."

"I'm sure I will manage, thank you, Mr Holmes." She stared at me curiously. "Taking me to this farm must bring back memories of what must have been a terrible ordeal for you. What you went through with Moriarty."

"Yes, it was indeed the worst of times, but I recovered. And thankfully London is now a safer place, devoid of the Napoleon of crime. But unfortunately, his brother Colonel Moriarty took against me, vowing revenge as he held me responsible for Professor Moriarty's death. He suffered a mental breakdown over three years ago and was incarcerated in Bedlam Mental Asylum in St. George's Fields, Lambeth. Ever since I dread to think what that man would be capable of if he was ever released." I stared at her intently.

"There was one other thing, Miss Adler."

"And what is that?" she asked.

"This is my plan," I continued, my voice low and intense. "First, I have informed the Espiritos that we are married."

She stared at me in utter astonishment, turning pale. "I'm sorry," she said. "But the very thought of being married to anyone ever again makes my stomach churn. Is this elaborate deception entirely necessary?"

"Yes, I'm afraid it must be so. Let me explain. We must avoid any scandal or small-town gossip. I honour the truth. However, now and again, a little deception is necessary. Only my friend Ludo Espirito will be aware of the pretence. I have not taken this decision lightly, Miss Adler. I must ensure this family's safety as well as our own. I hope you understand my position?"

She nodded. "Yes, I understand. That will not be a problem. But, to quote the Bard, *All the world's a stage*. We all have our entrances and exits, our parts to play. If I am under the pretence of being your wife, then you must call me Irene. However, I am affectionately known as Nene."

"Then that's what I shall call you." I flashed her a somewhat uneasy smile. "We must maintain continuity and alleviate ourselves from any undue suspicion."

"Ahh, then I suppose I must call you Sherlock. Unless you too have a preferred nickname?"

"No, I don't," I curtly replied. "You may call me Sherlock." That wasn't an invitation.

"I would advise you to get a good night's sleep, Miss Adler. We shall find that we have a rather long and complex day ahead of us."

I gently placed my hand on her forearm, patting it consolingly. "I realise you have endured a great deal. The road ahead will not be an easy one. We must be vigilant."

"I want you to know, Mr Holmes, that I appreciate your sagacious comments and your kindness. You are quite a friend."

"My pleasure, Miss Adler. You can rely on me to do all I can. I have arranged for a carriage to collect us in the morning. If you can make sure your luggage is ready for the porter, shall we say seven o'clock? We shall have breakfast on the train."

I escorted Miss Adler towards the connecting door and opened it for her. "Oh, Miss Adler, there is one more thing. You will need to travel in disguise until we get to Fiesole, just as a precaution. You understand?"

She raised an eyebrow. "Horatio?" she quizzed.

"Splendid," I replied.

"God help you in your undertaking, Mr Holmes. You know you are an inherently decent man."

I nodded. "Good night, Miss Adler."

I retired to bed, aware of the fact that Irene Adler and I would once again have to put our acting skills to good use. I had never imagined in my wildest dreams that I would turn out to be her knight in shining armour, our paths crossing once again.

Chapter Thirteen: Irene Adler

I was ready and waiting when the carriage arrived the following morning. Finally, the coachman pulled up at Milano Centrale railway station at precisely eight. We boarded the train, making our way to our first-class carriage.

Holmes spoke briefly to the porter, who secured our luggage through to Fiesole. The train eventually pulled out of the station. Holmes had little to offer in the way of conversation, appearing deep in thought. I was not yet aware this was a portent of things to come. I amused myself by reading a novel. Sunlight fell upon the carriage window as I looked out at endless fields and a melancholy cottage as yet another station with an indecipherable name streaked past. Finally, luncheon arrived and Holmes, at last, put down his newspaper.

"You appear to be reading the newspapers rather diligently this morning?" I said, determined to try and communicate with him, anything to break the languorous spell.

"I seldom read anything except the criminal news and the agony column. The latter is invariably the most informative." Holmes smiled dryly, glancing over at my novel, *Jane Eyre,* his lip curled.

"You surprise me, Miss Adler. I would not have suspected you to be one of those young ladies reading romantic fiction, yearning for Prince Charming to come along to sweep her off her feet."

I stared at Holmes with amused surprise, pondering if I could use this opportunity to understand him further. He was like a closed book to me. He could be sociable, it's true, but only when it suited him. Moreover, he had never married, which was unusual for a man of his age. Nevertheless, I was determined to try and get to know him better.

"It is the titular heroine herself who fascinates me, Mr Holmes. I am quite in awe of her rebellious spirit and humility. And as for the Byronic protagonist, well, he is most certainly no Prince Charming, I can assure you. I may have dreamed of a fairy tale ending when I was a young girl. However, I quickly learned not to expect them."

Holmes cracked a dry smile as I glanced down at the book on my lap. "I first read this novel when I was fifteen years old. I am still completely enthralled by it. I was instantly captivated, not only by Jane Eyre's story, which is rife with betrayals, but I was fascinated by Charlotte Bronte's interpretation of the protagonist. Aloof, intelligent, and sarcastic, his mercurial character often prone to multiplicity. And as a consequence, his personality changes, abrupt and brusque. His narrative is often offensive and offhand, described by the housekeeper as a peculiar character, yet underneath all that lies an inwardly sensitive and passionate soul."

Holmes stared at me. Although his smile was sardonic, his eyes held a glint of humour. "Forgive me, Miss Adler. I did not realise you were such a leading authority on the Bronte sisters?"

"In my humble opinion, Charlotte Bronte is the most gifted," I said. "I find her work's individualism and richness refreshingly different to the other writers. As for Prince Charming—well, as we all know, he simply does not exist. I have already met one prince, Mr Holmes, and he proved to be anything but charming."

"I am a prolific reader," said Holmes. "Although I am not in the habit of reading works of romantic fiction."

We continued the rest of the journey in silence. His breathtakingly caustic observations had done little for my confidence. His reluctance to extend elementary pleasantries astounded me at times. I felt as though I had embarked on a journey with two different people. Holmes pulled his billy-cock hat down over his eyes. I glanced across at his proud, unyielding mask, dignity showing on every line of his face. I was beginning to have grave reservations at the prospect of spending so much time alone with Sherlock Holmes. The remainder of the train journey was far from pleasant. The carriage was hot and humid, my travelling companion moody and silent, barely speaking save for an occasional grunt or sardonic remark.

Later that afternoon I breathed a sigh of relief when the train finally terminated at Santa Marna Railway Station. We disembarked to the sound of birdsong and chirping crickets. The sky was clear, the warm afternoon sun beat down. A brougham and a pair of splendid greys awaited us. Holmes looked relieved at the familiar sight of his old friend Ludo Espirito, with his shock of black wavy hair, great earnest blue eyes, and clean-shaven face. He broke into a wide grin upon seeing Holmes and me approach the brougham.

Holmes greeted his friend warmly. He shook his hand heartily and slapped him on the shoulder, all traces of irritation erased from his face. "How are you, my dear fellow?" said Holmes. "It does my heart good to see you again, although I wish it were under less trying circumstances." Holmes quietly introduced me to Ludo.

"It is a pleasure to meet you," said Ludo, touching the brim of his hat. "Please forgive me if my English is a little coarse. My daughter Ava is quite a fan. She can hardly wait to meet you."

I smiled back at Ludo. His courteous manner and genuine warmth immediately put me at ease. The porter loaded the luggage onto the brougham, engaging in a little friendly banter with Ludo. Holmes tipped the porter before I stepped into the carriage, whilst he sat at the front of the brougham. Ludo picked up the reins and our journey to Le Sole had begun. The men spoke along the way, Holmes no doubt updating Ludo of the events that had transpired so far.

I was grateful the carriage had three sides, giving me the opportunity to change out of my disguise, which I deftly removed to reveal a dove silk dress. Then I reached into my valise, removed my shoes, bonnet, fan and parasol, now transformed into the more than respectable Mrs Irene Holmes. I used a hand mirror to apply my makeup, sighing as I placed my mother's wedding ring on the third finger of my left hand, a necessary ploy in my mockery of marriage to Sherlock Holmes.

"Forgive me, Mama," I whispered. I felt warm from the heat of the sun and the burden of the additional clothing. I closed my eyes, allowing the hazy late afternoon sun to wash over me.

The distance to the farmhouse was approximately four miles. The brougham climbed up the steep hill with the city on one side and the spectacular panoramic views of the countryside and plain. The carriage passed several vineyards dotted with ancient hamlets and a scattering of picturesque renaissance-style villas. Eventually the brougham rounded a steep bend which brought us into a long winding lane. Just ahead, set back in the beautiful hills of Tuscany, stood the isolated grey stone detached farmhouse Le Sole. The brougham continued until the farmhouse appeared straight in front of us. A giant antique terracotta sundial stretched in front of two wrought iron gates that closed the entrance. On the right-hand side stood two hedges of lavender and a path leading to the stables. Beyond the stables were aromatic fields of saffron, grain, and barley and a large orchard. To the far end of the orchard stood an apiary containing eight cedarwood beehives, housing half a million bees, next to which stood a large wooden shed serving as a storage area and shop. The paddock's rear was a wildflower meadow, brimming with cowslip, knapweed, buttercups, ox eye daisy, and an abundance of clover.

The brougham pulled up outside the farmhouse. A scented breeze wafted over my face as I stepped out of the carriage. Lifting the handle of my parasol, I glanced around the courtyard, taking in my surroundings. Holmes offered a reassuring nod. I barely noticed, focused on the task at hand. Holmes had set the stage; the first act was about to commence. And I was the leading lady.

Ludo quickly beckoned two farmhands to tend to the horses and deliver the luggage to the barn before ushering us through the heavy-set front door and into a large old oak-panelled hallway. We continued through a mahogany door into a good-sized, well-appointed drawing room with a large, old-fashioned open fireplace. There were two sofas, a chaise lounge, and a sideboard adorned with ornaments and family photographs. An abundance of light streamed through two pairs of French windows that faced out onto established gardens. The wooden floors were highly polished and covered with Aubusson rugs.

Holmes moved forward to take Violetta Espirito's hand as well as that of her daughter Ava. Finally, he introduced the ladies to me.

"My dears." Violetta greeted us effusively, kissing us on both cheeks.

In her late thirties, Violetta was an attractive woman of medium height, with long dark hair tied up in a knot. She wore a blue velvet dress trimmed with cream-coloured lace. Twinkling almond-coloured eyes that were bright and full of life stared back at me from an intelligent, well-defined face. Holmes then introduced me to Violetta's daughter Ava, a striking olive-skinned girl of sixteen or so with a smattering of freckles, tall and willowy with braided soft light brown hair. Her long curling eyelashes and magnetic blue eyes looked at me before her face broke into a smile as sweet as a summer pear. Even at such a tender age, the elegance and femininity of her features were evident to see. Ava wore a blue-and-white gingham dress and a straw bonnet with a matching silk ribbon. She gave a slight bow, gazing at me in awe as if I was the most exciting person to ever arrive in Fiesole.

"I am so pleased to meet you. I am quite a fan of the opera," stuttered Ava.

"Thank you, Ava." I smiled warmly at the girl. "You are very kind. The pleasure is all mine."

Violetta gestured towards the chaise lounge. Holmes and I took a seat beside one another. I gently squeezed his arm.

"We are all delighted to see you again, Mr Holmes," said Violetta in her well-defined Florentine dialect. "And to meet you, of course, Mrs Holmes. My dear" — she gestured to me — "You must be tired. What a monotonous journey it must have been for you. May we offer you some light refreshment before tea? A small sherry, perhaps?" She beamed at her husband. "*Cuore mio,*" she said, gesturing to the sherry on the sideboard.

"*Vita mia,*" he replied, pouring the sherry.

We gladly accepted a glass of dry sherry. Then the domestic servants entered the drawing-room, bringing afternoon tea with cucumber sandwiches, scones, cream, honey, and saffron cake. Violetta asked if I would prefer tea or coffee.

"Well, I am American," I said. "I much prefer coffee to tea, although admittedly I do drink far too much of it. This afternoon I would quite like a cup of tea." So I watched as Violetta poured the tea into white china cups. I accepted a teacup of black Earl Grey with a slice of lemon, while Holmes took his with milk and sugar.

"Tell us, Mrs Holmes, do you prefer the country or the city?" Ludo quizzed.

"I believe I am a country girl at heart, Mr Espirito. I love to be surrounded by nature, although I must admit there are times when I do miss the sheer excitement of the city."

"May I ask how you and Mr Holmes met? Was it love at first sight?" Ava asked excitedly. Holmes spluttered into his teacup, mopping up the spilt liquid with a napkin.

I gave a melancholy smile. "I can honestly say that when I met my husband at La Scala, I was completely swept off my feet."

"Oh, that is so romantic, is it not, mama?" asked Ava.

"Yes, indeed, it is very romantic," Violetta replied.

"How many staff do you have, Mrs Espirito?" I asked in an attempt to change the subject.

"Oh, please do call me Violetta, Well let me see, we have two domestic servants who live in the farmhouse. The Ankas stay in the cottage next door. They've been with us ever since we got married, nearly twenty years ago." Violetta smiled at her husband.

"Gabriella Anka is our primary housekeeper. She'll be attending to you and Mr Holmes during your stay with us. Gabriella's husband Giovanni performs a few light duties. He mainly attends to the bees. In addition, we cultivate and sell honey, mead, and beeswax in our little farm shop."

"Yes, of course," said Holmes. "I remember the apiary from my last visit. I've always harboured a longing to keep bees. They are such fascinating creatures."

"You must go and see Giovanni after you have settled in. He'll be delighted to see you again, a fledgling fellow apiarist," said Ludo.

"Thank you. I'll look forward to paying him a visit," Holmes replied.

Violetta continued her conversation with me. "The Ankas'

nephew, Javier, is staying with them for the summer. He's a fine young man, a student at the Conservatory in Florence. Javier helps out every year with the harvesting and general odd jobs around the farm and so do a few other boys from the village. The fruit picking season is a short one, although our modest orchard produces over seventy tons of fruit each season."

"You have a busy household then?" I said,

"Well, yes, it can get a bit hectic, especially at this time of year." Violetta smiled at us. "You need to rest. Would you like to go through to the barn and see where you'll be staying? I shall send Clarissa over to help you unpack. After that, we would like you to join us for dinner tomorrow at eight. There will just be the five of us. We cannot wait to hear about the wedding, we are all rather intrigued."

"Oh, please say you will come," pleaded Ava.

"Oh, we would love to. Wouldn't we, darling?" I said, looking over at Holmes.

"Yes, of course," he replied. "It's the least we can do for your kind hospitality."

Violetta and Ava escorted us to the barn situated a hundred feet from the main house. Violetta told me the barn had been converted into accommodation over thirty years ago. The structure looked charming in the sunlight. Painted yellow, baskets of fern and honeysuckle adorned the doorway. Crossing the threshold, we entered a large drawing room with a separate dining area. My eyes immediately took in the gaping fireplace with a lovely arrangement of spring flowers—daffodils, crocus, and gladioli. Violetta had furnished the room with an elegant collection of furniture. A chaise lounge, two tufted Moroccan easy chairs with colourful throws, an occasional table, a mahogany dining table with four chairs, and a sideboard nestled in the far corner of the room well stocked with wine, whiskey, port, and sherry. A small bookcase and a gramophone were at the far end of the room. The polished wooden floors were all covered with Persian rugs. The drawing room boasted a grand piano draped with a dust sheet. I pulled back the cover to look closer and was astounded to discover an original Fazioli constructed in 1881, an astonishing piece of work. I ran my fingers over the keys, frowning at the unwavering sound. However, I was disappointed to find the piano was badly out of tune. Violetta explained the piano belonged to her late father. They had moved it into the barn after he died in the event any guests felt inclined to play.

I explored the rest of the barn. A small kitchen contained a table and chairs, while a study lay to the rear. Holmes said he was familiar with the room and the hours he had spent writing and contemplating. The study was as he remembered—a small chamber lined on two sides with books, a writing desk, and a chair facing the window that looked out onto the garden. I was relieved to find two double bed chambers, each with adjoining bathrooms, their walls varnished, and the floors covered with dark cork tiles.

Each bed chamber had a double white counterpane bed, mahogany bedstead and headboard, a brown chest of drawers, matching wardrobe, a dressing table close to the window, and a plain wooden chair next to each bed. The windows opened out onto a lawn.

We wandered outside to look at the enclosed rear garden, which was picture perfect. Sea green grasses, with pots of coral geraniums, purple and lemon petunias, heliotrope, jasmine, and honeysuckle trailing down the walls. Our senses were stirred by a wave of fragrance and the aromatic odours of rosemary, lavender, and roses. The barn had an attached wooden verandah with a canopy and patio area, holding a table with comfortable looking wicker chairs and cushions. To the left of the main farmhouse lay another terrace and patio area, its tables and benches overlooking the stupendous Tuscan landscapes and the old Etruscan village of Fiesole.

Violetta handed Holmes the keys to the barn, assuring him that Ludo had followed his instructions to the letter and attached two double padlocks to the mullioned window frames. An iron crossbar secured the front door.

With Clarissa's assistance, we spent the rest of the afternoon unpacking. When we had finished, Clarissa drew me a bath before returning to the farmhouse.

After a relaxing soak, I dried and powdered myself, dabbing eau de parfum onto my neck and behind my ears. I slipped into a dress of green brocade and tied my hair up in a knot before entering the kitchen. Pouring lemonade into two glasses, I took them outside onto the terrace. Holmes joined me on the patio, dressed in a dark suit and waistcoat. He took a seat across from me. We looked out onto the garden, which seemed beautiful and tranquil in the late afternoon sun. I drew Holmes's attention to the sky. We had both been disturbed by the hauntingly beautiful sound of the swifts, circling and screaming overhead, swooping with magnificent grace. We laughed at their antics, marvelling at their stunning performance against the backdrop of a majestic Tuscan sunset.

"Aren't they beautiful?" I whispered.

"Yes, beautiful," said Holmes.

We continued to watch the swifts until the sun began to set. One by one the birds retired for the night, nesting peripherally on the eaves and the inner roofs of the stables.

"I think it must be time for dinner," I said.

Holmes nodded in agreement as we entered the barn to find the housekeeper Gabriella had arrived with a supper consisting of roast lamb, potatoes, garden vegetables, and fresh fruit from the orchard.

Gabriella served us. She was a diminutive, slightly framed

woman in her mid-sixties, grey-haired with suspicious brown sidelong eyes, and a pair of gold pince-nez that rested at the tip of her nose.

We waited until Gabriella's bonnet had passed the window before we retired once more to the terrace on the patio. The gentle breeze in the moonlight cut through the trees, making for a perfect place to relax. I sighed. "There's something almost spiritual about being surrounded by natural beauty, don't you think, Mr Holmes? It brings out the melancholy in me."

Holmes agreed. He poured me a glass of wine and a whisky and soda for himself. Removing a cigar from a silver case, he pointed to it.

"Do you object to my smoking, Miss Adler? Feeding my addictions is indeed a filthy habit. However, I truly believe that it enhances my capacity to work."

I took a sip of my wine. "No, not at all, Mr Holmes. Please do go ahead. My father smokes cigars. I have always found the distinctive smell of tobacco to be somewhat comforting." Glancing over at him, I said, "I want to thank you again for keeping me safe. You know it fills me with hope to see Ludo and Violetta together. The way he looks at her after twenty years is quite remarkable. Violetta is a lucky woman."

"Indeed," said Holmes. "A more united couple would be difficult to find.

A peel of thunder suddenly flashed across the Tuscan sky.

"It looks as if a storm is brewing. I think we should go inside," said Holmes. So, we entered the drawing-room, Holmes shutting and locking the patio door behind him. I could sense his mood had changed. He appeared a little agitated. He hesitated for a moment before staring at me with his penetrating eyes.

"Miss Adler, before we retire for the evening, there are a few things that I need to make you aware of, certain peculiarities of my nature. I feel it only proper to discuss personal boundaries from the outset, so we are both aware of what is acceptable and unacceptable."

"Acceptable to whom, Mr Holmes?" I frowned.

"I have Bohemian habits." Holmes continued. "You will no doubt become used to my little idiosyncrasies. I am an insomniac. I do, on occasion, allow myself the luxury of a lie-in, but never when I am working on a case. I sometimes play the violin during the night when I cannot sleep, which will often be due to my insomnia. If for any reason you decide to leave the sanctuary of your bedroom during the evening hours, then I would appreciate a little decorum. And I really must insist that you wear slippers upon these wooden floors." He sighed before declaring with comical irony, "Apart from that, you will find me as easy going as the next man. Ludo Espirito has installed a lock to the inside of your bedroom door for your protection. Let me assure you, Miss Adler, there will be no need to fear any impropriety on my part." He chuckled. "If we were the last two people remaining on this spinning ball of rock, and procreation depended upon us, then as far as I am concerned, humankind would cease to exist. I do hope that removes any doubts, fears, or concerns from your mind?"

I looked at him askance. Holmes nodded back at me shamefaced as though realising the implications of his narrative.

"That was crass and extraordinarily rude of me. I'm so sorry. That was a misplaced feeble attempt at irony."

I glared at him indignantly. "I must say that, in your case, it's sometimes difficult to tell. But you are right. That was a thoughtless, insensitive remark. Tact and diplomacy are obviously skills you never mastered. May I remind you that I am only here with you now because I need you to protect me and not because I find you irresistible? As for playing your violin, have you considered sleeping pills to help with your insomnia? I think I have some in my bedroom. Would you like me to fetch them for you?"

"No, thank you, Miss Adler." Holmes held up his hand. "Tablets tend to numb the grey matter, and it is clear that I need all my faculties. It is most likely I will be up and about by the time you awake in the morning. I intend to drive down to the village to check in with the telegraph office. If you wish to write to your father, I will be happy to post the letter. If you can leave it on the kitchen table, I will collect it on my way out. Then, while I am gone, you may find yourself at liberty to come and go as you please, whilst under the constraints of this barn, of course."

"Thank you, Mr Holmes. That's very kind of you. Let's face facts. It's not as though I've got a great deal of options right now. I will be sure to write to my father this evening. That will no doubt distract me from the disturbance of your violin. How fortuitous that I am a heavy sleeper."

"You have great wit, Miss Adler. I'll give you that," said Holmes. "Although I must say I'm surprised you have time for frivolity. Leisure is, after all, the devil's playground."

"Well, I am American, Mr Holmes, and it would appear that I have nothing but time on my hands. It is just as well that I have no fear of solitude."

He bowed to me coldly. "I bid you goodnight then, Miss Adler. Unless there's anything else you would like me to add, clarify, or explain?"

"No, Mr Holmes, there will be nothing else. Goodnight." I smiled at him sweetly. I then retired to my bedroom, sitting on the bed and reflecting on the events of the day. *This is ridiculous. What on earth am I doing miles from my home, miles from reality, living under the same roof as Doctor Jekyll and Mr Hyde.*

I proceeded to write a long letter to my father. On my way back from the kitchen, where I had left the envelope on the table, I heard the distinct sound of a violin. The notes were ragged and full of discords, the long-drawn wailing notes wafting under my bedroom door. I sighed.

Day one with Mr Holmes, and already disillusionment had kicked in. I found myself alone in my room, reflecting on the irreparable ridiculousness of my situation, a situation so far removed from my gilded world. Mr Holmes was indeed a complex figure, brilliant yet mentally terrifying. Eccentricities bordering on disrespectful, incredibly formal, unbelievably uptight. I was still trying to decide if he was the rudest man I had ever met or just an arrogant boor. And yet there had been moments of extraordinary kindness. I brushed my long hair in the mirror. My eyes rolled as Holmes continued to play. I couldn't help wondering if his insomnia had been compounded by the fact that he lived and worked in London.

I spoke to myself into the mirror. "Still struggling to sleep, Mr Holmes. Why, that's a pity. If the violin is not working, might I suggest listening to one of your sanctimonious lectures? Yes, that should do it for you." I chuckled as I climbed into bed, face mask pulled over my eyes. Then, utterly exhausted, I drifted off into a deep sleep.

Chapter Fourteen: Irene Adler

Holmes was true to his word and was always first one stirring in the mornings. I would sometimes observe him from my bedroom window, sitting on the porch at dawn with a cup of fresh coffee and a cigarette. Then Holmes would drain his coffee cup, carefully stubbing out his cigarette before setting out on his journey to the village.

Holmes returned each day before luncheon, giving him ample time to relax in the drawing-room with his pipe rack and his slipper of tobacco as he studied the morning papers. First the *Corriere Della Sera,* and then the *il Sole 24 Ore.* Each publication sorely tested his command of the Italian language. Hence the floor around his chair would be randomly littered with cigarette ends, tobacco, and discarded newspaper cuttings.

Holmes' eccentric conduct had unfortunately caught the attention of Gabriella. She shot him a look of disdain each time he returned from his morning excursions. Holmes' steely grey eyes would glance to where Gabriella had tidied up after him, complaining that the room was ridiculously tidy. Then Holmes resumed where he had left off first, knocking the ashes out of his after-breakfast pipe onto the wooden floor then slowly refilling it, much to Gabriella's horror. Finally, she would lament to anyone who would listen that she was constantly removing tobacco from ridiculous places.

One morning Gabriella entered the barn with a basket of clean laundry and was shocked to discover the room where Holmes had sat once more in a state of wild disarray. Then, after an episode involving a particularly energetic emptying of ashtrays and slippers, things came to a head. Gabriella rushed into the drawing-room, her pince-nez pushed up onto her forehead and her cap strings flying around her chin. She complained to me, gesturing to the overflowing ashtray on the occasional table.

"God in heaven!" cried Gabriella. "Look at the state of this room. Your husband even keeps tobacco in his slipper. Why? It's enough to drive any woman out of her wits!"

I patted Gabriella's arm reassuringly. "My dear Gabriella. In the eyes of my husband, organisation is in the mind, not just the environment. Mr Holmes may be messy and untidy at times, but he is never disorganised. There is most certainly a method to his madness."

"Hmm, some might say there is madness in his method." Gabriella sniffed before dashing off to fetch the dustpan and brush. She swept up the tobacco remnants and cleaned the room before returning to her cottage, a look of the utmost perplexity upon her face.

I awoke each morning to the sound of the swifts singing outside my bedroom window, the sun streaming through the blinds, and the aromatic aroma of cafe noir. Gabriella arrived every morning with a breakfast of toast, butter, *cantucci*, honey, and fresh fruit. I took only coffee noir and dry toast, having little appetite in the morning. After breakfast, I sliced up the leftover bread before walking into the garden, calling out to the swifts. Tossing the bread onto the lawn, I laughed as I felt the winged feathers of the male birds brushing against my legs until every crumb was gone. Then the swifts flew back into the eaves of the barn, re-joining the females.

Gabriella returned after breakfast as part of her daily routine to collect the towels, sheets, and other laundry. To help pass the time, I would often engage in a little small talk with her. For example, I noticed the housekeeper raised an eyebrow at being expected to change two separate beds. Although it was customary for married couples to sleep in separate bedrooms during this period, it was inappropriate to do so during the honeymoon period, regarded by many as the most beautiful time in a couple's marriage. I sensed that Gabriella was suspicious. Nevertheless, I treated the housekeeper kindly, poured her a cup of tea from the pot and pushed a plate of *cantucci* towards her. We would sit at the kitchen table chatting until eventually Gabriella returned to her duties.

On the first morning, I gestured towards the second bedroom and shrugged. "Ah, Gabriella, my husband . . . he is quite the snorer, and a girl needs her sleep."

Chapter Fifteen: Sherlock Holmes

I routinely drove down to the village each morning, considering it only proper to give Irene Adler as much privacy as possible. I posted the letters, checking in with the telegraph office, before making an extensive tour of the neighbourhood I was so familiar with, taking in every detail, looking out for anything suspicious.

On the first morning, I stopped off on my way back from the village to visit Giovanni Anka at the apiary. The sight of Giovanni's face struck a chord with me, his deep-set brown eyes hidden behind round spectacles, the familiarity of the grizzled beard and his deeply lined features, the locks of grey hair curling from under his tattered straw hat. He was as I remembered, although his shoulders were more bowed, and he looked a little older.

He had at once recognised me as we shook hands. "How are you, Anka? Still tending your bees, I see."

"It's good to see you again, Mr Holmes," said Anka. "As you can see, I'm still here, not getting any younger. I'm beyond autumn, as my wife keeps reminding me. On a warm spring day, there are few places on earth I'd rather be than right here tending my bees."

We stood in silence for a moment as we listened in awe to the hum and murmur of the worker bees inside the hives which, mixed with the constant buzz of activity in the wildflower meadow close by, was an exhilarating experience. But then our eyes diverted to an apple tree engulfed by the whirring hum of a thousand tiny wings.

"A connection with nature that's a balm for the soul." I shook my head. "You must have spent many happy hours with these magnificent creatures."

"I have indeed, Mr Holmes. You know this has always been my favourite time of year. The bees perform a little waggle dance to signal where the best flowers are in the meadow. They love the clover and the apple and pear trees."

"I have always been fascinated by bees, ever since I was a young boy. Tell me, before you open a hive, do you still blow a little smoke into it?"

"Yes, Mr Holmes, it calms the swarm. But, like people, some colonies are more aggressive than others. We have to watch out for wasps and hornets, or they will destroy the hives. Tending the bees has become an almost religious experience. There is something rather spiritual about bees. I truly believe they have souls. They are the saviours of humanity." Anka lit a sprig of rosemary, wafting it gently over the comb.

I smiled at Anka. Half closing my eyes, I recited a poem from *The Tempest*:

Where the bee sucks, there suck I:
In a cowslip's bell, I lie,
There I crouch when owls do cry.
On the bat's back, I do fly.
After summer merrily.
Merrily, merrily shall I live now
Under the blossom that hangs on the bough.

"Well, thank you for your time, Anka." I extended my hand. "I had best be on my way. It has been a pleasure to see you again. And these magnificent creatures, of course."

"I understand that congratulations are in order." Anka stared at me curiously. "they told me you had recently married. Le Sole is rather an odd place to celebrate your nuptials. It wouldn't be my first choice." He chuckled.

"Yes, indeed," I replied. "As my wife and I recently married in Italy, it would have been churlish of me not to take the opportunity to call and pay my respects to the people who were instrumental in helping me when I was last here four years ago. I shall never forget the kindness bestowed upon me."

"We are all pleased to see you again, Mr Holmes. You are a sight for sore eyes, and that's a fact. I take it you are having a rest from all the sleuthing while you are here on a honeymoon?"

"I always keep my wits about me, Anka. I am no stranger to the unexpected. Evil is all around us, my friend. It can manifest itself as quickly as these magnificent creatures produce honey."

"Please feel free to visit the apiary at any time, Mr Holmes. There will always be a warm welcome for you here." I shook hands with Giovanni before returning to the brougham and making my way back to the barn.

Chapter Sixteen: Irene Adler

Later that evening, as Holmes and I prepared for dinner. I was distraught to discover I had mislaid my favourite ebony hair clip, a gift from Estelle. I knew I had packed it, as I remembered seeing it in my case in Milan. I decided to search for it later, otherwise, I would be late for dinner and had no wish to keep the celebrated detective waiting. Perish the thought. Attired in a white gown with a crochet lace bodice, my hair hung in rag curls, I entered the drawing room. Holmes acknowledged my presence with a curt nod.

"Good evening, Miss Adler. I hope you are feeling up to the interrogation you are most likely to receive from Violetta and Ava Espirito. I fancy the ladies will be far more interested in your narrative than mine."

"Ah, yes. Especially Ava," I said. "That young lady has such an enquiring mind. I will be fine, Mr Holmes. It is yet another opportunity to hone my acting skills. Although from what I can remember you are hardly devoid of talent in that department yourself."

Holmes flashed me a tight-lipped smile. Although his mood appeared to have changed again, I could feel the tension in the room. In truth, Holmes' mood had not improved since we arrived in Fiesole. He was no doubt pining for the hustle and bustle of London—the mess, the noise, and his bohemian lifestyle. Living in semi-isolation under the same roof as a woman, Holmes was clearly not a happy man. The thought that he was to be the subject of close personal scrutiny obviously did not bode well with him.

Holmes shrugged in an ungracious manner whenever I attempted to broach the subject. Little by little, I was discovering the uncertainty of his mood changes. Finally deciding to act, I gazed up at him with a smile. "Mr Holmes, do you not think we should devise a plan, some kind of strategy before we go to dinner? Our narrative surely ought to be believable." I held out my notebook. "I made a few notes this morning, which I have been memorising. I am more than happy to relay them to you. Do you have anything you would like to add?" I waited, expectantly.

He bowed to me coldly, avoiding my eyes. "Oh, I think it would be best to leave the salacious details of our married life in your more than capable hands, Miss Adler." He snorted. "Hopefully, it should not prove too trying. My ideas would not look out of place on the back of a Vestas matchbox!"

I stared at him in disbelief as, for the first time, I began to doubt my protector. The response from Holmes was indifference. He sighed deeply, staring at me coldly. "I hope you are not going to cry, Miss Adler?"

"No, I am not going to cry," I said. "First, I would not give you the satisfaction. And quite frankly, I find your disrespectful tone and lack of empathy completely underwhelming. I appreciate that this isn't easy for either of us, but even so, that doesn't give you poetic licence to treat me as such, leaving everything up to me just because you feel unhappy." I forced a smile and bit my quivering lip, then nodded. "If that's what you want, then so be it."

I was seething inside, and not at all happy with his insinuations that I was promiscuous. Still, I would set that aside for another time, a time when he was in a more pleasant mood. God knew when that would be. This elaborate deception was, after all, his idea. Even so, I was beginning to have grave reservations about the dinner. *He is going to hate this.* Living under the same roof with an egomaniac whose moods appeared to change more often than the weather was hardly my idea of fun. But if he was leaving the details of our marriage in my more than capable hands, then I must be sure not to disappoint him.

"Yes, Mr Holmes. You are right, of course. It is indeed fortuitous that we have my invaluable experience to draw upon. In the meantime, you could attempt to smile a little more. For appearance's sake, of course."

Holmes bowed with cold self-possession.

We walked over to the farmhouse together. I noticed Ava peering out of the drawing-room window, her face pressed against the windowpane. I casually touched Holmes's sleeve, linking my arm into his. Holmes recoiled at my touch. He looked at me in the startled fashion of a young stag facing the barrel of a gun, fixing me with an intense piercing stare.

"We are under scrutiny," I said,

A wry smile crossed my lips as Holmes returned a silent nod, retaining his pensive mood. Finally, we arrived at the farmhouse and were greeted at the front door by Antonia. She escorted us into the drawing-room. The Espirito family were all in attendance, anxiously waiting to greet their guests. "You are both very welcome." Ludo beamed. "Do come and join us in the drawing-room. We have been looking forward to seeing you."

We were seated together on a hard-backed couch. Ludo poured Holmes a whisky and soda. I accepted a small glass of dry sherry, aware that I needed to keep my wits about me for now.

Violetta smiled at us warmly. "I trust you both slept well?"

"Yes, we did, thank you," I said. "We were both exhausted after our long journey. However, I would like to take this opportunity to thank you all, on behalf of myself and my husband, for accommodating us at such short notice."

"It is not a problem," said Violetta. "You will both always

be welcome in our home at any time."

I took a sip from my glass, meeting Violetta's gaze. "You know Sherlock insisted on bringing me here to show me where he stayed in Fiesole and to introduce me to his friends. But I must say the farm is so beautiful and tranquil, it's just what we needed after our hectic schedules."

Ava was staring at me. Her face flushed, she was almost delirious with excitement. "What part of America are you from, Mrs Holmes?"

"Oh please, I must insist that you all call me Nene. Mrs Holmes is far too formal. We are all friends here, are we not? I am from Trenton in New Jersey. I miss my homeland so much. The rolling hills, the verdant forests . . . and of course my family."

"Nene, do you think you will ever return to live in America?"

"I doubt it, Ava. I will, of course, return from time to time to see my family. But, speaking as a performer, Americans chip away at you when you are successful, whereas in Europe they tend to put you on a pedestal. But of course, my rightful place is now in London with my beloved husband." I smiled at Holmes, gazed at him adoringly. He shifted uncomfortably in his seat.

"But surely you will miss performing at La Scala?" said Violetta.

"Yes, I will. I intend to return there one day, but for now, I must put my husband first. When you truly love someone, you want the best for them. Even if it's not always the right thing for you." I glanced across the table to observe Holmes arch an eyebrow. I tightly drew my lips, trying not to smile.

"Nene, may I ask, what's your favourite song?" asked a wide-eyed Ava.

"The hymn by John Newton, *Amazing Grace.*"

"Why that song?"

"Because it is so inspirational. Newton's inspiring lyrics will always retain their relevance. However, I have to say that Stephen Foster, the father of American music, was one of my most significant musical influences."

Violetta glanced over at her daughter, giving her a minute shake of her head. "Ava, you are bombarding our guest with far too many questions."

I laughed. "It's not a problem, Violetta. Ava is naturally curious, as was I at her age. So I don't mind."

Given carte blanche, Ava continued with her interrogation. "Why did you decide to become an opera singer, and did you enjoy your time at La Scala?"

"My father taught me to play the pianoforte when I was five years old. I remember the first time I heard him play *Für Elise* by Beethoven. I was completely captivated by the melody. After that, my inner diva emerged, and I demanded professional lessons. So I started piano lessons with a private tutor from age six. I took up singing lessons around the same time. The day I joined La Scala was the happiest of my life. When I became prima donna, I received letters from people suffering from many problems. They told me that my singing was like medicine to them and transported them from their unfortunate situations. That was quite a humbling experience."

"I have always yearned to visit La Scala," said Ava. "I have never been farther than Siena. But it must be quite something to be able to go out and spread joy into the lives of other people. How does it feel, being on the stage of that magnificent theatre, singing in front of all those people?"

"Special, extraordinary, standing amongst the greats. There is a high that is equal to nothing else. But you know you have to go out there and give a piece of yourself, your life, your soul. Then perhaps the *loggione* will accept you and give you an outstanding ovation at the end of your performance."

Ava stared at me excitedly. Finally, Violetta looked over at her daughter, holding up a warning finger. "Please make this your last question, young lady."

"I will, I promise. I am sorry, Mamma," Ava turned her attention back to me. "Nene, have you ever wondered what you would have done, what career you would have chosen if you hadn't become an opera singer?"

"Well, that's an excellent question, Ava, and an easy one for me to answer. I would have become an actress certainly. I always enjoyed reading plays, and when I was at school, I played Ophelia in *Hamlet*. Since then, I have always had a penchant for the *Sweet Swan of Avon*. I travelled to New York when I was eighteen and attended acting lessons on Broadway. The teachers were pretty tough. One day they ordered the students to go home and take a bath in ice-cold water to improve our mental resilience." I laughed out loud, observing Ava's shocked expression.

"I was fortunate to appear in two productions on Broadway. That was an exciting time for a young girl. My father insisted that I continue with my operatic training. I travelled to Warsaw later that year and spent the next three years receiving special training before taking up a position at the Warsaw governmental theatre. I studied and performed all the principal contralto roles to craft my versatility. A few months later, I finally achieved my dream of being accepted into the chorus at La Scala. I was there for three years before I was offered the prima donna's position at the Grand Opera house in Warsaw. In hindsight, that was the worst decision I ever made. After a disastrous love affair, I decided to try my luck and move to London. I performed in several concerts and took pupils under my tutelage in singing and the pianoforte. I met my first husband, Godfrey, in London. He died over two years ago. So, when I met Sherlock at La Scala, it felt as though fate had at last dealt me a winning hand. They say the third time's the charm!"

Violetta looked over at me in admiration. "My God, Nene, you have indeed led an adventurous life. You take my breath away. You are so confident, so polished."

Ludo paused from topping up my glass and smiled at me. "From what we read in the *giornali*, you were often under scrutiny, did you feel that you were treated differently because you are woman?"

"Oh, without a shadow of a doubt Ludo! But, of course, being discriminated against in public was all part and parcel of being in the limelight. I learned to trust my instincts in a profession where women's voices are seldom heard. Our male contemporaries get away with so much more than women. There were so many articles that began with Irene Adler and so and so. Any relationship I entered into, no matter how innocent, would take precedence over my success. And that was the main reason Sherlock and I have kept our marriage under wraps until now. In fact, at this moment in time, only you lovely people and a few of the villagers are privy to the fact we are married." I glanced across at Holmes.

He stared back at me pensively.

"Well," said Violetta. "You may have all the peace and tranquillity you desire here at Le Sole. And I speak for all of us when I say that you are both welcome to stay here with us for as long as you need."

Holmes turned his head and smiled at Violetta. "That is most kind of you, thank you."

Violetta beamed at him, waving a languid hand dismissively. "It's nothing. Our great pleasure."

Ava had never taken her eyes off me. "Nene, it must be wonderful to be famous."

"Fame is a funny business," I promptly rejoined. "Fickle too. It doesn't change who you are, it only changes people's perception of you."

"I would love to go to La Scala one day." Ava smiled wistfully.

"Well, Ava, we will have to see what we can do about that."

An ecstatic gleam shone upon Ava's face. Gabriella entered the drawing-room to announce dinner. She peered at Holmes over her pince-nez. He shifted uncomfortably in his chair. Then finally we retired to the dining room. The starter of arancini arrived. Ludo poured me a glass of Chianti, which I gratefully accepted. I sipped from my glass, badly in need of liquid refreshment after my interrogation. I drank it fast and hard, sitting back in my chair with a satisfied air as I deftly received a refill from Ludo.

Holmes stared at me in disbelief, his intense grey eyes glowing like embers. Finally, the main course of Florentine steak arrived. Violetta passed me the mustard before she asked the question I had been dreading. "How did you and Sherlock meet, and where did you get married?"

"Well, we met in Milan. One moment, we were just two people talking in the green room having a heated debate over Wagner, then we walked out together, and I accepted a kiss. I'm afraid I was smitten, right there and then. And then Sherlock wanted to marry me. So, we decided we must be married right away. You know how it is, Violetta. When you've met the love of your life, you want to start that life straight away. So, we travelled to Lake Como and were married by special licence just over three weeks from our first encounter. It was such a beautiful intimate ceremony, exactly what we wanted, wasn't it, darling?" I glanced over at Holmes.

Holmes nodded. "Oh yes, indeed," he said. "That intimate wedding ceremony will always remain indelibly imprinted on my memory."

Holmes laughed awkwardly, darting a glance at me. He sat with his legs crossed, shifting uncomfortably in his seat.

I smiled and said demurely, "After the wedding, we travelled to Lake Garda. We stayed there for several days—our little honeymoon."

I smiled shyly. "We then returned to Milan for my last performance at La Scala. After that we decided, we *must* come to Florence to meet you lovely people. The rest you already know. So far, it has all been rather wonderful." I bit my lip hard to stop myself from grinning.

"We are all so happy for you." Violetta beamed at us. "Such an engaging, charming story. You know, I still have the first letter and photograph Ludo gave to me." She gazed across at her husband. "*Cuore mio*," she said.

"*Vita mia*," Ludo replied, staring back at her adoringly.

I once again refilled my wine glass. Holmes flashed me a look of disdain and I stared at him with a brooding intensity. The Chianti was starting to take effect, my inhibitions disappearing faster than the wine I was consuming. I took a sip from my glass, licking my lips provocatively. Then finally I spoke softly, almost in a whisper, never once taking my eyes off Holmes, who was scolding me silently with his eyes.

"You know, they tell me it is quite a thing to save a photograph, and I believe it was Balzac who said a letter is a soul so faithful, an echo of the speaking voice, but that to the sensitive it is amongst the richest treasures of love." I glanced over at Holmes with a mocking smile. He returned my gaze with silent curiosity.

I looked around the table at Ava, Violetta, and Ludo, chatting and laughing together, their love for one another shining through. How I envied their unconditional, uncomplicated love for one another. I glanced over at Holmes again. He had lapsed into a sullen silence as the dinner dragged on. I could see from his tortured expression that he was most uncomfortable being forced to interact with a gaggle of women, finding the chitter-chatter no doubt tedious and irrelevant. Sensing his vulnerability, I took a deep breath. "Please excuse me, ladies, Ludo. I have a terrible headache. I can feel one of my migraines coming on. I must go and lie down. I am so dreadfully sorry. We were having such a wonderful time."

Violetta frowned, a concerned look upon her face. "Can we get you anything, Nene? I know that migraines can be awful."

"No, thank you, Violetta. My prescription is back at the barn. Thank you so much for your hospitality. Sherlock will escort me back. He'll look after me, won't you darling?"

Holmes smiled, a look of begrudging gratitude upon his face as he nodded in agreement. "Yes, of course." We bid farewell to the family and made our way to the barn in silence.

As we entered the drawing-room, I looked at Holmes with some trepidation. "I don't know about you, Mr Holmes, but I could sure do with a nightcap."

He nodded curtly, walked over to the sideboard, and poured out a glass of wine and a whiskey and soda. He handed me the wine, staring at me hard. "I don't like surprises, Miss Adler."

"I'm not crazy about them myself, Mr Holmes. Let me assure you this was hardly a whirl of fun for me."

"Believe me, Miss Adler, when I say the feeling is entirely mutual."

I raised my glass. "I think we need this little liquid stimulation after the Spanish inquisition we just endured." I laughed nervously. "At least it's over now. My narrative was, for the most part, the actual truth. I had to try and make our married life appear realistic. We are, after all, supposed to be newlyweds."

"Do you think they believed you?" quizzed Holmes.

"Yes," I said softly. "I rather think they did. Although I must say you don't appear best pleased, Mr Holmes?"

He fixed me with his piercing eyes. "I've had better nights, I can assure you. I must, however, congratulate you on your impressive thespian skills. You even surpassed my expectations."

"Why, thank you, Mr Holmes. How kind of you to point that out," I muttered.

"That wasn't a compliment," Holmes scoffed. "Speaking frankly, I found most of your narrative this evening to be quite discomfiting. And I wasn't expecting you to consume quite so much Chianti."

I glared at him, astounded by his astonishing chutzpah. "I'm sorry, I didn't realise we'd returned to the world of Sherlock Holmes, where all kind words and considerations remain unacknowledged. If you want my advice, which I'm sure you don't, you appear far more adept at giving out so-called wise counsel rather than listening to it. Still, please allow me to give some to you anyway."

"I am on the edge of my seat, Miss Adler, giddy in anticipation. Pray, do enlighten me."

I glared at Holmes. "My advice to you, Mr Holmes, is to live for the moment. Who knows what the future will hold? You really ought to engage with the world and discover new experiences. What's the worst that could happen? However, I would hardly expect you to lower yourself to the level of my licentious behaviour, my debaucheries. Not all women are inscrutable. Our marriage of pretence was going along just fine until your inflated ego got in the way. I realise I am a long way from your never-ending hill of Calvary because, in your eyes, you don't believe that Irene Adler is good enough to be the wife of the celebrated detective Sherlock Holmes, albeit a pretend one. You are the worst kind of pretentious snob, Mr Holmes. You believe yourself in a class above the rest of us."

Holmes' face turned white with rage. He stared at me with a brooding fury. "I'm afraid you are taking this far too personally."

I turned to Holmes, narrowing my eyes. "It *is* personal,

godammit!"

Holmes sat back in his chair, a weary, heavy expression on his face. He made no answer for some time. Then, at last, he spoke in a tone of utmost solemnity. "Enough! Enough of this nonsense! If I wanted your opinion, I would ask for it. But while I consider your narrative, you consider—love makes fools of clever men. Perhaps you can stitch that sentiment onto a pillow." He spoke in an impersonal tone, his voice sharp and clear, freezing me with another cold stare.

"I may well do that, Mr Holmes," I said, tears of anguish stinging my eyes. "Why, you are no better than Godfrey! At least he had an excuse for bullying me. He was a hopeless addict, while you, sir, are a pompous ass *and* an addict. Your behaviour this evening has been reminiscent of a petulant child. All you have done all day is to moan and complain while leaving everything to me. I have had my fair share of challenges in life, Mr Holmes, but I'm still here, and I don't deserve to be treated this way. Sometimes you make it difficult for me to like you."

His face softened for a moment. "I'm sorry. I never intended to make you feel uncomfortable, Miss Adler. On the contrary, I wasn't trying to make you feel anything at all. Shall we call a halt to this now?" He held up his hands. "Before one of us says something else we may well regret."

I flashed him a look of contempt. This response was like a red rag to a bull.

"Be careful, young lady," he said. "As far as I'm concerned, this matter will bear no further discussions. I don't want to hear another word from you. Do I make myself clear?"

"Duly noted," I rejoined, once again fighting back tears. "I believe you have made yourself abundantly clear, Mr Holmes. I've had all the incandescent conversation I can take for one evening. I bid you goodnight." I glared at him. Holmes stared back at me in exasperation and so the conversation ended. He did not speak again, his parting shot a bitter smile.

I was once again stunned by his outrageous behaviour. Realising it would be futile to argue or even attempt to discuss the matter further, I retired to my room, flushed and trembling. As I slammed the door behind me, I found it difficult to comprehend why he could have such an effect upon me. I sat on the bed and let out a gut-wrenching sob. Our altercation, my dressing down from Sherlock Holmes, had deeply affected me. I immediately regretted my actions, conceding I had gone too far.

Opening the bedroom door, I walked back into the drawing-room and hesitated in the doorway only to hear the distinct sound of a door opening. Then the sound of the back door closing, a turning in the lock. I let out a deep sigh, and reluctantly retired to my bedroom. Sitting on the bed, I stared at the ceiling. A single tear fell from my eye, caressing my cheek before rolling off my chin. I lay down on the bed and fell asleep.

Chapter Seventeen: Sherlock Holmes

After our altercation I strolled outside to the garden to reflect on the events of the evening. Then, finally sitting down at a bench in the courtyard, I solaced myself with a cigarette, thick blue cloud wreaths spinning up as I collected my thoughts. I wasn't used to dealing with feisty opinionated women. To me, women had always been mysterious, inscrutable creatures to be tolerated only when it was impossible to avoid them. In all the years I'd spent on this planet, I rarely came across a woman I was even remotely interested in. Yet something about Irene Adler intrigued me in the way she stood up for herself. How her eyes had flashed with fire during our altercation. I was aware I'd upset her deeply. Watson was forever reminding me that my levels of bluntness and honesty often caused offence. Not that I took much notice of Watson's observations . . . or anyone else's for that matter. But this time was different. The more time I spent with her, the more difficult I found it to suppress my emotions. My hostility and bluntness were my way of addressing the situation and keeping that barrier between us, although I had not envisaged Irene Adler leaping over it. Eventually I returned to the barn, closed the door then bolted it with the crossbar before I retired to the drawing-room.

CHAPTER EIGHTEEN: IRENE ADLER

I jolted awake at two o'clock, my heart pounding. I was shaken from a bad dream and a troubled sleep. I slipped on my silk matching robe and slippers before entering the drawing-room. I found Holmes fast asleep, his long frame curled up in the recess of the chaise lounge, his newspaper resting upon his knee. I stared at him for a moment, feeling an aching need to be back in his good graces. Going back into my bedroom, I returned with a pillow and blanket, gently removed the newspaper, and took the empty glass from his hand before stubbing out the cigarette into the ashtray. I then tenderly covered him with the blanket, stroking his thick black hair from his forehead. My pulse quickened as my fingertips gently traced the lines around his mouth and eyes. Placing the pillow under his head, I took a deep breath in response to the startling wave of heat coursing through my body.

Then, fighting tears, very softly, I whispered, "Goodnight, Mr Holmes." I heard movement behind me and turned around to find he had half-opened his eyes. A faint smile appeared on his face. Observing the pillow and blanket, he closed his eyes. Entering my bedroom, I sat on my bed pondering the events of the evening. I had retorted a little too much, it was true. But there appeared to be a pattern forming, as I found myself once again retiring to my bed, angry with him, disappointed with myself. Alas, Mr Holmes remained an insufferable prig.

Chapter Nineteen: Irene Adler

I awoke anxious the following day after another restless night and toyed with my breakfast. I managed only a little dry toast and a cup of cafe noir. Finally, I decided to sit in the garden to take in some fresh air to help clear my head. I entered the parlour before luncheon to find Holmes, seemingly ensconced in his newspapers. His brow darkened and he scowled, clearly in no mood for polite conversation.

Eventually he looked up and nodded with a curt good afternoon. "You are looking a little peaky, Nene. I hope you are not imbibing again. The drink is a good servant but a poor master." Holmes spoke in a condescending tone as he turned over his newspaper, his lips tightly drawn. Gabriella served us luncheon in silence.

Later that evening, Holmes joined me for dinner. I felt relieved when he invited me onto the patio to partake in our evening ritual of drinks. He sat opposite me, lit a cigarette, and continued to read his newspapers, not once looking up or offering anything in the way of conversation. Finally, I admitted defeat, conceding that we made a volatile combination. I wondered how we could fight yet have so much in common.

I took a sip from my glass before turning to face him. "Mr Holmes, do you not think we are a little old for the silent routine? Can we please call a truce and talk for a moment? This friction between us has to end. Otherwise, I fear I may get frostbite from your cold shoulder!" I laughed nervously.

"If you will allow me, I would like to offer you an explanation. I was feeling stressed and then, fortified with too much wine, which clouded my judgement, I took my mood out on you, which was unforgivable of me. I wish to make amends if you will only allow it."

"Miss Adler, I am glad you reached this cleansing moment of clarity. An explanation is often more potent than an apology in such matters. I realise that I should have been of greater assistance to you in our deception, and if I was high handed and intransigent, I sincerely apologise. However, I suggest we put the matter behind us. I have one goal, and that is to get you home safely. We will make no further progress if we concentrate only on our differences."

"I appreciate that we had our differences, Mr Holmes. Unfortunately, neither of us appears to be coping very well with confinement. Can we pretend that yesterday didn't happen?"

"Consider it erased from my mind."

"I hope you don't regret helping me. I'd hate for you to think that you're wasting your time."

"No, you are not wasting my time. I am here because you need me to be, not just as your protector but also as your friend. I intend to bring this dreadful business to a swift and successful conclusion so that we may return to normality. In the meantime, we are where we are. We should make the best of it." He smiled at me gently.

I nodded in agreement. Staring at Holmes with a bemused expression, I was grateful that his demeanour had changed, even if it was only from icy to tepid. "Thank you, Mr Holmes. I would like you to know I don't always have to agree with you to like and respect you. So please bear that in mind if, God forbid, we have any further altercations."

I felt overwhelmed by our newfound rapprochement. I rose from my seat and entered the drawing-room, placing a record on the gramophone. Our conversation continued with Richard Wagner's *Der Ring des Nibelungen* playing in the background. Even though my self-confidence had sunk to an all-time low, I was struck by an overwhelming sense of certainty that he cared for me, albeit in his way. Yet I could not help but feel the strain of his loneliness and the struggles that lay behind his genius.

Chapter Twenty: Sherlock Holmes

After luncheon, I took Miss Adler out for a ride in the brougham to take in some fresh air the following day. The afternoon was perfect as we drove through the Tuscan hills. I pointed out various landmarks and places of interest along the way, such as the Mure Etrusche, the Convento di San Francesco, and the caves, finally stopping for a while at an archaeological area, home to the historical ruin of a Roman amphitheatre, which offered breath-taking scenic views of the countryside. Miss Adler appeared fascinated by the massive stones that made up the Etruscan walls, the remains of Roman baths. The amphitheatre had all the hallmarks of a classical stage set in a semi-circle around which people would have sat and watched the performances. Encompassed by green hills, the theatre looked spectacular in the glow of the afternoon sun.

I pointed out the green hilltop where Leonardo da Vinci first experimented with flight.

"This is so beautiful." She sighed.

I smiled at her. "It is indeed a place of natural beauty. Could you possibly imagine performing here all those years ago? I am told you are a fine actress amongst your other remarkable talents. Tell me, do you prefer music to the stage?"

"Oh, music by far Mr Holmes. For me acting tends to start with what's already written on the page. The actor has little control over the narrative. But music can and should, in my opinion, begin anywhere."

I nodded. "Indeed. I have so far only seen a glimpse of your remarkable talent. But that is something I intend to put right once all this madness is behind us. I shall look forward to seeing you perform again in concert."

"Thank you. I shall look forward to it," she said. We spent the remainder of the afternoon sitting in quiet contemplation, taking in the magnificent scenery.

After our afternoon excursion to the ruins, we stopped off at Ricardo's in the village for a glass of wine. We sat in the beer garden, observing a wedding party spilling out from the marquee.

"They look happy," I said, acknowledging the blushing bride and groom.

"Yes, until one of them messes it up."

I left her briefly to call into the little telegraph office. A telegram had arrived from Mycroft which went thus:

My dear brother, I implore you to be extra vigilant. I'm afraid you may no longer only have Palmer to deal with. I have just discovered the shocking news that Colonel Moriarty escaped his asylum. I'm not sure how or why as yet, but you can rest assured I will be making rigorous inquiries with the help of Lestrade and the Metropolitan Police. It is unlikely Moriarty will know you are in Florence, but I think it best not to take any chances. I will report back to you shortly. In the meantime, take good care. Yours Mycroft.

I quickly returned to the beer garden, relieved to find Miss Adler sitting waiting for me. I decided not to tell her about Moriarty, at least not yet. I beckoned the waiter to bring over the bill. He deftly arrived to inform me that a gentleman in the bar had already taken care of it.

He handed Irene Adler a single red rose. "The gentleman in the bar asked me to give you this. He said he is quite a fan."

"What gentleman, can you show me where he is?" I asked.

"He left about ten minutes ago," said the waiter.

"Can you describe him?" I quizzed.

"Yes, he's not a regular. He was English, I think. Tall and slim. He was wearing a cap pulled down over his face and thick horn-rimmed glasses." I ran outside and looked all around the surrounding area. There was no sign of anyone fitting the man's description.

"Is something wrong, Mr Holmes?" asked Miss Adler when I eventually returned to the bar. She stared at me anxiously.

"I'm not sure. I suppose he could have been a fan. If so, why did he not present the flower to you himself?"

"Perhaps he was shy. That happens sometimes," she replied.

I smiled at her reassuringly. I had no wish to alarm her unnecessarily. "Of course. I think we should head back to Le Sole."

Chapter Twenty-One: Irene Adler

After dinner each evening, Holmes and I would retire to the verandah. The nights would slip smoothly along as Holmes enjoyed a glass of whisky or port and a pipe of tobacco, with me partaking of an occasional glass of dry sherry or Chianti. Fortified by the whisky and port, his mood brightened. We engaged in deep, meaningful conversations on a variety of subjects. I considered him an extraordinary individual—brilliant, intelligent, and eccentric. I came to recognise his little peculiarities. Although I hadn't liked him much on first impression, finding him arrogant and self-absorbed, my opinion changed as I came to know him. I was instinctively aware when Holmes needed his own space and quiet time for contemplation, discreetly retiring to my bedroom when I sensed his need for solitude. There was no doubt that most women would find his behaviour odd, strange even, but I revelled in his company. Holmes only had my best interests at heart. He put himself at risk trying to protect me. I knew of no one else who would be prepared to do that. Consequently, I felt strangely drawn to him, like a moth to a flame.

I was under no illusions that our adventure would continue. I was aware that we would go our separate ways as soon as the case was solved and the perpetrator found. It was unlikely that I would ever see him again. I felt profound sadness at the thought. To Holmes, I was a mere factor in a problem, just a number from his extensive case book. So many of those had made their way into Dr Watson's chronicles. I wondered if I would ever become part of that collection. No doubt

Holmes would lose interest in me once the case was closed. Part of me hoped that Palmer was not apprehended too quickly. I had even considered suggesting that we remain friends and write to each other occasionally. I would have liked that. I had not yet plucked up the courage to make the suggestion as I was afraid he would reject the idea out of hand.

A few of the local boys came over to Le Sole to help out around the farm in the evenings. We would observe them from a distance, whetting their scythes and harvesting the fields against the backdrop of the beautiful Tuscan sunset. The smell of newly cut grain in the moonlight was intoxicating. Javier Anka would often join them. He was six feet tall, remarkably handsome, with jet black curly hair and deep-set brown eyes. He would glance over to us from time to time, smiling and waving, much to Holmes' disdain. I laughed in amusement. I was immune to his charms. Indeed, I was far more interested in the swifts. I would sit for hours marvelling at the birds, preening and screeching out to each other as they built their nests of grasses, leaves, and feathers. Holmes observed me watch them with mild amusement.

Left to my own devices, often for long periods, I amused myself by reading or sketching. Finally, after much persuasion, explaining that I felt like a wasp in a jar, Holmes reluctantly agreed that I could go outside to take some exercise on the proviso that I stayed within the confines of the farm and went in disguise. I agreed to his terms. So, the following day I ventured out on my walk, determined to make the most of the tiny crumbs of freedom bestowed on me by Sherlock Holmes. The blissful rays of the Tuscan sunshine touched my face with the promise of a new day. The smell of nature amidst the spring blooms was an exhilarating experience. As I approached the stables, I was disturbed by the sound of the swifts brawling in the eaves and then by the sight of a slim athletic-looking youth walking out of the stable block, leading a powerful looking bay colt. I was surprised to see it was Javier. I stared at the horse, a beautiful Anglo Arab Sardinian with four white socks and a star on his forehead. His coat gleamed, shining like a barn door in the Tuscan sunshine.

I watched as Javier led the colt over to the mounting block, tentatively easing himself into the saddle. He was about to place his boots into the stirrups when the colt became fractious and reared up, flinging his jockey unceremoniously out of the saddle. Javier landed on the ground with a thud, nibbling the Tuscan turf. Now rid of his jockey, the colt casually walked away to graze nearby.

I ran over to Javier. "Are you hurt?" I asked.

"No, just my pride," said Javier. He stared at the colt, shaking his head.

"He has only recently been broken in. Clearly, he has a mind of his own."

I slowly walked over to the colt. His head jarred up at my approach and he flicked back his ears, swishing his tail.

"Hey," I said in a slow, soothing voice. "Steady, my beauty."

I chuckled softly, taking hold of the bridle, and blowing gently into the colt's nostrils, which seemed to calm him down. I slowly moved my hands over the colt's head, neck, and withers, gently slipping my fingers under the girth which was holding the saddle in place. Unfortunately, the band was far too tight, as I realized from my time at my uncle's ranch in the Catskills. I learnt that a twisted girth could often lead to anxiety in a horse.

I readjusted the saddle, unfastened the girth, and loosened it a couple of notches. I waved over Pietro, the stable boy, a keen-faced youth with protruding ears. He held the colt's head and gave me a leg up until I was safely in the saddle. I purposely kept my feet out of the stirrups.

Pietro stared at me in disbelief, snickering to himself. "I'd keep one finger on the neck strap if I were you. He's got quite a reputation."

"Walk on," I said. After a while, I placed my boots into the stirrups.

The colt broke into a trot. We continued trotting until we reached the far end of the meadow. I leant forward in the saddle, squeezing my thighs. The colt immediately picked up the snaffle bit and broke into a canter. We continued steadily around the field's perimeter, passing the farmhands and Ludo in the adjoining meadow. He was leaning on his pitchfork and shouted out to me.

"Quello che una Donna." What a woman"

Finally, we approached the stables where Javier stood waiting for us open-mouthed. Upon seeing the stables, the colt's herding instinct kicked in and he slowed down to a trot. I crouched down low in the saddle, whispering words of encouragement.

"Come on, boy. Show me what you've got." I kicked the colt's belly. We quickly extended to a gallop.

I felt as though I was floating on air as the colt's long powerful stride ate up the ground. He was by far the quickest horse I'd ever ridden, in a different league to the sturdy quarter horses of the Catskills. We completed an entire circuit of the meadow, eventually coming to a halt next to the stables, where Javier and Pietro stood waiting for us. Javier wore a look of considerable astonishment. I laughed.

I dismounted the colt and spoke to Javier until Pietro opened the loose box and led the colt back into the stable where he unsaddled him, replacing the bridle with a head collar. The colt was sweating profusely, steam coming from his body as a result of our exertions. Pietro pulled a sponge from a nearby bucket and began to wash down the colt. Javier and

I stood to one side, watching them.

"What is his name?" I quizzed.

"Allegro," Javier replied. "He is Violetta's pride and joy. What you say . . . the apple of her eye. His dam died when he was a foal, and Violetta hand-reared him until Ludo managed to borrow a foster mother from one of the neighbouring farms. Allegro is very special to her."

I patted the colt and spoke to him softly, stroking his head under his forelock.

"Well, Allegro, you certainly live up to your name. There was an old saying back in the Catskills. – One white sock buy him, two white socks try him, three white socks be on the sly, four white socks pass him by – but I never put much store in that old wives tale. All the best horses have quirks." I laughed. "He's a lovely horse, Javier. He has such a beautiful way about him. Tell me, did you break him in?"

"Yes," Javier said with an air of pride and conviction. A flush of colour appeared on his cheeks.

"Well, you should be very proud of yourself. You've done an excellent job. He skips along the ground like a ballet dancer." We continued chatting about horses, music, and family.

I found our conversation surprisingly heartfelt, and Javier to be an agreeable, sensitive young man. I suspected that he had a sneaking regard for Ava, the way he looked at her with such profound tenderness. Realising I would be late for luncheon, I made my excuses and returned to the barn.

Chapter Twenty-Two: Sherlock Holmes

I was on my way back from the village, approaching Le Sole when my eyes took in the haunting image of Irene Adler astride a colt cantering through the fields. I stopped the brougham and watched as they gathered momentum and galloped past. The colt's hooves rattled over the turf, snorting and straining every sinew. Adler's cap had flown off. Her long auburn hair glistened in the sun like burnished copper hanging loose upon her shoulders. I watched as she rode back to the stables and dismounted the colt. I continued to observe as she spoke to the Anka boy, the two of them laughing and joking together for several minutes before they entered the stables together. I sat contemplating for several minutes before I finally picked up the reins and proceeded on my way back to Le Sole, the sound of their laughter ringing in my ears.

CHAPTER TWENTY-THREE: IRENE ADLER

Holmes and I were preparing to dine with Ludo and Violetta. There would be four of us this evening. Ava was away visiting her cousin. Entering the drawing-room in a pastel green evening dress, my hair piled high in a pompadour, unrecognisable from my earlier equestrian activities, I found Holmes dressed in a full suit, fiddling with his tie.

"I do apologise for keeping you waiting," said Holmes. "I am struggling with this darned cravat."

"Please let me help you." I unfastened the mother-of-pearl pin on his black satin cravat.

We gazed into each other's eyes for a brief moment. I could smell the soap on his skin, the faint aroma of his cologne. "You know, Mr Holmes, you're holding a lot of tension in your shoulders. You would sleep much better if you could let it out."

"Thank you, Miss Adler. I will bear that in mind."

We strolled over to the farmhouse where Ludo greeted us warmly and escorted us into the drawing-room for pre-dinner drinks. I accepted a dry sherry, Holmes a whiskey and soda.

Ludo raised his glass to me. "I saw you riding in the fields earlier today, most impressive. You ride as well as any man." He chuckled, turning his attention to Holmes. "Were you aware that your wife was quite the equestrienne?"

"I am discovering that there is no end to my wife's indisputable talents," said Holmes.

"Where did you learn to ride?" asked Violetta.

"I used to stay with my uncle and his family during the holidays. They had a ranch in the Catskills. That's where I learned my equestrian skills and how to use a gun."

"Well, we're very fortunate to have your expertise," said Violetta. "Please feel free to ride Allegro any time you want. He could do with the exercise. Javier does his best, but he struggles to handle him sometimes. Ludo doesn't want me to ride Allegro at the moment."

"No, that's right," said Ludo, shaking his head. "Allegro is far too robust for you right now, Violetta."

"I would love to take him out for a ride," I said. "It will no doubt keep me occupied, thank you."

Ludo nodded. "It is our pleasure, and you would really be doing us a favour. Violetta and I have some exciting news to share with you both." Ludo beamed at his wife. "The reason why my Violetta cannot ride at the moment is that we are expecting a bambino. After fifteen years of trying for a second precious child, Violetta is finally expecting."

Violetta laughed, pointing to her belly, hidden underneath her dress. "We have managed to keep it a secret until now because we didn't want to tempt fate. I miscarried a child the year after Ava was born."

"Many congratulations to you both." Holmes slapped Ludo on the back. "Well, my boy, I believe that a cigar is in order. Shall we?"

Holmes and Ludo excused themselves, retiring to the courtyard.

"I am delighted for you and Ludo. It couldn't happen to a more deserving couple," I said.

"Oh, I nearly forgot. I have something for you, Nene. I won't be a moment."

Violetta returned after a few minutes with two pairs of riding trousers and a velvet slimline black riding habit exquisitely tailored, with a high buttoned bodice and deep pockets.

She passed the clothes to me.

"Nene, I would like you to have these trousers. I'm afraid I can only lend you the jacket. That was a gift from Ludo. He would be upset if I gave it away, although it isn't of much use to me at the moment." She laughed.

"Thank you," I said, accepting the clothes. "I quite understand. The jacket is beautiful. I'll be sure to take good care of it. You are too kind."

"Nonsense, it's the least I can do." Violetta reached into her pocket. "This is a key to the lumber room. It's at the far end of the stable block, where I keep Allegro's tack. There's a side-saddle there if you wish to make use of it, but please be sure to lock the door behind you. Ludo keeps his gun in there. There is an influx of children running around at this time of year, what with the fruit picking, you can never be too careful."

"Thank you so much." I accepted the key from Violetta. "I'll be sure to keep the door locked. As for the saddle, I much prefer to use a good English saddle because it offers more control. Allegro was a joy to ride, but he's not the most straightforward conveyance. I hope that is agreeable with you?"

"It's more than agreeable with me," said Violetta. "Come, let me get you another drink."

Holmes and Ludo returned to the drawing-room. Holmes fixed his eyes on me, his face a mask of concern. "Are you all right, Nene?"

"I am fine, Sherlock," I whispered. "I'm not about to fall apart because someone else is pregnant. I'm delighted for Violetta and Ludo."

A flush of colour appeared on Holmes's sallow cheeks, and he gave my shoulder a sympathetic pat. Taken by surprise at his rare display of empathy, I instinctively kissed him on the cheek. Staring at him, I was shocked by the realisation of my actions. Holmes looked at me in stunned silence before taking my arm in his and we retired to the dining room.

During dinner, Violetta and Ludo extended a warm invitation for us to join them at their twentieth-anniversary supper to be held at the farm on Saturday. Ludo reassured Holmes that this would be a private function, by invitation only, for close friends, relatives, and a handful of the farmhands and their families who help with the harvest. Ludo explained this was their annual custom. To do otherwise, he said, would only evoke resentment and suspicion.

Chapter Twenty-Four: Irene Adler

The following morning, I arrived at the stables to find Allegro tacked up and ready to go. I was about to lead him out of the stable when I noticed the colt had cast a shoe. I would be unable to ride that day. Removing the bridle and replacing it with a head collar, I unfastened the girth and was shocked to discover it had been cut through and was hanging by a thread. I wondered if Pietro was trying to teach me a lesson. I patted the colt down the neck, filling his manger with grass hay, which he happily munched on.

"Hey, I hope you enjoy your sweet feed. I'll see you tomorrow." I let myself out of the stable, bolting the door behind me.

I found Pietro in the lumber room and showed him the girth. He appeared as shocked as I but denied all knowledge, instead blaming the incident on a group of children who often came fruit-picking with their parents. Pietro said they were a wild bunch who were always up to mischief, although he admitted it was his responsibility to keep an eye on them. I considered telling Violetta and Ludo, then decided they had enough to worry about with the farm and their impending arrival. Pietro assured me he would take care of it, begging me not to tell the Espiritos, explaining that he'd already received a warning for tardiness and was terrified he would lose his job. He promised to speak to the children and ensure it never happened again. Looking at the distraught expression on Pietro's face, I decided to give him the benefit of the doubt. But. I warned him I would not be quite so forgiving if there were any further incidents.

Setting off on my way back to the barn, I raised an eyebrow upon hearing the sound of a soprano. The voice appeared to be coming from the direction of the orchard. I spotted Ava through the trees, collecting quinces, while singing Luigiii Denza's "Funiculi, Funicula." I stopped in my tracks, taken aback by the joyous melody and Ava's mellifluous sweet-sounding voice. I waited until Ava had sung the last note before walking over to join her.

Ava appeared startled at my approach, failing to recognise me until I removed my cap.

"My riding attire is very fetching, don't you agree?" I laughed. "How long have you been singing?"

"I love to sing," said Ava. "I've been captivated by music ever since I was a little girl when I heard my first recording on the gramophone."

"Your voice is outstanding for your age, Ava. Were you aware you have a beautiful soprano voice?"

Ava blushed. "I have been practising Mama's favourite song, but I find it rather difficult."

"What song is that?"

"Drink to me only with thine eyes," said Ava. "I would love to be able to sing it for my parents on their wedding anniversary. That would mean so much to Mamma. Her sister Adriana died last year in childbirth. Mamma was devastated. She was very close to her sister. Adriana's husband was grief-stricken and inconsolable. He's an Intelligence officer in the navy. He returned to his ship, the *Regia Marina,* straight after Adriana's funeral, and we haven't heard from him since. So you see, Nene, I need to try and perfect this song as best I can. I want Mamma to feel happy again."

"What a lovely gesture," I said. "You must allow me to help you with your task. It's certainly not the easiest song choice. I performed the song at one of my early recitals. It brings back fond memories."

Ava stared at me in disbelief. "The great Irene Adler is to be my tutor? I don't believe it."

I took hold of Ava's hand, offering her a reassuring smile. "Come with me, Ava, back to the barn."

I rummaged through the bookshelves until I found Ben Johnson's book of poetry nestled between Shakespeare's *Romeo and Juliet* and Mark Twain's *Huckleberry Finn,* and I handed the book to Ava.

"The poem is on page twelve," I said. "I want you to read it. That will help you focus and comprehend the actual meaning of the song. Then I want you to tell me your thoughts on the text tomorrow."

Ava thanked me before returning to the farmhouse in wild euphoria. I had no sooner come back, fresh from my morning exercise the following day, when Ava knocked on my door. I poured us a glass of lemonade. We sat in the kitchen chatting for a while.

I took a sip from my glass, staring at Ava curiously. "Well, Ava, what are your thoughts on the poem, or as my husband would say, what have you deduced?"

"I believe it's obvious that the man is in love with the woman. He appears to be saying that if she leaves a kiss in the cup, he won't need wine. He doesn't feel the need to drink to be happy, although it's unclear if she returns his admiration."

I smiled at the girl. "You know, you are right. It's not easy to perceive. When I studied this poem, I deduced that she did love him. The reader can feel the speaker's ardent adulation. She sent the flowers back to him after breathing on them. Now the flowers grow and can never die. That could mean that even though they couldn't be together, she wanted him to know that their love was forever. The speaker appears to hold her in very high regard."

"Yes, thank you, Nene. I feel that I understand it much

better now."

"Please come and see me tomorrow morning after breakfast. We'll need a few things from the village. Would you be kind enough to accompany me?"

"Yes, of course."

"Good, then I will ask Sherlock to drive us. Please ensure you ask Violetta for permission." Ava nodded before dashing back to the farmhouse to speak to her mamma. Violetta raised no objections to Ava's request. She was delighted that I took such an avid interest in her daughter.

Chapter Twenty-Five: Irene Adler

The following morning, Holmes drove Ava and me to the village. I wore a white dress and matching parasol, my hair arranged in kiss curls. Ava looked fetching in a plain blue dress with a yellow yoke, a straw boater perched jauntily on her head. Holmes checked in with Mario at the telegraph office. A telegram had arrived from Lestrade, stating there had been no recent sightings of Palmer, although the Metropolitan Police were actively pursuing several lines of inquiries.

Meanwhile, Ava and I entered the cobbled market, where we rummaged our way through the stalls. We finally emerged with a selection of items—perfume, stockings, hair clips, satin, and ribbon, new shoes for Ava, and various makeup items completed our purchases. We then entered the florist where I ordered a basket of spring flowers. The assistant promised to deliver the blooms to Violetta and Ludo on their wedding anniversary. Our next stop was the modiste. A little bell peeled as Ava and I entered the shop. The proprietor, Madama Passarello, appeared. She was an elegant lady in her early forties, attired in a blue taffeta suit, her dark hair tied up in a knot. Madame Passarello smiled at us warmly.

"Good morning, ladies. How may I be of service?" she asked.

"We are looking for some pretty material for an evening dress for this lovely young lady." I gestured towards Ava. "Do you have anything suitable in white nun's veiling?"

Madame Passarello placed a ream of material on the countertop. "This is our bespoke collection."

My fingers quickly searched through the reams. "Could we please see this one unfurled?"

"Of course, madame." Madama Passarello duly obliged.

"Well, what do you think, Ava? Do you like this one?" I quizzed, rubbing the material back and forth between my fingers.

"Like it? Nene, I love it." Ava's brow furrowed. "But it's more expensive than the others."

"Don't worry about that." I gestured to Madame Passarello. "Well, that's settled, thank you. We shall take this one."

Ava's face broke into a wide grin. Madame Passarello took out her measuring tape and guided Ava towards the dressing room, where two assistants deftly cut and measured.

Afterwards we looked through the window of the local jeweller before finally entering the shop. Ava was utterly overwhelmed. In addition to the dress and the shoes, I also bought her a black ebony choker with a silver ivory cameo. I was delighted with my own purchases—a solid silver powder case and an additional item I arranged to have engraved. We eventually emerged from the market with all our required purchases either on order or already in hand. We found Holmes waiting for us in the brougham, impatiently puffing away on his pipe. He helped us into the carriage then picked up the reins, setting off to Le Sole.

Later that evening, while partaking of drinks on the patio, I spoke to Holmes of Ava's desire to sing for her parents on their wedding anniversary. I explained I had offered to help and that rehearsals would commence the following morning on the pretence that I would teach Ava a little French.

Holmes stared at me oddly. "I see that you have added lies to our list of deceptions, Miss Adler."

"Yes, but for a noble cause, Mr Holmes, don't you think?"

Holmes agreed. He was curled up on his chair, his eyes half-closed, smoking his black clay pipe. His demeanour had greatly improved since our altercation. He appeared amused when I explained I wanted to take on a more active role and, to my surprise, agreed to my request that I take Allegro out every morning and ride through the fields to check for anything suspicious.

I watched him curiously. "Do you have any plans when you return to London?"

He laughed. "I daresay I will continue with my consultations until I drop dead. I hope that's not too shallow an answer for you."

"Not at all. But is it not depressing to be constantly faced with murderers and the worst possible versions of people? That must be a cold world to live in." I frowned.

"Yes, at times it can be," Holmes agreed. "The world is full of dreadful, detestable people. Inhumanity is like a drug. It's all around us. The worst criminals are often the ones people least suspect. Take women, for instance. Katie Webster, Marie Manning, and Lizzie Borden, to name a few. Although, admittedly, when most women kill, it's usually for or because of men."

"It's a wonder that such women actually impressed you," I said. "What about the likes of Anne Boleyn, Joan of Arc, Margaret Beaufort, and Josephine Butler? Many men have vilified such inspirational women throughout history, but I have always thought there was something rather noble about their self-effacement. Surely even you can't believe them to be inscrutable? Well, Anne Boleyn may not be the best example. She is said to have lived a life of sexual intrigue and political scandal, but even so, she didn't deserve to go down in history as a harlot."

"According to the poem by Lancelot Du Lac, there is strong evidence to suggest that Anne Boleyn did, in fact, commit adultery. But you are right, of course, not all women are inscrutable. Only most of the ones I have been unfortunate to come into contact with during my career."

"Mr Holmes, it must be quite a thing to observe what no one else can. You see solutions to problems that others cannot even begin to understand. People are fascinated by you because not only do you see straight through the obvious, but you do it in such a way that makes it, well, obvious. The way I see it, you are a righter of wrongs, a friend to the friendless."

"It all sounds very romantic when you put it like that. Believe me, Miss Adler, detective work is anything but."

"How would you define intelligence in a person, Mr Holmes? What would impress you about someone intellectually?"

Holmes looked at me in amusement. "A person is intelligent if they can process information well and not procrastinate while they do so. To me, what defines intellect in somebody is how quickly it takes them to arrive at the correct conclusion after considering all the facts. A single misunderstood clue has the power to destabilise even the most discerning observer. It's so easy to be carried away by preconceptions, which is why the police so often get it wrong. Confidence, of course, is the key. Nothing dispels perceptiveness as much as self-doubt. Pray, tell me, what is your own view of intelligence?"

"Well, I would agree with you, Mr Holmes. Although I think intelligent people have a keen look about them, they tend to react to subtle things more quickly than others. Little shifts and changes—nothing scares them, nothing slips past them."

He flashed me a wry smile. "Except you, Miss Adler. You slipped past me seven years ago."

"Tell me, does anything scare you, Mr Holmes?"

"Failure scares me," Holmes admitted. "And the fear of

losing my faculties, the thought of being mentally incapacitated, horrifies me. But other than that, not really. I've seen it all in my line of work. You know, you are very perceptive, Miss Adler. I truly value your intelligent observations. Come, let me get you another drink."

CHAPTER TWENTY-SIX: IRENE ADLER

Ava waited impatiently for Gabriella Anka to leave the barn before joining me the following day. She was disappointed to learn I would not be accompanying her on the piano.

I poured her a glass of lemonade. "We must have a little patience, Ava. We shall begin acapella. Then, when I am happy, we will slowly introduce the chords."

We spent the morning practising vocal exercises and breathing techniques until at last I felt satisfied with Ava's progress.

"Well," I said. "That was your first vocal examination. I am pleased to tell you that your voice is in fair condition for rapid development, but you must have patience. You will not become a great performer overnight. No one expects to pick up a paintbrush and recreate the Mona Lisa. You must learn to sing from your diaphragm. The more you practice, the better you will become. You know, when I was a young girl, I aspired to be Agnes Huntington. She was my heroine."

"*You* are my heroine, Nene."

"Thank you, Ava, you are very kind." Looking at Ava, I detected a desire in the girl that I recognised in myself at such a tender age. "I know how it feels to be young, ambitious and talented. I want to help enable you so you can realise your dreams."

The rehearsal continued for some time. I noticed Ava appeared a little downcast, so I held up my hand to stop her from singing.

"Ava, I want you to look at me when you sing. At the moment, your eyes are on the floor. If you're going to sing for people, you need to connect with them and stay focused."

"I'm sorry, I'm just so nervous."

"It's all right, my dear girl. It is good to have nerves. That shows you care. There's an intrinsic beauty to your voice that is truly captivating. You know I couldn't sing as well as you at your age."

"Really?" gasped Ava.

"Really. And now you will learn to sing with your eyes."

Later that evening, Holmes and I enjoyed after-dinner drinks on the patio. I poured myself a glass of wine, taking a few sips before plucking up the courage to ask Holmes if he would consider accompanying Ava on the violin, explaining the predicament regarding the piano. To my astonishment, he agreed to my request.

"I was unaware the young lady could sing. Does she possess any talent?" he asked.

"Oh, Ava has talent, all right. Her voice has a vulnerability which is extraordinary to listen to. She will make her parents proud, I am certain."

"You appear to have become very fond of the young lady."

"I have indeed. She has such a lively, engaging personality. And she is such a striking girl for her age, don't you think?"

"Is she? I hadn't really noticed. But now you come to mention it, I suppose she is."

"Mr Holmes, are you familiar with the song *Drink to Me Only With Thine Eyes*?"

"Hmm, Ben Johnson." He raised an eyebrow. "That was a particular favourite of my late mother's. I will have no problem remembering the score."

The following day I spoke to Ava about the unfortunate situation with the piano, and how it was badly out of tune.

But all was not lost as Mr Holmes had kindly agreed to accompany her on the violin.

Holmes opened his violin case to reveal a beautiful Stradivarius. We were amazed to hear he was such an accomplished musician, a far cry from his ghastly cat wailing during the midnight hours.

The day before the anniversary supper was a Friday, and the final rehearsals were underway. Holmes gestured to the piano and asked me to play a few notes.

I did as he asked and was astounded to hear the piano play perfectly in tune.

Ava was ecstatic, crying tears of joy. She flung her arms around Holmes. I ran my fingers over the piano, playing the first few chords of "The Old Folks at Home."

"Thank you. That was unbelievably generous and gracious of you." I smiled at Holmes.

"You play beautifully, Nene," said Holmes. "Your technique and the delicacy of your expression are quite remarkable."

Unbeknownst to Ava and me, Holmes later revealed that he'd had the piano tuned earlier that morning. After making extensive enquiries in the village, he was eventually pointed in the direction of a retired piano tuner, Frederico Colletti, being reliably informed that Colleti could be found most days propping up the bar at Ricardo's Inn. Holmes made his acquaintance there the day before. At first, Colletti proved a reluctant accomplice.

Only after Holmes plied Coletti with whisky, cigars, and the promise of a substantial tip did he begrudgingly agree to accompany Holmes to Le Sole the following morning. He carried out a splendid job of restoring the piano to its former glory, managing to complete the task before I returned from the stables.

CHAPTER TWENTY-SEVEN: IRENE ADLER

After dinner that evening, Holmes and I retired to the patio for our evening ritual of drinks and conversation. The evening was balmy, the end to a perfect spring day. We settled into the cushioned wicker chairs, gazing out into the garden and the stunning Tuscan sunset. I could tell from the twinkle in his eyes and the welcoming smile on his lips that Holmes was in a congenial mood.

"You fill me with interest, Miss Adler. Tell me more about your childhood."

I sighed before meeting his gaze. "I was just a baby when my mother died, and my father employed a parade of governesses. I'm afraid none of them lasted very long. They were all ghastly. My father didn't know what to do with me. So, on my aunt Eileen's advice, I was sent to my uncle's ranch in the Catskills. I went there every summer and ran wild and free through the fields and mountains. I became a spiritual orphan."

"Who else lived at the ranch?"

"My uncle, aunt, and cousins. They taught me to ride and shoot. Then my aunt's son from her first marriage, Beau, came to stay with us. We got on well, at first. He was four years older than me, and I really looked up to him. And then one night he made a pass at me, and when I rejected his advances, he changed. I realised he was far from wonderful." I scoffed. "He never missed an opportunity to undermine me in front of my family. Then, when I was fifteen, my aunt intervened. She told my father I was a wilful, reckless child and should be sent away to school. In despair, my father, shipped me off to a private boarding school for girls in New York."

"What were your first thoughts of the school?"

"My *only* thought was how could I get out of there. I was lucky enough to share a dorm on the top floor with just one other girl, Hilary Bilby. She became my only friend."

"How about your academic life?"

"We each stood in line at assembly every morning. The formidable headmistress, Miss Ackers, stared down at us over her horn-rimmed spectacles, her shrill didactic voice ringing in our ears. *Girls, pull those shoulders back, heads erect, no slouching. Remember to always carry yourselves with confidence, dignity. and grace.*

"I hated every minute of school life. I was smart, all right, but I was a friendless outsider. Girls were expected to be compliant, obedient, and enthusiastic. I'm afraid I was none of those things. The other girls were preoccupied with their own vanity and self-importance. I was the one they gossiped about, the new girl from Trenton. There I developed my carapace so as not to allow things to bother me too much. After an altercation with one of the girls, something snapped in me. In an act of extreme defiance—or in the words of Miss Ackers *extreme foolishness,*—I fought back. That was not my finest hour, Mr Holmes."

"What happened next?"

"Miss Ackers hauled me into her office. The other girls were terrified of her, but not me. She remarked that according to the other girls, I was difficult to get along with, considering myself superior to everyone else. I laughed at the absurdity of her accusation."

"Admirable." Holmes chuckled. "Standing up to authority at such a tender age. Stupid, perhaps, but admirable. What else did she say?"

"She peered over her glasses at me with a look of disdain and said, *Irene Adler, this school expects its students to adhere to specific standards. You are undoubtedly one of our brightest students. However, character is as important as academic achievement. You must try to remember you're a lady and not all of us are fortunate enough to be born into a life of privilege."*

"How did you respond?"

"I said I didn't believe I was better than anyone else because of wealth or birth, and surely being different was preferable to being something you're not. I refused to apologise for being who I am. Instead, I asked Miss Ackers if she intended to interview the other girl."

"Did she?"

"No, I ended up with detention for insubordination and was confined to my dorm for the rest of the week."

"Troublemakers and bullies are invariably unhappy people," said Holmes. "Filled with inexcusable anger and rage. I fancy those girls and that teacher were jealous. You are never afraid to challenge authority, always in search of the truth."

"Thank you, Mr Holmes," I said. "As much as those girls tried, they could never break my spirit. That experience left me with an innate hunger to succeed. I finished school with the highest marks in our examinations."

"What of your mother?"

"Unfortunately, she tragically died from heart failure shortly after I was born. No one was aware she had a problem until it was too late. You know, it's strange, I always felt like my mother was with me in some capacity."

Holmes raised an eyebrow. "My mother was one of twenty women to graduate as a doctor from the Medical Institution of Geneva College in New York. Of course, Elizabeth Blackwell paved the way to become the first woman to graduate from the same college.

'I realise how difficult all this is. You must miss your family and friends." He drew on his cigarette. "It would be a pity if we lost touch after all this business is behind us. Indeed, I fancy it would be quite something to know you as a friend."

I stared at him. "Thank you, Mr Holmes. I would like that. I appreciate that we will be living in different countries, different worlds even. Perhaps we may correspond?"

"That would be capital. I fancy it would be interesting for me to keep track of your career." He looked at me thoughtfully. "Do you see yourself getting married again in the future?"

"My independent lifestyle is a conscious choice. I'm better alone, it's safer." I smiled. "I am determined to return to La Scala one day. I want to be happy again, although I don't think true happiness lasts very long, but I believe that tranquillity might, and I'll be glad to settle for that."

"Your determination is admirable, Miss Adler. I tend to think the worst of people. However, even an old cynic like me believes a few good people are left in the world. So, you must pursue your dream and return to Milan. Nobody deserves it more than you."

"Thank you." I took a sip from my wine glass. "I want to rediscover all that I am. I have come to terms with my infertility. If only I could find a way to have a child without involving a man, that would be perfect."

"A physical impossibility, I would fancy."

"My cousin Estelle has three children, and they are all quite adorable. I try to spend as much time with them as possible whenever I go home. I love sneaking into their bedrooms at night to read to them. I introduced them to the worlds of Lewis Carroll and Edward Lear. Their particular favourite was Alice's Adventures in Wonderland, which I must admit was one of mine too. That's a book that never loses its relevance, mainly due to Alice's intellectual curiosity and her courage to speak out. My favourite part was when the gardeners rushed in to paint the white roses red and avoid those immortal words, *off with their heads*!" I laughed, observing Holmes's bemused expression. "That logic may appear insane to you, but sometimes a light-handed cosmic touch can make all the difference. Life can be that uncomplicated, Mr Holmes, if only we allow it."

"If life were uncomplicated, I'd be out of a job."

"May I ask you a personal question, Mr Holmes?"

"Yes, of course." He raised an eyebrow.

"Have you ever been in love?"

Holmes shook his head. "I'm delighted to categorically and absolutely say that love has so far eluded me. That being said, I don't feel I am capable of love, not in the same way as other people. In any case, I would make a terrible husband. I play the violin far too loudly."

"Yes, I've noticed."

"I drove Watson to distraction when we first shared rooms." He shook his head. "No, I don't think there is a woman alive who would put up with my Bohemian lifestyle. Don't get me wrong, I have had dalliances in the past. However, I was always reluctant to take things any further."

"Why?"

"I'm not sure," he said. "Too fussy. Too busy solving crimes. Mainly due to the lack of anyone drawing my attention. I have little experience with children, although I sometimes wonder what it would have been like to have a son. He may have gone to Eton. I believe education opens the gateway to success. But alas, that was not to be."

I shook my head. "I long to live in a house filled with the laughter of children, but that's not meant to be either. It's not too late for you, Mr Holmes. Do you ever wonder what might have been if you had pursued a relationship? It may have led to marriage and children. How would you have felt back then if the lady in question told you she was expecting your child? How wonderful would it be to hear those words?"

Holmes took a sip of whisky, coughed and spluttered, staring at me in baffled bemusement. "I would have been as intrigued then as I am now. Sadly, that ship has long since sailed."

"That's a pity, Mr Holmes. I think it would be a crime not to reproduce your genes."

"My gifts are often a hindrance and a burden. I'm not sure if it would be fair to pass them on to an innocent child."

"But tell me, do you never feel lonely?"

"Lonely in the middle of London with all those crimes to solve? It suits me to live alone, and I know that I will most likely die alone. But to answer your question, Miss Adler, yes, sometimes I feel lonely, but only when I have nothing to occupy my mind. Please don't tell anyone I said that. I've got a reputation to uphold. I prefer to walk alone. That is the path I have chosen for myself. Forgive me if I appear cynical, but from what I've seen over the years, most women seem to view relationships more about what they can get out of them – possessions, wealth, and status. They marry well as a means to an end and have no clue what the end is, but they love the means."

"I'd rather not speculate about that."

"Oh, please do. I believe you should." A flicker of a smile appeared on his face.

"I know you believe most women to be inscrutable, Mr Holmes, but let me tell you from personal experience, men are far worse. They are capable of faking an entire relationship."

"I have always looked upon marriage as an invasion of privacy."

"You don't get married just to live with someone," I said, looking at him aghast. "True love is priceless and can never be bought. People marry because they simply can't live without each other, well, most people do. Love is, after all, an act of courage. A faithful heart must surely be worth the wait?"

"Ah, but what is faith? Only a leap in the dark," said Holmes. "I have an irreverent attitude towards marriage. It is, in my opinion, the greatest test of character a man will ever have to endure. It never ceases to amaze me that so many are prepared to participate in the ridiculous nonsense of it all so willingly, when it is almost certain that they will be hurt and betrayed. Admittedly a few find the lifetime encumbrance fulfilling. But of course, it's a societal expectation that dictates we should be with the same person for life."

"You appear to regard love as a sign of weakness, which is an interesting concept, but nothing could be further from the truth. Tell me, Mr Holmes, what is your perception of love?"

"As far as I'm concerned, Miss Adler, we can't be everything to someone and still be true to ourselves. It's as simple as that. In any case, I don't believe that love, whatever love is, should be measured in feelings."

"You don't?"

"No," he said. "It should be based on facts. Feelings are inconsistent and unpredictable. Emotions and feelings are a product of a chemical reaction at a physical level. In my line of work, they would become a hindrance and interfere with my efficiency and strategic decision-making. I would never make a decision based on emotion. I couldn't allow it to cloud my professional judgement. But you can always rely on logic—feelings and people are far too unreliable." He stared at me curiously. "Here is a question for you, Miss Adler. What is your perception of love?"

I stared at him defiantly. "Love isn't something to be explained away or justified. No amount of logic can talk you in or out of love, love is only distinguishable when felt. That said, I'm afraid that love has become a rather violated word and has lost all meaning. If you had to ask the question of what love is, Mr Holmes, then the argument is already lost. You haven't yet felt its all-consuming power. Humanity cannot yet offer a rational explanation for why we love, although many have tried and failed, of course. The romantic poets, the great composers, have all been mesmerised by its potency. However, I believe Mozart came close when he said *Love, love, love, that is the soul of genius.*"

Holmes looked into my eyes with a peculiarly mischievous gaze. "If you would allow me to be so bold and beg your indulgence for one moment, Miss Adler. Let's pretend by process of smoke and mirrors, and in an imaginary universe not unlike Wonderland, you and I have decided to embark on a relationship. Of course, having declared our undying love for one another, we might feel happy right now. Still, happiness is fleeting. In a few hours, we may argue and then feel angry. So, if we predict our love based on feelings, is it not possible that I could love you today and feel that I didn't love you tomorrow? Feelings are far too inconsistent, and therefore can never be the proper foundation of any true relationship."

I stared at him. "Let me get this straight, Mr Holmes. In this private Wonderland, I am to play the imaginary role of your lover? Pray tell me, how would your love for me, or your perfect woman, if she does in fact exist, manifest itself, and what would you be looking for in your ideal woman?"

"I believe you are mocking me, Miss Adler." Holmes leaned forward in his chair. "But I will let that go for now. It amuses me to play this little game with you, as long as you are happy to continue, of course."

"Oh, I'm more than happy to play along."

Holmes half-closed his eyes. "Let's see, this woman, would have to be intelligent, of course, and devoid of intellectual disparity. That should narrow the field down somewhat. But I would need to feel a mental connection and stimulation. She should possess the ability to accept all of my quirks."

I smiled at him sardonically.

"Yes, Miss Adler, I'm aware that I have them. This woman would need to be interesting enough to challenge me in the verbal repertoire of wits, yet at the same time, she must not be shallow or superficial. In my world, values count. So, I would choose someone who could show me how to live in the moment and come to terms with my own emotions without analysing them. Now that would be quite something."

I frowned. "You fail to mention passion, Mr Holmes. I believe that a couple should be equal in love, friendship, and passion. If you don't have passion in a relationship, then indeed it's not a genuine relationship?"

"You told me there was no passion in the relationship with your late husband."

"You are right, of course." I nodded. "Godfrey was no more in love with me than I was with him. But tell me this, Mr Holmes, what would your perfect woman hope to get out of a relationship with you?"

"I beg your pardon, Miss Adler?"

"I'm merely curious, Mr Holmes, what could she expect from you in return?"

"Hmm, what could she expect? Why, I would move heaven and earth for her. Her problems would become mine and I would solve them before she was even aware they existed. I would not only allow this woman into my world by including her in the inner sanctum of my notoriously private life and by sharing my deepest innermost feelings. I would, however, be prepared to say goodbye if she broke my trust for any reason. I would distance myself and walk away. And that's how I view love, Miss Adler. It requires a commitment and consistency that is way beyond feelings. It requires constant communication. However, just like your Prince Charming and Alice in Wonderland, this perfect woman simply does not exist, and that is why I choose not to be in such a relationship."

"Well, thank you for the depressingly pragmatic hypothesis. You tend to mock love, you appear sceptical, but you may well find love when you are least expecting it. And when that happens, your entire world will be shaken, with all of its logic, and you will be left questioning everything."

"How on earth could I be expected to recognise this phenomenon, being the man that I am?"

"Oh, you will be aware when it happens, Mr Holmes, trust me. Nothing is unknowable, you have taught me that. You have to be aware of what you are looking for and watch out for the signs. Everything is out there, waiting for you."

Holmes stared at me, a faint smile on his lips. He removed a cigar from his case. Striking a vesta match, he lit his cigar and blew circles of blue smoke up into the air.

"You appear quite the expert on the subject, Miss Adler. Perhaps you can advise a cynical old man like me on how I would go about finding love, and what to look out for?"

I paused for a moment, realising that Holmes was revealing a side to me he would never divulge to anyone else. Although I didn't always agree with him, I adored listening to his pragmatic perspectives. "The most important advice I can give is to be prepared to compromise with the person with whom you fall in love and be flexible. And know this, Mr Holmes, someone you may not even be aware of may love you right now but remains anonymous. Life is fleeting. We should embrace its moments, not walk away from them."

"You presume to know a great deal about relationships, Miss Adler."

"I speak as I find, Mr Holmes. My honesty gets me into trouble at times. I sincerely believe that genuine attraction, the meeting of minds, goes beyond the physical. Sexuality is fluid and can change with time." I stared at him searchingly.

He responded with a mocking smile. "Well, Miss Adler, in this imaginary world, that is what I must do."

"I believe that you are mocking me now, Mr Holmes."

"I was merely making an observation, Miss Adler. This is just a game, after all."

After a pause, he picked up again. "Well then let me tell you something that you don't know. I was once engaged, although it wasn't common knowledge, albeit for a short period. Her name was Victoria, the daughter of my university professor. Alas, that did not end well. One moment, we were engaged, and then we were not. It was as simple as that."

"Why, whatever happened? Did she break your heart?" I asked, eyes wide.

"She had her head turned by the charms of an affluent lawyer. He was much older and, unfortunately for me, much wealthier than I was. She broke off our engagement and returned my ring. Of course she blamed me. Victoria told me she could no longer consider marrying a man who thought only of himself. In short, I was by far the most selfish person she had ever had the misfortune to encounter."

A sputtering sound escaped from my mouth. "I'm sorry, Mr Holmes. I don't want you to think that I'm laughing at you."

"You're not?" he quizzed. "Then perhaps you can explain that alarming noise escaping your mouth? Anyway, I digress. Victoria then became angry and told me in no uncertain terms that I was too much of a maverick for her tastes, and that I was a difficult man to deal with!"

"What did you say?"

"I advised the young lady not to end sentences with a preposition and that was the end of the affair. After that humiliating experience, I reasoned that it was far better to look forward than dwell in the past. Thinking rationally and not being led by emotions was preferable to being vulnerable. Emotional intelligence was not high up on my agenda back then. Perhaps if it was, I might have gone on to marry. Still, now I know I'll never marry, as I'm much more set in my ways and unapologetically so."

"Well, I think that lady was quite right about you being a

maverick, but the rest I find quite harsh."

"As is life, Miss Adler."

"I'm sorry to hear about your broken engagement. You obviously must have loved her."

"I seldom allude to that time in my past. She was my fiancée for a short period. I'm not sure about love, but I did like her. She was beautiful and intelligent, but I noticed aspects of her personality that were not so attractive. She was attention-seeking, manipulative, and was possessed of a penchant for the finer things in life. And I speak as one of the finer things in life. I was already beginning to have serious reservations about marriage before she called off the engagement. I was, of course, initially mortified—no one likes to be forsaken. But then I felt relieved and realised the relationship had run its course. I had received all I wanted from it."

"I bet you did," I said sarcastically. "Marriage is not for everyone, you know."

Holmes was no more in need of a wife than I was a husband. Nevertheless, his private life fascinated me. I had the feeling he wasn't telling me everything, but I knew better than to push him further on the matter.

He leaned forward in his chair, stretching out his long limbs, a sardonic look on his face. "I detect an undertone of sarcasm in your tone. While we are on the subject of failed relationships, might I mention Wilhelm Ormstein?"

"Well, that's unscrupulous, Mr Holmes!" I glared at him indignantly.

He shrugged with an air of comic resignation before we both burst into laughter.

"I long ago forfeited my right to take the moral high ground, I can assure you. And yes, Wilhelm let me down badly. He attempted to bestow precious gems upon me. I resisted all temptation, although you know how I feel about jewellery. As young and naive as I was, I realised that if I accepted what he offered, there would be expectations and repercussions. I was no fool. I was simply a girl who loved a young man."

"Who just happened to be a Crown Prince?"

"Let people think what they will." I narrowed my eyes. "People assumed I was only with Wilhelm because of his wealth and position, but nothing could have been further from the truth. I naively believed him when he promised to marry me, but I was devastated after learning of his engagement to Clotide Von Saxe Meiningen, and outraged when Wilhelm suggested I become his mistress. I couldn't get away from Warsaw quickly enough. I travelled to London with my honour intact but with my reputation in tatters. I took with me the photograph of us as leverage just in case there were any repercussions. I avoided Wilhelm's agents on several occasions before he engaged your services. Bad choices leave you in bad places, Mr Holmes. Mind you, I will say this for Wilhelm—he was slow with his promises but fast on his feet. He was an excellent dancer, and dancing is perfect for the soul. I'm so glad we got to share our mutual disappointments."

Holmes took another sip from his glass, sitting back in his chair. "Did it ever bother you what people thought?"

"No, it never bothered me. I cannot express enough how little I care about what people think. I had to work hard to unsully my reputation."

"Did you not feel liberated after your experience?"

"No, I didn't feel liberated because that would have implied that I was concerned, and to be brutally honest, I was not. Of course, I was aware I was the subject of scandal and gossip. When choosing a public career, one must be open to certain critiques. So I was expecting repercussions. But even so, I was unprepared for the onslaught of insults over the years. I'd learned to despise the press, the lowest bastion of an acceptable form of prejudice. For the most part, they are superficial opportunists, utterly unconcerned about the truth. To have your character assassinated, accused of things you did not do, is the most corrosive of human experiences. All the alleged allegations were, of course, unfounded. Still, they made for excellent broadsheet drama. I'm sure even you must have read about me at some point, Mr Holmes. I couldn't help but be reminded of all the people I was terrified of at school and how awful it was to be fifteen. There I was thrust into the limelight for all the wrong reasons, only instead of people writing about me on blackboards, now they were reporting in newspapers."

"I am acutely aware that the newspapers are not always blameless. The press is a powerful entity. They print whatever they can get away with."

"I have never flaunted myself in public. Don't get me wrong, it's nice to be recognised now and again, but to be more famous than that has never been an aspiration of mine. With that said, it does sometimes help to secure a reservation at your favourite restaurant." I laughed.

"I've never much cared about recognition and accolades. I have never performed an aria in order to win an award, and I'm sure Wagner never composed a symphony with a trophy in mind. I believe there is an imperative in everyone to make a mark in the world, but I haven't done that yet, and that's the thing that burns away at me after all this time. I should have done something of meaning, and I think that's important before one becomes irrelevant!"

"You are an incredible artist, with a huge talent. The best of the best. I doubt you could ever become irrelevant. I fancy that Irene Adler is capable of achieving anything she sets her mind to. You have unexplored possibilities. You have beauty, brains, and talent. There is ample time for you to make your mark on this world."

"Yes, but what mark and where is the question," I said. "So you see, Mr Holmes, I didn't care for a moment. I had no interest in pandering to the negative thoughts of others. I was never happier than when I was surrounded by my friends and family when I met Godfrey. He appeared utterly unconcerned about my past. He professed to love me unconditionally. I cannot tell you how good that felt, but of course we both know how that ended. Since then, I have concluded that human relationships are unpredictable and futile. Of course, I'm aware that there are a few exceptions, but sadly not for me. My past relationships have brought nothing but misery and despair."

Holmes shook his head and smiled at me with profound tenderness. "Thank you for sharing that with me, Miss Adler." He held out his splendid gold snuff box with a great amethyst at the centre of the lid. "Do you like this?"

"Why, it's beautiful."

"Yes." Holmes stared at me pointedly. "Sometimes it takes time to see the true beauty in something. This was a gift from the man himself, the King of Bohemia, for investigating the scandal in Bohemia – the only time a woman has ever outwitted me."

"Well, what was a girl to do when pursued by such a formidable antagonist as yourself? I do hope that your fee was extortionate."

"It was indeed." We laughed.

"You know, I have come to look forward to our evening discussions. I enjoy your astute observations, your advice, and your thoughts on life. You are an amazing orator and an excellent listener. I feel that I could talk to you about anything. You're hell to live with, mind, with your insistent violin playing throughout the night."

"I was unaware that my violin bothered you."

"Mr Holmes, I have appeared in operas with less music.

And don't get me started on your over-inflated self-importance and your untidiness. But your conversation is quite sublime."

"You mock me, Miss Adler?"

"Why not? Someone must," I glibly replied before bursting into a peal of laughter.

"I am just teasing you, of course. I have no wish to offend you of all people. There's no one's company I enjoy more than yours. But then I think you already know that."

There was no doubt I would miss Sherlock Holmes once our adventure was over. Still, most of all, I would miss the intimacy of our private conversations. While here in Fiesole, we had not only created a subtle bond, a good and stimulating friendship had been forged. Holmes nodded to me with a wry smile, clapping in amusement.

"You don't offend me. On the contrary, you rather amuse me. I look forward to your little epigrams. You are by far the wittiest, funniest person that I have ever met."

Chapter Twenty-Eight: Irene Adler

The sounds of hustle and bustle echoed around the courtyard as the domestic servants prepared for the wedding anniversary festivities. They scrubbed and dried the outside patio area on Violetta's instructions in case anyone felt inclined to dance later that evening. The benches were covered with freshly laundered white linen tablecloths, each with a bouquet of fresh flowers from the gardens. Ava and Clarissa decorated the courtyard with paper garlands, flowers, and balloons. Gabriella, Antonia, and Violetta were in the kitchen, busy preparing the food.

Ava arrived at the barn just after breakfast with a basket of flowers and a parcel.

I embraced Ava, kissing her on the cheek. "My goodness, such beautiful flowers. I'm sure Violetta will love them."

"No, Nene." Ava shook her head. "Mama already has her flowers. These blooms are for you. They must be from Mr Holmes." She smiled at me curiously. "What's it like being married? I imagine it must be wonderful to be with someone you genuinely love."

I hesitated, taken aback by Ava's question. "Well, it has its moments. What's brought this on, young lady? Do you have a secret admirer?"

Ava blushed before nodding. "Yes, it's Javier. I think I love him."

"What makes you say that?"

"Because every time I see or speak to him, I get butterflies in my tummy, and I cannot wait to see him again."

"Ah, then I think you may well be in love, and there's nothing wrong with that. Javier is a fine young man. He'd be lucky to have you."

"Do you still get butterflies when you see Mr Holmes?"

"My feelings for my husband are unlike anything I have ever experienced before. And yes, I did get butterflies when I first saw him, but that was before I even knew him . . ."

Ava hugged me before running back to the farmhouse in a state of girlish excitement.

I placed the parcel in my bedroom drawer, then examined the flowers. I couldn't help thinking that Ava had wildly exaggerated Holmes' romantic tendencies. It seemed odd that he would send me flowers. I opened the card and the ebony hair clip I thought I had lost fell into the palm of my hand. My eyes scanned the card, which read:

Until next time,

Jx

I was taken aback, realising with a start that they must be from Javier. But if that was the case, why on earth would he have my hair clip?

Later that evening, Ava and I peered out of her bedroom window to find a gathering of guests had piled into the courtyard. The Anka family were amongst them. Several farm labourers, along with the regulars and their families, had also arrived.

The domestic servants had done splendidly, laying outside benches with a feast of lampredotto Tuscan pork, provolone cheese, spiced olives, bowls of fresh fruit, saffron cake, honey, and sweetbread. Drinks flowed—beer, vin santo, and homemade lemonade for the children. Champagne was provided for the toast with the compliments of Sherlock Holmes.

The sun was beginning to set in the courtyard and the gardens illuminated with oil lamps and taper candles created a welcoming, cosy atmosphere. Giovanni played his banjo, accompanied by Javier on the harpsichord.

Meanwhile, upstairs in the bedroom, I helped Ava change into her evening dress of white nun's veiling. The dress was a perfect fit, a lovely contrast to her beautiful olive skin. Next, I sugar curled Ava's hair with curling tongs. She was amazed how I had managed to make the curls so tight and small. She admired them in the pier glass. I showed Ava the small pair of bespoke curling tongs.

"I bought them when I lived in New York. They cost a week's salary. If a lady can have one indulgence, then in my opinion it should be her hair, her crowning glory."

"I wish I could afford a pair," said Ava. A mournful expression appeared on her face.

I smiled. "Ava, a determined woman will find a way to get whatever she wants."

I tied a small bouquet of white roses into Ava's hair. They perfectly matched her dress. Next, I applied Ava's makeup before presenting her with an opera mask and a pair of white evening gloves. I pinned a brooch onto her dress as a finishing touch, a mosaic antique Italian fan in blue and gold, engraved on the back. *From La Scala Irene Adler 1884 – 1887.*

Ava stared at the broach in awe. "It's beautiful, Nene. Thank you so much for allowing me to borrow it. I promise to take good care of it."

I kissed the top of Ava's head. "You are very welcome, my dear. I only bring it out on special occasions, and this is your night, your time to shine. I don't think it's precious, but what it does have is great sentimental value. And at least it's Italian."

"Thank you," said Ava. "This is such a strange feeling, terrifying yet exciting at the same time. I must admit I do feel a little apprehensive having to follow you, Nene. You are *so* talented. I'm worried about what people will think of me."

I took Ava by the shoulder. "Ava, listen to me. Sometimes feeling scared is good because it lights a fire within you.

Everyone has the right to criticise you; it is your right to prove them wrong."

I pointed Ava towards the pier glass. "Ava, my darling, you are a chrysalis just bursting with potential. You'll make quite the impression. Your mama and papa will be so proud."

Downstairs the guests had assembled. Many sat outside on the wooden benches, chatting indiscriminately, partaking of the lovely food and drinks.

Two days earlier, Ludo had asked if I would consider playing at the anniversary supper and dedicate a song to Violetta. I happily agreed.

Holmes raised his concerns with me when we discussed the matter over luncheon the following day. He remarked that accompanying Ava on the piano was one thing, but singing in public was quite another. I shrugged and told him I felt unable to let the family down, given the kindness they'd bestowed upon us. In the end, Holmes conceded, albeit reluctantly.

Holmes had returned from the village earlier than expected the following day to find me alone at breakfast. He sat beside me to show me a telegram that had arrived that morning. The wire was from his brother Mycroft, relaying the news that Palmer's lifeless body had been fished out of the Thames by the dredger men.

"Thank god," I cried out in relief. "Does this mean it's safe to go home now?"

"It would appear so," said Holmes. "Although my brother has asked that we stay on for a few more days until the Metropolitan police establish who is responsible for Palmer's death."

I nodded. "Then tonight at least we can celebrate with Ludo and Violetta. I can sing for them without worry."

"Yes, of course, why not." Holmes offered me a smile. "I need to go out again. I have a few matters to attend to, but I will be back in time for the festivities."

"Thank you, Mr Holmes, for everything," I said, tears in my eyes.

I stepped forward and kissed him lightly on the cheek, but I resisted the urge to throw my arms around his neck and hug him. I had mixed feelings about Palmer's demise. I was, of course, relieved that he could no longer pursue us. But the thought of never seeing Holmes again hit me like a sledgehammer. Imagining my world without him in it was an impossible concept.

I walked into the courtyard attired in a midnight blue sleeveless evening gown, my hair concealed in an elaborate chignon. The murmurs and indistinct chatter began to fade. Giovanni and Javier Anka looked up at my entrance, laying their instruments down as I approached the piano.

As I addressed the audience, there was a hush in the courtyard, an air of expectation. "Ladies and gentlemen, I have been asked to play a medley of romantic music for you this evening. Of course, being classically trained, I have a vast repertoire to choose from. I have selected some of my favourites. I hope they are yours, too. Well, ladies and gentlemen, I sincerely hope my husband and I will be as happy as Ludo and Violetta when we have been married for twenty years." The audience laughed.

I overheard Gabriella mutter to her husband, "Twenty years? They will be lucky if they last twenty weeks."

Gabriella Anka glanced at Holmes. He had the grace to blush.

I sat down at the piano and began to play Beethoven's "Für Elise." You could hear a pin drop in the courtyard as I reached the last chord of the song before effortlessly moving onto Liszt's "Liebestraum in A-flat Major" to the delight of the thrilled audience. They gasped in awe at the fast cadenza requiring dexterous finger-work. At the end of the piece, I stood up for a moment and smiled at the audience before sitting back down again to play Stephen Foster's "Beautiful Dreamer," singing the beautiful melody. At the end of my performance, the audience burst into delighted applause.

"Well, that was fun," I said. "The songs I sing in my professional routine can often be a little static. This is a significant change. Ladies and gentlemen, we now come to the highlight of the evening. It is my great privilege to introduce our mystery performer, who will be dedicating a song for someone extraordinary. I understand this particular song is very close to Violetta's heart. She even insisted on playing it at her wedding."

The lights dimmed, and a young lady, her identity concealed in an opera mask, glided into the courtyard. She stood beside me at the piano, the audience gasping in admiration. I began to play the opening chords of "Drink To Me Only With Thine Eyes." I was shocked to hear the distinct sound of a violin. I swung round on my seat to discover Holmes, who was seated close by, accompanying me. I composed myself and took a deep breath. I smiled at the audience and shrugged nonchalantly, as though Sherlock Holmes and I played a duet every day of our lives. Ava began to sing in all the power and beauty of youth.

A hush fell in the courtyard as the song ended and the audience erupted into applause. Ava removed her mask, laughing nervously. The audience and her parents stared at her in stunned disbelief. Violetta and Ludo were astounded to discover their beloved daughter had sung to them. Ava ran over to her parents and embraced them. Her beautiful eyes shone like stars.

I glanced over to Holmes and whispered, "Thank you." He nodded.

Looking up from the piano, I found Violetta beaming at me. "Thank you so much, Nene, for all you have done for

Ava. My god, I was unaware my daughter could sing like an angel! I knew she could carry a tune. I've heard her singing in the bath, but nothing like this. I've never heard a finer rendition of that song."

"You've done very well, Ava. I am so proud of you," I said.

"You are such an inspirational teacher," Ava replied. "Thank you for everything. You have made Mamma so happy."

"My pleasure," I said, beaming at the girl.

Ava found herself surrounded by friends congratulating her on her performance.

I took the opportunity to speak to Violetta and Ludo confidentially.

"Ava has a shining natural talent," I said. "However, she will need extensive tuition and development to reach her full potential. Nevertheless, I would like to put her name forward for an audition at La Scala in September. Despite her tender years, I'm convinced your daughter has what it takes to become part of the theatre chorus. I am more than happy to write a letter of recommendation. However, for this endorsement to be effective, Ava must first showcase a high level of talent at the audition, which she has, of course, in abundance. When I leave here, Ava must continue to practise. I would like to arrange this as a parting gift. Javier informed me there is such a teacher in the village, a retired soprano. And no, Violetta, I will not take no for an answer.

"If you and Ludo agree, I would like to arrange for my good friend Sophia to act as Ava's mentor. I have many friends at La Scala. They will keep a watchful eye on your daughter. I don't want either of you to worry regarding the financial aspects. Should Ava be accepted, she would automatically qualify for a bursary to assist with her studies and living expenses."

Ludo stared at me pensively, stroking his chin. "Does such

a fund exist for our stellina?" He asked.

"Yes, of course." I crossed my fingers behind my back, determined that Ava would not lose her place due to financial reasons.

I was more than happy to help. Ludo and Violetta would feel uncomfortable accepting charity. They were proud people, but a bursary was a bursary, irrespective of who was funding it.

"Thank you so much," said Violetta. "For what you did for Ava. The generosity of your spirit and time is overwhelming. Ludo and I already know the answer to your question, but we need a little more time to mull it over. We will miss her dreadfully if she should be accepted by La Scala."

"I know you will," I said. "But you know, Milan is only a train ride away, so Ava would be able to come home on the weekends and the holidays. Can you imagine her first professional appearance at La Scala? It will be amazing, and you will love Milan, Violetta."

"Hmm, sounds like it's going to cost me a pretty penny," said Ludo, shaking his head. "Thank god we have good crops this year."

Chapter Twenty-Nine: Irene Adler

Venturing outside to search for Holmes, I scanned the courtyard, but he was nowhere in sight.

Clarissa approached with a tray of champagne, and I gratefully accepted a glass. Sitting at a bench, I soon struck up a conversation with a couple from a neighbouring farm. A pleasant-looking woman of middle-aged years, slim built, with light brown hair and deep-set blue eyes, introduced herself as Rachel and her paramour as Gino. He was a small shifty-looking man with a handlebar moustache and dark piercing eyes. I was about to leave when I noticed a lady in a black silk georgette dress and a scarlet cloak approach.

The lady sat down across from Rachel and Gino, nodding to them. "Good evening," she said, staring at Rachel with a pair of magnetic deep-set brown eyes. "My name is Maria. I have come to read your palm. All I ask is for a little change, not for me. All proceeds from this evening will be donated to the Ospedale Degli Innocenti for the abandoned bambinos."

Maria wore a black bandana and a rosary as a necklace, but this wasn't the only reason for my sudden interest. A young pocket-sized version of Gabriella Anka sat before me, the same eyes, glasses, and facial features.

Firmly clasping Rachel's hand in her own, Maria recited her rosary in Italian before continuing. "You have lost someone close to you recently?"

"Yes," said Rachel. "My husband, Alfonso. He tragically died last year under mysterious circumstances. The coroner recorded an open verdict."

"You have found a new love?" Maria gestured to Gino, raising an eyebrow.

Not too tricky, Maria, the man is sitting beside her.

"Yes indeed." Rachel smiled at Gino. "Fortune has smiled down on me. I have found love for the second time." Rachel paused for a moment. "I have no wish to speak ill of the dead, but Alfonso was a very mean man. He only took me out when the shops were closed, whereas Gino has been more than generous."

"Gino was your late husband's business partner and the best man at your wedding," said Maria. "Your husband is not happy. He will not rest until the perpetrator has been found and brought to justice."

"What does he have to say?" Rachel asked suspiciously, a shocked expression on her face.

"I want my wife," said Maria, suddenly speaking in a manly tone.

The blood drained from Rachel's face. "You can tell my husband that I'm not ready to come yet," she cried.

Rachel stood, almost knocking the bench over, before flouncing off into the night. Gino reached into his pocket, threw Maria a handful of change, then ran after the stricken Rachel.

"Nobody wants to hear the truth. They cross my palm with silver and tell me they do, but most can't handle it." Maria stood up, smiling at me. "Over the years, I have learnt never to question my gifts. They have been bestowed upon me by a higher order. At least the money is going to a good cause."

"Do I know you?" I quizzed. "Are you related to Gabriella Anka? You look very much like her."

"Yes, Gabriella is my sister," Maria replied. "May I speak to you confidentially?"

"Yes, of course. Let me introduce myself. My name is Irene Adler."

"Yes, I know who you are," Maria said. "I saw your

performance earlier this evening. You and the girl were naturally magnificent."

"Well, thank you, Maria, you are very kind. Do you live nearby? I don't remember seeing you before."

Maria stared at me. "I am the seventh daughter of a seventh daughter. People say I have the gift of prophecy. I detect pain in your eyes. May I?"

"Please go ahead, Maria. As you say, it's for a worthy cause." Endeavouring to enter into the spirit of the occasion, I took a sip of champagne.

Maria turned my hand over. She rubbed my palm with the tips of her fingers then grasped it tightly. I took in a sharp intake of breath and then, just as suddenly, Maria released her grip, gazing intently at my palm.

"Many challenges have consumed your life," she said. "You have suffered immeasurable heartache at the hands of men."

"You can say that again." I scoffed.

"A man pursues you. I see a conflict with fire and smoke. The reaper waits at the end, but not for you, my dear." Maria smiled at me reassuringly. "As for matters of the heart, love will manifest itself from an unexpected source. This man will travel over water in pursuit of the truth in this quest of you, my dear. He is a man of no equal, supremely gifted and confident in his own sagacity. True soul mates are like sunrise and sunset, they live amongst us every day, yet we rarely see them."

I stared at Maria curiously. "Do you know who this man is?"

"His identity will soon become apparent to you, my dear. When the ball starts to roll, you must be ready. He waits by an open doorway and all you need to do is walk through the doorway to meet him. You see this man as no woman has seen him before, and that unnerves him. You will conceive a child together, a son, born of great love on the twelfth day of the first month, at the stroke of six o'clock, under the sign of Capricorn. The same birth sign as his father and his father before him. This child will possess many talents and make his mark in history. That is fate."

"Is this boy to be my only child?"

Maria shook her head. "The Lord is mysterious, and we must await his intentions. I am merely a humble vessel." She smiled at my bemused expression. "You doubt my words? I see you have already lost an infant."

"Tell me, Maria, will I ever see my child again?"

Maria sighed. "When we have endured the unendurable, it is only through the dark night of the soul that we come to speak, to understand, and to see through the eyes of Christ. Your daughter lives inside you. Her soul shines as bright as the crimson on my cloak. You will meet again, for her memory can never be erased. I must take my leave of you now. *Buona Fortuna, mia cara.*" Maria stood abruptly as if to go.

"Please wait." I looked at her anxiously. "I have something for you to cross your palm."

Bending down to open my bag, I took out some change before I noticed Maria had disappeared into the night. I sighed. Part of me felt relieved Maria had moved on to her next victim. The other part wondered how she could have known about Rosemary.

I removed a compact from my bag and gazed at my reflection, reapplying my lipstick.

If I were to give birth in nine months, it would have to be by immaculate conception. Otherwise, where is he, my lover, the father of my unborn child? I giggled at the absurd notion.

Just then a tall man approached me. He looked vaguely familiar, and I assumed he was one of the casual farm labourers. The man removed his cap to reveal a bald head, pale skin and a long, thin face with sideburns. His light blue eyes were covered by horn-rimmed glasses. Something about the way he presented himself made me feel uncomfortable.

The man introduced himself as Ben Masterson, an artist from Mellis, a tiny village just outside Somerset. He said he was staying in Fiesole during the summer months on a sabbatical to paint and meditate, labouring at the farm a few hours here and there to supplement his income. I breathed a sigh of relief. At least he was not another soothsayer. Ben told me how much he enjoyed my performance and asked if I would sign an autograph, handing me a black fountain pen and a commonplace book, which I happily signed. I noticed the signature had a slightly blurred look to it. Ben thanked me for the autograph and apologised about the pen, which he said needed a new nib, bidding me a good evening before rejoining the festivities.

I stared after him for a few moments, remembering where I had seen him before. He was one of the men who helped Javier take the piano out onto the courtyard.

Turning around, I noticed Javier by my side, congratulating me on my performance. We spoke about music and Ava's spectacular debut. The boy appeared a little intoxicated. He spoke to me in Italian, explaining how he desperately loved Ava in an agitated tone. But it was hopeless, she seemed oblivious to his ardent admiration. He didn't know what to do. I placed my hand soothingly on Javier's, attempting to console the love-stricken boy. I told him Ava had been distracted recently with rehearsals, but she spoke to me in the confidence of her affection and deep admiration for him. I suggested he return home for an early night, explaining it would be far better to declare his feelings in the morning when he was sober and refreshed. I quizzed Javier on the flowers, and the hair clip, he swore he knew nothing about either.

"Well, maybe I should." Javier jokingly replied, his mood brightening. He kissed me on the cheek before making his way back to the cottage.

Chapter Thirty: Sherlock Holmes

After Ava's stunning performance, I decided to go for a walk and ponder over the events of the evening.

When I returned, I found Miss Adler sitting at a bench with the Anka boy. They appeared engrossed in intimate conversation, although I was too far away to make out what they were saying.

Nevertheless, I continued to observe them for some time. Finally I took one last look before turning on my heels and returning to the barn.

Arriving back at the barn in a sombre mood, I entered the drawing-room, my eyes immediately drawn to the flowers. I removed the card, digesting the contents, and became incensed that Anka dared to send flowers to an allegedly married woman. Then pouring a whiskey and soda, I entered the bedroom and removed a case from the drawer. A tiny hypodermic needle glittered in the moonlight. I hesitated for a moment, but without Watson there to counsel me, the temptation proved impossible to resist. I injected myself with cocaine, the single weakness of my nature. My mood soon skewed into a fit of jealous rage and wild imaginings, feelings alien to me until now, brooding on the occasions Anka waved to Nene while working in the fields, their intimate conversations at the stables. I managed to convince myself that the two of them were lovers. I lit a cigarette, attempting to calm myself. Sadly, whisky, nicotine, and cocaine did little to alleviate the pain.

The night air had grown exceptionally still and humid, almost suffocating. I rose and opened the window. I took off my jacket, waistcoat, and cravat, unfastening the top two buttons of my shirt in an attempt to cool myself down. Finally, I sat on the bed, reflecting on my sombre mood. I dozed off, then awoke with a jolt, disturbed by the sound of a key turning in the latch.

Chapter Thirty-One: Irene Adler

After bidding Javier goodnight, I returned to the barn, stopping to speak to a group of children playing football on the lawn. I returned to find everything in darkness, save for a taper lamp shining through the bedroom window. Half expecting to find Holmes sitting on the patio, I was disappointed when there was no sign of him. I retired to my bedroom with a heavy heart.

I changed into a pale blue silk chemise and a matching dressing gown with satin slippers. Then I untied my hair and brushed it, allowing it to fall loose upon my shoulders. Sitting on the bed, pessimistic thoughts flooded my brain. I had failed in my fight for Holmes' attention. As our camaraderie flourished, I'd been hoping for more. Whenever I thought I was getting close to him, the part of himself he held back closed down and shut me out.

Entering the kitchen, I noticed a carafe of wine on the side and poured myself a drink. I sipped slowly from the glass, pondering the events of the evening. I had developed feelings for the celebrated detective, feelings I knew he would never reciprocate. Holmes could never be interested in someone like me, a woman of the world. Albeit a world that was getting smaller every day.

Turning around, I was startled to find Holmes standing in the doorway. The top two buttons of his shirt were unfastened, exposing his chest. Long muscular arms rested on the door frame.

I was shocked by his dishevelled appearance. His eyes

were dilated as he looked at me with a dark, brooding intensity. His hair was swept back from his face, giving him a rugged sultry appearance, his usual sallow cheeks flushed with colour. The tension in the room had dissipated. I took in the faint scent of his cologne, overwhelmed by the power of his physicality. I felt vulnerable, scared, and hopelessly lost.

"Ah, you have returned, I see?" Holmes spoke in a deprecating tone, an air of sarcasm in his manner. "I was under the impression you had absconded for the evening with your lover, Javier Anka. I have to say he is an intriguing choice, although not the most quick-witted youth. But admittedly he is comely. Such a handsome young man to look at, I'll give him that. He's undoubtedly an ardent lover full of youthful vigour, I would fancy. Tell me, do you find him handsome, Miss Adler?"

Although I was shocked by Holmes's expostulation, the ferocity of his anger surprised me. Observing his livid eyes, I'd never seen Holmes so riled. Suddenly I felt afraid, reminding myself that Holmes would never dream of raising a hand to me, not like Godfrey.

"I have never professed to have a high aesthetic bar. I fail to see the point you're making, Mr Holmes."

"That is because I have not yet arrived at it. Why, it beggars belief. Underestimate me at your peril, especially when I have unleashed my full powers. Do you really want to risk that?"

"I have never underestimated you, Mr Holmes!"

Holmes paced around the kitchen, hands behind his back, as though an advocate in a court of law. "Don't play me for a fool. Do you think I haven't noticed how the two of you talk, the way he looks at you? So tell me, when did this rigmarole begin, this fait accompli? By God, I ought to lay a whip upon that boy's shoulders and thrash the hide off him!"

A baleful light shone in his imperious stare, cutting me down to size. The intensity of sound heightened, and I began to shake with humiliation and anger. Then I realised I needn't be afraid of Holmes. I knew he would never dream of hurting me physically. That would be abhorrent to his robust personal code of chivalry and high moral compass.

His narrative, however, was a different matter. Reassured in that knowledge, I stood my ground, staring at him defiantly. "First of all, Mr Holmes, I am not a fan of rhetorical questions. Nor was I aware that it was a crime to meet someone in public for a friendly discussion of a mutual love of horses and music?"

"There is a difference between being friendly and making a public spectacle of yourself, Madame. You were speaking to him in Italian, for God's sake."

"And that's a crime!" I scoffed at his impertinence. "My affairs are none of your concern, sir. I don't have to explain myself to you or anyone else. Do you think that I am incapable of making my own decisions because I am a woman?"

"The matter is not open for discussion. May I remind you that while we remain in this village, to all intents and purposes you are the wife of a celebrated detective. You *will* behave like it."

"Aah," I said. "You think that because I am your assumed wife, that entitles you to take the moral high ground? Are you out of your godforsaken mind? You have no evidence to substantiate your spurious claim. Javier is not my lover. He is of no interest to me in the way you so impudently imply."

I threw up my hands in a despairing gesture, finding little relief in a gush of tears.

Holmes smiled at me sardonically. "Was that an embarrassed shudder of recognition, Miss Adler? Why does your moral outrage amuse me, I wonder? If it was not Javier Anka, then it must be someone else from the supper party who was privy to your ardent admiration. Tell me, was there anyone else there this evening with the initial J?"

In a desperate attempt to gather my thoughts, I remained silent for a moment. Holmes stared at me, his face filled with exasperation.

"With all due respect, I'm talking to you, Miss Adler. Please tell me that I am heard?"

"Yes, I heard you, but you're not telling me anything." I turned to face him. "Without respect, Mr Holmes, you are talking over me. You are raising your voice. I find your attitude offensive." I paused for several moments, astounded by his haughty arrogance.

Picking up my wine glass, I swallowed the contents in one large gulp. "That's what bothers you, isn't it?" I sneered. "The fact that I could have lain with Javier if I'd wanted to. Not that Javier could have lain with me. Why, this isn't about Javier, or any other man for that matter. I am so disappointed in you. Who do you think you are?"

Holmes stared at me. He let out a long sigh of despair, as his face slowly contorted into a grimace of sober contemplation.

"You are delusional. It's clear to see that you are intoxicated. Pray tell how much wine have you consumed this evening?"

"Not nearly enough," I scoffed. "And that's rich, coming from you. You are drunk yourself. From my experience, when a man's had a drink, that's when the truth comes out. He says what he thinks. What a cruel man you are. I thought I'd seen my fair share of such men in my lifetime."

"I must say that I find your answer rather impertinent, Miss Adler."

"Well, your accusations may come under the same heading, Mr Holmes."

I couldn't believe this was happening. I felt drained and demoralised, as though I was in a dreadful nightmare I would never wake from. In a moment of madness and pure frustration, I threw the glass at the wall, narrowly missing Holmes, who ducked when he saw it hurtling towards him. The glass hit the wall and shattered.

I glared at him, my nostrils flaring. "Oh, yes, Mr Sherlock Holmes, as you so rightly deduce, there is someone from the supper party whom I greatly admire. Why, I am astounded that I've been able to conceal his identity for so long, especially from you, the all-seeing detective. Please allow me to give you a clue, as you are so clearly in need of one. His name does not begin with the letter J, although he is undoubtedly a conundrum to me."

Holmes stood motionless.

"You know all the people at the supper party are under the misapprehension that I am married to you, the celebrated detective Sherlock Holmes. Your egotism, your breath-taking level of arrogance, your condescending manner . . . I am repelled by it, by all of it. Why, I believe your coldness to be nothing more than a calculated, unwavering self-correction."

With the brooding of his deep-set and inscrutable eyes, Holmes laughed. "You mean I am incapable of connecting with you? I am immune from sentiment, as you are well aware, and am hardly the gay Lothario one would expect. We're different people, you and I."

"You're not incorrect," I scoffed. "I think, Mr Holmes, you are more than capable of liking people as long as it's on your terms. You remove feelings from your mind because you believe, in doing so, you no longer have to deal with emotions. You turn your back on spontaneity, burying your intuition. However, there's a massive consequence to that action, because when you lose your intuition, you lose your strongest function." I paused for a moment. "The real value of having intuition, of course, is knowing how to use it."

"I don't appreciate your directness. I hope I am making myself clear."

"On the contrary, you are making yourself very unclear. You are the living definition of a man who lives in a world where he considers love and affection to be trite and frivolous. With all your cleverness, you have no understanding at all about love and the frailty of the human heart. What difference does it make? What's it to you, anyway, if I sleep with the whole village, especially all men with the initials J? I'm surprised you haven't carried out a census."

I paused for a moment. "You don't get it, do you? Goddammit, do I have to spell it out for you? I like you quite a lot. In fact, and considering the issues you clearly have, your highhandedness, your lack of tact, telling you was not easy for me. Of course, you are far too self-absorbed and emotionally detached to notice. You are the most infuriating man I have ever had the misfortune to come across. Why, you are Edward Fairfax Rochester without the charisma and charm!" I paused for a moment, gazing directly into his eyes. "I do have one question, though."

"I am breathless with anticipation. What, I shudder to ask, is your question?" he asked, a wary expression on his face.

"What did Victoria do to burn you, to make you this way? Your meticulous self-directed journey must get very lonely and somewhat taxing. Damn you and all your logic. I wish to retire to my bedroom now. This toxic conversation is crushing my soul!"

Holmes had by no means relaxed his rigid attitude, but instead lapsed into a gloomy silence.

I poured myself another glass of wine and flounced past him, retiring to my bedroom. Blind with fury, I slammed the door shut with such force it almost came off its hinges. I lay down on the bed, crying with frustration and rage. I made up my mind that I would go home in the morning. I would prefer to sleep on a park bench rather than spend another night under the same roof as Sherlock Holmes.

Sitting up, I sipped the wine in an attempt to calm myself when I heard the sound of footsteps approaching, then a knocking on my bedroom door. I remained silent, hoping he would go away, but he rapped again, this time more urgently.

"Please go away. I don't want to talk to you. My God, is this night ever going to end?"

Holmes opened the door and walked towards me, sinking into the chair beside the bed and placing a glass of water on the table. He clasped his hands together, his eyes focused on the ceiling.

"I am so sorry, Miss Adler. My behaviour this evening has been utterly atrocious. I offer you my most heartfelt apologies. I had no idea you would be so affected."

I turned to him. "Well, here we are again . . . you upsetting me then finding yourself having to apologise. Perhaps you need to take a closer look at yourself. And as for your apology, it's as pathetic as you are, Mr Holmes."

"I concede that you have every right to feel angry. I have upset you very deeply, which is unforgivable, even if it was unintended. I freely admit that I drank far too much whisky and took a little cocaine, of which I'm not proud. However, given what happened to your late husband, this is quite unacceptable. Therefore, if you agree, I think we should head back to London tomorrow. I can then place you in the safe hands of Inspector Lestrade and my brother, Mycroft. Whatever your feelings may be towards me, your safety and well-being will always be of paramount importance."

He stood and walked towards the door then turned to face me. "Your description of me being emotionally detached and self-absorbed is an accurate assessment. It's a harsh truth, but a truth nevertheless. I'm fundamentally a cold, unfeeling person. There's a reason I'm alone in the world." He flashed me a dry smile.

I scoffed. "You know something? I have enough regrets.

My life has been one unmitigated disaster after another, constantly living through a vale of tears. But then you come along and take it to a whole new level. You know, despite it all, during our intimate conversations when I bared my soul to you, there were moments of breath-taking tenderness and joy. Yet despite all of that, you still expect me to tell you everything, while at the same time, you say nothing at all. Am I really to be the narrator of your silence? Walk away from me, by all means, but don't pretend for one moment that you don't have feelings for me. I know beneath that icy exterior lies a complex and profoundly feeling man, whom I believe likes me too. Perhaps you should allow people to see that occasionally."

Holmes stared at me incredulously. "*Like* you? If it were only that simple. I more than like you. I can't stop thinking of you. By God, Nene, I love you, I have always loved you. I am barely controlling my feelings and you were always good enough." He turned towards the door. 'I will take my leave of you now, for I have nothing further to say on the matter.'

I pulled myself up from the bed, all my strength and bravado evaporating at that precise moment. "Wait!" I cried. "Mr Holmes, please wait before you go. There's something of great importance that I need you to do for me."

"Name it."

"I would very much like you to repeat what you said. If it is as I thought, then I must insist you kiss me without any delay."

Holmes walked towards me, his eyes fixed on mine. With a profound tenderness he cradled my face, softly brushing my lips with his, before we rapturously fell into each other's arms.

"I wasn't sure if this is what you wanted."

"Oh, it's what I wanted, Mr Holmes."

He took me in his arms, kissing me passionately. "I've dreamed of doing this since the moment I first laid eyes on you."

"And do I fulfil your expectations?"

"Precisely so," he whispered, pulling me to him.

We kissed again as though it was the most natural thing in the world, holding each other tightly. I was moved to tears by his declaration of love, the anguish I had felt just a few moments ago now erased from my mind.

I spoke softly to Holmes, whispering in his ear. "So, you think that I am the most exceptional woman you have ever met? Why, that's quite a compliment, coming from you, Mr Holmes."

"Yes, you are indeed exceptional. The only thing that stops you from being the most perfect is your obstinacy. I must say that it's not your most endearing feature."

"Well, I suppose a half compliment is better than none at all." I scoffed. "You need to work on your flattery. Promise me to never become a therapist."

"There is no such thing as a bad compliment."

"All right, if you say so. Tell me, have you been here with Victoria?"

"It's been a while," he said. "There have been other women in my past, as you are aware, but never like this. I have no interest in pursuing a personal relationship for the sake of it. My brain needs to be mentally stimulated before I could consider it, and that rarely happens, except of course when I am with you."

"Nice recovery Mr Holmes," I said, laughing. "Why, that could be the finest compliment a man could ever bestow upon a woman. There may be hope for you yet."

Sitting down on the bed, I stared at him, my heart beating wildly. Holmes sat beside me, taking my hand in his. "I don't think you want to become involved with a man like me, not really. You come from a different, sweeter, purer world than me."

"Let me be the judge of that. Although I do have it on excellent authority that you are a highly complex man." I gestured towards the bed.

He shook his head, a concerned look on his face. "We don't have to rush into anything. As I have said, this is not about the physical for me." Holmes paused for a moment, gazing into my eyes. "Perhaps we can return to being friends? We can leave it at that, if you want. I am not a steady man, and you deserve to be loved wholeheartedly."

"I have not been put on this earth to be your friend, Sherlock. Friends don't feel for each other the way I feel about you."

"Your deduction is as accurate as ever. You certainly have potential to make an admirable detective. You should consider taking it up professionally."

"I am naturally observant, as you may have commented. You do realise that he who hesitates is lost?"

"You had my attention from our first encounter at La Scala. The moment you appeared on stage, I was lost."

"You had me from Wagner." I sighed, stroking his face. "You have evoked a passion in me that I have never felt before. So why don't we take the next step?"

Holmes stared at me in disbelief. "Are you quite sure?"

"Yes. Is that a problem for you?"

"No."

I slowly began to unbutton his shirt. "I only ask one thing of you."

"And what is that?"

"Please don't do this unless you mean it."

"Oh, I mean it," he said, his voice hoarse with emotion.

I gently placed my hand on his thigh. He flinched at my touch and moved away from me.

Holmes looked into my eyes in the thoughtful manner I had become familiar with and lowered his head. That look said it all. Overcome with emotion and disappointment, I bit my top lip to stop myself from crying.

"I'm sorry I cannot do this," said Holmes. "Forgive me, but you are my client, for God's sake, I promised your father I would protect you."

Smiling, I tried holding back the tears. "We are way beyond regrets, and well past the age of consent. I don't care if this is right or wrong, I only know that I'm drowning here."

"I don't think I can give you what you need. I'm not even sure if I want a relationship," he said.

I gasped, shocked by the callousness of his words, tears stinging my eyes. "I can take rejection, that's nothing new to me, but you're right, this is never going to work." I began to laugh hysterically. "Oh, my god, what is wrong with me? Why can't I be with someone normal for once? How on earth can I expect to embark on a personal relationship with a man who professes his love for me, cannot bear the thought of me being with anyone else, yet recoils at my touch? What do you want from me, Sherlock?"

Holmes looked up at me, shaking his head. "No, you are quite wrong. Please hear me out." He took my hand and entwined my fingers with his. "I realise that being with me is never going to be easy, but I want you to know that, although I didn't want to and I've tried to fight it with every fibre of my being, I love you ardently. I cannot express the magnitude of my feelings for you. I want to change the concept of your world until you no longer feel any pain, until I have erased every negative thought and memory. We are both in uncharted territory, but neither of us is ever going to settle for normal, for the mundane." He stared at me with burning intensity before continuing. "But what I really want to do is to lay with you. You have no idea how much I want to do that."

My eyes glistened with tears. "Well, if you're sure. I know how prickly you are about personal boundaries."

Holmes gently stroked my face with his fingertips. "Pray, tell me one thing, who the hell is Edward Fairfax Rochester?"

I chuckled. "All you need to know, my love, is that he won the heroine in the end." I paused for a moment. "Sherlock, would you be so kind as to turn down the lamp?"

"Yes, of course, but why?" he asked.

"Because if we leave it on, it will advocate a level of confidence I don't have."

I was beginning to feel a little apprehensive. The last time I was touched by a man was over two years ago when Godfrey violated me. I still carried a scar under my left breast from that encounter.

As though somehow aware of my thoughts, Holmes dimmed the taper lamp, turning it down so low that there was scarcely any light at all. Then, taking me into his arms, he pulled me closer, tracing every area of my body with his fingers. I unbuttoned his shirt, revealing a fit, moderately haired torso, and ran my hands up and down his taut stomach, stroking his chest and muscular arms. Holmes caressed the nape of my neck with his fingertips. His touch sent a shiver down my spine as he stroked the fine silky hair on my arms, trailing downwards to my breasts. His caresses became more urgent, extending over my belly. I could feel his heart beating wildly as though it would burst through his chest. We undressed until we were lying beside each other naked. His mouth moved downwards, and my breathing became shallow.

"Nene, are you sure?" he whispered. "I don't want our first time together to make you uncomfortable. Tell me to stop at any time and you have my word that I will."

"I don't want you to stop." I surrendered into his arms for a melting kiss.

We made love slowly and tenderly, until the light from the taper lamp flickered and died. He stirred my senses in a way I never thought possible, and we held onto each other long after the point of our sweet surrender.

Later that evening, we lay naked under the sheets, our bodies entwined, when he said, "When I was a young boy, my mother told me that those who want never got, but she was wrong. You have bestowed something in me I never knew I wanted, Nene."

We lay in bed whispering to each other softly until the sun came up. Much to Holmes's amusement, I did everything I could to engage him in conversation, literally fighting to keep my eyes open. I wanted to be held in his arms forever. Eventually, my lids became so heavy I finally fell into a deep sleep.

Chapter Thirty-Two: Sherlock Holmes

I emerged from the bathroom early the following day, showered, dressed, and prepared for the day ahead. I glanced over at Nene. She was sleeping soundly. She stirred for a moment, half opened her lids and smiled at me before turning over and drifting back to sleep. I left the bedroom, shut the door quietly behind me, and placed a letter on the kitchen table before making my way to the farmhouse.

Finding the front door ajar, I walked into the kitchen, relieved to find Ludo Espirito sitting alone at the kitchen table. He nodded to me, gesturing for me to sit down as he poured coffee into a mug. I gratefully accepted the cup of hot steaming liquid, sipping from it slowly.

I explained to Ludo how somebody had sent the flowers under mysterious circumstances. I asked if there had been anyone else at the supper party with the initials *J*.

He appeared deep in thought for a moment before shaking his head. "Javier is not the culprit. He is a fine, staunch lad, nothing would induce him to disrespect either you or Nene." Ludo scratched his head. "I cannot think of anyone else with that initial."

I stared at him gravely. "My dear fellow, I have a favour to ask, I need you to accompany me to the village. I have a few matters to attend to, and I wish to speak to you in confidence on a delicate matter."

"I will get my jacket and cap. The brougham is outside. I

will drive."

I sat alongside Ludo as we set off down to the village, confiding with him my fledgling romance with Nene. He stared at me incredulously,

"You and Nene?" He whistled. "Well, it's about time. The two of you have been performing this dance for a while."

"She's a remarkable woman," I said. "It's a rare thing indeed for beauty and virtue to go hand in hand."

Ludo glanced over at me. "Trust me from a man who's been in love for many years, I recognise that look, my friend. You are in love with this woman, and you, the great detective, cannot see it."

"Oh, I can see it. I am completely out of my depth."

"You are only human, my friend."

"So I'm discovering."

"Let me tell you," said Ludo. "You cannot control how you feel about someone, but you can control how you deal with those feelings. The more you suppress them, the unhappier you will become. Now, my friend, what you must do is woo this woman and show her what she means to you. Of course, a romantic gesture is always good. Compliment her, women love spontaneity. But, for God's sake, take her out somewhere, away from the barn. That's not the most romantic of settings, eh?"

"I don't know," I said. "It's had its moments."

When we arrived at the village, Ludo tethered the horses before walking over to the florist. Madame Luna, the proprietor, rushed over to greet us. She was a small dark-haired woman with expressive and well-defined brows.

"Good morning, gentlemen. How may I help you?" she asked.

Introducing myself, I questioned Madame Luna about the flowers.

"Oh, I am certain I can find the answer to your question by

checking our sales book." Madame Luna looked through her ledger. "Why, this is the entry right here," she said. "Yes, indeed, I can see we made two deliveries yesterday. But, unfortunately, no name is registered against the second delivery."

"Can you describe the person who ordered the flowers?" I asked.

"My daughter Isabella dealt with this particular order, sir. I shall go fetch her."

Madame Luna returned after a few minutes with a nervous young girl with large brown eyes and long dark hair worn in silver fillets.

"Go on Isabella," said Madame Luna. "Tell the gentleman what you told me."

Isabella looked at me anxiously. "The man came into the shop before noon on Friday. First, he purchased a basket of spring flowers. Then he wrote out a card to go inside the basket. As we were already making a delivery to Le Sole, I offered him a small discount."

"Can you describe this man?" I asked.

"He was of slim build, with blue eyes. I remember his eyes were quite striking. He was sallow-skinned, clean-shaven, but he didn't have much to say for himself. He simply paid for the flowers and left. I'm sure I have seen him somewhere in the village, but I cannot remember where or when. Why, have I done something wrong?" she asked, tears welling in her eyes.

"Thank you, Isabella," I said. "Quite the contrary, you have been of great assistance to me. Did this man indicate where he had come from or where he might be staying?"

Isabella shook her head. "No, but some of the local farmers take in lodgers at this time of year."

Thanking Isabella, I turned my attention to her mother. "Your daughter's description is quite detailed for one of such tender years."

"This is a tranquil place, Mr Holmes. Any fresh faces

would likely cause comment."

After a brief discussion with Ludo, I called into the confectioners next door before returning to the florists, where I selected a bouquet of red roses and handed Madame Luna a box of candies.

"For your daughter," I said. "As a thank you. I apologise if I have upset her in any way, I appear to have a habit of reducing young women to tears."

Madame Luna smiled at me, pointing to the flowers she had just wrapped. "Are these another apology?"

"Something like that," I said, bowing to Madame Luna before leaving the shop.

"Well, that's an admirable start, my friend. Perfecto." Ludo laughed at my bemused expression.

Our next stop was the telegraph office. I sent a wire to Mycroft. There were no incoming telegrams for me that day. We called into Ricardo's for a cold beer before embarking on our journey back to Le Sole.

"Well, you have the flowers. All you need now is a nice ristorante with a certain ambience." Ludo chuckled. "Do not look so worried, my friend. You are taking this romance business far too seriously. My late mother's advice, God bless her soul, was to never worry about your heart until it stops beating. Embarking on a personal relationship with a young lady is really quite simple. All you can do is ask the question, and she can say yes or no, the outcome a two-in-one chance of being in your favour!"

Ludo stopped the brougham and pointed to an impressive white stone building. "Welcome to Othello's," he said. "The finest ristorante in the area. To be honest, it's the only decent ristorante in the area. Sophisticated, elegant, yet at the same time relaxing. It comes with an excellent reputation for the quality of the food and stunning views. They even have a stringed quartet. What more could you want?"

Jumping down from the brougham, I entered the ristorante, which was charming and rustic. The ristorante's rear was an enclosed courtyard filled with summer flowers, outdoor seating, and tables with crisp white tablecloths underneath glass canopies reflecting the sunlight. Engaging in a brief conversation with the head waiter, I made dinner reservation for later that evening before continuing to Le Sole.

Chapter Thirty-Three: Irene Adler

I woke to the sound of bird song, a burst of bright sunshine streaming in through the bedroom window, and a headache. I felt sick with apprehension, annoyed with myself for letting things go this far.

Adler, you have a headache, you're not stupid. I scolded myself. *Holmes, with a clear head, will realise it was all a dreadful mistake.* You *were a dreadful mistake.*

Closing my eyes, I recalled the night before when I had wallowed in his sweet smell. The odour of his cologne and the texture of his skin still lingered on the sheets. Opening my eyes, I pulled the covers back from the bed, revealing my naked body. I glanced around the bedroom, observing the empty wine glass on the dressing table and my nightdress discarded on the floor. With a weary sigh, I dragged myself out of bed and stepped into the shower. The warm water cascading down my naked body felt invigorating. I took aspirin before getting dressed to prepare for Holmes's return. Good god, how embarrassing would that be? I chastised myself in the bathroom mirror, tying my hair up in a knot, and practising what I would say to him.

I walked into the drawing-room to discover the broken glass had disappeared along with the basket of flowers.

Gabriella had left breakfast in the kitchen. My stomach churning, I couldn't eat a thing, pouring myself a cup of cafe noir. I noticed an envelope addressed to me on the kitchen table.

I sighed, rolling my eyes. "Well, here we go. Not exactly

original, Mr Holmes." With some trepidation, I tentatively opened the envelope and read the letter.

My dearest Nene,

Please forgive me for leaving so early. You were sleeping so peacefully; I had no wish to disturb you.

I shall be driving down to the village this morning with Ludo Espirito, as I have several matters to attend to and we expect to return before luncheon.

I want you to know that last night was incomparable to anything I have ever experienced, and I look forward to discovering new experiences with you.

Yours SH x

I read the letter several times, feeling giddy with girlish excitement. I spent the rest of the morning pampering myself, carefully removing body hair, exfoliating every inch of my skin, manicuring my nails, taking extra care with my hair and makeup, dabbing a liberal amount of Eau de Parfum behind my ears. I changed my clothes several times before finally slipping into a navy silk dress.

Holmes returned to the barn before luncheon. I heard the brougham returning from the village, the sound of the horses neighing, their hooves stamping, the grind of a wheel as it rasped against the path.

Walking onto the verandah, Holmes stood in the doorway. Looking up from my novel, I smiled at him.

"Are you enjoying the book?" Holmes asked. "I can see you are reading the *Adventures of Huckleberry Finn* by Mark Twain. I suppose it makes a change from Charlotte Bronte." There was even a touch of colour upon his sallow cheeks.

"Yes, I am, Mr Holmes. Why do you ask?"

"Because you are reading it upside down. I am a celebrated detective for a good reason, you know."

Setting the book down, I rose to my feet and walked over to him. "I wasn't sure what to do with myself. It's as if I'm afraid to be happy."

"You deserve happiness more than anyone I know." Holmes gestured to the beautiful bouquet of red roses he held in his hand. "I hope this is not too much for our first . . . whatever you wish to call it. I'm sorry, I'm woefully out of practice."

"Thank you," I said, accepting the flowers. "Such beautiful roses. They've always been my favourites. I will ask Clarissa to put them in water." Looking in his eyes, I said, "I want you to know that last night meant a great deal to me."

"It did for me, too," he said.

"Sherlock, I need to ask you a question."

"What is it?"

"What is your birth sign? What date were you born?"

"I didn't realise you were interested in astrology. I was born on the sixth of January, a Capricorn, if you believe in all that poppycock. I wouldn't normally waste a minute on that kind of nonsense, I can assure you."

I frowned. "Oh, the sixth of January, not the twelfth?"

Holmes stared at me with an amused expression. "I seldom celebrate the day, but I think I can remember my own date of birth."

"Yes, but that year?"

"Every year, Miss Adler."

"Hilarious, Mr Holmes, very droll."

Holmes stared at me in amusement. "I was born in 1854."

"Thank you, Sherlock. I misunderstood you, that's all. I will be sure to remember that date. I will note it in my diary. Tell me, was your father by any chance born on the twelfth of January?"

"You appear to have a fixation with the twelfth of January, Miss Adler," he said. "But you are only one day out. He was born on the eleventh of January, a fellow Capricorn." Holmes clapped his hand to his head. "Good god, you are going to expect me to remember your birthday now. Well, go on then, when is it?"

"I was born on the first of July, my birth sign is Cancer. I thought you would have already known that."

"I am a man of science," said Holmes. "I am no astrologer. Tell me, in matters of astromancy, are we compatible?"

"You may well mock." I raised an eyebrow. "But I'll have you know that I'm an avid follower of Sepharial and have read several of his books. You must, no doubt, be familiar with his articles in the Society Times?"

"I have heard of them," Holmes replied. "But it's not a publication I would typically read."

"Well, in that case, allow me to enlighten you. We are both water signs, opposite one another in the zodiac. Different, but better when together. Considered natural partners, opposite signs can be apt. If the suns are well aspected at birth, my independent thinking and capabilities are intended to impress you, as was my dazzling wit and individuality. But, at the same time, you are my perfect man, impressive and strong, and I must say that you are unique."

"Hmm, I'll take that as a compliment."

"We share many traits in common, such as loyalty and integrity. Our lovemaking has an earthy sensuality.'

"Well, we are a couple, albeit an unconventional one," said Holmes.

"The Cancer women can be stubborn and moody at times."

Holmes raised an eyebrow. "Well, there's a small but beautifully performed understatement."

"The Capricorn man can be prone to terrible mood swings. He can be an extremely complicated man. Are you getting the picture?" I doubled over with laughter.

"Oh, very mature, Miss Adler. I am sure you're making this up as you are going along. Your talents are wasted as an opera singer. Do you expect people from all over the world to share traits such as these? Why, it's a ridiculous notion."

Holmes looked at me thoughtfully for a moment.

Gabriella and Clarissa arrived with the luncheon. Holmes took my hand, and I followed him into the dining room.

"We will talk later. We have much to discuss," he said.

Chapter Thirty-Four: Irene Adler

Luncheon was over and the table cleared before Holmes alluded to the matter again. "Shall we retire to the verandah?" he asked.

I noticed Holmes appeared a little agitated as he updated me on his enquiries at the florist. "Do you think it was one of Palmer's agents who sent the flowers?" I quizzed.

"It is a distinct possibility," said Holmes. "There is another theory, but I will need further data before I can come to any definitive conclusions. I have sent an urgent telegram to my brother, so hopefully we will know more within the next day or so."

"You told me your brother worked for the government. In what capacity? Is he also a detective?"

"No," said Holmes. "My brother has a rather lethargic disposition that would make him unsuitable for detective work. Which is a pity as he is by far the superior thinker. Mycroft has a powerful occupation. He is totally indispensable to the British government. If my brother cannot garner the information I have requested, then no one can."

"What an achieving family you are." I looked at him curiously. "Sherlock, I don't understand the initial J on the flowers. What can it mean? It doesn't make any sense?"

"If I receive the answer I'm expecting from my brother, then it will make sense to me. I pray to God that my theory is wrong, but, for now, we keep our powder dry."

Holmes pulled out the card from the basket of flowers he had kept in his pocket. "This little card indeed throws new light on the situation. I perceive that our anonymous scribbler wrote with a fountain pen. The nib has become splayed, giving it a double-visioned look. Observe the bold hand of the message, and the letter T which has lost its crossing here." He pointed to the writing. "We are looking for a middle-aged man. Does anything else about the writing strike you as odd?"

I shook my head, staring hard at the card. "Well, I can see that the writing slants to the left. Is that significant?"

"Yes, well spotted," said Holmes. "The left-hand slant indicates that the writer seeks solitude and anonymity. And then we look at the capital I in your name, which is much bigger than the other letters. This man is overconfident." He pointed to the letters. "The narrow loop here indicates tension. Then finally, there is a thin loop in the letter E, indicating scepticism or suspicion towards others. It may well be a secret admirer. Or it's very possible that it's another antagonist we are not yet aware of. One of Palmer's agents, perhaps. Unfortunately, I don't have my materials, which I will need before I can give a definitive answer."

I stared at him in awe. "You know all this from the short message on the card? Unbelievable."

"Don't worry, Nene, I promise you that we will get to the bottom of this dreadful business. Tell me, have you been out this morning?"

"No, but I did promise Violetta that I would take Allegro for a canter. I can ask Javier to ride him if you wish?"

"No need," said Holmes, shaking his head. "If you get changed, we can walk down to the stables. It will be nice to take a stroll in nature together." He took my hand in his, gazing at me solemnly. "I fear I may have compromised you last night. I did not observe all precautions."

I shrugged. "The chances of me conceiving are nil. I have no regrets."

"You are certainly a progressive thinker," said Holmes.

"You have always struck me as being ahead of your time. As long as you are sure." Holmes gazed at me. "If you had said to me this time last week that I would have concerns about the hazards of illicit lovemaking, I would have thought you quite mad." Holmes laughed, his eyes radiant and shining with a light I'd never seen before.

"Sherlock, I don't care about any scandal, or what other people think, for that matter. I only care what you think. But none of this, whatever this is, will ever work unless I'm honest with you." Holmes looked at me questioningly and I took a breath before continuing. "I don't feel I can cope if the cocaine is a long-term habit. I know that addiction and secrecy are not a good combination, but I cannot put myself through all of that again. You are not Godfrey, God forbid, but I need to know if you are dependent upon it."

Holmes stared at me, holding my face in his hands. "No, it's . . ." He paused for a moment. "It's recreational. I am sorry, Nene. I cannot lie and promise you I will completely abstain from cocaine, but I swear to you that I will never take it while we are together."

"All right, I can accept that." I took his hand in mine. "Come, let's go for a walk."

We strolled through the fields towards the stables. Javier had already saddled Allegro. The colt waited patiently in his box, whickering at my approach. Holmes gave me a leg up into the saddle and I cantered gently round the perimeter of the field. When we returned, Javier unsaddled the colt and rubbed him down, agreeing to my request that he would ride him out for the next few days.

I walked over to the cypress tree close to the stables to find Holmes sitting on a blanket. He appeared relaxed, his hands behind his head. I sat down beside him, resting my head on his shoulders.

"Lying down on the job, Mr Holmes?" I teased.

"I was pondering where we're going to live when we return to England. I own several properties in London, but none of them are suitable. I shall instruct Mycroft to sell two properties as he knows all the right contacts. Then when we arrive in London, we can look for something more fitting for our needs."

I stared at him in disbelief. "Sherlock, I think we are moving too fast. It's improbable I will ever be able to conceive a child. Does that not bother you?"

"I'm happy just to have you."

"Well, I hope you mean that."

"I do. I am not with you to increase the population."

I frowned. "I did not realise I was going back to London with you."

"Forgive me for being so presumptuous."

"Do you not think that your brother, your housekeeper, and your good friend Dr Watson may all be shocked when you introduce me as your lover?"

"Oh god, no, that would never do. Mrs Hudson would have a fit. And as for Watson, well, he would be more surprised than shocked. No, I will need to arrange things properly. We will have to live apart until we have found somewhere suitable to live."

I stared at him with a look of bewilderment.

"What is wrong?"

I shook my head. "Sherlock, I have just discovered that I am to return to London with you, where I am to live alone so as not to shock your housekeeper. Then, as an afterthought, you tell me that you, a man who loathes women, want to live with me and be my lover? It's all too much!"

"I don't loathe women. Well, not all of them." Holmes chuckled softly. "I am sorry, my mind is racing. I realise that I need to slow down and share things with you."

"Yes, you do, my love. Anyway, living with a man didn't

exactly work in my favour last time."

Holmes looked at me thoughtfully. "There is a question I would like to ask of you. When you think of me, what is your first thought? What word comes to mind to describe me?"

"Hmm, if you had asked me that question a few days ago, I would have said irritating."

"And now?" he quizzed, staring at me keenly.

"Intoxicating," I replied, smiling at him. "You want to embark on a personal relationship with me? Ah, is that not what dull, conventional people do? Only yesterday you told me you didn't want a relationship at all. You are a figure of mystery to me, Mr Holmes. Why change anything? Mind you, I quite like being your lover."

"Yes, I've noticed."

"In the darkest moments of my life, you have become a ray of light. I wish we'd met years ago."

"We did, you just married someone else."

"Very funny, very droll, Mr Holmes."

"Are you turning me down, Miss Adler?"

"I need to think about it."

"Well, thinking is good," said Holmes. "I can accept that. It means I have hope. I am trying, Nene. However, I need to warn you that when I have little to occupy my mind, I become listless and annoying."

"Well, in that case, I will be sure to think of something to occupy your mind." I paused for a moment, gazing into his eyes. "You know Sherlock, we could be good together. Imagine that."

"Yes," said Holmes. "I believe we could. I have a surprise for you. This evening, I shall be taking you out for dinner to Othello's Ristorante, an establishment that comes highly recommended."

"You mean it's the only one for miles around."

"I am reliably informed they have a string quartet."

"I love how you manage to keep the romance alive."

"I am attempting to impress you, and you are not making it easy for me."

"You don't need to do anything to impress me. You already impress me immensely."

"Thank you, Nene, that's very kind. I have made a reservation for eight, I hope that is acceptable? Forgive me, I should have asked before making arrangements. My God, I'm so hopeless at all of this."

"You're all right, do you know that?"

"You're not too bad yourself. I hope you know what you are letting yourself in for. There will be times when I will say things without thinking, which will upset you. And while I will rarely compliment you or be tactile in public places, I shall never lie to you. And on the rare occasions when I tell you that I love you, you will know without even having to ask that I mean every word."

"No," I said, shaking my head. "I don't want that. I'm afraid that's not good enough for me."

"Then what do you want?"

"I have no idea what's going to happen between us, but I know this. If you love me half as much as you profess, then give me the same attention and passion that you extend to your other projects. At least while we are together, that's all I ask of you."

Holmes stared at me hard. "You demand a lot from me, Nene," he said. "I cannot promise what you ask, but I am prepared to try, starting with this evening, if you are happy to take a chance and come to dinner with me."

"The food is bound to be far more palatable than Gabriella's offerings, which can at times be less than flavoursome." I took his hand in mine. "Forgive me, I wasn't trying to back you into a corner, but I have never felt like this about anyone else before."

"Really, not even Wilhelm Ormstein?"

"Especially not Wilhelm. In matters of love, you are quite the virtuoso."

Holmes looked at me in amused surprise. "Well, there's a sentence I don't hear every day," he said, eyes crinkling at the corners. "Never in a million years did I think I would develop feelings for you, Nene. And it's not just about the pleasures of the flesh, as wonderful as they are. I am attracted to your other fine qualities. Your individuality, flair and imagination. Your kindness and consideration to others. What you have done for the Espirito family takes my breath away. These are rare qualities indeed."

"My father taught me never to look down on anyone unless you are helping them up," I said. "And never to judge anyone irrespective of their status or appearance. Do you mind if we return to the barn? I need to prepare myself. For tonight I am to walk out with the celebrated detective, Mr Sherlock Holmes, and I fear I may take some time."

Chapter Thirty-Five: Irene Adler

Our carriage arrived at Othello's Ristorante at eight o'clock that evening. The night was pleasant with a bright half-moon shining in the sky.

We were greeted by the head waiter, Franco, who seated us at a table for two on the illuminated terrace with breathtaking views of Florence, overlooking the Duomo and the Palazzo Vecchio.

"I will be back shortly with the menus and some water for the table," said Franco.

The sommelier arrived with the wine list, giving us a few minutes before returning. "May I take your order, sir?"

"A dry sherry for the lady and a cognac for myself. Can you put a bottle of Armand De Brignac on ice?" asked Holmes.

I ordered the chicken liver pate and the *frittura di paranza,* whilst Holmes ordered the *ribollita* soup and fillet. A lovely, relaxed ambience ran throughout the ristorante as a quartet played in the background. The sommelier opened the champagne and poured a little into Holmes's glass. He took a sip, nodding his approval. The sommelier filled the glasses before resting the bottle in the wine cooler. I gestured towards the champagne.

"This is lovely, very intimate. Did you bring me here to celebrate?"

"The two of us finding each other again is a cause to celebrate," said Holmes."

I paused for a moment. "Sherlock, there's something I need

to tell you. I want no subterfuge between us. I believe that's how it should be if we are to embark upon a serious relationship." Holmes listened with an interested and concerned expression as I continued my narrative.

"Something strange happened to me when I joined La Scala. On our first day, as we were queuing for registration, I noticed Sophia walk into the room. Immediately, I was drawn to her in a way that I cannot describe. After registration, the students were introduced to each other, all vying for attention from the maestros. That reminded me of school, where I was constantly out of tune with the other girls, like being fifteen all over again. Then one girl approaches. She listens, she comprehends. There was an instant rapport when we spoke, which I believe is the true nature of friendship. Sophia's acerbic wit was the perfect foil for my rebellious spirit. And that's how our friendship began. I discovered what I already suspected—that Sophia was this remarkable person who, when I had given up on life, told me that one day I would find the one when I least expected it, that he would be there waiting for me. And then, of course, I started to develop feelings for this man who was trying to save me. And here he is, just as Sophia predicted."

"And you felt it again with me?"

"Yes, except this time the feeling was much stronger. Mark Twain said the two most important days in your life are the day you were born and the day you find out why. Part of me knew that we would meet that night. In fact, I truly believe that God put me on Planet Earth so our paths would cross one day, like lovers dancing in the night. I realise how ridiculous that must sound to you, a man of science and logic."

"No, it doesn't sound ridiculous at all. Tell me about this feeling. Did it happen during our conversation in the green room?" He stared at me searchingly.

"No, when we met, you took me completely by surprise. I

was immediately taken aback, your formidable reputation, your thunderous ego. To be honest, at first I thought you a little pompous, a little arrogant, until our conversation at the carriage. Do you remember we spoke of Wagner?"

"How could I ever forget?"

"That's when the feeling overcame me," I said. "You have no idea how affected I was. My desire to kiss you was so strong, and I didn't want the evening to end, but I had to leave. I couldn't trust myself not to do anything silly. I cried on the way back to the hotel, and I didn't know why. I put it down to being fatigued from the boat journey."

"You think that I am an incredible, exceptional person, just like Sophia Stephanato? Why, that's quite the compliment, I know how close you are to Sophia. You were very fortunate to find such a friend. It would appear that we both owe her a debt of gratitude."

"Yes, I certainly was fortunate to find Sophia, to find you both. But I don't think you quite understand, Sherlock, my relationship with Sophia." I hesitated for a moment, speaking almost in a whisper. "We were more than friends. Sophia filled the void in my life caused by my mother's early demise. She fulfilled a need. I craved to love and be loved in those early days. We were very discreet. We had clear boundaries, and from the outset, we never allowed our relationship to intrude on our careers. I don't care what the rest of the world thinks of me. I only care what you think." I stared into his eyes, on tenterhooks awaiting his response.

A moment passed and he offered an awkward smile. "You never fail to surprise me, Nene. In a dismal world, you are a beacon of light." Holmes laughed. "I understand that life can be complicated, and sexual character can sometimes be misleading. Especially when we are young and impressionable. When it comes down to it, I don't believe that anyone is entirely one way. One day, humanity will come to celebrate diversity, not turn their backs on it. Sadly, I don't think that will ever happen in our lifetime. You did the right thing to be discreet at such a tender age. It takes courage to live outside the traditional confines of Victorian society. You know, a young lady once told me that sometimes you just have to take a leap of faith."

Covering my hand with his, I stared at him. "You and me, that is all that matters," I whispered. "At the end of the day, attraction is not about looks or status, but about who keeps you up at night."

Holmes nodded.

The waiter appeared at the table, deftly removing the starter plates. "Are you ready for your main course, sir?" He asked.

Holmes glanced across at me. "Yes, I believe we are."

The quartet had advanced to the terrace, playing Concertino in B minor by Franz Lehár.

"Impressive," I whispered.

We finished our main courses. As the sommelier refilled the glasses, I noticed the quartet had stopped playing. They approached our table and introduced themselves, then they began playing the first few chords of "Amazing Grace." The violinist sang the first verse. He gestured for me to stand up to sing for them. I refused at first, finally relented after shouts of encouragement, and continued to sing the rest of the song. The diners erupted into applause when I reached the end.

I thanked the quartet. Antonio, the violinist, bowed to me. "We are thrilled that you enjoyed our music this evening. It is my responsibility to find the most charming lady in the Ristorante and to present her with this single red rose. Beautiful lady, your evening has just begun." He winked, handing me the flower.

"Compliments of the house," said Antonio.

The quartet gave a final bow before walking back to the

podium. I glanced over at Holmes. "This has been such a wonderful evening, thank you. I am so happy."

Chapter Thirty-Six: Irene Adler

After dinner, we returned to the barn, resuming our positions at our table for two on the patio, Beethoven's music playing in the background.

"I love this piece." I sighed. "It's one of my favourites, Beethoven's Fourth Symphony in B Flat Major. He was in love when he wrote it at a friend's house in the countryside. It's about a countess Beethoven proposed to. Sadly, she turned him down in favour of an Austrian nobleman. More fool her, I say. Beethoven would have been around your age, Sherlock when he fell in love again, this time with a mysterious married woman, known today as Immortal Beloved. Beethoven wrote numerous love letters to her. Tragically they were never posted. It must be the worst feeling to be in love with someone you know you can never be with."

"Yes indeed," said Holmes. "That's why he wrote the letters. He had to find a way to express his admiration, so he used his brain, the most important sexual organ in the body. Your friend Toscanini told me you had a particular penchant for Beethoven."

"Oh, indeed I do. Did you know that he was the most famous composer in the world by the time he died? And of course, he was tragically, heartbreakingly deaf. The man had to turn around to see his audience applauding. Nevertheless, he premiered his fifth and sixth symphonies and fourth piano concerto all in one concert. Now that's my definition of talent. Beethoven loved his coffee, like me. Mind you, I have a long way to go to reach the dizzy heights of Balzac. Apparently, he drank up to fifty cups a day. When Sophia and I were on tour in New York, we visited Beethoven's memorial in Central Park. You know, the one created by the American sculptor Henry Baer." I sighed. "Such was our humble pilgrimage to the great man. I freely admit that Beethoven has long been my secret crush and is at the top of my list of imaginary honorary dinner guests."

"And who else would be invited to this imaginary dinner party?"

"Well, let me see," I said. "It would have to be Stephen Foster, Charlotte Bronte, William Shakespeare . . . and you too, of course. Now that would be quite the dinner party, don't you think?"

"I do indeed. Should I be jealous?"

"Fortunately for you, Sherlock, Beethoven died. So, no, you need not be jealous of a dead man. Mind you, it might be a close call if he were still alive." I laughed, observing his bemused expression.

"Pray, do tell me, aside from Beethoven, do you have a penchant for any other type of music?"

"I love to listen to everything. I enjoy the symphony, concerts, arias, operas, recitals, and even string quartets. And of course, the music composed by the American music legend Stephen Foster. I have an enduring love for his music. Foster's lyrics have all the wild exaggeration and rustic charm of folklore."

Holmes took my hand in his. "If you have any concerns, or are having second thoughts about embarking upon a relationship together, then please tell me now." He stared at me intently.

"No, Sherlock, it's what I want. However, I want you to promise me two things."

"Name them."

"Have a care with my heart. And whenever we argue, you

know we will, don't punish me with silence. You hurt me when you did that. Promise me that you will never do that again."

Holmes paused for a moment before he spoke. "I would never intentionally hurt you, Nene. As for the silent treatment, yes, I can do that. I promise you I will never ignore you again." Holmes looked over at the gramophone, where the music was still playing. "What do you think? Miss Adler? Would you like to take a spin?"

"I don't mind if I do, Mr Holmes."

Chapter Thirty-Seven: Irene Adler

The following evening Holmes and I sat on the patio, watching the sun go down.

"Are you all right?" he asked.

"I'm always all right when I'm with you. You know I love it here, in this humble barn. It's as if the rest of the world doesn't exist."

"Yes, I entirely agree. Tell me, are you happy?"

"Yes, I'm happy. Why wouldn't I be? I can promise you a future, Sherlock, if you can forgive me my past."

"Whatever do you mean?"

"I'm not perfect, far from it. I'm a little afraid I won't be able to live up to your impossibly high standards."

"We all have ghosts, Nene. There is nothing you can do or say that will stop me from wanting to be with you, as long as you want me. Do you?" he quizzed.

"Why ask me a question when you already know the answer? I reciprocate with ardour."

"The only people's opinion I would be remotely interested in are Watson and Mrs Hudson, and they are going to love you. Dr Watson is quite a fan."

"He is?"

"Oh yes, he has always thought very highly of you. I want to see the look of surprise on their faces when I tell Watson and Mrs Hudson that we are in a serious relationship. You know I am forty-one years old, which is mature for a love affair?"

"It is mature for many things. As for me, I'll never pass for twenty-five again."

"We will show these young ones a thing or two, I fancy."

"In that case, to quote Oliver Cromwell, you can have me, warts and all. Oh, I nearly forgot I have something for you."

"What's this?" he asked, feigning impatience.

Reaching into my bag, I pulled out a small box wrapped in gold paper and passed it to him. "It's a gift for you. I wanted to get you something to show my appreciation for all you have done for me. It's nothing, really."

"You have kept this quiet."

"A lady must be allowed to have some secrets."

He quickly removed the paper to reveal a wooden box. "And what, pray tell, is this?"

"Open it," I said.

Holmes opened the box underneath the paper to reveal a Sampson Mordan antique silver hand-chased dip pen. He removed the pen from the box, inspecting it with keen grey eyes. He turned it over to read an inscription on the other side that read: *l'Homme C'est, Rien L'oeuvre C'est Tout.*

He glanced over at me, eyes shining bright. "Thank you. There is no lighter burden more agreeable to me than the humble pen. I think it is quite possibly the most thoughtful gift that has ever been given to me, but how on earth did you know?"

"Dr Watson told me on the train that it was one of your favourite quotes, amongst other things. I thought that you could use the pen to write to me when you are away solving crimes."

"Yes, indeed. I will treasure it forever. And every time I use it, I will think of you. What else did Watson tell you?" he asked, a mischievous glint appearing in his eyes.

"He warned me that you had bohemian habits, and that you could be impatient and difficult at times. He was concerned I might not be able to cope with your moods and brooding intensity. But he also told me that I could trust you with my life, that you would never let me down."

Holmes's expression turned serious. "I was hoping you would consider Paris a suitable venue for our first vacation together. That is not only one of the most romantic cities in the world, it's also where my grand uncle, the military artist Horace Vernet, was born in the Louvre in 1789. So, it's a place that I have always intended to visit."

"Paris would be wonderful," I said. "I shall look forward to it, but there is one thing I need to make you aware of." I paused for a moment, tears welling in my eyes. "I am so sorry, Sherlock. I have been agonising over this since you first mentioned it, but I can't move to London. That place holds so many terrible memories for me, and I simply cannot do it, not even for you."

He smiled at me gently. "It's all right, I understand. We shall have to think of something else. We can find a place on the outskirts, on the Sussex Downs, perhaps. In fact, I'd like to take you there before we make a definitive decision regarding our future. I want you to be happy, and at least this way I can commute to London whenever I need to work. We will find a compromise, of that I'm certain."

"There is one more thing." I stared at him apprehensively. "I have no wish to be a kept woman. My intention is to continue with my singing career. I already have an agent in England."

Holmes relaxed into his chair, putting his fingers together as was his custom when in a judicial mood. "Hmm, not very conventional, Nene. However, I respect your wishes. I have no wish to curtail your remarkable talent. You are a free spirit who must be allowed to fly."

I nodded. "I am also thinking of taking on some private pupils when we eventually find a place to live, so I could work from home. We wouldn't disturb you, of course." I smiled at the thought of Holmes finding a group of small children running amok infuriating.

Holmes smiled at me, as though reading my mind. "I think it will be a good idea to continue with my consulting rooms at Baker Street, all the better not to mix our private lives with work. At times we do get some dubious characters knocking on the door, and I do have to consider your safety."

"Thank you for being so understanding," I said, stroking his face. "Your clients will have access to your brilliant mind, but only I will have access to your heart."

"Of course." He nodded. "My work consumes me. There will be times when we will be apart for long periods. Do you think you will be able to cope with that?"

"Yes, of course. I understand that our relationship will be far from conventional, but at least it won't be boring. And, if we are to buy a house on the outskirts of London, my father would be more than happy to contribute. I don't feel that it is fair for you to foot the bill."

"I appreciate the gesture, Nene, but no, that is out of the question. It is my job to provide for you. As soon as there is a suitable property available that you are happy with, then I will buy it without any undue delay."

"You know I really don't care where we live, as long as it's not the centre of London and we can be together. I would live in a cave with you."

"Well, I think I can do a little better than that." He laughed. "Or I would not hear the last of it from your father. Speaking of your father, I will write to him tomorrow morning, although I am not sure if he would consider me an ideal suitor. I can only profess to him my love and ardent admiration for his beloved daughter. I must admit I do have some reservations about corresponding with him."

"Why?"

"Nene, I am supposed to be protecting you. I sincerely

hope your father can find it in his heart to forgive me."

"Nonsense, Sherlock. My father will adore you. In my letters, I have made him aware of how well you have looked after me during all of this madness. None of us can help who we fall in love with." Holmes nodded in agreement.

I breathed a sigh of relief; telling Holmes I couldn't move to London had taken everything I had. In fact, the very thought had filled me with dread. I would have preferred instead to stay in Italy with its beautiful memories, its endless possibilities. However, I was aware of how impractical that would be. And, of course, Sherlock must return to England. Still, I would be alone for the most part while he gave himself up to his next case. I realised that few women would cope with being married to the celebrated detective, whilst I would be there waiting for the most incredible human being I had ever met when he returned and called out for me at the end of a long day. We sat on the patio, hands held together until darkness fell.

Holmes kissed me gently on the lips. "And so to bed," he whispered.

Chapter Thirty-Eight: Irene Adler

I saw little of Holmes over the next few days. He set off to the village by the time I awoke and did not return to the barn until late afternoon. I amused myself by baking biscotti and panettone with Violetta and Ava in the farm kitchen.

Holmes and I had dinner together later that night. I could sense he was distracted, as though the weight of the world were on his shoulders. Aware that this was one of those times he needed to be alone, I decided to retire early. Although I struggled to get off to sleep, I was worried about Holmes and figured we needed some light relief. I was disturbed when he came to bed in the early hours. I reached out for him, nestling my head into his back. He slipped his hand into mine, squeezing it gently.

"You don't always find life easy do you, Sherlock?" I whispered. "I wish I could help you with that."

He turned round to face me, pulling me close until I was cradled in his muscular arms. "You already have, Nene. Finding you has brought new meaning and purpose into my life." I lay in his arms until, eventually, we both fell asleep.

Holmes opened his eyes the following morning to find me smiling down at him.

"Good morning," I whispered.

"Nene!" Holmes cried. "What on earth are you doing?" He spoke in an exasperated tone. "I know that look. What is it?" He raised an eyebrow.

"I have a complaint to make. You are not paying me enough attention. You are going to have to do a whole lot better."

"I wondered when you were going to bring that up." He groaned. "Forgive me if I have been distracted."

"Sherlock, please don't go down to the village this morning. Can we not forget our troubles for once and spend the day together? Let us pretend we're a commonplace couple doing things that commonplace people do."

Holmes stared at me for a moment, a flicker of amusement on his face. "All right," he conceded. "We'll do what you want, only for today. Pray tell me how you wish to spend the day?"

I brightened at his reply, gesturing to the sun streaming in through the open window. "After breakfast we could take a walk, maybe have a picnic, and visit the ruins of the amphitheatre. It's such a lovely day today."

"All right," he agreed, pulling me to him.

After breakfast, we took a leisurely walk through the fields, exploring the wildflower meadow under a warm, cloudless sky. We returned to the barn to discover Gabriella had left a picnic basket containing ham, cheese, bread, fresh fruit, and wine. I added two slices of the panettone loaf I had baked the day before. To my great relief, it was delicious. Thanks to Violetta and Ava, my culinary skills were definitely improving. We set off in the brougham and spent a glorious afternoon at the amphitheatre, eating the contents of our picnic and soaking up the atmosphere amid the stunning scenery, which looked magnificent against the backdrop of a beautiful Tuscan sky.

Holmes took my hand in his and stared into my eyes, his mood turning serious. "During our last altercation you asked what really happened between Victoria and me. By God Nene, you of all people deserve to know the truth." He sighed before continuing. "We had been seeing each other for around four months. I made it clear from the outset that our relationship was not exclusive. And then she came to see me one night in a state of agitation and told me she was expecting my child. I wasn't happy.; I thought we had been careful. We were both far too young to even contemplate marriage, but then I realised I had no choice but to do the right thing, by Victoria and my child, so I proposed to her."

"And what happened next?"

I'm ashamed to say that a part of me felt jealous. I would have loved to have known Holmes back then, as a young man embracing his bohemian lifestyle.

"I wanted us to be married straight away in a registry office," Holmes continued. "But Victoria insisted on a church wedding. The banns were out, we were due to be married four weeks hence, when tragically Victoria suffered a miscarriage. A week later, she returned my ring and told me she was releasing me from my promise. She had met someone else, a better man than me, and that was the end of our relationship. I felt relieved, although sad about the child. I realised I lost my one and only chance to become a father as I vowed never to lie with another woman." He signed deeply. "You see, I hadn't been faithful to Victoria."

"You were unfaithful?" I exclaimed.

"I was young, brash and arrogant, even more so than I am now. I wanted to experiment and see what all the fuss was about, although I never liked what I found. A month later, I heard that Victoria and the lawyer John Parkinson had married. I thought it all rather sudden, but I saw them together three months later. It was obvious Victoria was heavily pregnant. After making extensive inquiries, I discovered that Parkinson had been married before. I eventually tracked down his ex-wife, Anne Goldsmith, and she told me they divorced four years earlier, as they had been unable to conceive a child. You see, Parkinson had kept from her the fact that he was infertile. Apparently, he contracted mumps as a child, then developed complications. Later, I confronted Parkinson and Victoria at their home in Knightsbridge, but they denied everything, of course. What was I to do? They say he is a wise man who knows his own child. Shortly after, Parkinson came to see me and told me that Victoria had suffered a catastrophic postpartum haemorrhage. She and the child, a boy, both died, the infant starved of oxygen in the womb. Parkinson admitted the child was mine. He apologised, but it was far too late. Apparently, the boy was perfect, not a mark on him. But I never had a chance to lay eyes on my own son."

Holmes shook his head and smiled at me, his eyes filled with tears. "Because of my cavalier attitude, I was indirectly responsible for the death of two people. After that, how could I ever feel worthy of being a father and ask any woman to marry me, least of all you? I often think of my son and how he would have turned out. He would be eighteen now. Ready to go off to university, his whole life ahead of him. But tragically that was not to be."

Taking a deep breath, I kissed him tenderly on the cheek, my heart breaking at the sight of him consumed by grief. "I am sorry you had to endure that, but you need to stop torturing yourself. It wasn't your fault. At least I got to see my child before she was so cruelly taken from me." I smiled at him, tears running down my face. "Shall we head back to Le Sole? Perhaps I can think of a way to put a smile back on your face."

"Yes, I would like that." Holmes squeezed my hand tightly. "What I have just told you, I never wish to speak of again."

I knew exactly how he felt. I recognised that horrible, agonising pain, the feeling of despair that never leaves you, our sorrow shared.

We returned to Le Sole and spent the remainder of the afternoon sitting on the porch in quiet contemplation. I poured Holmes a whisky and soda as he retained his pensive mood, staring out onto the garden. After dinner, he asked if I would play the piano for him. I was happy to oblige . . . anything to lift his sombre mood. First, I played "Song from The Evening Star" from Tannhauser, also known as "The Star of Eve," as I knew it was one of his favourites. When I glanced across at Holmes as I hit the last note, he smiled at me appreciatively, his mood far more relaxed as I drew him further into my world with piano and voice. I moved on to Branganan's song from act two of Wagner's *Tristan and Isolde*, a piece I had performed many times in concert and never grew tired of. Who could grow weary of Richard Wagner?

Later that evening, I gazed into Holmes's eyes as we lay on the bed, my head upon his shoulder.

"Thank you for humouring me," I said. "I hope it didn't put you out too much, being ordinary, even if it was only for one day."

"Overall, it's been a good day," said Holmes. "There's a joy to be found in the simplest of places."

Chapter Thirty-Nine: Irene Adler

Two days passed before a wire arrived from Lestrade conveying the news that Colonel James Moriarty was now the main suspect for the murder of William Palmer. The Metropolitan Police had issued a warrant for his arrest.

I was as shocked as Holmes when he relayed the news to me. "Sherlock, if Palmer's dead, then who is pursuing us? My god, whoever this man is, it's not just me he's after, is it?"

Holmes nodded, pushing his lunch to one side. "I have suddenly lost my appetite."

"You have to eat something to keep up your strength."

"I cannot spare energy for digestion, Nene. My faculties become more concentrated when I starve them. And at this moment I clearly need all my faculties about me."

Holmes smoked incessantly for the rest of the day, barely touching any food and unable to sleep. When Holmes and I arrived in the village the following day, he was relieved to find a telegram from Mycroft had come at last. He read out the contents to me, which were several pages long.

Mycroft discovered Colonel Moriarty's escape from Bedlam Mental Asylum had been orchestrated by Palmer's henchmen, the Tooley Street gang. Apparently, the gang plotted Moriarty's escape after learning of Sherlock's shock return to London after being presumed dead for three years. An eyewitness had come forward, Ronnie Williams, who was an ex-gang member. The latter had turned informant after being arrested by Lestrade in Camden for robbery and causing grievous bodily harm. Williams confessed to Lestrade that he was one of the three gang members responsible for springing Moriarty out of Bedlam after Palmer bribed two security guards. Moriarty was subsequently held in a safe house by Palmer's gang, where according to Williams, he plotted an act of wicked and deadly revenge. Moreover, the Metropolitan police connected Moriarty with Palmer's murder after identifying the bullet removed from Palmer's body had been fired from an old Remington army revolver of the same calibre Moriarty used during his time in the armed forces.

Holmes was staggered to learn that Moriarty was still at large. He told me that although Moriarty was by no means in the same intellectual league as his late brother, nevertheless, he still remained an intelligent and dangerous antagonist. When we returned to the barn, Holmes read Mycroft's message for a second time, digesting the extraordinary story.

Later that afternoon, I returned from the stables to find Holmes sitting on the chaise lounge. I was shocked to see his shoulders bowed and his head sunk into his hand.

In a state of agitation, I sat beside him, taking his hand in mine. "What is it, Sherlock? You don't look well at all."

"This infernal problem consumes me," said Holmes. "You are aware that it has always been an old maxim of mine that when you have excluded the impossible, whatever remains, however improbable, has to be the truth. Given the fact that Palmer is already dead, Moriarty is on our trail and there is little doubt he has vengeance in mind."

"But why is this man so fixated on you?"

"Because he constantly wrote to the newspapers, making threats, and spreading malicious rumours of my guilt while professing his brother's innocence. He broke out of the asylum with the assistance of Palmer and his gang. It is no coincidence that he escaped from the institution that incarcerated him for over three years upon discovering I was back in London. He undoubtedly used his contacts with the railways to follow Watson and me to Milan. Then for some reason, he turned his attention to you, Nene. Perhaps having seen us together, he was under the illusion that there was something between us, his senses no doubt inflamed by his fragile mental state, and more likely, the reason he attempted to poison you was to get to me. He knows about us. My god, Professor Moriarty has turned his own death into an enigma. Even though he burns in hell, he continues to torment me."

I gasped. "My god, that means he must have followed us here from Milan!"

Holmes nodded. "It would appear so. Moriarty used Palmer as a scapegoat and then as a decoy to try and put me off the scent. While I suspected Palmer, Moriarty was aware that I would not be looking elsewhere. His main advantage, of course, was that I had never seen him before."

"Did Mycroft give you a physical description of this man?"

"Yes. He is similar in stature to his late brother. He obviously used makeup to create and disguise Palmer's scar."

"You must not blame yourself, Sherlock. How could you have known?"

"It's my job to know, Nene. As it is my job to protect you. I was too slow at the outset, culpably so."

"This man has been planning and fantasising about our demise. I assume he will be armed."

"Yes, he will be armed all right," said Holmes. "What we do know is that he is ruthless. He shot Palmer and threw his body in to the Thames. He is most certainly already here in Fiesole. But this is not your mountain to climb, it's me he wants. If you remain here, you will be in mortal danger. I need to get you away from here."

"I am *not* going anywhere. As far as I'm concerned, *we* are in this together. Javier is working outside. I can ask him to escort me to the lumber room. That's where Ludo keeps his pistol. I take it you still have your revolver?"

Holmes nodded.

"Good," I said. "You know everybody has gone to a wedding in the village today. Only Javier and a few of the farmhands remain behind." I paused for a moment, staring at Holmes, horrified. "Oh, my god, I believe this man is much nearer than we first anticipated. On the night of the supper party, one of the casual labourers asked for my autograph. His physical description matches that of Moriarty, except for a shaved head and side whisker. He said his name was Ben Masterson, an artist from the West Country. I borrowed his fountain pen to sign my autograph, and I remember thinking it appeared odd. The signature had a slightly blurred appearance, not unlike the card from the flowers. I am so sorry, I have only just remembered."

"Do not reproach yourself for a second," said Holmes. "This is not your fault. At least we know what we are dealing with."

Holmes opened the barn door and called out to Javier, beckoning him to come inside. He quizzed Javier, asking if he had seen Ben Masterson. Javier shook his head, claiming he had not seen Masterson for several days. Finally, Holmes took Javier by the shoulders.

"Now, my boy," he said. "I need you to accompany Nene to the lumber room. I take it the brougham is still outside?" Javier nodded, and Holmes continued. "When you get to the stables, wait for Nene. Don't let her out of your sight for one second. Then I want you to return her here to me, do you understand?"

Javier nodded, a grave expression on his face. Holmes smiled at him grimly. "Good man. There's no time to be lost. You must ride like the devil down to the village and take this letter to the local constabulary." I watched as Holmes quickly scribbled out a letter onto his notebook then handed it to Javier

The letter was for Chief Inspector Montalabo. In the note, Holmes insisted that Montalabo return to Le Sole with an escort as though their lives depended upon it as he would have a particularly dangerous fugitive to deal with, one who was most certainly armed and who had murder in mind.

Holmes whispered in Javier's ear and patted him on the shoulder. Javier and I jumped into the brougham and set off on our journey to the lumber room. Javier watched in stunned silence as I expertly loaded the pistol, a Schonberger Laumann semi-automatic. Before placing it into the pocket of my riding habit, I noticed a small bottle of blue vitriol nestled in the box containing the bullets. I carefully poured a small amount into an empty phial and then firmly closed the lid before placing it into my pocket alongside the gun.

Javier helped me into the brougham. Lashing the horses until they broke into a gallop, we passed the barn and the farmhouse at speed until we were outside on the lane.

I gasped in shock. "Javier, what on earth are you doing? You were supposed to drop me off at the barn. You must stop at once!"

"I am sorry, Nene, but I have to follow Mr Holmes's orders and take you to the village where you will be safe."

I stared at him in disbelief, tears flooding my face. "Javier, if you don't stop this carriage right now, I swear to god I will jump out. Do you want to be responsible for my death?"

Javier looked round, mortified to find my hand on the carriage door, trying to force it open with a sharp tug. Javier reigned in the horses, until the carriage eventually came to a halt, and I quickly jumped out of the brougham.

Javier stared at me, a stunned expression on his face. "I cannot leave you here, Nene. It's not safe. Please get back in and I promise that I will take you back to the barn, but only if you are sure that's what you want?"

"Yes, it's what I want." I nodded. "Thank you, Javier. I

know I'm a nightmare, but please don't worry. I will speak to Mr Holmes, and I will explain it's all my fault."

Javier turned the horses around and we made our way back to the barn. Javier helped me out of the carriage, and I kissed him on the cheek.

"Thank you, be careful," I whispered.

Javier waited in silence until I reached the door before whipping the horses to move. In a moment he had disappeared into the night.

CHAPTER FORTY: SHERLOCK HOLMES

Ensuring every door and shutter was closed, I checked the rooms in the barn. As I opened the door to the study, I noticed the window was half-open. Within seconds I was outside, my eyes scanning the garden. Large masculine footprints were imprinted in the flower bed. I searched amongst the grass and leaves, finally discovering a discarded Bowie army knife. I turned over the blade, examining it closely.

"Moriarty," I muttered.

Walking back into the barn, I heard running water coming from the direction of the bathroom. Pushing the door open, I found the taps running. I switched them off and my eyes were immediately drawn to the mirror. The initials *JM* and the word *retribution* traced into the steamy condensation. Closing the door, I quietly entered the bedroom, removing Watson's revolver from the drawer. Checking the chamber, I was staggered to discover it was empty, the bullets removed. A faint sound echoed in the stillness, one that appeared to be coming from the direction of the drawing-room.

Picking up my riding crop from the dressing table, I moved along the passageway. I was about to enter the drawing-room when I heard the definite noise of another human being. The space was undoubtedly empty, save for one strange figure ahead. I felt as though I'd seen a ghost at the sight of a tall, bald-headed man with a high forehead and protruding chin who sat in an armchair. He was the mirror image of Professor Moriarty. There was a roguish snap in his sunken blue eyes that continued to stare at me. His head swayed from side to side in a curiously reptilian manner, reminiscent of his late brother. He was dressed in a grey suit of tweed, with gaiters and a soft cloth cap. There was no doubt it was Moriarty's brother who pointed a revolver at me.

"Good afternoon, Holmes. Were you perchance looking for these?" Moriarty opened his left hand to reveal the missing shells. "Sit down, for god's sake. You're giving me a migraine with your hovering."

Sitting down on the chaise lounge, I slowly pulled out my silver cigarette case from my pocket. "Do you mind?" I asked. Moriarty nodded.

I lit the cigarette with a vestas match before throwing the case over to Moriarty. He removed a cigarette from the case and struck a match, blowing circles of smoke into the air. Leaning my head back on the chaise lounge, I stared at the bilious face in front of me, drawing on my cigarette.

"You're a skulking rascal, Moriarty."

"You worked it out then, Holmes? I knew you would eventually realise it was me."

"Apart from your physical description, which was only recently made known to me, your clothes gave it away. Why, your whole outfit is quintessentially English. From the cut of your coat, frayed at the elbows, and the trousers bagged at the knee. I can see that you cycled here today. There's a slight indentation to your knees caused by the bicycle clips."

Moriarty stared at me thoughtfully. "I don't even begin to understand you, Holmes. I followed you and Watson to Milan and intended to kill you both there and then, but then I discovered your budding romance with the enchanting Miss Adler at La Scala. And I recognised the opportunity for what it was, to remove someone from your life who you actually gave a damn about. Watson had a very fortunate escape. Although I do have to say that you are a fortunate man Holmes. Miss Adler is a lovely woman. No doubt you've kept her entertained, and who could blame you? A smile like hers would melt ice. I would have been sorely tempted myself under different circumstances. The drugs they administer at the asylum do little for your libido. You have no idea what it was like, Holmes, to be deprived of your dignity day after day. Having to listen to the meandering screams of the other inmates being forcibly injected with antipsychotics. Bedlam is hardly a bastion of recovery and rehabilitation."

Moriarty continued to stare at me, his blue eyes as cold as ice. He shuffled in his seat before adding with grim levity, "As for the poisoning episode, well, I must admit I couldn't resist. Once I knew the both of you were to attend the celebration dinner, I wasted no time in offering my services to the hotel manager, who was delighted with my impeccable references. As to the actual poisoning, well, that was most regrettable. How could one know the young lady would switch seats? Then I followed you here. You must surely remember that nice grey-haired old porter who loaded your luggage onto the brougham? Why, you even gave me a tip. I was in disguise, of course. I didn't want your friend Mr Espirito to recognise me when I applied for a job posing as my make-believe brother. I shaved my head and faked side whiskers for that interview. He's such a charming man, but he unwittingly revealed your destination after I enquired about possible employment for my brother, Ben . . . which was me in disguise, once again. I tricked you into thinking it was Palmer pursuing you and your lady friend, looking for some ridiculous carbuncle that he told me of before I shot him and dumped his body into the Thames.

"Oh, Palmer had to go, I'm afraid. It would have ruined everything if the Metropolitan Police had found him in London. But it was rather exhilarating impersonating a dead man. You should try it, Holmes. It removes the strain from the living. Oh, I nearly forgot, you already have. Fortunately,

Palmer and I were of a similar build and height. Why, we could have been brothers in another life. I used makeup, of course, to copy his scar. I have always been artistically gifted. But please don't blame yourself, Holmes. How could you be expected to recognise someone you'd never met before? Even with all your cleverness that would have proven impossible."

I smiled sardonically at Moriarty, leaning forward in my chair. "I must say that I am a little puzzled by your allegiance to your late brother, the man who robbed you of your inheritance."

Moriarty looked at me in surprise. "What exactly do you mean by that?"

"When your father, Richard, discovered your brother's evil intentions, there was an altercation between the two of them at your father's country estate in Elmridge. Richard threatened to cut your brother off without a penny and leave everything to you. Your brother stormed out, but he returned a few months later, cap in hand, begging for forgiveness. He soon struck up a relationship with your father's nurse, Sybil Dexter. She was flattered by his attentions and naively allowed him to charm his way into her affections. Your brother tricked Sybil and your father into believing he was a reformed character. Then he slowly began to poison Richard, lacing his tea with thallium until your father became delirious and your brother took advantage of his fragile state of mind, forcing your father to change his will in his favour."

"How could you possibly know that?" cried Moriarty.

I sighed. "Sybil Dexter came to see me at Baker Street. After witnessing him pouring a liquid into his tea then finding out he was forcing your father to sign a new will, she realised what your brother was up to. She explained to me how your father started to suffer from alopecia and complained of burning feet and palms. Sybil called for the doctor, despite your brother's protestations. Unfortunately, your father was misdiagnosed with gastroenteritis and diabetic peripheral neuropathy. I suspected your father had been poisoned by thallium, which can be found in most country houses, often used as a rat poison. It's a colourless, odourless and tasteless toxin, difficult to detect in small doses, as it's slow-acting, producing numerous symptoms often suggestive of other illnesses, hence the misdiagnosis.

"Desperately worried about him, Sybil implored me to help your father. By the time Lestrade and I arrived at Elmridge, it was too late. Your father was already dead. Giving a lecture on the treatise he wrote on binomial theorem, your brother ensured he was nowhere near the scene of the crime, of course. An autopsy was later carried out. Although small traces of the toxin were detected in your father's urine and blood, we had little proof that it was your brother who had committed the crime. We only had the word of Sybil. She bravely agreed to testify against your brother, but the day before the preliminary hearing, she disappeared. Without its key witness, the prosecution fell apart, leaving your brother free to claim his inheritance."

I drew on my cigarette. "Sybil Dexter was later found overdosed on heroin at her home in Kentish Town. The Metropolitan Police found a suicide note and confession next to her body, claiming she was solely responsible for your father's death." I hesitated for a moment, before continuing. "She was four months pregnant at the time with your brother's child. Supposing Professor Moriarty was capable of having an innocent woman murdered, destroying his own child in the process, do you think he would think twice about swindling you out of your inheritance?" I shook my head. "Moriarty was a highly ruthless individual, totally devoid of humanity, an epitome of evil. And, of course, he used his ill-gotten gains to launch his empire, his network of crime when he moved to London."

"You're lying," shrieked Moriarty. "My brother told me the police closed the case after Sybil's confession. They would never have done that if they thought my brother was responsible for my father's death."

"I have never lied to you," I said. "The truth can hurt, but if you don't believe me, you are even more disillusioned than I first gave you credit for."

Moriarty laughed. "This changes nothing, Holmes. I still intend to kill you and the woman."

At that moment, the clatter of a carriage and horse drawing up outside sounded.

"Ah," said Moriarty. "I wondered what was keeping Miss Adler."

"You're too late, Moriarty!" I cried. "She is long gone by now, away from your evil clutches!"

Moriarty smirked at me. "You know very little of women, Holmes, if you think a woman like Miss Adler would leave you. I was banking on her high regard for you, and it would appear she has justified my faith." He laughed again as the front door opened and Nene entered the drawing-room, pausing for a moment, taking in the scene in front of her.

"Moriarty, I presume?" said Nene, glaring at him.

Moriarty smiled, pointing the gun at her. "Welcome to the party, Miss Adler. How lovely to see you again. Tell me, have you come to glorify me?"

"Hardly," Nene retorted, making no attempt to hide the contempt in her voice.

"Why, this is turning into quite the reunion. Do take a seat next to your lover." Moriarty gestured to the chaise lounge.

"You may as well let her go. There is nothing between this woman and me. We are friends, nothing more."

"Please don't insult my intelligence," said Moriarty, his head swaying from side to side. "You are asking me to believe this woman is your friend? You don't have friends, especially not women. I've observed your shining intimacy with Miss Adler for some time, your romantic moonlight rendezvous." Moriarty smirked at Nene. "When you catch such a fish, you don't throw it back into the ocean. You know I'm going to have to kill you? However, I must say I'm impressed with your tenacity."

Nene glared at Moriarty, her cheeks flushed and eyes ablaze. "You tragedy of a man, there's nothing you can take from me that I have not already lost. There are worse things than death. I'm not afraid of you, Moriarty."

"Oh, you will be in the end, my dear. That I promise."

Nene scowled at Moriarty. "God set my heart beating and he will be the one to decide when it stops. You have no right to decide who lives and dies."

Moriarty appeared amused by her narrative. "We are all dying, Miss Adler. Life contains death. However, I do think that a little celebratory drink is called for to acknowledge my late brother's retribution, so to speak. Would you be kind enough to do the honours?" Moriarty gestured towards the drinks on the sideboard.

Nene flashed him a dry smile. "If these are to be my last moments on earth, I prefer to go out with a bang. As you can see, I have recently returned from the stables." She pointed to her riding habit. "This is a new jacket which does not belong to me. I would hate for it to be ruined. Would you mind if I take it off?"

Moriarty nodded. Nene took her left arm out of the jacket, quickly turning the pocket inside out so I could see the outline of Ludo's gun, then promptly removed a tiny vial and placed it into her gloved hand, quickly closing it to make a fist, before laying the jacket beside me on the chaise lounge. I watched closely as she carefully removed her gloves, the vial remaining concealed in her fist. Finally, she slowly walked over to the sideboard, her face dripping with perspiration.

"Tell me, Moriarty, what's your poison?" she asked, fixing him with a steely gaze.

"Whiskey for me, Miss Adler," said Moriarty, a flicker of a smile on his face.

Nene decanted the whiskey, pouring it into three separate tumblers. She brought one over to me. Despair branded every line of her face as she smiled at me sadly before returning to the sideboard. I observed her topping up her own glass with a splash of soda water, quickly adding a liberal dash of liquid from the vial. I had no way of knowing what was in the vial, but suspected vitriol, as I knew Ludo kept it in at the stables. My eyes darted over to Moriarty, who sat back in his chair, unaware of the deception.

He looked up as Nene walked toward him and passed him a glass. "Thank you, my dear," he said, taking a swig of whisky.

Nene remained standing next to him, pretending to sip from her own glass, narrowing her eyes, before fixing Moriarty with a cold stare.

"I ask only one thing. If you insist on shooting me like a dog, then aim for my heart, not my head. It would kill my family if they were called upon to identify my body."

"I will see what I can do." Moriarty looked at Nene with amused surprise. "I must say I find your courage remarkable, my dear. Even now you don't desist." He flashed her a wry smile before turning his attention back to me, pointing the gun at my head.

"Not all will weep for you, Holmes." Moriarty sneered. "You've made some powerful enemies during your time at Baker Street. There are plenty from the underworld who would line up to take my place. I've seen to it that they know about your alliance with Miss Adler, of course. My little insurance policy." He laughed menacingly. "You and the young lady would be rather vulnerable if you were to return to

London." He raised his glass, a glazed expression upon his face.

"Count no man happy until he has had a good death."

I glared at Moriarty, my eyes narrowed. "You leave very little room for misinterpretation, Moriarty. You are culpable all right, but know this. If you lay one finger on this woman, I swear I will finish you, and I promise you it will hurt. Your brother was a giant of evil, and with your blatant disregard for human life it appears the rotten apple doesn't fall far from the tree. Professor Moriarty fell to his death attempting to murder me, and that is the absolute truth of the matter."

"Spare yourself the indignity of denial, Holmes!" cried Moriarty. "Tell the truth and shame the devil, why don't you?"

"You may as well give it up," I cried. "It's finished, there's nowhere to run. The police will be here any moment. They are surrounding this establishment even as we speak!" A cold, gnawing feeling knotted in the pit of my stomach.

I looked over to Nene. Tears of anguish flooded her face, as she addressed me. "There are things between us that remain unsaid, but I want you to know that I love you with my whole heart. What you said to me at the Amphitheatre . . . you were wrong. Any woman should be proud to call you her husband. I know I would."

"Thank you, that is quite the compliment." I smiled at her. "What an incredible fortune it was to have found you again."

Moriarty laughed. "Such impassioned speeches," he exclaimed, pointing the gun at Nene's head as he cocked the pistol. "Please don't take this personally, Miss Adler. I rather like you."

I shot to my feet. Running between the two, I turned to face Moriarty. "You are right about one thing, Moriarty. If you want to kill this woman, then you will have to go through me first. For I would sooner slit my own throat than allow you to harm her. Few people are worth dying for, but she is the exception. Prepare for your descent straight into hell you pathetic runt. Why, I believe you are the devil himself."

"I'm hardly the devil," Moriarty quipped. "Perhaps an aspiring deviant."

"Do your worst, Moriarty," Nene exclaimed, throwing her drink in his face.

Moriarty screamed out in agony. His right hand shot up in the air. The gun fired, missing Nene by a hair's breadth. She stumbled and fell onto the floor, stunned by the bullet's passage as it went whistling past her and ricocheted against the edge of the window, shattering the glass. I quickly removed Ludo's gun from its hiding place and fired without hesitation. The bullet hit Moriarty in the shoulder. He howled in pain before falling back. The gun flew out of his hand and clattered to the floor.

Nene lunged towards the gun. Out of the corner of my eye, I saw Moriarty, blood running down his face, his left eye swollen shut, kick the gun out of Nene's reach.

"You poisonous little bitch!" he snarled, grabbing for her.

Moriarty picked up the gun and pointed it at Nene's head with his right hand, his other around her neck.

I aimed Ludo's gun at Moriarty's head. "Drop it. Let her go! " I cried.

Moriarty glared at me. "No, *you* drop it, Holmes . . . or I swear I will kill her right in front of you."

Nene looked at me. "You have a clear shot, Sherlock. Take it. You *must* shoot him. We both don't need to die today."

I shook my head. A tear rolled down my face. I heard Moriarty cock the barrel of the gun. I took aim at Moriarty's head. My hand was on the trigger when gunfire sounded. Moriarty fell to the floor, his head mutilated by a bullet fired from Inspector Montalbano's pistol.

Looking over to Nene, I noticed she was still on the floor. I dropped the gun and ran to her. I had spent most of my adult life avoiding emotional interaction with women, but when I saw Nene lying on the ground I felt as though my world had ended.

Reaching for her hand, I checked her pulse, crying out in anguish. "Nene, look at me. I've got you and I'm going to take care of you."

She slowly opened her eyes and smiled at me. "Are we dead? Have we made it to heaven?"

"Hardly. Not unless I'm God, and I think that's highly unlikely, don't you?" I breathed a sigh of relief. "You fainted for a moment."

"Are you all right, my love?" She gazed up at me with a concerned expression.

"I'm fine." Sweeping her up in my arms, I sat her down on the chaise lounge. My hands gripped her waist, pulling her to me. "Why didn't you go with Javier while you had the chance?"

"I couldn't bear to leave you."

Inspector Montalbano's constables burst into the room, taking in the body on the floor, the blood-spattered walls, and the room thick with smoke and fire. I spoke to Montalbano, who was considerably astonished when I revealed our identity and the chain of events leading to its bloody conclusion.

"Thank you for your help, Inspector," I said, shaking his hand. "If you hadn't arrived when you did, I would have been responsible for his demise."

Helping Nene to her feet, we held onto each other as I whispered, "You do realise that was the only time you have ever told me you love me?"

Nene laughed, her eyes bright with tears. "Now is not the time to be fishing for compliments, Mr Holmes. I have spent enough time massaging your ego."

"I want you to pack an overnight bag," I said. "I'm taking you to a hotel."

"Surely we have to give a statement to the police?" she quizzed.

I shook my head. "I will go and see Montalabo in the morning to make a formal statement. The rest they can work out for themselves. The police don't retain me to supply their deficiencies."

Nene quickly packed a bag while I wrote a note for the Espiritos. Soon we were safely ensconced in Montalabo's carriage, and when we arrived at the village, I booked us into a suite at the Athena hotel under the name of Mr and Mrs Holmes.

Chapter Forty-One: Irene Adler

The whole of our extraordinary journey seemed like a dream, as though something had tilted the world off its axis.

Holmes sat beside me, looking concerned. "Can I get you anything?" He asked.

"May I have one of those, please?" I gestured to his cigarette.

Holmes lit another and passed it to me. I puffed on it, blowing a circle of smoke into the air. "Perhaps one day they will invent a cigarette that lights itself, wouldn't that be something? I need a bath; I can smell Moriarty on my skin."

Holmes stood. "Stay here," he said. "I will be back in a moment."

The pungent aroma of Castile soap lingered in the air as I climbed into the bath Holmes had drawn for me. Resting my head on the backrest, I closed my eyes as Holmes tenderly sponged my body.

"I'm going to order drinks from room service. What would you like?" he asked.

"Mmmm," I murmured sleepily. "Hot chocolate would be good . . . with a dash of brandy."

I must have fallen asleep, because when I woke, I was lying on the bed, wrapped in a soft Egyptian towel and a sheet that covered my body. Holmes was sitting in an armchair watching over me.

Sitting up on my elbows, I gazed at Holmes. "What time is it?"

He looked at his watch chain. "It's seven o'clock."

Holmes's action had inadvertently drawn my attention to his watch. I noticed something glittering on the chain. I stared at him curiously. "What was that shining on your watch chain?" I quizzed.

"Surely you must remember." Holmes placed a gold coin in the palm of his hand. "This sovereign was given to me by a young lady at the church of Saint Monica as a reward for standing witness to her marriage seven years ago. I wear it every now and again to remind me of the occasion."

I stared at him, shocked. "Of course, you were the witness at the church. I remember giving it to you. And you kept it after all this time?"

"Yes, even then I had a premonition that our paths would cross again."

I smiled at him. "You were willing to sacrifice yourself for me today. I shall never forget that. I was once told that true bravery wears an invisible cloak without ever being suspected."

"I would do it all again in a heartbeat," said Holmes. "I would rip up the world to keep you safe. You know, we made quite a team today. Perhaps we should attempt to save the world together more often."

"You and me against the world? That has a nice ring to it." I gazed into his eyes. "You know, Sherlock, there's nothing like the fear of death for making you question the meaning of life. When Moriarty pointed that gun at me, I wasn't afraid of dying—I was scared I'd never see you again. The thought you might die in front of me . . . like Rosemary . . . was terrifying. When you spoke to me earlier and questioned whether I loved you, your words broke my heart. I could no more not love you than I could stop breathing. If today has taught us anything, it's that we need to make the most of our time together."

"If there's any reason we cannot be together, I promise you

this—I will find you again someday. Of that, you must have no doubt."

"You can't get rid of me that easily. I'm here for the duration, although I don't want you to make any promises you don't want to keep. I have no expectations."

"I pride myself on being a man of my word. When I say that I will do something, then I will do everything within my power to make it happen."

I put my arms around his neck, kissing him softly on the lips. "Can I be with you tonight? I need to be close to you."

"Yes, of course. Are you hungry?"

"Strangely enough, I am. Our brush with death has given me quite an appetite."

"Good, dinner will arrive at eight o'clock. Come, let's have a drink." He handed me a brandy.

I took a sip from the glass. "I'd better get dressed," I said. "I have no wish to shock the waiter."

Holmes kept his appointment with Montalabo the following day. He called in at the telegraph office to send messages to Mycroft, Watson, and Lestrade, informing them of Moriarty's demise. He returned to the hotel in time for breakfast to find me already dressed. Although I had little appetite, I was feeling nauseous. I blamed my affliction on the chicken we'd consumed for dinner the night before, although Sherlock appeared unaffected.

Later that morning, we ordered a carriage and arrived at the farmhouse before luncheon. Holmes looked at me anxiously as he helped me down from the carriage. "Are you sure you're up to this?" he asked.

"I'm fine." I squeezed his hand reassuringly. "We need to face the music together."

We walked over to the farmhouse. I hugged Violetta, taking her hand in mine.

"I am so sorry we deceived you, Violetta. We were not married when we first arrived. We lied to you, and for that we are truly sorry. We hope you can forgive us."

"I must admit I thought the situation strange at first," said Violetta. "But then I reasoned that whatever was going on, Sherlock must hold you in high regard to bring you here. You are an outstanding actress, Nene."

"Oh, it was not all acting, I can assure you. We've made a commitment to each other and have decided to live together when we return to England."

Violetta embraced me, tears in her eyes. "I am so very sorry for everything you have endured, but at least you came through it unscathed. That man can never hurt you again." Violetta stared at me curiously. "Tell me, when do you and Sherlock plan to return to London?"

I chuckled softly. "Well, Violetta, your baby is due any moment now. I'd like to be around when the happy event takes place, if that's agreeable with you and Ludo of course. I want to say thank you from the bottom of my heart for everything you've done for us."

"I'm delighted that you're going to be here for the birth," said Violetta. "I'm afraid Ludo will not be of much use."

Holmes agreed we could stay on, but only for a few more days. His services were required back in London, where according to Mycroft, an intriguing case of the utmost importance awaited.

"I believe that you miss the foggy streets of London, am I right?" I quizzed.

"Your intuition is once again correct," said Holmes.

"Thank you, Sherlock."

"Whatever for?"

"For indulging me."

"It is my pleasure."

Chapter Forty-Two: Irene Adler

The following morning, I waited until Holmes left for the village before dragging myself out of bed. Once again, I was feeling nauseous. Stepping out of the shower, I stared at my naked body in the bathroom mirror. I inspected my breasts. They were sensitive and tender and the rose-coloured circles around my nipples were enlarged and had assumed a darker hue. I'd only just gotten dressed when I heard a knock on the barn door. I was surprised to find Violetta standing on the doorstep with fresh laundry and towels. She explained Gabriella was unwell that morning. Entering the bedroom together, we sat on the bed and chatted for a while.

Violetta took my hand in hers. "Nene, you need to let me know if you need any rags. You have not asked for any since you first came here."

"I'm afraid my courses are irregular due to a long-standing medical condition, Violetta."

Violetta stared at me with a concerned expression. "You don't look well these days."

"It's just a cold."

"This is more than a head cold; it could be a stomach bug. Should I fetch a doctor?"

"No, thank you. Please excuse me, Violetta." I jumped up from the bed as a wave of nausea overcame me.

Running into the bathroom, I was violently sick. Violetta had followed me. She gently wiped my mouth with a face towel and pushed my hair back from my face before passing me a glass of water.

"It's not a stomach bug," I whispered. "I think I'm pregnant. This must be morning sickness."

Violetta wrapped her arms around my shoulders with motherly tenderness, leading me back into the bedroom. "I don't know why they call it morning sickness," said Violetta, shaking her head. "It will soon pass, you'll see. You need some of Gabriella's ginger tea to alleviate the symptoms." Violetta glanced around the room. "Sherlock will be thrilled."

"Violetta, I cannot tell him!"

"Why not?"

"I lost a baby due to complications during my first marriage, and I will likely lose this child. Every time I go to the bathroom, I expect to see blood. I cannot put Sherlock through that. I couldn't deliver him such a crushing blow." I took hold of Violetta's arm. "Promise me you will not tell anyone, Violetta, not even Ludo."

Violetta nodded. "I promise, Nene. But you are going to have to tell Sherlock before you start to show. I'm sure he will be thrilled, even under such trying circumstances. I know from personal experience that keeping a secret is exhausting, and it rarely ends well. The more you keep something to yourself, the more difficult it becomes to reveal the truth."

"If I can get past the first few months, Violetta, I will be more than happy to tell him. I want us to be able to celebrate without worry." I sighed. "This will not be an easy secret to keep. Sherlock has a mind that can see around corners. But I can endure anything as long as my baby is safe. That is what matters."

Violetta smiled as she put her arm around me. "Life is the most incredible, extraordinary gift there is. There may be bad times ahead, but every precious second is a wondrous miracle, and every beat of our heart gives us reason to celebrate. You only need to look at what happened for Ludo and me after all these years. You know, Nene, what you and Sherlock have is special. I can tell you are a good fit."

I nodded. "Yes, we are. I freely admit that there are challenging aspects to Sherlock's personality. His lack of tact and his superior intelligence can at times be intimidating to others, but underneath that icy exterior is a lovely man. He does not like to show his emotions in public, but when we're alone together we have this fire. I need to protect him as he has protected me. I will pray to God and hope for the best. That's all I can do."

"God is good, Nene, he came through for Ludo and me. Why not you and Sherlock?"

"Why not, indeed, Violetta. Come join me for breakfast. We're both eating for two."

I somehow managed to keep my pregnancy a secret. The morning sickness gradually wore off by late morning and with careful makeup application I worked hard to appear my usual self when Holmes returned from the village. I spent sleepless nights agonising over whether to tell him of our child, but decided not to for two reasons. First, the child was unlikely to survive, and it would be much better to bleed out on my own and spare Holmes that unspeakable agony. The second was that I was sure if I told him, he would ask me to marry him, and the last thing I wanted was for him to feel trapped in marriage. I would never want him to propose to me under such circumstances.

So, on the first night after discovering I was with child, I accepted a small glass of dry sherry, but refused further alcohol.

Holmes nodded at the bottle. "Are you sure you won't have another?"

"No, thank you," I said. "I've been drinking far too much lately. That has led to arguments between us. I'll stick with the one glass, for now. But I will take a glass of lemonade."

Holmes stared at me for a moment then nodded. "All right, if that's what you want. Never the bottle, never the way." He laughed, and I felt relieved he had accepted my explanation.

Violetta went into labour the following afternoon. Ludo was pacing up and down the hallway in a fever of impatience until Giovanni finally shouted over to him. "Ludo, come outside at once for a cigarette. You don't want to be troubling the women when a bambino is arriving. Rachel, the midwife, said only the women are allowed in the birthing room."

Ludo nodded in resignation and joined Giovanni outside for a much-needed cigarette. Violetta was exhausted but happy when her newborn son eventually entered the world. The midwife handed him to Violetta.

"I have been waiting for you for such a long time," she whispered.

I beamed at my friend. "My God, he's so beautiful, Violetta. Look at his eyes. They're like liquid pools."

Violetta nodded. "Yes, he is indeed handsome, But you know every child is unique in their mother's eyes."

Ludo and Holmes tentatively entered the room. Ludo gazed at his son with infinite affection and pride. "Welcome to the world, my beautiful son. Well, Mr Holmes, what do you think of my boy Francesco?"

Holmes smiled, staring keenly at the baby. "He is a splendid child. You must be a very proud man, and rightly so. Many congratulations to both of you."

Ludo embraced Violetta, speaking to her softly. "*Grazie Bella signora per avermi dato un figlio.*"

Ava entered the room with a silver tray loaded with champagne flutes, and we raised our glasses in a toast to Francesco.

Violetta raised her glass to Holmes and me. "Ludo will ask Father Amati if he will perform the christening on Saturday. If he agrees, then we would very much like you to be the godparents to our son."

I pressed my hand to my mouth, crying tears of joy. "Are you sure?"

"We cannot think of a finer couple to be godparents," said Ludo.

"We would consider it a privilege and an honour," said Holmes, gesturing to Ludo. "You need to come with me, Mr Espirito. Let's leave the ladies in peace. We will go and seek out the infamous Father Amati. And then my dear fellow, we must find Giovanni and go wet the baby's head."

Chapter Forty-Three: Irene Adler

The following evening Clarissa, Antonio, and Gabriella were busy preparing a delicious dinner of muscles, followed by Violetta's favourite dish Peposo Alla Fiorentina, a peppery Tuscan beef stew. Holmes and I decided to have pre-dinner drinks on the patio to take in some fresh air.

"Sherlock, there is one thing that has been puzzling me."

Holmes glanced at me curiously. "What is it?" He asked.

"The carbuncle. I don't understand what happened to it. How can it just disappear?"

"Ah, well it was hardly a mystery to me. Let me expound that when your late husband hid the stone, he chose a place that he knew would be safe and where he could recover it without suspicion."

"I don't understand."

"Your brooch from La Scala, forgive me." Holmes unclipped the brooch from my dress.

Turning it over, he revealed a catch at the back. He carefully unfastened the clasp and the brooch opened up to reveal a dazzling green gemstone which fell out into the palm of his hand.

I gasped with shock. "No, it cannot be!"

"I would stake my life on it," said Holmes.

He placed the stone on the table. Under the sparkling night sky, the rock slowly began to change colour until it had turned into a deep ruby red. "Let me introduce you to the infamous Alexandrite Carbuncle from Russia, a gemstone so rare and precious that men have died attempting to possess it." A flush of colour rose to Holmes's pale cheeks. "It's part of the chrysoberyl family with an optical reflectance effect. Because of the way it absorbs the light it is described as an emerald by day and a ruby by night. A marvel of nature. The rarity of its material and its chameleon-like qualities make alexandrite one of the world's most desirable gemstones."

Holmes gazed into my eyes. "My dearest Nene, you have been the custodian of this illustrious treasure all this time. If not for this stone, I would never have found you." He laughed, giving the stone one last look before placing it in his pocket.

I stared at him in disbelief. "Why, it's inconceivable. Unbelievable. How on earth did you know it was there?"

"Because I knew it was nowhere else," said Holmes. "After our conversation in Milan, there was never any doubt. Jones only had a limited amount of time to hide this valuable prize. Even the burglars turned their noses up at it when they broke into your house. Mind you, we needed to hold onto it to give us leverage in case Palmer ever caught up with us."

"Sherlock Holmes, you never cease to amaze me," I said, staring at him in awe.

Linking my arm in his, we walked to the farmhouse, taking our places at the dining table. Ludo filled our glasses, and Holmes proposed a toast to *molte congratulazioni*.

I smiled at Holmes. "I'm delighted you found the stone," I said, gesturing to Violetta, Ludo, and Ava. "But you know, true friends are the rare jewels of life . . . difficult to find and impossible to replace. A toast—to true friends." We all raised our glasses, repeating the sentiment.

Chapter Forty-Four: Irene Adler

It was a perfect summer's day for the christening of Francesco Alessandro Espirito.

Holmes rose early, as usual, bringing me a cup of cafe noir. "Come on, Nene, it's time to get up," he whispered.

I slowly opened one eye, glancing at the clock on the wall. "Good morning to you too," I replied defensively, still a little groggy from my peaceful slumber. "It's only seven o'clock. Why on earth do you insist on getting me out of bed at such a ridiculous hour?"

"We must start the day. How are you this morning?"

"Overtired from sleep deprivation. You know I'm not human until I have had my first cup of coffee."

"I thought you might appreciate a cup," said Holmes. "And then I must insist you get up. Clarissa has drawn you a bath."

I yawned, stretching out my arms. "All right, you are right." I arched an eyebrow. "Why don't you come back to bed? I'd like to hold you here for a week."

"Nice try." Holmes chuckled as he handed me the cup. "But it's not going to work, I'm afraid, not this morning. Drink your coffee while it's hot."

I accepted the cup, sipping from it slowly. In truth, I was still feeling a little aggrieved by Violetta's insistence that we arrive at the church an hour before the ceremony. Ludo had hired a professional photographer to take photographs of family and godparents before the other guests arrived. Instead, I would have preferred to spend the extra hour in bed, wrapped around Sherlock Holmes. Then I felt guilty, knowing how much the christening meant to Violetta. She'd waited so long for her beloved son, and she wanted everything to be perfect.

I got out of bed and drained my coffee cup before taking my bath, emerging two and a half hours later with my hair braided to the sides and attired in my favourite dress, a beautiful cream and white silk satin gown. I had purchased the gown from the House of Worth when touring France and had saved it for a special occasion. Well, becoming a godmother was notable enough in my book. Entering the drawing-room, I found Holmes waiting for me, dressed in a full suit and silk waistcoat. I helped him with his tie.

"Well, I must say, you look rather handsome, Mr Holmes."

"You look stunning yourself, Miss Adler."

"I'm glad you approve. You don't think that this dress is too much?"

"Not at all, Nene. It's perfect. You have far too much class to make anyone feel second rate."

"We're going to be early," I grumbled. "The photographs shouldn't take that long. What can we possibly do in the meantime?"

"Oh, I'm sure we will think of something," he said. "It's such a beautiful day. We can wander around the grounds and take a look at the church. It's the oldest one in Fiesole, built on the site of an Etruscan temple." Holmes paused for a moment, smiling at me gently. "I thought we might take the opportunity to light a candle for our lost children. That should keep us occupied for a while."

Surprised, I looked at him. "What a lovely thought, Sherlock. Yes, I'd like to do that a lot."

Holmes stared out of the window. "I believe our carriage has arrived." He checked the time on his watch. It read ten o'clock. The christening would commence at eleven o'clock, one hour hence.

Chapter Forty-Five: Irene Adler

Later that morning, the guests congregated to attend the christening of Francesco Alessandro Espirito at the Basilica of Sant Alessandro Church. The proud godparents—Holmes, Ava, and I—stood next to the font, prepared to pledge our *sponder*—our promise to encourage the child's spiritual growth.

The choir boys sang "Loving Shepherd of Thy Sheep." Francesco, the very picture of infantile dignity, neither cried nor fussed until the holy water was sprinkled onto his forehead. Then he let out an indignant yell, much to the amusement of his proud parents and the rest of the congregation. Outside the church, the carriages waited to transport the guests back to Le Sole to attend a private reception. Back at the farmhouse, Violetta and I were in conversation while fussing over Francesco.

"I want to thank you, Violetta," I said. "For being my confidant. I never had a sister, and I love you dearly."

"Thank you, Nene. That means so much to me. You know that I love you too."

Ludo approached us. "Violetta and I have come to a decision," he said. "We agree that Ava must have her chance to audition for La Scala."

"Well, that *is* wonderful news." I beamed at them. "I shall write at once to my dear friend Sophia and ask her to chaperone Ava at her audition."

Returning to the barn, I quickly wrote a letter to Sophia, enclosing a cheque to cover Ava's audition fee. I returned to the farmhouse with a parcel under my arm, handing Clarissa the letter for posting before re-joining the celebrations. Holmes and I presented Ludo and Violetta with a cheque to be used at their discretion to set up a trust fund for Francesco.

Violetta stared at the cheque in disbelief. "I shouldn't be so bold as to tell you how to spend your money, but this is far too generous. We cannot accept it," she stuttered.

I shook my head. "Nonsense, Violetta. Francesco is our godson, and it's our moral duty to help provide for his future. You've looked after us during all this madness, and you refused to accept a single lira. It's the least we can do."

Holmes laughed. "I know from personal experience there is little point in arguing with the lady. However, we both owe you a great deal, so please consider this recompense for services rendered. Not only for now but from four years ago, when you helped a total stranger."

Ludo and Violetta reluctantly accepted the cheque.

I caught Ava's eye and beckoned to her. "Come, Ava. I have something for you."

Ava walked over to join me. "What is it, Nene?" she asked, staring at the package in anticipation.

"Well, open it, please," I said, handing the parcel to Ava.

Ava opened the package and was stunned to discover my bespoke curling tongs. She gasped with shock, shaking her head. "Nene, I cannot accept them. I know they cost a fortune. You have given me so much already."

"Don't be silly," I said. "Consider it an investment in your future. I want you to promise me you'll take them with you to Milan. Be sure to ask Sophia to dress your hair. she is a dab hand with tongs. Don't worry, I have an identical pair back in Trenton."

A telegram waited for me when I awoke the following morning. My cousin, Estelle, relayed the news that my father had taken ill. There had been complications with his diabetes. I explained the situation to Holmes and after much deliberation, we agreed to travel to London together. From there, I would make my way to Southampton to board the boat to New Jersey. Holmes offered to accompany me, but I politely declined his kind gesture.

"There's no rush," I said. "We have all the time in the world."

"I sincerely hope your father makes a speedy recovery," said Holmes. "As soon as I get matters in hand and attend to Mycroft's so-called urgent case, I intend to travel to see you and your father. It doesn't sit right with me, leaving you alone to cope with everything."

"Nonsense, I won't be alone. I have the full support of my family. I don't want you to worry. As soon as I am convinced my father is recovering, I will come back to England."

"I suppose while you are in New Jersey, that will allow me to put my own affairs in order."

"Well, in that case," I said. "You had better let me show you what you will be missing."

Chapter Forty-Six: Irene Adler

Holmes had set off to the village by the time I awoke the following morning. Stepping into the shower, I stared at my reflection in the mirror. The woman who stared back looked pale and drawn, with dark circles under her eyes. I tied my hair up in a knot. I was just about to put the finishing touches on my makeup when I was disturbed by a knock on the door. I opened it expecting to find Violetta or Ava. Instead, a tall, well-built man stood before me, his corpulent frame spanning the doorway. He smiled at me before removing his hat.

"Good morning, Miss Adler. Please allow me to introduce myself, my name is Mycroft Holmes. I am Sherlock's brother. May I come in?" he asked, offering a soft but purposeful handshake.

"Please do come in, Mr Holmes." I stared at him with a puzzled expression, inviting him to take a seat in the drawing-room. Mycroft took off his overcoat, placing it on the chair next to him.

"May I offer you a drink?" I smiled at him nervously.

"A glass of port would be more than acceptable. And perhaps a glass of water. I'm not used to this infernal heat.; This will be the death of me."

Mycroft's face glistened from the heat of the morning sun. He pulled a handkerchief from his pocket and wiped his chubby cheeks in an attempt to cool himself down before lighting a cigarette. I handed Mycroft a glass of port, along with the water. I stared at the bottle for a moment, sorely tempted. What I wouldn't give to have a drink right now. But instead, I put the cork back in the bottle, returning it to the sideboard. Then, pouring a glass of water from the pitcher, I took a seat across from Mycroft.

He was a tall, portly man. From what Sherlock had told me, Mycroft was seven years older than his brother, although he appeared much older, his dark hair going grey at the temples. His grey deep-set eyes darted around the room and seemed to retain that far away retrospective look that I have often observed in Sherlock. He wore a sombre but well-cut pearl-grey suit, with a cravat and a gold watch chain burrowed into his waistcoat, his shining black hat rested on his knee. The Inverness draped over the chair appeared far too warm for the Tuscan weather.

I was desperately trying to remember what Sherlock had told me of his brother. I knew they had a strained relationship, and Mycroft was dedicated to his work. He served his country diligently and did his duty, never afraid to make difficult decisions. Sherlock said his brother had the most orderly brain of any man living. A man of habit, he lived in rooms at Pall Mall. His regular routine was to walk around the corner every morning to Whitehall to his place of employment, then in the evening he would walk back to Pall Mall, to The Diogenes Club, where Mycroft was a founding member. Sherlock said his brother seldom broke his routine. But if that was the case, what was he doing here in Fiesole?

"I am sorry, Mr Holmes, was Sherlock expecting you? He never mentioned anything." I sat back in my chair, instinctively covering my stomach with my hands.

"No, he was not expecting me, Miss Adler. On the contrary, I ensured he would be out before making myself known to you."

I immediately had an overwhelming feeling of dread as a wave of nausea engulfed me.

Mycroft stood. "This really will not do, Miss Adler. Do you seriously believe that you and Sherlock can return to London and live together? Why, that is quite an absurd notion. I don't doubt that he is smitten with you. your charms are evident to see. But Sherlock would soon weary of domestic bliss and inevitably end up resenting you." He sighed deeply. "My brother is the greatest detective of his time. He must be allowed to continue with his work, his *raison d'etre*." Mycroft stared at me intently.

"I speak to you confidentially, Miss Adler. Archibald Primrose has personally intervened and demanded my brother's immediate return to London. Sherlock's enemies are many, and there have been several attempts on his life. There's always a backlash for someone classed as a genius flaunting himself in the public eye. My brother collects enemies as others collect stamps, and if he continues his relationship with you, you and your unborn child will become targets. I'm sorry, but I simply cannot stand by and allow that to happen."

"How on earth could you possibly know I am with child?" I stared at him aghast.

"I assume my brother does not know about the child?"

I shook my head.

Mycroft stared at me incredulously. "I rest my case. The situation is far worse than I first anticipated."

"The facts are these, Miss Adler. You have recently lost weight and are habitually afflicted by nausea. You begrudgingly abstain from alcohol. Your body language, and the way you protect yourself and your unborn child when you feel you are in danger, is indicative of a woman with child. You have the pale, drawn look that is so familiar in pregnant women. Well, it hardly takes a genius to work it out, and I speak to you as one. The fact that Sherlock has no idea is of grave concern to me. They say that love is blind. Well, it is certainly true in this case."

I felt sick to my stomach. "I have already lost one child, Mr Holmes. The chances of me carrying this child to full term are negligible. I had no wish to raise Sherlock's expectations. Did you know that Sherlock saved my life?"

Mycroft stared at me stony-faced, nodding curtly. "Yes, I am well aware that my brother saved your life, Miss Adler. And now you must repay the debt and save his. If my brother finds out about this child, he will follow you to the ends of the earth. On the other hand, if you love him as much as you profess, you must do the right thing and let him go. It is your moral duty to release him from any obligations or reckless promises." Mycroft paused for a moment. "If the pregnancy proves viable, then you have my assurance that the child will be provided for." He grimaced. "My carriage will return to collect you and your luggage in precisely one hour. I understand Sherlock is not expected back before lunchtime?"

Mycroft placed a large envelope down beside me. "These are return tickets for your train journey to Southampton and your subsequent passage to New York. First class, of course. The coachman will return on the hour with instructions to wait ten minutes, giving you ample time to acknowledge his presence. You will either come or stay, it will be entirely your decision."

Mycroft stood as if to go. "Perhaps I may get to see my nephew or niece someday?" He appeared to soften for a moment. He put on his hat and coat, walking towards the door. There he turned, fixing me with his steel-grey eyes.

"Miss Adler, in case you decide to stay, you need to know that my brother is unaware that I'm in Florence. Best not to mention it, don't you think?" Mycroft placed his card on the table next to me.

I stared at it in stunned disbelief. This couldn't be happening. I opened my mouth in an attempt to speak, but no words were forthcoming. My voice didn't appear to be working.

"Please don't hesitate to contact me if you need anything. No need to show me out." Mycroft took one last look around him before leaving the room, shutting the door behind him.

I was utterly bereft. I lay down on the bed, wailing uncontrollably. Until, finally, I dragged myself up from the bed and pulled my cases down from the top of the wardrobe—realizing what I had always known. I could not stay with Sherlock Holmes, as much as I wanted to. I must let go of him to protect him and our unborn child. Walking into the kitchen, I placed a letter on the table before stepping out onto the patio.

Lost in reflection, I recalled our intimate conversations, every glorious moment we had spent together, before once more entering the bedroom we'd shared. I picked up his shirt, inhaled his manly smell, tears welling in my eyes. I was disturbed by the sound of the coachman's whip and the creaking of the wheels as the horses galloped into the courtyard.

Chapter Forty-Seven: Sherlock Holmes

Before luncheon, I returned to the barn to find the nest empty and a letter waiting for me on the kitchen table.

I tore open the envelope, removing the letter.

My darling Sherlock,

I am writing this letter to ease your mind. To avoid any conversation regarding our relationship and release you from any unconditional promise. First of all, thank you for saving my life. In my time of darkness, you were a ray of light. I hope to repay the debt someday.

I am sure that when you return to London, your life will resume as it did before. It makes me happy knowing that you will continue with what you do best, what you were born to do. I would have only let you down in the end, and I couldn't accept that.

I leave with this letter my brooch from La Scala, the vessel used by Godfrey to conceal the alexandrite stone to remind you of our time together. Dr Watson confided that you kept my photograph and letter, and whenever you spoke of me, it was always The Woman *as a term of endearment.*

Let me tell you now, Sherlock, that if I am The Woman, you are most certainly The Man. Any other would pale into insignificance in my eyes. I intend to return to La Scala one day, and my dearest wish is to meet you there if you ever find it in your heart to forgive me. If you ever think of me, let it be as a light in the darkness, removing the shadows from your face and steering you away from danger.

I leave you with this quote by Tennyson and my favourite poem by Percy Shelley:

I believe that every life holds one great love,
One face to take into the dark.
You are mine. You always will be.

Music when soft voices die

Music when soft voices die
Vibrates in the memory
Odours when sweet violets sicken
Live within the sense they quicken.
Rose leaves, when the rose is dead
Are heaped for the beloved's bed.
And so thy thoughts, when thou art gone.
Love itself shall slumber on.

Remember me with a rose. I love you now and always.
Nene xx

Tears rolled down my face as I read her letter, falling back into my chair as an overwhelming sense of despondency flooded over me.

"Why on earth would she leave me? What did I do?" I cried, running into her bedroom, and flinging the wardrobe open to find everything gone.

My eyes darted around the room when they landed on a card on the floor. I picked it up and examined it with shaking hands, staggered by what I saw.

"Mycroft!" I cried out in anguish.

I sat on the bed, trying to make sense of the sordid situation. Slowly the tawdry conspiracy unfolded in my mind. In an act of devastating cruelty, I had been comprehensively betrayed by the two people I trusted. Aided and abetted by my brother, the woman I had dreamed of for the past seven years had left me without a moment's thought.

I ran to the farmhouse. Violetta showed me a note that Nene had pushed through her door.

She read it out to me:

Violetta, I am so sorry to leave this way. Please forgive me. I promise I will be in touch to explain everything. I love you. Nene. x.

I jumped into the brougham, lashing the horses until we arrived at the railway station, only to be told by the porter that the last train had departed an hour ago. I returned to the barn with a heavy heart, vowing never to trust anyone again.

Chapter Forty-Eight: Sherlock Holmes

To the delight of Watson, Mrs Hudson, and the various clients seeking my help and representation, I arrived safely back in London, where I was soon ensconced in the familiar congenial surroundings of Baker Street for what was to be a particularly hectic period. Around this time, Miss Violet Smith, from Farnham, contacted me. Her visit was most unwelcome, for I was busy working on the case Mycroft had asked me to look into, a very abstruse and complicated problem concerning the peculiar persecution of the well-known tobacco millionaire John Vincent Harden.

Miss Smith presented herself late one evening at Baker Street and implored my help. Despite my protestations, Miss Smith was adamant that I hear her story. With a resigned air and a somewhat weary smile, I begged her to take a seat and inform Watson and me what was troubling her. Violet Smith's presence—beautiful, tall, and graceful—reminded me so much of Nene. Violet had an intriguing story regarding an unusual turn in her and her mother's lives.

I reluctantly agreed to accept the case, which would become known as "The Solitary Cyclist." Unable to break off the necessary research, I sent Watson ahead to Carlington Heath in Farnham to make enquiries regarding the occupants of Carlington Hall. Not surprisingly, I was disappointed by Watson's meagre observations, forcing me to travel to Farnham for what I described as a quiet day in the country. Heading to the local pub, I had a drink at the bar. Striking up a conversation with the pub landlord gave me all I wanted concerning Williamson, one of the antagonists in the case. What I didn't realize was that Woodley, a fellow antagonist, was drinking beer in the taproom next door and had eavesdropped on the entire conversation. Woodley confronted me, ending a string of abuse with a vicious backhand.

I emerged from the confrontation with a cut lip, my face marred, and a discoloured lump on my forehead. At the same time, Woodley's face took the full brunt of my anger and frustration, the unspeakable agony at losing the only woman I'd ever loved. A red fog descended upon me as I threw my last knockout punch, a straight left against a slogging ruffian. Unfortunately for Woodley, his opponent was no slogger. He was facing a fit, athletic man, a champion boxer in my youth. And I wanted to hurt him. I wanted him to feel pain as I had felt pain. Throughout the altercation, all I could see in front of me was Mycroft's mocking face tormenting me and the words of my old boxing coach ringing in my ears,—Only step into the ring if you are ready to ring the bell, for it's a bell you can never unring—advice I had never forgotten and which boded me well in my adventures as a detective. I was eventually dragged off Woodley, who was rendered unconscious and carried home in a cart.

The police arrested two brutal rogues and an unscrupulous clergy member in the dramatic conclusion of this particular tale. Even though the heroine, like Nene, was an independent, strong-willed woman, nevertheless she still needed saving from the worst fate that can befall a woman. There was at least one happy ending. Violet Smith inherited a large fortune and married her fiancée Cyril Morton, the senior partner of Morton and Kennedy, the famous Westminster electricians.

Chapter Forty-Nine: Irene Adler

When I returned to New Jersey, my father and Estelle received me with open arms. I explained what had transpired with Holmes and Mycroft and the news of my impending birth. Although devastated and angry, my father fully supported me. He bravely tried to hang on to see his first grandchild born. But alas that was not to be. My father suffered a stroke at the beginning of October and lay gravely ill in hospital. He begged me to take him home as he wished to end his days within his own four walls. Estelle and I arranged for him to come home, where he lay in our care for a month. Early one morning, I came to relieve Estelle from her nursing duties. Sadly, my father's condition had deteriorated overnight. A priest was called in to give his last rites.

I recited the poems of Percy Shelley as he lay on his bed. His eyes half-closed, he spoke to me in a soft voice. "I am an old man, at the end of my journey." He squeezed my hand. "My darling girl, you have always been very special to me. I've done a terrible thing, please forgive me." My father began drifting in and out of consciousness.

"There's nothing to forgive," I whispered. "Please don't go. Don't leave me," I begged, powerless to do anything except hold his hand as the life of one of the most important relationships in my life slipped quietly away.

My father lay silently on the bed in the bedroom he had shared with my mother, Marianne. The bed where I'd been born in the absolute stillness of death. I told Estelle of my father's passing as tears streamed down my face.

"I sang and read to him as he lay dying. I held his hand and told him I loved him. I'm not sure if he could hear me."

Estelle put her hand on my arm, smiling at me reassuringly, wiping away her own tears. "Yes, he would have, Nene. I promise you, hearing is the last thing to go. The pain he was in was untenable and had been for a long time. But at least he is at peace now."

I was seven months pregnant when my father passed away, my stomach burgeoning as my miracle baby, a blessing in disguise, grew within me. My physician visited me regularly. The first time he came to my home, I found a darkly handsome face smiling back at me, his black hair flecked with a tinge of grey. His kind dark brown eyes, and his self-deprecating Jewish sense of humour warmed me to him.

After numerous examinations, and consultations, Doctor Burstyn was finally able to reassure me. "That's a healthy, strong heartbeat," he said. "I have never before seen such strong will and determination like yours. Most of the pregnant women who consult me complain of weight gain, swollen ankles, and varicose veins."

I laughed. "I have cherished every minute of my confinement," I said. "I realise that this is my one and only chance to have a child."

He nodded. "You need to relax. The memories of the child you lost are making this pregnancy a time of anxiety when it should be a time of great joy."

"Doctor Burstyn, I have only reached this stage of my confinement because of you. I want to thank you for that."

"Please call me Abe," he said. "I feel that we have become good friends over the last few months. My wife died just over two years ago. Sadly, we were unable to have children. I have been alone ever since."

"I'm sorry to hear that, Abe. I must insist that you call me Nene."

"Thank you, Nene." He smiled at me gently. "The truth is I have fallen in love with you." He laughed. "I accept that you don't reciprocate my feelings. However, I want you to know that it doesn't matter to me. I can deal with this. I would like to offer you my hand in marriage, I am happy to accept you and the child."

"Your kind offer deeply touches me deeply," I said. "You are a lovely man, but sadly I have been here before with my late husband. That did not end well. But I would like us to remain friends. I truly value your friendship. In fact, I have come to depend upon it."

He smiled at me resignedly. "Thank you for being honest with me. You know where I am if you should ever change your mind. My proposal will stand. There is no time limit on my feelings."

"Thank you, Abe." I stood, kissing him on the cheek.

"I look forward to seeing you at our next appointment."

Exhilarated by the favourable prognosis, I took up my pen and wrote a long letter to Holmes, informing him of my confinement and the confrontation with Mycroft. But, although I waited anxiously for his reply, it was to be in vain.

Chapter Fifty: Irene Adler

A week after my father's funeral, my mind still in a haze, I found myself in the offices of Aboudi Hyde, accompanied by Estelle, for the reading of my father's last will and codicils. We were greeted at the entrance by my father's friend and attorney David Bateson, a middle-aged tall, imposing looking man with an engaging manner. He was dressed conservatively in a neat well-cut black suit. Mr Bateson shook hands with us, offering his condolences before inviting us into his office where we were seated on a brown leather Chesterfield settee. Mr Bateson stared at his papers for a moment as though deep in thought. Then, looking up at me with his clear blue eyes, he smiled.

"I'm delighted to say that the primary beneficiaries, Irene Adler and Estelle Conlin, are here with us this morning." He nodded to me. "Unfortunately, the other beneficiaries of your father's estate, your relatives in the Catskills, and your aunt Eileen Allen are unable to join us this morning. However, your uncle hopes to be able to catch up with you both soon."

"Over my dead body," I muttered to myself.

Having to be civil at the funeral for appearance's sake was hard enough as the encounter had brought back old memories that I wanted to forget.

David Bateson paused for a moment. "As for your aunt Eileen Allen, I am reliably informed that she is cruising around Egypt, so no message from her, I'm afraid."

"Just as well," I said, breathing a sigh of relief. "We have never seen eye to eye. She was the source of a great deal of conflict between my father and me in the past."

Mr Bateson read through the contents of my father's will, which was relatively straightforward. He had left five thousand dollars each to his brother, Aloysius, and Eileen Allen. In addition, his nephews Denis and Desmond would receive one thousand six hundred dollars, while Estelle was bequeathed two thousand dollars for her help and support over the years, which my father said went above and beyond the call of duty. He had left the rest of his estate with its advantages and disadvantages to his beloved daughter Irene Aerona Adler. Finally, an additional sum of ten thousand dollars was to accumulate in the hands of trustees to fund Alfred's grandchild's education and any other subsequent expenses. This would be at the discretion of Irene Adler, the sole executor of said trust.

"Are you all right, my dear?" Estelle asked as she squeezed my hand.

"Yes, I'm fine, Estelle. I'm so glad my father gave you the recognition you so rightly deserve. He would never have managed all these months without you, and neither would I."

"Thank you, Nene. That means a great deal to me. He was such a lovely man. I miss him so much."

"As do I, Estelle. I wasn't ready to lose him yet." I placed my hand on my stomach. "You know I really feel for this little one. He or she will never get to see their grandfather, and it appears unlikely they will ever see their own father. All the money in the world cannot compensate for that."

David Bateson smiled at me warmly before speaking. "The rest of your father's estate includes the house. Therefore, in addition to the money your father had in stocks and shares, and all his various holdings and investments, there will be a sum available to you of approximately twenty-five thousand dollars."

I collapsed in my chair, rendered speechless for a moment.

I stared back at Mr Bateson in disbelief. "I am shocked, Mr Bateson. I was always aware that my father was comfortable, but not to that extent!"

"Marianne left a substantial amount of money when she died, which your father inherited, of course. Alfred refused to touch any of it. With interest, it has accrued over such a long period. Your father left clear instructions that the money was to go to you and any subsequent grandchildren he may have at the time of his death."

Estelle and I stood and shook hands with Mr Bateson.

"Do you have any plans for your good fortune, Miss Adler?" He smiled at me curiously.

"Oh yes, indeed. I will be sure to put the money to good use. We bid you a good day, Mr Bateson."

Chapter Fifty-One: Irene Adler

The morning of the 11th of January, I was sitting quietly in the library reading the poetry of Thomas Moore. After a while, I put the book down on my knee. I could feel the baby kicking, so I placed my hand on my stomach. "Hey, I'm looking forward to meeting you," I whispered.

Laying my head back on the cushion and closing my eyes, I was immediately transported back to Fiesole. I could almost feel the sun on my face, the smell of the roses, and the intoxicating sweet smell of the grass in the fields. I could hear the swifts chirp, smell the familiar aroma of Sherlock's cologne, taste his lips on mine.

My thoughts took me back to the familiar sound of classical music playing on the gramophone, the vision of Holmes playing his violin naked, and how I missed our intimacy. I suddenly awoke from the fantasies playing in the theatre of my mind to feel a sharp pain in my side. I rang the bell. When Mary, the maid, arrived, I asked her to send for my cousin.

Estelle came in swiftly. "Are you all right, Nene?"

"I have this horrible pain." I grimaced. "Surely the baby cannot be coming yet?"

"Babies come when they are ready, Nene. It looks like today may well be the day." Estelle gave my hand a reassuring squeeze.

I sighed. "Do you think I'll be any good as a mother, Estelle? Do you think the baby will like me?"

"I think you will be an exceptional mother. Everyone likes you, my dear."

My waters broke the following afternoon. I was in labour for four hours. Estelle was by my side, holding my hand during each excruciating contraction which became more frequent. When I felt I could not endure any further pain, Estelle asked me to push. "Right, Nene, I can see the head. When the next contraction comes, I need you to push as hard as you can." The next contraction deftly arrived, along with the worst pain I had ever experienced, and I promised myself that if I got through this, I would never lie with a man again. I took a deep breath, did as Estelle asked, and gave an almighty push.

"The head is out, Nene. You're doing well," said Estelle. "I need you to give me one more push, but wait for the next contraction."

I looked at Estelle aghast. "I don't think I have enough strength to push again." I cried tears of frustration. Nothing had prepared me for such pain. It had ultimately slipped my mind that after pushing out the head, I would have to push again to free the baby's shoulders.

Estelle squeezed my hand tightly. "Come on, Nene, you can do this. Your baby's going to arrive any moment now."

I summoned all of my strength and gave one last push. The baby slid out, and there we were, mother and child, sweaty, slimy, exhausted, but happy.

Estelle cut the cord, after clamping it first, and then she beamed at me. "Congratulations, Nene, you just delivered a baby boy."

I breathed a sigh of relief as tears of joy streamed down my face. There was a deathly silence, no baby's cry.

I called out to Estelle. "He isn't crying! Why is my son silent?"

Estelle looked across at me with an ashen face. "I'm sorry, your baby isn't breathing."

I felt as though I was in a bad dream. Taking a deep breath,

I began to pray. "Please God, don't let my baby die. Take *me*, just don't let him die."

Then, out of the corner of my eye, as if in a trance. I could hardly bear to watch as Estelle picked up my baby. She threw cold water onto his face. Holding him by the legs, Estelle smacked him hard on the bottom . . . more silence. Then, finally, the shrill indignant cry of a baby, the unmistakable sound of life. Estelle gently washed the child before wrapping him up in a blanket while I watched anxiously.

"Is everything all right?" I asked.

Estelle gently placed the baby in my arms. "Here is your baby boy. He has a fine set of lungs on him, and everything is as it should be. Nene, you just need to get some rest."

"Thank you so much, that's the best directive I've ever had." I beamed at Estelle as she proceeded to deliver the placenta.

When I gazed down at my son, gone were all the negative feelings from my past. I remembered Harvey Walpole's words from our final consultation. "Present exultations thrive on the traumas of our past. They can only exist if we let them."

Estelle kissed me on the cheek. 'Nene, Just look at him, he's perfect. May I hold him?"

I passed my son to Estelle. She held the baby gently in her arms, gazing down at his beautiful little scrunched-up face. "Hello, young man. Welcome to Trenton." Estelle kissed the baby before passing him back to me.

"Have you decided on a name yet?"

"I'm not sure yet, although I do have a few ideas."

Estelle picked up her Kodak Box camera and took several snapshots of the baby while I counted my son's fingers and toes. I stared in wonder at his mop of soft downy black hair, the dimples in his chin, the long slender limbs. His tiny feet and hands, kicking aimlessly in the air. I gasped as he opened his lids, looking up at me with piercing eyes that reminded me of his father. I leaned in to kiss him, gasping in wonder at the sensation of his soft little hands touching my face. To me, a sweeter, better-looking child would be hard to imagine. I chuckled, recalling Violetta's words of wisdom when Francesco was born.

Glancing down at my son, I whispered to him softly, "Hello, precious little man. Welcome to the world. You and I are going to be fine. I promise to always keep you safe."

I held him to my breast and looked over at Estelle. "What day is this?" I asked.

"Why, it's Sunday. Your child was born on the Sabbath day. He is going to be bonny, blithe, good, and gay."

"Thank you, but I meant what date is this."

"It's the twelfth of January, of course."

"Thank you," I said, gazing lovingly at my son. "Well, little man. Maria Anka was right about you all along. You are a God-given gift born of great love, but I didn't need her to tell me that. Let's hope she was right about your father."

"Can I get you anything?" asked Estelle.

"No, thank you, I have everything I need right here."

Chapter Fifty-Two: Sherlock Holmes

I awoke from a troubled sleep and sharp pain in my stomach. Outside was cold and frosty. My limbs felt numb and chilled, yet I was sweating profusely. I rose from my bed and entered the drawing-room, glancing up at the clock on the wall which was striking eleven. Pouring a glass of water from the pitcher, I lit a cigarette before taking a sip.

Sitting in my chair by the fire, I was in a melancholy mood. All I could think about was the son I had lost nearly nineteen years ago. My eyes focused on the photograph of Nene, and I suddenly remembered why today's date, the 12th of January, had struck a chord in my memory, reminding me of how much I missed the engaging smile that never failed to get my attention. But, more than that, I missed her presence in my life. Glancing once more at the clock, I frowned. It had stopped at 11 o'clock. Wiping a tear from my eye, I rewound the clock, checking the time with my pocket watch, which said 11:30. Then, carefully stubbing out my cigarette in the ashtray, I retired to my bedroom.

Chapter Fifty-Three: Irene Adler

After my confinement, I returned home to Red Oaks. Settling into my new life with a newborn kept me busy. I tried not to think of Holmes as I was determined to get on with my life, but every now and then a memory would knock the wind from me . . . slow dancing to Wagner, the feel of his body beside mine as we slept. There was no escaping him. He was even there every time I looked into the eyes of our son.

Several months passed before I finally felt strong enough to deal with my father's personal effects. One fine spring morning, accompanied by Estella, we tentatively entered my father's bedroom, which had remained untouched since he died. We painstakingly sorted through his belongings, making two piles. The first was for clothes to go to charity and the poor, the second for any personal effects I wished to keep, including his watch chain and wedding ring. Estelle opened Father's ottoman, while I checked his bureau. I rummaged around to find a large leather wallet full of documents and old letters from my mother. I noticed a white envelope tucked away at the back of the wallet. Pulling it out, I at once recognized my own handwriting. The envelope was addressed to Sherlock Holmes. I stared at the faded envelope in disbelief before going through the rest of the papers. I gasped as yet another faded envelope fell out, only this time it was addressed to me and bore a London postmark.

I recognized Holmes's unmistakable handwriting and felt the room spin. "Estelle, why would my father do this to me?" I cried.

"To protect you, Nene. The last thing he wanted was for you to be hurt again. He was concerned you were going to have another breakdown."

"My father was set against Sherlock and me getting back together. He made me promise I would not pursue our relationship."

Estelle shook her head. She appeared close to tears. "Nene, there is something else you need to know. He came for you, Sherlock Holmes did."

I stared at Estelle. "What are you talking about? Sherlock would never come here. In his eyes I broke his trust, I betrayed him."

"He came at the end of May. You were at a doctor's appointment. I did not see him, but I overheard him talking to your father in his study. He said he came to Trenton because he was concerned for your welfare after receiving no response to his letter."

"The letter my father kept from me?" I said.

Estelle nodded. "Yes. I'm so sorry I didn't tell you earlier, but your father swore me to secrecy. He was so angry. He said the children and I would have to leave the house if you ever found out. I couldn't risk that." Estelle began to sob.

"It's all right, Estelle, don't get upset. I understand you were placed in an impossible position, but what happened between Sherlock and my father?"

"Your father told him you had met someone else. That you had no interest in pursuing your relationship with him. Your father turned him away and told him never to come back."

"What about Nicco? Did my father tell him of the child?" I asked.

"No, he had no idea, and your father never mentioned anything."

"Estelle, please forgive me. I need to be alone right now."

"Yes, of course, Nene. I'll watch over the baby. Take all the time you need. I am so sorry." Estelle embraced me before leaving the room.

I retreated to my bedroom, sitting at my desk. Then, I opened the envelope addressed to me from Sherlock Holmes with trembling hands. My heart was beating uncontrollably as my eyes absorbed the letter, the testament of an extraordinary human being. He explained how he had discovered Mycroft's card and came to understand why I felt compelled to leave him.

You must come back to me. I swear I will never again allow anyone to come between us.

I read the letter repeatedly, including a poem Holmes had written, which moved me to tears and went thus:

She is gone, yet this incomparable woman's very essence remains indelibly in my memory.

For where else in this universe am I to find beauty without conceit, courage without the want of recognition, friendship without envy, talent devoid of arrogance.

She loved unconditionally, with tenderness and empathy without jealousy.

She offered the air from her lungs to this wretched man who knew nothing of love until he found her.

She, who epitomised all that was good in humanity, eclipsed and predominated her whole sex.

My best friend, lover, and soul mate, there can be no other, Nene.

Then, finally, I picked up a pen and wrote a letter to Holmes, explaining how my father had intercepted our mutual correspondence. I sealed the envelope, enclosing a recent photograph of our son, running out of the house into the rain, to post the letter. I waited anxiously for several weeks, devastated when there was no response. The thought of going to my grave without seeing or hearing from Holmes ever again totally broke my heart, but I decided that I must carry on as best I could for the sake of my son. I was determined to be strong for him and build a new life for both of us.

Chapter Fifty-Four: Irene Adler

Three years later in 1899, having accepted a teaching position at La Scala, my son Nicco and I moved to Milan.

The six-bedroomed Georgian villa we lived in was light, airy, well-appointed, and set in two acres of immaculate cultivated gardens. With the assistance of Robert, Sophia, and the domestic servants, Nicco and I moved into the villa with minimum fuss.

My days burst into life as I found solace and joy in my role as a teacher. I also took on several private pupils in singing and piano. At my happiest when performing and interacting with the children, I now had the best of both worlds. With the assistance of Sophia and Violetta, I used some of my father's inheritance to set up a children's charity. I bought an abandoned church in the old town, and at the end of six months we had a new roof and kitchen. The interior had been replastered and decorated, and made into three separate school rooms with desks and chairs. We also had a separate dining room where the children were served a hot meal twice a day, offering respite to parents who were struggling financially. The three classrooms offered tuition in reading, writing, singing, and music. I was as proud of that achievement as anything else I'd ever done.

Ava Espirito was by now in her third year at La Scala, an outstanding pupil, widely tipped by the maestros to be the next principal Soprano at the prestigious opera house. In addition, Ava was the first recipient of the Alfred Adler bursary, the other charity I set up to assist musicians who would be unable to afford the fees. I was thrilled when Ava accepted my invitation to move into the villa. Violetta often visited, bringing her son Francesco, a welcome playmate for Nicco. The two boys became best friends.

In the middle of June, two weeks before Ava's debut performance, Violetta and Francesco arrived at the villa. In the gardens, the children played with my latest acquisitions, two beautiful Persian blue kittens. Nicco doted on them, solemnly naming them Junior and Miss Millie, much to Violetta's amusement. After lunch, the children asked if they could draw. Violetta and I sat on the lawn, watching over them while we drank coffee.

I glanced over her son's shoulder and took in a sharp intake of breath. Nicco had drawn two identical pictures of the sun. "What lovely pictures, Nicco. Tell me, did you draw these yourself? Are you sure you didn't hire a professional artist?" I laughed, observing Nicco's bemused expression, which reminded me so much of his father.

"Do not be silly, mamma. It was me, Nicco."

"Mamma was just teasing you, my darling. Was one of those for me?"

Nicco looked up at me, bright-eyed, happy with his exquisite little drawings. "Yes, mummy." Nicco handed me one of the drawings, smiling broadly.

He pointed to the second picture. "This one is for my daddy," he said proudly

"I'm sure he will love it," I whispered, smiling down at my son, tears stinging my eyes. I felt an overwhelming urge to scoop him up in my arms and hug him. I knew he would not like that one bit, so I put my arms around him, holding him closely.

"Mummy, too tight! "Nicco complained, wriggling from my grasp.

"I'm sorry." I kissed Nicco on the top of his head. "I love

you."

"I love you too, Mummy."

"You should be proud of yourself."

"Do you think my daddy would be proud of me?" asked Nicco, his wide-eyed expression focused on my face.

"Yes, I know he would be."

"Do you miss my daddy?" he quizzed.

"Yes, of course. If it hadn't been for your daddy, I wouldn't have you."

Nicco suddenly turned his attention to Francesco, who was knelt on the grass, digging up the soil. Francesco held out his hands and showed Nicco the worms wriggling on his palms, his chubby cheeks flushed with colour.

"Look Mummy. Francesco's found some worms," cried Nicco.

We encouraged the children onto the lawns to play hop-scotch and football and then into the bushes for hide and seek. Eventually Dara, the maid, came to collect the children to take them into the nursery for tea, leaving Violetta and me free to retire and change for dinner.

Chapter Fifty-Five: Irene Adler

Sophia arrived later that evening, joining us for pre-dinner drinks on the patio. I asked the maid to replenish the wine glasses before dismissing her.

"Ladies, may I have your attention. There is a matter I wish to discuss with you."

Violetta looked over at me with a concerned expression on her face. "What is it, Nene?"

I removed a letter from my handbag, placing it on my lap. "This is a letter from Sherlock Holmes. He wrote to me shortly after I left Fiesole. My father, unfortunately, intercepted the letter before I had a chance to read it. However, I would like to read some of it to you."

The ladies nodded in agreement. After reading the letter, I looked at my friends and said, "When I discovered Nicco's birth was likely to be viable, I wrote to Sherlock. I realised it was time to let him know."

"I take it you received no response?" said Violetta.

I shook my head. "No, Violetta. My father also intercepted my letter to Sherlock. But, do you see, this is the reason I heard nothing from him. He believes that I rejected him, not once, but twice. Any deception to Sherlock would be completely unacceptable. He could never forgive any deceit or betrayal." I paused for a moment. "But I feel that I must at least try for Nicco's sake."

Sophia glanced across at me, a look of grave concern etched upon her lovely face. "Nene, why are you dredging this up again after all this time? I'm sorry about your letters. Your father had no right to conceal them from you, God bless his soul. But to bring up Sherlock Holmes again after all this time, why it is madness. You are going to be hurt all over again. Why would you do it?"

"Because, Sophia, earlier this week my son looked me in the eyes and asked *why don't I see my daddy like the other children?* It broke my heart."

"And what did you tell him?"

"I told him the truth, of course. That his father lived in England, where he had a significant job helping people who were in trouble. Nicco is naturally curious. He doesn't understand why he cannot see his father." I sighed. "Sophia, this is why I need to try to contact Sherlock. I could not look Nicco in the eyes again if I didn't at least try. I don't want my son to suffer because of my personal failings."

"Nene, you know that I adore you." Sophia wrinkled her nose. "But I'm afraid you have a blind spot where that man is concerned. Sherlock Holmes cut you off like a decaying limb and never looked back. He may be married by now, or at least have another woman, although I have to say that he is rather an acquired taste. I fail to understand what attracted you to him in the first place."

Violetta flashed Sophia a look of disdain. "You may have met Sherlock Holmes, Sophia, but you never knew him. He is a man of conviction and principle, decisive, honest and smart. Honesty is such an underestimated trait in a man, don't you think? They seem like pretty good qualities to me."

"I didn't realise you were such an avid fan of his," said Sophia.

"I know a good man when I see one. He is also godfather to my son."

"Sherlock was unlike any other man I have ever known," I said. "He always told you the absolute naked truth, whether you were ready for it or not. And after all the bullshit from the other men in my life, I found that to be so refreshing. Don't get me wrong, being with him could be challenging at times. We had disagreements and debates just like any other couple. Our relationship was unusually intense, filled with passion and a deep abiding love for one another."

Sophia stared at me, aghast. "Nene, he was supposed to be protecting you, not seducing you."

"Well, let me tell you, Sophia, he managed to do both with considerable aplomb." The ladies burst into a peal of laughter. "I became a whetstone for his mind. I stimulated him mentally and physically. Neither of us set out looking for love, far from it. But it crept up on us unexpectedly."

Sophia stared at me hard. "I don't doubt that it was a serious love affair, Nene, but what about Nicco? That man must have a heart of stone to turn his back on his child."

I shook my head. "No, you're wrong, Sophia, and there will be no other woman. Sherlock may well have washed his hands of me. One can hardly abandon someone, travel halfway across the world, and then expect to pick up where you left off. There are few second chances in life. Sherlock would never turn his back on his son, of that I'm sure. He never replied to my last letter. I wrote to him again after Nicco was born and even sent him a photograph."

"And you still heard nothing from him?" said Sophia.

"No, not a word. I don't believe he even opened the envelope. I keep turning over in my mind the events that could have transpired and how Sherlock would address the situation. After much deliberation, I have deduced that there can only be two possible explanations. One, he destroyed the letter without opening it. The other is that he kept it without reading it. If I were a betting woman, that's the one I would go for. If he had read my letter, I would have heard from him by now. He is still angry with me for leaving Fiesole and is blissfully unaware that it took everything I had to close the door on our relationship. Still, of course, I have no way of knowing. That is mere speculation." I paused for a moment. "There is one thing I can do to get his undivided attention, another way to reach him."

Sophia stared at me, aghast, shaking her head.

I frowned. "Oh Sophia, I know that look. You're looking at me askance, please don't do that."

Sophia slowly sipped from her glass, her eyes narrowed. "For god's sake, Nene, there is a fine line between love and madness. But please tell me you will not travel to London to see this man. I find your dismissal of him having no other woman to be naive and fanciful. You couldn't possibly know that."

Violetta held up her hand, interrupting the conversation. "Sophia, Nene is right. If I had not seen how they interacted together with my own eyes, I would never have believed it. I have never seen Sherlock look at anyone the way he looked at Nene." Violetta glanced over at me, smiling affectionately, before continuing. "It was obvious he was deeply in love with you, Nene. No, it's not arrogance. Call it women's intuition."

I smiled at Violetta. "Don't worry, Sophia. I have no intentions of returning to the gloomy ruthless streets of London. God, how I hate that place. I would not travel all that way to be unsure of a welcome. But go I would if I thought for one second that Sherlock would see me."

"But, why him?" Sophia exclaimed. "You've become fixated on this man. Look in the mirror. You are stunning, witty and bright . . . the funniest person I have ever met. You could have any man you want."

I glared at Sophia, arching an eyebrow almost to the point of snapping. "You have no idea how many times in my life I've heard that expression, Sophia. Sherlock was the only man who ever saw me as a person in my own right. He's not a gargoyle made of stone. He's human, just like you and me. I'm aware that you find him cold, standoffish, and aloof. And yes, of course, he can be all of those things. But that is not the true measure of the man. He is also clever, complicated, kind, and compassionate, and so powerfully full of life."

Sophia looked at me with an exasperated expression. "You must try not to allow him to consume you like this, Nene. I love you like a sister, and I know I can say anything to you, so please believe me when I tell you that he's never coming back. Those embers are never going to flame up again. You need to accept that."

I shook my head and glared at Sophia defiantly. "I don't want to reunite with him, Sophia. That ship has long sailed. I've managed to build a new life, and with the help of you and my wonderful friends, I am finally moving forward. I love my job. I love working with the little ones, especially the underprivileged children I help with my charities. But, that said, I still need to get in touch with Sherlock. He must see his son. He deserves that at least. Sherlock said something to me while we were on the train to Florence that gave me an idea. Ladies, the answer to my quest lies in the gossip columns of the Times and the Telegraph."

The ladies stared at me with bemused expressions. I returned their gaze, giddy with excitement. "What will Mr Holmes most look forward to every morning? Why, the arrival of his newspapers, of course. He scans the gossip columns religiously every day."

Sophia raised an eyebrow, a smirk replacing her frown of suspicion. "Hmm, he sounds like a real catch. Why does he read them?"

"Oh Sophia, for reasons too tangled to go into just now, I'll explain to you later over dinner." I smiled at the ladies. "I am determined to send him a message. Incognito, of course, but he will be aware it's from me. Sherlock rarely plays games, so if I want to get his attention, I must use words. The gossip columns are the ideal vessel, but of course, I must be careful how I word my message. It cannot be so direct that others would notice. The press would have a field day if they discovered Nicco was Sherlock's son. I have no wish to embarrass him."

Sophia turned to me aghast. "Embarrassed, Nene? My God, you were the one left holding the baby. Would it not just have been easier to have told him about the child when you were in Fiesole?"

"Sophia, I didn't know if my baby would live or die at that stage. You're aware of my medical condition. I had to protect Sherlock and my child. I was, in truth, about to tell him. Then I received a visit from his brother, the formidable Mycroft Holmes, warning me that I would be putting all our lives at risk if I returned to England with Sherlock and continued our relationship. Mycroft gave me no choice. Of course, I couldn't tell Sherlock then. I had to leave Fiesole to protect him and Nicco. When I received the news that Nicco's birth was likely to be viable, I knew then that I must tell him. It was the right thing for Sherlock *and* my son. I don't want Nicco to live a life of subterfuge and deception. He deserves to know the truth."

I glanced around the patio at my friends and stood, refilling their glasses with wine. I raised my glass. "A toast, ladies. To my calamitous history. Let's drink to fate, let the chips fall where they may."

Sophia and Violetta raised their glasses. "To fate!"

"Ladies," I continued. "I understand I must be driving you to distraction, but at least this way I will have closure. All I want is for Sherlock to acknowledge his son. I realise that this must be hard for you all to comprehend, but I promise you this—if nothing comes of my advert, I will never again mention his name."

"Can we have that in writing, please?" quipped Sophia. She rolled her eyes at me, which sent us into fits of laughter.

"Ladies," I said. "We're going to change the subject now to something far more light-hearted, I promise. Did I mention that I had a secret admirer?"

Sophia laughed. "You've kept that quiet. Who is he?"

"My physician from New Jersey, Abe Burstyn. He has professed his undying love for me on several occasions. He's a lovely man, a widower. Abe asked me to marry him before Nicco was born. I turned him down, of course. But now, he has become quite a friend. He is travelling to Italy for a vacation to tour the lakes. He asked if he could take me out to dinner after the performance at La Scala and I said yes, of course. I only hope he isn't going to propose again!" I rolled my eyes in mock humour.

Sophia flashed me a knowing look. "Well, we shall all look forward to meeting the elusive Doctor Burstyn. But, hmm, what a coincidence that he's coming to see you on your birthday. How romantic. Are we not to be invited to this birthday soiree, or would we be in the way?"

"No, not at all," I said. "The more people, the merrier as far as I'm concerned. I want to avoid any awkward moments at all costs." Sophia and Violetta stared at each other with perplexed expressions.

"Where is Dr Burstyn taking you to dinner?" asked Violetta.

"Lafayette, I believe. Why? Would you like to join us?"

A look of relief appeared on Sophia's face. She made a silent gesture to Violetta.

"What am I missing here, ladies? What's going on?" I quizzed.

Sophia looked at me sheepishly. "You need to know that Lafayette already has a reservation for your birthday dinner. It was meant to be a surprise."

"What a lovely gesture, ladies. Thank you very much indeed," I said, overcome for a moment with emotion.

"Heavens, we're going to have quite a reunion. At least I won't have to be alone with Abe. I'm sure he'll understand when I explain the situation to him."

"Would it be so bad if Doctor Burstyn proposed to you again? He sounds like a decent man. He may be fretting for you," said Sophia.

"Yes, he may well be Sophia, but I only love him as a friend. Although I am very fond of him, I've always made that abundantly clear."

"Yet he still pursues you. He appears smitten. Are you certain you could not consider him as a husband?" A mischievous expression appeared on Sophia's face.

"Sophia, I have already married someone I was not in love with. Look how well that ended. Anyway, I couldn't marry him even if I wanted to."

Sophia looked at me suspiciously. "Why ever not?"

"A promise I made. It's complicated."

"It always is with you, my dear."

I turned my attention to Violetta. "You must be looking forward to Ava's debut at La Scala. I've been listening to her at rehearsals, and my god, her vocal interpretation is magnificent. You have quite a treat in store. Is Ludo still coming?"

"Yes, of course," said Violetta. "He wouldn't miss it for the world, not his little girl."

Sophia glanced over at Violetta. "Robert has organised a private box for you and Ludo as a special surprise, but please don't tell him I told you."

"Thank you so much, Sophia." Violetta nodded. "I really appreciate it. You and Robert have been all kindness itself to Ava. My brother-in-law has been in touch with me recently and would love to come and hear Ava sing. Is it possible he could join us in the private box? We haven't seen him for several years, so it would be a real family reunion. He has no living siblings and his parents died years ago. We're the only family he has left."

"That is not a problem," said Sophia. "I will arrange it myself. There will be ample room."

"Thank you," said Violetta. "I won't mention anything to Ava just in case he doesn't turn up. He's a lovely man, but not the most reliable of people. I would hate for Ava to be disappointed. They were extremely close."

I interrupted the conversation. "Listen to me, ladies. I have a macabre tale for you. I don't think I've ever told you this before, Violetta, but Gabriella Anka's sister Maria predicted the birth of Nicco. She approached me at your anniversary supper. She said she was the seventh sister of a seventh sister, whatever that means. She told me the exact date and time Nicco was born. Do you not find that spooky?"

"Nene, it's true that Gabriella had six sisters, but if you had been speaking to Maria, you would have needed a shovel." Violetta stared at me oddly. "Maria was Gabriella's youngest sister. She passed away over five years ago. She was a seer, a shamanistic visionary. I laughed when she told me I would have a son. Ludo and I had given up all hope after so many years. I rather impudently asked her how she knew, and Maria told me that what she saw engulfed her. It is well documented in Fiesole that Maria had the gift of second sight. She was very godly, very devout. It is said that she sometimes appears in spirit, but only to those in need of her help."

I looked at Violetta's askance. "I don't believe it." I gasped.

"Perhaps it was someone playing a trick," said Violetta. "Yes, it must be. There can be no other possible explanation."

"Well, whoever it was, whether ghost or a trickster, her predictions have been strangely accurate. She even knew about Moriarty."

"What else did Maria say to you?"

"She spoke of the father of my unborn child," I said softly, almost in a whisper. "She said our souls hovered in flight, and he would cross over the water to find me."

"Well, she got that prediction wrong," said Sophia.

Ava entered the room attired in a stunning olive-green dress, her hair pinioned with hair grips. She broke into a wide grin upon seeing her mama and friends.

"Good evening, ladies. I've been asked to inform you that dinner is to be served in ten minutes." Ava glanced over at me. "Don't worry, Nene, the children are bathed and tucked up in bed and have said their prayers. I read them a nursery rhyme, although Nicco insisted on interrupting halfway through and narrating it himself."

"That little boy's genius is no accident," interrupted Violetta, looking knowingly at me. "That child had learned the alphabet by the time he was fourteen months old. He's always asking for new books. And he can identify every single dinosaur from that encyclopaedia I bought him."

"Yes, he loves to read about dinosaurs" I laughed. "I'm well aware of where his genius comes from. I felt life was such a blessing when Nicco was born. That little boy is my entire world. When I began to teach the younger children, Nicco would watch, and one day he asked if he could play the pianoforte. Of course, I agreed to teach him, but it was never with any assumption that he possessed any aptitude until the other children started to comment on how talented he was. I will always strive to be supportive and encouraging in anything Nicco wants to do, but most of all I want my son to grow up understanding that his happiness is what matters to me."

Sophia smiled at me. "I must admit there's a skip in your step these days that I hadn't seen in a long time. A newfound *joie de vivre*. What you have achieved with your charities in such a short time is phenomenal. You deserve to be happy again. There is no question that you're a wonderful mother, Nene. However, Nicco is exceptional for his age. You should have him tested and sent to a special school. They'll be able to provide private tutors who can channel his intellect."

I shook my head. "There will be no testing or special school, Sophia. I don't want my son to be singled out and made to feel different at such a tender age. Nicco will be home-schooled for now, until he is older, then I will see what he wants to do. I want to give my son the best possible childhood and be the best mother I can be."

"Well, the boy genius is now happily ensconced in the nursery with my brother, sleeping like little angels. They're the best of friends, those two. Inseparable," said Ava.

"Some angels!" Violetta rolled her eyes.

The gong sounded to announce dinner. I smiled warmly at my friends. "Come, ladies, let's go in. The wine has given me quite an appetite."

Sophia and Ava entered the dining room. Violetta held back for a moment. She approached me and took my arm, a concerned expression upon her face. "You have had a hard time these past few years, Nene. You must get lonely."

"Yes, I sometimes do, Violetta. But you know I have my little man to comfort me. And teaching the children, especially the younger ones, has brought some much-needed normality and focus into my life. I realise I have much to be thankful for."

Violetta nodded in agreement. "I don't believe we ever get over those who are special or memorable to us. Some people are not meant to be forgotten. You and Sherlock have an unbreakable bond. You understand each other." Violetta smiled, taking my hand in hers. "To understand all is to forgive all. I truly believe that you will see him again one day. I know that Sophia disapproves, but speaking as a mother, I think that you're right to pursue Sherlock. You should do everything you can to make peace with him. But most of all, Nene, you have to make peace and forgive yourself. For your own sake and Nicco's, I hope you finally allow yourself some happiness. Would you like me to write to him?"

"Good god, no, thank you, Violetta," I said, taken aback for a moment by Violetta's gesture. "I love you for offering, though. But I cannot allow you to get embroiled in the mess that is my life. Anyway, Sherlock would not be impressed if I tried to reach him through a third party. He would consider that rude. But at least you're well-intentioned, thank you."

Violetta stared at me curiously. "Do you regret meeting him?"

"No, I don't regret it." I shook my head. "Sherlock and I are responsible for bringing a beautiful boy into the world. I will treasure forever the time we spent together and the memories we made. Our relationship cut deep, it was bittersweet, and I miss him."

"And if you receive a reply from your message, and it's not the answer you're looking for, what then?"

"Then it will be over." I shrugged. "But at least I will have known love with a man who has no equal. How many can say that?" I gazed into Violetta's eyes, smiling at her through tears. "From all the sad words of tongue and pen, the saddest are these, it might have been. Come, Violetta, we must not be late for dinner, or we will not hear the end of it from Sophia."

I had composed my adverts and signed two cheques for the Times and the Telegraph well before breakfast. I ran out of the villa to post the envelopes, ensuring I was in time to catch the early morning collection. I was happy in the knowledge that my adverts would appear in the Times and the Telegraph in ten days.

Chapter Fifty-Six: Sherlock Holmes

Watson and I enjoyed a lazy morning relaxing in bachelor comfort in the lounge at Baker Street. I was, as usual, ensconced in my morning papers.

Watson glanced across to me as he lit his pipe. "Holmes, were you aware Irene Adler has returned to Milan? Good for her, I say. I received a letter from Moon only yesterday. Miss Adler has secured a position teaching as well as performing at La Scala. The Moons' helped her secure a villa close to the theatre where she lives with her son. I wasn't aware that Irene Adler had any children, were you?"

Looking up from my newspaper, I glanced over at Watson. Trying to maintain an expression of nonchalance, I shrugged in a desperate attempt to hide my shock.

"Apart from the child, does she live there alone?" I casually asked, appearing ensconced in my newspaper.

"Hmm, according to Moon, a friend Ava, a talented student at La Scala, has recently moved in with Miss Adler, no doubt for companionship. But surely there must be some chap on the scene if she has a child?"

"A son, you say. How old is the boy?"

"Why, he's three years old."

I hesitated, struggling to keep my composure. "And pray, what is this child's name?"

Watson glanced over at me, bemused by my sudden interest in matters which would not usually concern me. "His name is Niccolo, although his mother calls him Nicco." Watson chuckled. "That is an unusual name, Holmes. It sounds familiar. Now where have I heard it before?"

I closed my eyes for a moment, taking a breath. "Paganini, the celebrated virtuoso. You've heard me mention him on numerous occasions, Niccolo was his Christian name."

"Yes, I remember now, of course. He played the violin. Hmm, Miss Adler must have met the boy's father just after she returned from Fiesole. I keep saying it's a small world, Holmes."

"It is indeed, Watson."

Watson stared at me curiously. "Tell me, why the sudden interest in Irene Adler and her child? It's unlike you, Holmes, to delve into people's private lives. You refused to let me write about her adventures in my chronicles. However, you offered no reasonable explanation at the time."

"You know my methods by now, Watson. It's all about data for future reference, nothing more, nothing less. I'm glad you had not forgotten Miss Adler was once . . . ." I paused for a moment. "She was once a client. Miss Adler asked for anonymity after the case, and this was why she can never feature in your chronicles. We must respect her privacy. I hope I have made myself clear, Watson."

Watson glanced across at me with a look of concern. "You are looking a little peaky, Holmes. Are you sure you're not coming down with something?"

I picked up my Inverness and cap. "I'm not ill, Watson. I need some fresh air. Come, let's go out for a walk."

Chapter Fifty-Seven: Sherlock Holmes

I rose early the following morning and took a cab to Victoria Station in order to book my ticket to Milano Centrale. I was desperate to get there, to find Nene and my son as soon as possible. Frustratingly, as it was the holiday season, the earliest passage I could secure was the day after next. I walked back to Baker Street, where I had breakfast alone. I was musing at the breakfast table when Mrs Hudson entered the room to deliver the newspapers. I picked up the Times, scanning the gossip column, scribbling random notes with the pen Nene had presented to me. My eyes kept diverting to one particular advert. I sat up alertly in my chair. Removing my pipe from my lips, I read the advert.

Still a long way from your hill of Calvary. I would implore you to read my latest correspondence. There you will find data of the utmost importance, all will become clear.

Yours,

the stubborn one.

I sat for a while, collapsed in my chair. The advert had left me in a state of profound agitation. "Clever, very clever, Nene," I muttered. "Endeavouring to establish true concord between us."

I sat for several minutes in deep contemplation. Eventually, I rose from my chair and opened my strongbox, tentatively removing the unopened envelopes from Nene and placing them on my knee. Then, reaching for the brass letter opener on the table beside me, I carefully opened the envelopes. I read a passage from Nene's first letter informing me of her pregnancy and the altercation with Mycroft, professing her deep abiding love for me.

The intensity of my feelings for you scares me sometimes. Yet, wherever I am, whatever I do, your presence never leaves me.

My eyes were continually drawn back to one particular sentence.

The skin on my stomach flutters like a butterfly, each little tumbling motion an incredible miracle.

I turned over the picture enclosed with Nene's second letter. It was a photograph of a newborn, my secret child. I studied it carefully. My son's magnetic eyes stared back at me. I re-read Nene's letters once more. At the bottom of the page on the second letter, next to her signature, was a carbon impression of our son's footprint, his Christian name printed alongside it. A postscript from Nene went as follows:

I want you to know that not a day goes by when I don't speak to our son of his father. He's like you, Sherlock. Curious about everything. The things I've taught him, I learned them all from you.

Then, I remembered the words Nene had spoken to me, of forgiveness, and I felt ashamed.

I took in a sharp intake of breath once again, taking in my son's Christian name, the name Nene had chosen for him. A single tear rolled down my cheek.

Chapter Fifty-Eight: Sherlock Holmes

I dined alone at Baker Street that evening and had just finished packing my valise when Mrs Hudson came in to collect the tray.

"Thank you, Mrs Hudson. Dinner was delicious. You have quite surpassed yourself this evening." I gestured towards the armchair next to the fire. "Would you please take a seat for a moment? There is a pressing matter that I wish to discuss with you."

Mrs Hudson stared at me in surprise but did as I asked. She smoothed down her black cotton dress, pushing her grey hair under her bonnet, taking a seat across from me next to the fire

"Let's have a drink, Mrs Hudson." I rose briskly from my chair. "I'll get it. Would a dry sherry be acceptable?"

"That's very kind of you, Mr Holmes." She smiled, accepting the glass of sherry.

I sat down across from her, a glass of port in hand and raised my glass. "To your excellent health, Mrs Hudson."

"Thank you, Mr Holmes, and the same to you." She looked at me anxiously. "Was there something in particular that you wanted to talk to me about?"

"Yes, indeed." I nodded. "It is rather a delicate matter."

Mrs Hudson shuffled on her feet. It was unlike me to invite her for drinks and clandestine conversation.

"I see," she said. "Is it something you could discuss with Dr Watson, perhaps?"

"No, Mrs Hudson. What I am about to tell you no one else can ever know, especially Watson, and this conversation can never leave this room. Do you understand?"

She nodded, taken aback.

"A little over four years ago, I embarked on a personal relationship with a young lady."

She stared at me, a startled expression upon her face. "Goodness me, I am shocked. You certainly kept that quiet."

"The liaison took place when I was in Florence." I pointed to the mantelpiece, towards the photo of Irene Adler. "This is the lady in question."

Mrs Hudson's jaw fell open as she stared at the photograph on the mantelpiece, the picture she polished every morning. "You were in a relationship with Irene Adler? The opera singer?" She shook her head in disbelief.

"Surely it's not that difficult to comprehend?"

"Oh no, Mr Holmes, it's not that. You've taken me completely by surprise, that's all. I have never known you to be involved with a young lady before, not in a romantic way."

"That's a fair comment, Mrs Hudson. But, you know, I can hardly believe it happened myself. It suffices to say that outside influences clouded her judgement. Otherwise, we would still be together. We subsequently wrote to each other, but unfortunately our correspondence was cruelly intercepted. That deception has only recently come to my attention." I shrugged. "And now I am at a loss as to what to do."

"Goodness, Mr Holmes, such a tragic story. Why you and Miss Adler are star crossed lovers, just like Shakespeare's Romeo and Juliet."

I smiled at her dryly. "I wouldn't go quite that far. We all know how that story ended. But there is an additional complication. I recently discovered Irene Adler gave birth to a child." I removed the photo of my son from my desk drawer and handed it to her. "This is my son, Niccolo. What do you think of him?" I stared at her keenly, trying to gauge her reaction.

Mrs Hudson stared at the photo, a look of astonishment on her face. "What a fine boy he is, Mr Holmes. You are fortunate to have such a child. He looks like you, he does. He has your eyes."

I smiled softly at the housekeeper. "Yes, I believe he does. Thank you, Mrs Hudson. Tell me, what would you suggest I do? I would appreciate a woman's perspective. You're the only one I can trust."

Smiling at me, her cheeks flushed with colour. "That's very kind of you to say so, Mr Holmes. I'm flattered that you feel able to confide in me."

"I don't believe that took too much effort on my part."

She stared at me hard. "Do you still love this woman?"

I paused for a moment. "Yes," I said. "I believe I do."

"Then you have answered your own question. It's evident to me that you love your son, even if you have not yet met him. I can tell from the way you looked at him in that photograph. If you care for them as much as you say you do, then you have no choice. You have to fight for them. Even if you face rejection. Otherwise, their loss will burn within you until the day you die. My husband and I became estranged before we had a chance to have children, but I know if we had I would have done anything for them."

"I believe you're right." I nodded in agreement. "You know, Irene Adler told me once it was possible to miss someone you never met. I was sceptical at the time, but she was right, of course. She was right about everything. I have to find them, I need to make things right and be a father to my son. Although I'm unsure what kind of reception to expect. Nene has been let down by men for most of her life and I made her a promise, and if Sherlock Holmes cannot keep his word, then what is left? I want to thank you for your advice, Mrs Hudson, and for being my confidante."

"You are more than welcome, Mr Holmes. And I promise you I will never speak to a living soul of what you have just told me. I will take your secret to the grave. But what will you do now?"

"I've already made plans to travel to Milan. I would have gone today, but the earliest passage I could secure was the day after tomorrow. But before I embark upon my journey, there is someone I need to speak to."

"Shall I bring you up a glass of milk and some biscuits?"

I beamed at her. "That would be most agreeable. Thank you, Mrs Hudson."

Chapter Fifty-Nine: Sherlock Holmes

The following day, before noon, I arrived in a hansom at the Diogenes Club in Pall Mall. I jumped out of the cab and knocked on the door with my cane. The chief steward, John Rochford, silently escorted me into the inner sanctum of the stranger's room to await my brother. I paced up and down like a caged animal until my brother eventually entered the room.

Mycroft nodded to me, taking a seat in a comfortable-looking leather armchair. The steward came in with a tray containing two glasses of port which he placed on the table before leaving the room, quietly closing the door behind him. Mycroft handed one of the glasses to me which I reluctantly accepted.

"Please take a seat, Sherlock."

"I prefer to stand if it's all the same to you, Mycroft."

"Well, Sherlock, you appear a little paler than usual. I can see that you've lost a little weight since our last encounter. Five pounds, I would fancy."

"Four."

"You're troubled by insomnia, and I see you intend to travel abroad quite soon."

"I am in no mood for banter today, Mycroft. Although you are, of course, quite correct on all three counts. Insomnia has troubled me for some time. And of course, we both know the reason for that. You are solely responsible for the fact that I've never seen my son. You have kept him from me, my own flesh and blood. If I did not know you better, I would suspect you were jealous that I have a child and have found someone to share my life with. You have no idea how difficult that was. By God, Mycroft, our mother would have been ashamed of you. The fact that you're capable of casting out her grandson—your nephew. Have you any idea how much harm you have caused? The lives you have affected?"

Mycroft shook his head. "Blame me, why don't you?"

"Oh, I do blame you, Mycroft!"

"Come, Sherlock, enough of the dramatics. You need to think about this logically. What use would a woman and child be to you? Why, they would be a hindrance to what you were born to do. You can rant all you like, but you know deep down that I speak the truth. People like us don't have normal relationships."

"If our mother had that mentality, then neither of us would have been born. She found love, managed to combine the two with considerable aplomb. And let's face facts, her genius was far superior to ours."

"Yes, you're right. I'll give you that." Mycroft nodded in agreement. "But then our mother was a remarkable woman. You must have known that you couldn't hold onto a prize like Irene Adler. You would not be the first man to have his judgement melted by the face of a pretty woman."

I flashed my brother a contemptuous look. "If you think I was only interested in Irene Adler because of the way she looked, then you don't know me at all. Nene was beautiful, all right, but she was much more than that to me. She's also the mother of my child!"

Mycroft laughed softly. "Sherlock, the boy is hardly running barefoot through the streets of London with the Baker Street Irregulars. Do you not think it best to leave well enough alone? Can you really see yourself living your life through the prism of fatherhood? I think not, my dear brother. I understand Miss Adler is an exceptional mother. And as for the boy, well, he is remarkable. as smart as a whip by all accounts. If you're concerned because the child is illegitimate, then remove such concerns from your mind. We are living in the age of transition. The spirit of the world is changing. Your son is not the first and he will not be the last child to be born out of wedlock. It certainly didn't do William the Conqueror any harm." Mycroft drew on his cigarette.

I glared at my brother, barely suppressing the rage that tensed my jaw. "You show not one modicum of respect, Mycroft. With your condescending attitude, you dared to have Irene Adler monitored. Why, it's outrageous!"

"I am not completely heartless, Sherlock. I wrote to Irene Adler on several occasions offering financial support, and she returned my letters and cheques. You don't know me as well as you might think."

"Your behaviour in this matter has been utterly contemptible, Mycroft. Please don't judge me by your inadequacies."

"Be careful what you wish for, Sherlock. There's always a price to pay for happiness, which is inevitably short-lived. However, I must say that I'm surprised that you intend to pursue this woman and her child. A lot of dirty water will have flowed under the old bridge. A great deal will have happened after all this time." Mycroft stared at me curiously.

"You don't get it, do you?" He scoffed. "You cannot handle the fact that Irene Adler rejected you. In your mind's eye, loyalty has a breaking point . . . and you refuse to see the facts for what they are. Irene Adler did not forsake you. She left Fiesole to protect you and the child. Her sacrifice was the highest mark of love. My point is, my dear Sherlock, the story cannot always be about you."

"Yes, she felt compelled to leave me, but only under duress from *you*, Mycroft."

"I merely pointed out the risks, the decision was entirely her own, I can assure you." Mycroft raised his glass. "A toast, Sherlock. To water under the bridge."

Staring at my brother, I raised my glass, as he continued his narrative.

"I begrudgingly admit that your ex-fiancée is an exceptional woman. I can see why you were attracted to her. And to give credit where it's due, she has never revealed the identity of her son's father to the press, despite being under considerable pressure to do so."

I glared at my brother with contempt. "Nene would never reveal anything to the press. That's the last thing she would do. She despises them. I loved her and I'm not ashamed to say it. She will remain forever in my memory as the most remarkable of women."

Mycroft shook his head, a pained expression on his face. "The best thing you can do for this woman and her child is to leave them be, where they will be safe. You must not put the child at risk. Do you understand me, Sherlock? The boy has never been in danger, and I saw to that. Don't go making waves, brother."

I stared at Mycroft in disbelief. "You are no brother of mine, Mycroft. I can never forgive you for this. Why, I can hardly bear to look at you. If it were not for the fact that we are unfortunately related, I would thrash you to within an inch of your life!" I walked over to the door then turned back to confront my brother. "Oh, by the way, Mycroft, you are not nearly quite as clever as you might imagine." I smiled at him sardonically.

Mycroft arched an eyebrow, staring at me suspiciously. The glass of port he had been holding fell from his hands onto the marble floor, shattering into pieces. Mycroft recoiled in his seat, appearing just as horrified by the noise of the broken glass as my narrative. Any noise was indeed a grave offence at the Diogenes Club, with its strict rules and emphasis on exclusivity. No talking was allowed under any circumstances outside the stranger's room. There would be grave repercussions if the incident came to the committee's attention. Mycroft would have a lot of explaining to do.

Before Mycroft had a chance to respond. I stormed out of the room, slamming the door behind me. I walked down the corridor. Passed the sign demanding *Silence at all times*. Brandished my cane and banged it along the wall as I walked out of the building.

The following morning, I received a wire from my brother notifying me of Irene Adler's address in Milan, imploring me not to put his nephew at risk.

If you insist on pursuing this woman then there may be a solution to keep everyone safe. However you're not going to like it. If it's going to work, we need to act quickly. My dear brother, you must speak to me before you travel to Milan and do something that you may well regret.

"Hmmm, too little too late, Mycroft," I muttered, shaking my head in disbelief. I scribbled down Irene's address, throwing the telegram into a bin.

Chapter Sixty: Irene Adler

The scene was La Scala on Friday morning, the first of July. Although it was the day of Ava Espirito's debut performance, the notices are all out that there would be a special guest appearance by yours truly, the acclaimed contralto Irene Adler.

There was a knock on my dressing room door. Robert Moon appeared in the doorway. "I'm sorry to bother you, Nene, but the press is here, asking for an interview."

"Who is it this time, Robert?"

"It's Mateo Madini. Should I send him away?"

I shook my head. "It's all right, Robert. Can you give me a couple of minutes and then send him in, please?"

Robert left the room, closing the door behind him. I composed myself. I rarely granted interviews with reporters. As far as I was concerned, they were all parasites. And yet a part of me hoped Holmes might read the article. A few minutes later, there came a knock at the door.

"Come in."

Mateo Madini entered the room. He was a tall, pale-faced man in a dark coat, in his later forties with piercing brown eyes. His dark brown hair was going a little grey around the temples. I was aware Madini always had a little tenderness for me, feelings I never reciprocated. I shook hands with Madini, inviting him to take a seat. Glancing at me nervously, he placed a bouquet on the table. I acknowledged the gesture with a silent nod.

"Miss Adler, first of all, I would like to thank you for

granting me this interview."

"It will be a short one, Mr Madini. I rarely speak to the press, as you are aware."

"I am. Everyone is looking forward to your appearance this evening. How do you feel about performing once again in this legendary theatre?"

"It's my great pleasure, Signor Madini. La Scala is by far my favourite opera house. However, I'm also looking forward to the debut of my protégé, Miss Ava. She's the one you really should be interviewing."

"Yes, we understand that you have been instrumental in the nurturing of that talent."

"I have known Ava since she started, but it's the maestros at La Scala who are responsible for her remarkable progress. She has much to thank them for."

"May I ask about your future plans?"

"I intend to stay in Milan and teach at the theatre school. I have my charity work to keep me busy, and I hope to make more appearances on stage. Well, if that is all, Signor Madini, I must be getting on." I gestured towards the door. "Oh, please be sure to thank your editor for the flowers."

"Oh, they are not from my newspaper. The flowers are from me, Miss Adle. A token of my ardent admiration. I wonder if you would allow me the honour of taking you to dinner one evening? I believe we have much in common."

"Oh, I do hope not!" I replied, shaking my head. "I'm sorry, but I have a very tight schedule and have plans to meet with friends this evening. Other than that, I'm afraid I don't have time to go to dinner with you. Or anyone else, for that matter."

Madini glared at me, clearly rattled by my reply, his cheeks flushed with anger. "Well, yes, I suppose you are busy with your son. What did you say his name was again?"

"I didn't."

Madini stared at me, his dark eyes narrowed. "You never divulged the identity of your child's father. Rumours abounded, of course. There has been a great deal of consternation amongst our readers. Would you now like to take this opportunity to reveal who he is? I am simply allowing you to put forward your side of the story. Until then, as far as our readers are concerned, your boy will merely be the natural child of an opera singer. Assuming, of course, you know who the father is."

I glared at him, my cheeks pink with rage. "You have all the morals of a back street journalist, Madini. Life is far too short for long-term grudges, but I'm prepared to make an exception in your case. As for my son, he is not fodder for your unscrupulous editor. I'm sure you must have more pressing things to deal with than second-guessing the lineage of an innocent child. The identity of my son's father is none of your damned business. And I would like you to get the hell out of my dressing room. Should you dare to print even one derogatory word about my son, or insult him in any way, you and your editor will be dealing with my lawyer, you perfidious little man." I glared at Madini defiantly, my eyes flashing with anger.

Robert Moon suddenly appeared in the doorway, his brow furrowed. "Is this man disturbing you, Nene?" He looked at me anxiously.

"Thank you, Robert." I nodded. "Signor Madini was just leaving. Would you mind showing him out?"

Robert accompanied Madini out of the dressing room. Madini paused for a moment as he edged towards the door. "Perhaps another time, Miss Adler. I won't give up, you know, I intend to make you mine one day and I'm prepared to wait. But, in the meantime, I sincerely apologise if I have offended you in any way. I wouldn't want you to think any less of me."

I stared at him in disbelief. "I doubt that's possible, Madini, and you can stop waiting for me. I wouldn't consider marrying you even if you were the last man on earth."

Madini gave me a defiant nod. "Well, I shall take that as a maybe. I like a challenge." He laughed nervously before both men left the room, closing the door behind them.

I picked up the flowers and threw them into the bin. Sighing deeply, I wished Sherlock was with me, the only man apart from my father who'd ever been capable of calming, protecting, and reassuring me.

Chapter Sixty-One: Irene Adler

Later that evening, my dressing room was alive with chatter and laughter. I wore a low-cut gold lame evening gown with a sweeping train. My hair was dressed in an arrangement of braids and curls. Sophia said I looked every inch the diva. She was putting the finishing touches on my makeup when there was a knock at the door. Robert stood in the doorway with a large bouquet of mixed blooms and a small box wrapped in gold paper with a single red rose. He glanced around the dressing room, a bemused smile on his face, taking in the numerous bouquets and baskets of flowers which already adorned the room.

"Well, someone's popular." He laughed.

"They just keep on coming!" said Sophia.

"Well, it *is* the birthday of an extraordinary diva," said Robert.

He said his goodbyes, kissing us each on the cheek before closing the door behind him. I opened the card nestling in the flowers to discover they were from Abe.

"How lovely. He's such a sweet man." I stared at the little box and the single red rose with a brief note attached. I frowned. There was no signature, just a quote from Rumi: *Lovers don't finally meet somewhere; they're in each other all along.* I unwrapped the gold paper, then took a sharp intake of breath. Underneath lay a ring box. I slowly opened it to reveal a beautiful antique eighteen karat gold wedding ring.

Sophia giggled. "Well, Nene, I'll say this for your friend. He is very persistent."

"This is not funny, Sophia. What on earth am I going to say to him when we go to dinner? Thank God you're all coming. I am clearly in need of moral support."

Sophia stared at the ring. "Are you sure it's from Abe? Could it not be from your other ardent admirer, Madini?"

"You're hilarious, Sophia. Well, whoever it is will be getting it back. Although I must admit it's a beautiful piece, almost worth getting married for, if I was inclined to do so. I'll put it here in my jewellery case until the sender reveals himself. Dear god, please don't let it be Madini."

Backstage in the main theatre, I peeped through the curtains to observe Ludo, Violetta, and Violetta's brother-in-law sitting together in a private box. Then, to the left of the stage, Abe and Madini took their seats in the stalls. The evening was about to get underway. Arturo, now the principal conductor at La Scala, took up his position in the orchestra pit.

I walked out onto the stage to rapturous applause. Arturo picked up his baton and the orchestra played "Happy Birthday." The audience sang along. I laughed with delight. Glancing over to the front stalls, I could see Abe smiling as he gazed at me adoringly. I returned his smile then glanced over to the press box. My not-so-secret admirer, Madini, smirked back at me.

I turned away to address the captive audience. "Thank you so much, ladies and gentlemen. It's wonderful to be back with you once again in this magnificent theatre." I glanced upwards, winking at the logiona. "I realise my visits to La Scala have been sporadic over the years, but I hope to stay a little longer this time, if you will have me. My friend, Mr Toscanini, has invited me to come sing for you this evening. On more than one occasion, he has remarked how I am an admired interpreter of Wagnerian roles and has asked why I seldom perform Wagner."

The audience laughed. I glanced over to Arturo in the

orchestra pit and shrugged, looking at him questioningly.

Arturo blew a kiss, shouting back. "Venire Irene." The audience whooped with delight.

I once again addressed the audience. "Well, ladies and gentlemen, who am I to defy the great man, my good friend, Arturo Toscanini, now principal conductor at La Scala?"

Arturo took a bow, flashing me an enigmatic smile, as I rejoined my narrative.

"My friend is right, of course. When one thinks of Richard Wagner, it's not difficult to appreciate the passion, the soaring melodies, and the sheer power of his music. But don't worry, ladies and gentlemen, I will not be performing all the Wagnerian roles this evening, only one of them. I wish to dedicate this next piece to an extraordinary man who is sadly no longer in my life. Still, wherever he is right now, I would like him to know that he will always have my heart. Ladies and gentlemen, I give you Richard Wagner's "Mignonne," I hope you enjoy it."

Jean Claude began to play as I sang to a hushed audience. The performance ended and the audience rose to their feet, applauding.

I turned to face Jean Claude. "Thank you." I gestured to the audience, encouraging them to show their appreciation. Jean Claude stood from the piano to take a bow. The audience applauded ecstatically. I bowed to them, waiting patiently for the applause to die down.

"Ladies and gentlemen, thank you so much. La Scala is exceptionally proud to introduce to you this evening our new principal soprano on her professional debut. Ladies and gentlemen, please welcome onto the stage a very dear friend of mine, the sublimely talented Miss Ava."

Ava entered the stage in a stunning sleeveless petrol blue tulle lace gown. She walked over to me and presented me with a beautiful bouquet of long-stemmed red roses. I glanced at the flowers and card and quickly read the short message:

Things that never made sense before have now become evident.

I looked at Ava. "They are beautiful, Ava, my favourite flowers."

Ava glanced upwards, and my eyes followed her gaze. Looking up into the box to Ava's family, Violetta, Ludo, and Violetta's brother-in-law, Lucca, a tall, grey-haired distinguished-looking gentleman dressed in a black bowler hat and suit. His eyes were concealed behind grey-tinted glasses, set in gold frames. I stared at him. I'd never met Lucca Sapori before, but there was something vaguely familiar about him. He removed his glasses for a moment, wiping his eyes with a handkerchief, before he glanced down, staring at me. A faint smile appeared on his face. I would recognise those steel grey eyes anywhere. I was shocked to find Sherlock Holmes looking at me. I closed my eyes for a moment, trying to take it all in. Then, opening my lids slowly, my focus moved around the box. Violetta and Ludo smiled down at me. Looking to my right, I gasped, Sherlock Holmes was still there, looking at me. His eyes bore into mine for several long seconds.

Then suddenly, as though having a sixth sense of déjà vu, my mind was immediately transported back to Fiesole.

And there we were on the day of the christening, in our carriage, approaching the church. Beautiful stained-glass windows, with a great spire reaching to the heavens, came into view as the carriage rolled to a stop and Holmes helped me out of the Brougham.

"Shall we light a candle before or after the photographs?" I asked.

"I thought we could do the marrying thing," said he.

"My God, Sherlock, you're serious, aren't you? Baptisms obviously bring out the romantic in you."

"I have never been more serious."

"Why the change of heart? You told me you would never marry."

"Because when I saw you after our altercation with Moriarty, I had never felt such pain, and I knew then that I would be a fool to

allow even one glorious moment of being with you to slip through my fingers. I want you for my wife if you will have me. Although I know I will most likely make a terrible husband, and if I were you, I'd be heading for the hills right now."

I laughed. "You are not selling this terribly well, Mr Holmes. But why this church? Do you even believe in God?"

"I believe in us," he said. "I have arranged a special licence. We only need to take the next definitive step and turn up."

"Are you completely sure I'm going to be enough for you?"

"You are everything I could ever want."

"I cannot believe this is happening. What about witnesses?"

"Mr and Mrs Espirito have kindly agreed to be our witnesses."

"What about a ring?"

"You will forgive me if I don't go down on one knee. I fear I may never get up again. My intention was to buy you a wedding ring, but then I thought we could make use of Mariane's, only until we return to England, where I intend to replace it with my late mother's. If that is acceptable, of course. In the meantime, I have bought you this." He reached into his pocket and pulled out a box, opening the lid to reveal a beautiful six-carat vintage Celtic knot diamond-and-sapphire engagement ring in a yellow-and-white band. He slipped it onto my finger. It was a perfect fit.

"My God, it's beautiful!" I gasped. "You have thought of everything?"

"Yes, indeed, I have. But was there something you wanted to tell me?" He stared at me curiously.

"I'm so sorry." I spluttered. I could feel my face grow warm. "There was something I had been meaning to discuss with you." I stared at Holmes.

He was obviously aware I was keeping something from him. My mounting apprehension made my head spin. I wasn't ready to tell Holmes about the child, not yet. I was entirely thrown off guard by what he said next.

"It's all right, Nene. I know that something terrible happened to you back in the Catskills." He paused for a moment. "You know you can confide in me about anything. We don't have to talk about it

now, not if you don't want to. Although I can hazard a guess as to what transpired."

"Sherlock, you never guess," I said as tears filled my eyes. "You knew all along, didn't you?"

"Yes." He nodded. "Ever since our conversation at the barn. When you spoke to me of your childhood, the childhood you are still locked inside, still traumatised by its fears."

"I have never dared to speak of it to a living soul. My Aunt Susannah found us." I took a deep breath. "I remember he was very drunk. When I refused to do what he wanted, he put a knife to my throat. I said no, he didn't listen. I was fifteen." I paused for a moment. "He intended to violate me."

"What happened?" asked Holmes, his face a mask of anger and concern. "Who did this to you? Was it your cousin Beau?" he quizzed.

"Yes, it was Beau." I swallowed hard. "He took me completely by surprise. I never thought for a moment he was interested in me, not in that way. It was common knowledge he had a penchant for men. My aunt put a rifle to his head. She threatened to shoot him if he ever came near me again. We never spoke of it after that. It was as if it never happened. My aunt said it was the drink that made him do it and that no one would believe me if I told anyone. It would just be the words of a headstrong wilful young girl against Beau, a straight-A student, a pillar of the community." I shook my head. "Then my aunt Eileen intervened, and it was she who persuaded my father to send me away. So I was packed off to boarding school shortly after. I shall never forget that night. It was my fifteenth birthday." I scoffed. "But there was nothing to celebrate. I lost more than my childhood that day."

I looked Holmes straight in the eye. "After everything, I didn't expect to feel happy again, but you changed that. So, if you are having second thoughts about marrying me, I will understand." My eyes were streaming tears.

"Nothing is going to stop me from marrying you, I love you. You must know that." Holmes gazed into my eyes. "When you are ready, I swear to God I will find a way to punish him. Revenge is always a

dish best served cold."

He paused for a moment as though deep in thought, then took my hand in his. "Abuse comes in all shapes and forms. Those who experience it first-hand often perceive it in others. But I promise you this . . . you will no longer walk that path alone. We will face your demons together." He smiled softly, offering me his arm.

"Are you ready?" he asked, smiling down at me.

I wiped a tear from my eye. "I am as ready as I'll ever be, Mr Holmes. You have just reminded me why I love you. Give me time and I will tell you everything. No more secrets, I promise."

"That can keep for now," said Holmes. "It will all keep for now." He gestured towards the church. "You and I have a wedding to attend, not to mention a christening, shall we?"

I felt humbled by his narrative. I knew his words were heartfelt, just in the same way I was sure he would never speak of it again. I took his arm as we walked over to the church. Violetta appeared in the vestry doorway. She held a bouquet of wild meadow flowers and offered me a reassuring smile as she handed them to me. We entered the church and walked towards the chapel. The clergyman and Ludo were there waiting for us.

As clear as day, standing at the altar, I could remember the priest reciting the grave importance of the vows we were about to make.

Looking up at the box in La Scala, I walked towards the wings of the theatre. Instinctively, I clutched the muff chain around my neck, the chain that held my engagement ring. My eyes were fixed on Holmes. Four years ago, we stood in front of an altar together. There are few moments in life that are precious and profoundly memorable—that was one of them. My eyes had been bright with wonder on what would forever remain the most joyous day of my life. I would have given anything to be back on that beautiful sunny day in Fiesole, my hand in his. That had genuinely been a shared mission, a search for what we both needed and finally found. Although we were no longer together, my heart would always belong to him. The beautiful secret that few people knew. The mystery the rest of the world would never discover, that he was my beloved husband, Sherlock Holmes. Looking up once again into the box I recalled a line from Jane Eyre. *Reader, I married him.*

Chapter Sixty-Two: Irene Adler

I returned to the dressing room in a state of wild agitation. I had barely finished changing when I noticed a shadow in the doorway, a tall, imposing presence, and then Sherlock Holmes was standing before me.

"Hello, Nene," he said. "It's good to see you again. You look well."

"You look older," I replied, struggling to keep my composure. "I take it you are here to see your son?"

"I am here to see you both." Holmes fixed me with his penetrating eyes.

"Where are you staying?"

"I am booked in at The Grand. I was hoping we could go there for dinner to talk."

I shook my head. "I'm sorry, Sherlock, but I already have plans for this evening. My friends have organised a birthday dinner. I shall send a carriage tomorrow morning. You can come to the villa and spend the day with Nicco. He would like that. He takes a nap in the afternoon. We can talk then."

He nodded. "Yes, of course. I shall look forward to it. I hope you enjoy your birthday celebrations with your gentleman friend. I couldn't help but notice the way he looked at you in the audience."

I shook my head in disbelief. "My gentleman friend, as you call him, is exactly that. His name is Abe Burstyn, the doctor who was instrumental in ensuring our son was safely delivered into the world. If it were not for him, Nicco might not even be here!"

"I'm sorry," said Holmes. "Forgive me. I had no right to say that. I cannot even imagine what your life must have been like these past few years."

"Difficult!" I forced a smile. "Did you hate me when I left you?"

"Hate you? By god, Nene, I could never hate you. I know what Mycroft did was unforgivable, but I promise you this. If you come back to me, I will never allow anything to come between us again."

I shook my head. "I will never return to London with you. You know how I feel about that place. Mycroft was right. That would not be safe for any of us. I will always care for you, Sherlock, but I am no longer that vulnerable woman who was hopelessly besotted with you in Fiesole. When I was forced to leave, I felt as if I'd fallen into a black hole from which I would never escape. But I did. I had to fight hard to rebuild my life. Raising our son while juggling my career, teaching, setting up two charities. I did those things independently. I've become a strong woman, and I choose to stay here in Milan. There are people here, children, who depend on me. And I need to be surrounded by my friends, in a place where Nicco and I can feel safe and be happy."

He nodded. "Yes, you're right, of course. None of us would be safe if the underworld discovered Sherlock Holmes and Irene Adler were together. But there *is* another way. Mycroft suggested I take on Lucca Sapori's identity. I would, of course, have to return to London, but I would come and see you as often as possible? I can buy us a second home in England, in the countryside. Or wherever you wish. However, for this to work, first we would have to be married and become known as Mr and Mrs Sapori."

I stared at him incredulously. "Ah, yet another fake marriage!" I scoffed. "And one orchestrated by your brother, even better." I shook my head. "No, Sherlock, I'm not prepared to do that. You ask too much. That would be too difficult."

"I'm sorry," said Holmes. "I was being selfish. I don't know what I was thinking." He sighed deeply. "In that case, the only logical thing to do is to divorce. That way, you'll be free to be with someone who can give you what you deserve, give you their undivided attention. I'll arrange everything when I get back to London. I don't want you to worry. My lawyer is very discreet. If you have any questions, then we can discuss them tomorrow. You need to go, your friends will be wondering where you are."

He reached into his pocket. "I need to return this to you." He placed my brooch from La Scala into the palm of my hand.

I shuddered as his signet ring brushed my fingers, sending shock waves throughout my body. I felt so choked I could hardly speak.

"There is one more thing," he said. "When you see your doctor friend, please shake his hand for me."

I kissed him lightly on the cheek, expecting him to put his arms around me, but he didn't respond. I left the room and made my way to the ristorante, tears flooding my face.

The ristorante was full. My friends were all waiting for me by the time I arrived. The atmosphere and the food were all marvellous, but my mind was in turmoil. I couldn't stop thinking of Holmes. Even though we were no longer together, the thought of us getting a divorce made me feel physically sick. Abe did his best to engage in polite conversation, but he could sense I was distracted. He was such a lovely man, but he was never going to make my heart sing. I knew that my life would be so much easier if I could feel for him a fraction of what I felt for Sherlock. I glanced across the table at Sophia and Robert laughing and joking together. They had recently announced Sophia was expecting their second child and she looked radiant. Something about the way she and Robert looked at each other cast no doubt in my mind that they were indeed a couple in love. I recognised that look. I ached to experience it again.

After we finished the meal, I made my excuses and retired for the evening. I was getting into my cab when I felt a hand on my arm. I turned round to discover Violetta smiling at me, a puzzled expression on her face.

"I'm sorry, Nene, but I couldn't ask you in the ristorante while you were with Abe. Have you spoken to Sherlock?"

I nodded. "Yes," I said. "I have spoken to him. 'We've arranged to meet up tomorrow to discuss our divorce."

Violetta shook her head. "If you want him, then you have to fight for him. He has not come all this way to ask you for a divorce."

"No, that's true," I agreed. "But what he suggested as an alternative was too ridiculous for words and I couldn't agree to it, so we are where we are. I think it's probably for the best. I will ensure that Sherlock gets regular access to Nicco, so at least something good will have come out of this. My son will be able to see his father. And hopefully Sherlock and I can remain friends."

"I don't believe for a second that's what either of you wants," said Violetta. "That man loves you inside and out, although it's unlikely he will ever tell you that." Violetta took my hand in hers. "Nene, promise me you'll talk to him before you close the door on everything and make a decision you'll most likely regret for the rest of your life. You need to follow your heart. But if you do decide to reunite with him, then promise me one thing."

"And what is that?" I stared at her curiously.

"Embrace his originality and eccentricity. Do not try to mould him into something he isn't, because he will try to, if you ask, and he will fail. If you truly love him, then you must accept him as he is—the man you fell in love with, flaws and all. Otherwise, it will drive a wedge between the two of you and you will both end up unhappy."

I hugged Violetta, kissed her on the cheek. "All right," I said. "Wish me luck for tomorrow."

When I arrived at the villa, I sat in the cab for a while, reflecting on my conversation with Violetta and what I would say to Holmes in the morning. Finally realising that Violetta was right, and I couldn't wait that long, I asked the puzzled cab driver to turn around and take me to the Grand Hotel. I found Holmes alone in the hotel restaurant, nursing a brandy. He looked up at me, a strange expression on his face.

I took a seat across from him. "Sherlock," I said. "I know we have much to discuss tomorrow, but what I'm about to say cannot wait." I stared deeply into his eyes. "I need you to know that I was never unfaithful to you. My father told you a lie. He was misguidedly trying to protect me. What about you, have you found someone else?" I asked, reluctantly conceding that I still loved this man who was irreplaceable in my life with a passion that took my breath away.

He started to laugh, shaking his head. "I have hardly been beating them off with a stick. Obviously your father was lying. He could barely look me in the eye. Although he made it perfectly clear I was no longer welcome in your life, he said it would be unsafe to pursue our relationship and that if I truly loved you, I should let you go. I could say or do nothing to convince him otherwise because he was right, of course. If I had known of our child, I never would have left."

Holmes paused for a moment. Then he put his hand on mine and I knew that I wanted to spend the rest of my life with him. Yes, he could at times be insensitive, abrasive, and arrogant, but underneath that blunt and often breathtakingly rude exterior lay a man with a good heart capable of extreme acts of kindness who I knew loved me more than anything in the world. Even though we could never be fully together, above everything else, he was still my husband, and I was determined to be with him till death us do part.

"I don't want a divorce." I spluttered.

"Then what do you want?" he looked at me searchingly.

"I want you to kiss me." He stared at me oddly, a flicker of amusement on his face. "What, in front of everybody? Come to my room, I can kiss you there."

Glancing across the ristorante, I laughed. There were only four other people there. an elderly couple sitting at a table across from us, a waiter, and the bartender.

I smiled at Holmes. "You have no idea how much I want to, but I have no intention of laying with you. At least, not until we are married."

"What on earth do you mean? We are married!"

I took his hand. "I must have taken leave of my senses, and Sophia is unlikely to speak to me ever again, but if this is going to work, then we have to do it my way."

"Absolutely. Whatever you want. I can't lose you again."

"You need to tell me about Lucca Sapori. I hope, for your sake, he knows how to propose to a lady and isn't too prickly about personal boundaries. Although I have to say I love the new look." I removed my engagement ring from the chain around my neck and placed it on the table next to Holmes. He stared at it for a moment before picking it up.

He stood up and smiled at me. "Don't go anywhere. I need a moment." Holmes walked over to the bartender. Then within minutes, he knelt down in front of me with his left knee on the ground and his right knee up. Then, taking my hand in his, he proposed to me in Italian. *"Ti amo Vuoi sposarmi."*

"Accetto La tua proposta!" I exclaimed in a bubble of pure joy and happiness. And then he kissed me. And it was the most sensational kiss, raising an eyebrow and a chuckle from the elderly couple in the corner.

"I do have one condition," I whispered. "I am not going to obey."

"I didn't think for one moment that you would." He laughed.

"I will respect, though," I said, staring into his eyes. "I promise you I will always do that. And I don't want you to change, not for me or anyone, not ever."

"Ah," said Holmes, with a twinkle in his eyes. "Does this mean I get to treat you with the same lofty disdain as everyone else?"

"Don't push your luck," I said before we both burst into a peal of laughter. The bartender deftly arrived with a bottle of vintage champagne and two glasses.

"I believe congratulations are in order." He beamed at us.

Taking Holmes's hand in mine, I realised that loving him would be easy, but to be with him, to make that commitment under such trying circumstances, would take courage, and that was a choice I would have to make every day for the rest of our lives. Patience and understanding would be required. But most of all, trust and unconditional love. The only kind that truly matters. I didn't know then what the future would hold, but I was sure of three things. Holmes and I would never again allow distance to dim our relationship, I would never be bored, and when life became problematic my friends would be there for me, helping me through whatever adventures were to come.

There would be many, of that I was certain.

Holmes squeezed my hand. "I couldn't be sure if you still wanted me," he said, speaking softly, almost a whisper. "Your body language gave it away. I knew then that you would come back to me. Because despite telling yourself this is a ludicrous idea, not only do you find the thought of living this ambiguous life an intriguing, daunting prospect, I can see that it also excites and fascinates you. Like me, you find yourself unable to think of anything else. Come hell or high water, we will be together."

He motioned to the bartender. "Can you please charge the champagne to my room? The name is Lucca Sapori. Please allow me to introduce you to my fiancée, Miss Irene Adler."

Epilogue: Charlotte Sapori

It was Sunday morning, the day after the memorial service. I rose to the sounds of birds chirping outside my bedroom window, church bells tolling in the distance, and the clatter of hooves along the lane. The brougham had set off on the journey to the railway station, transporting Ava, Javier, Sophia, and Robert to the morning train that would take them to the Milano Centrale. Even though we had said our farewells the night before, I still felt a profound sense of sadness at their departure. I quickly dressed, deciding to skip breakfast as I still felt a little delicate from the wake.

I checked on Nicco, who was sleeping soundly, like a baby. I quietly closed the door behind me, not wishing to disturb my brother. Letting myself out of the barn, I walked over to the stables to find Francesco waiting for me, holding onto a bay gelding and a dapple-grey mare. Francesco helped me into the saddle, and we set off on our journey to the little church where my mother's memorial service had taken place the day before. The journey was pleasant in the early morning sunshine.

Francesco, Nicco and I had been best friends from the first time we played together as children in Milan, and we'd maintained a constant correspondence ever since. I spoke to Francesco of my parent's memoirs, my mother's voice haunting me on that journey to the church. Francesco listened attentively to my narrative, hardly saying a word. We could see the church at the top of a steep hill from a distance, the sunlight glinting brilliantly off the spires. The horses broke into a trot at the bottom of the hill until we finally arrived at our destination.

I left Francesco to tend to the horses and slipped into the side entrance. The morning service was still in progress. The eight benches on either side of the aisle were all full. I managed to find a seat at the back, joining the rest of the congregation. The priest delivered a stirring sermon, a powerful message of love, hope, and better times ahead. I glanced around. I hadn't noticed during the memorial service that three naves flanked the church's interior. The central nave was twice as big as the side naves, and on either side stood eight columns made up of Cipollino marble. To the left of the chapel's centre stood Renaissance frescoes and a sixteenth-century panel created by Gerimo D. Postia.

I waited for the congregation to leave before I stood and gestured to the parish priest, Father Abatenglo. He smiled as I approached. "Good morning, Signora Sapori. May I say it is a great pleasure to see you again. I trust you were happy with the memorial ceremony?" He was an older man in his late sixties with a mane of thick silver hair, mutton-chop whiskers, and the most striking blue eyes. I imagined he must have cut quite a dash in his youth.

"Yes, thank you, Father. It was a beautiful service," I said. "I wanted to come back to thank you personally, and to make a donation to the church on behalf of my family."

He beamed as I handed over thirty lire, which he deftly placed on the collection plate. "Father, I need to beg a favour."

"How may I be of assistance?"

"I understand that my mother was married here in 1895. Would you have kept any records?"

"That's long before my time." He scratched his head. "I've only been here for ten years. But if such a ceremony took place, then yes, we should still have a record of it. If you would like to come with me, we can take a look."

Father Abatenglo ushered me into the vestry, gesturing for me to sit down on a hard-backed chair next to a large oak table. He pulled out a pair of rickety-looking steps. then climbed onto them. He wobbled perilously for a moment or two before he reached up and took down a large dusty book from the top shelf of an old oaken bookcase. Father Abatenglo gently blew the dust and cobwebs away from the cover and wiped it with his handkerchief before placing it on the table beside me.

"This is a record of all the marriages here from 1890-1900. Please feel free to take a look. I have a christening to officiate this afternoon, so I must go and prepare. Please leave the book on the table when you have finished. God bless you, my dear child." He stooped down to kiss my hand before leaving the vestry.

I opened the book and painstakingly read through the entries until I eventually found what I was looking for, the entry of marriage dated April 1895. Tears welled in my eyes as I stared at the signatures for several minutes before I finally closed the book, leaving it on the table as Father Abatenglo had asked. Francesco was waiting patiently for me. I was shaking with emotion, so much I could hardly speak.

But as soon as we reached the quiet country lane, Francesco grabbed the mare's reins. "What's wrong, Charley?" he asked, his handsome face a mask of concern.

"It's all right, Francesco. Life just gets in the way sometimes." I smiled at him through my tears. "I'm finding it hard to come to terms with the fact that not only is Lucca Sapori not my biological father, but my brother and I are both the offspring of the celebrated detective Sherlock Holmes. It feels surreal."

Francesco smiled at me. "Well, he's still your father, whatever he calls himself. He is also my godfather. And I know this. Sherlock Holmes is a good man, a special man, and should be treated as such. What your parents endured to protect you and Nicco is incredible. You must trust your father. He will never let you down." Francesco stroked my tear-stained face, kissing me tenderly on the cheek

"I have yet to broach the subject with him," I said. "I intend to speak to him this evening after dinner. I'm not looking forward to that conversation. Why are the British always uptight?" We laughed.

"Look, Charley, we don't have to go back straight away. Why don't we go exploring, like we used to do when we were children?"

"Ah," I said. "Why not? I would quite like a trip down memory lane."

I looked at Francesco for a moment—this wonderful boy who had always looked out for me ever since we first played together in my mother's garden in Milan. Whenever I fell over, or had an altercation with my brother, or with the other children who sometimes came to play with us, Francesco was always there to console and comfort me. The years had been kind to him. He was a handsome man—thirty-two years old, six-foot-tall, with beautiful brown eyes, long curling eyelashes, and a tanned complexion. I'd watched him grow from a charming child to a polite young man who worked for his parents.

Our bond with the Espiritos endured over the years mainly thanks to our mother's close relationship with Violetta and Ava. There had always been an intimate understanding and friendship between our two families. When my mother returned from New Jersey to perform at La Scala in the summertime, Nicco and I would often go with her. Violetta and Francesco would visit us, and Francesco and I would spend endless happy hours playing together, just like old times.

We rode up to the ruins of the old Roman amphitheatre amidst the Roman baths and the Etruscan temple. The place my parents visited all those years ago. Tethering the horses under the shade of a cypress tree, we wandered freely. We explored the entire area and wondered what the location would have been like all those centuries ago. Francesco bought two bottles of lemonade from a café, and we sat on the grass on a blanket, soaking up the atmosphere. A mew of swifts flew overhead, screeching and squealing as we sat chatting, basking in the late morning sun.

Francesco took a sip from his lemonade and gestured to the ruins. "All the buildings on this site were built from the natural rock of the Fiesole hills. The Romans carried all the stones to this site. Every single man who laid these rocks has a story to tell. Just as I have a tale to tell you." I listened as Francesco spoke to me of his plans for a better future. His parents, Ludo and Violetta, were soon to retire. Ava had bought them a villa in Milan close to their grandchildren, Ava and Javier's twin girls, Chiara and Claudia.

With a heavy heart, Francesco had informed his parents that he had no wish to continue managing the farm. Ludo and Violetta reluctantly agreed to put the farm up for sale and they already had an interested party. Only years later, after my father passed away, did Nicco and I discover Sherlock Holmes had not only bought the farm, but he also instructed a local land agent to rent it out to tenant farmers—the grandchildren of Frederico Colletti, a retired piano tuner. The Colletti family did a splendid job of managing the farm, paying a peppercorn rent on the proviso that an apiarist was employed to tend to the bees. The barn was to remain untouched, except for the gardens, which were regularly maintained.

Francesco told me he intended to travel and study farm operation management in agriculture. Encouraged by my father, Francesco had expressed an interest in the science and technical side of farming. From an early age, Francesco had made up his mind that he would teach the subject to others. His parents had promised him fifteen percent of the proceeds from the farm as an acknowledgement for all his hard work and dedication, along with the trust fund that my parents had set up for him. Francesco would be quite a wealthy young man, but he was a proud man and was determined to make his own way in the world.

"You can't buy a life," Francesco said. "You must build one. No amount of money can give you the feeling of self-worth from knowing you've achieved something on your own."

I laughed, reflecting that was something my father would have said. "Oh, Francesco," I said. "You are quite the catch, a very eligible bachelor. You must watch out for gold diggers."

Francesco stared at me strangely for a moment and flushed crimson as a look of profound tenderness suffused his face. "I'll have a lot of things, but I won't have you. Come with me," he said.

I stared at him, taken aback for a moment.

There had always been a poise and idealism about Francisco that was so endearing. I'd always felt able to talk to him about anything. Finally, I took hold of his hand and told him in almost a whisper that it couldn't happen. I had worked so hard to prove myself in a man's world. I was going to be a doctor, not some man's wife.

"Francesco," I said. "I'm sorry, I cannot expect you to wait for me, not when you have the whole of your life ahead of you."

"I have no wish to interfere with your medical studies, Charley. Perhaps when you've completed your placement, you might reconsider. That's if you haven't already been swept off your feet by a handsome consultant."

"I think that is highly unlikely," I said. "There will be little time for socialising, I can assure you. It's much more likely that you will find someone before me."

"I don't think so." Francesco shook his head. "I love what we have, and I don't want our friendship to ever end." He paused for a moment. "I think it's time we went back. Your father will be wondering where we are."

We packed everything up and set off back to Le Sole. We had dinner in the farmhouse that evening. Father, Nicco, and I joined Ludo, Violetta, and Francesco for our last meal together. After dinner Ludo, Francesco and Nicco decided to take the brougham and head down to the village to have drinks at Ricardo's inn. They asked if any of us felt inclined to join them. Violetta shook her head, explaining she was still tired from the wake, and she needed an early night. My father also declined the invitation, protesting that he too was tired and wished to spend his last evening on the patio at the barn. I offered to keep him company which appeared to please him.

We waited until we could hear the sound of the brougham and horses trotting down the lane before we said goodnight to Violetta and walked over to the barn. Stars shone in the sky as we sat on the patio. Father poured us a drink and we made polite conversation for a while.

I was a mass of nerves as I took a large gulp from my glass of wine and stared at him defiantly. "I went to the church this morning to see the priest, to thank him for mother's memorial service."

My father nodded. "Yes, Charlotte, it was indeed a remarkable event. Violetta wondered why you didn't join us for breakfast, but I daresay that was not the only reason you went to the church."

He stared at me keenly with his penetrating grey eyes, which I knew from personal experience never missed a thing. "No," I said. "It wasn't the only reason. While I was there, Father Abatenglo kindly allowed me to look through the old marriage register. You told me that you and my mother were married in Milan in 1899. But that ceremony was a complete sham, because my mother had already married in April 1895, but not to Lucca Sapori. Oh no, she married the celebrated private detective Sherlock Holmes. Were you and mother ever going to tell Nicco and me?"

My father nodded. All of a sudden, he looked tired and weary, although he didn't appear at all surprised at my expulsion. "Yes, of course. Nene and I always intended to tell you and Nicco when the time was right. You've read our journals. You must realise how difficult it was for us."

I stared at my father, struggling to hide the emotion in my voice. "Nicco and I are no longer children. You and mother should have told us when we came of age. You kept it from us all this time."

"Yes, we did, Charlotte, and with good reason. I have always been your father. I have always been there for you and your brother. Don't ever forget that, young lady."

"I understand you had enemies, and you and mother did it all to protect us, but what about Nicco? What on earth is my brother going to think about all this, and what are we supposed to call you now? Father? Mr Sapori? Sherlock Holmes?"

"You can call me Father just as you have always done. And as for your brother, he already knows."

"How? And why did he not tell me?" I asked, staring at him askance.

"Because I asked him not to, and he worked it out for himself. You must be aware that your brother has a photographic memory, amongst his other fine qualities. He read my newspapers and Watson's chronicles from an early age. Then one year, you probably won't remember, as you would only have been four years old when we celebrated Christmas for the first time at the farm. Nene invited my brother Mycroft to join us. I was against it, of course, but Mycroft was desperate to meet his nephew and niece. He also wished to atone to Nene for his behaviour towards her in Fiesole, although I don't think I would have been as forgiving if I'd been her.

So, I introduced Mycroft to you and Nicco as a work colleague from the government offices where I was employed. I remember your mother telling you and Nicco that one of Mycroft's many claims to fame was being the brother of the celebrated detective Sherlock Holmes. You and Nicco were excited to meet him. But as clever as Mycroft and I thought we were, we didn't fool Nicco for one second. Even at such a tender age he quickly put two and two together. I am not sure how. Our body language, our mannerisms, which according to my late mother can be quite similar on occasions, made him aware. The following morning Nicco confronted me in my study." He sighed. "Sherlock Holmes cross-examined by an eight-year-old. I instinctively knew I couldn't lie to him. He would know if I tried to deceive him, and I wasn't prepared to risk that. So I swore him to secrecy, I made him promise he would not breathe a single word about it to you or your mother. He agreed to do so, to protect you both. Charlotte, you have no idea how wretched I felt, asking my child, my own flesh and blood, to do that. And of course, Nicco did not let me down, he was as good as his word."

I stared at my father, speechless. "I was so angry with you at first," I retorted. "I felt badly let down. But then I read your journals about this incredible second act of your lives and I came to realise what you had both sacrificed for us. What you went through took my breath away. Why did you stay together? It must have been so difficult, leading a life of deception and duplicity?"

"Yes, it was at times," said father. "But you see, by then, it was too late. Our dalliance had not only produced a beautiful boy while we were here in Fiesole, but we also forged an unbreakable bond. Although we were apart for over four years, that would have made no difference if it had been forty years. Nene helped me face up to my shortcomings in a way I never thought possible. It might have been an unconventional liaison, but it worked for us."

"You and mom sacrificed everything for Nicco and me to make it work. We owe you so much."

"We can only give what we have, Charlotte. It only worked for us because of your mother. She was a remarkable woman. Our relationship reignited with each gripping encounter. Of course, your mother was forever the actress. She would often meet me at a railway station or a hotel, dressed in disguise. We would book a room under a nom de guerre. We would spend a few days alone together before we came home to catch up and talk."

Father glanced around the barn, his lids half-closed, a lugubrious expression upon his face. "Oh Charlotte, if the walls of this humble barn could only talk, what delicious misdemeanours they would speak of. I doubt that any guests who stayed here before or since could have quite the same affection for this humble dwelling." Father wiped a tear away from his eye before continuing. "A long-distance relationship isn't for everyone, but we both had our careers to keep us occupied. And of course, your mother had her family and friends to support her. I came to realise that the secret to any relationship is trust. If one of you has jealous tendencies, then separation can sometimes inflame insecurities. But your mother never once gave me cause to doubt her."

"Did you not find it strange that mother went on to have two healthy children? It was most unusual with her medical condition." I stared at him curiously.

"I took Nene to a private clinic in Milan shortly after you were born to check everything was as it should be, Charlotte." Father leaned forward in his chair. "There was no sign of any adhesions, apart from the old scar tissue. The consultant was baffled. He was aware of your mother's medical history, but he couldn't explain it. Being a man of science, I, too, found it difficult to comprehend. No matter how hard we try, there are some things in life we may never fully understand."

I paused for a moment, deeply humbled by his words. "Why did you choose the identity of Lucca Sapori?" I asked.

"Lucca Sapori was Violetta Espirito's brother-in law. An intelligence officer in the Royal Italian navy, Sapori disappeared under mysterious circumstances. While I was in Fiesole, Ava Espirito asked me to try and find him on behalf of her mother. With the help of my brother, we eventually managed to find him in Canada under the assumed name of Sergio Regio." Father shook his head. "I thought it wonderfully ironic to be impersonating a man who was already impersonating someone else. Sapori had fallen in love and married an heiress from Toronto, Judith Sladen. Sapori wrote back to my brother, imploring him to leave him be. He explained he was happy with his new life and had no plans to return to Italy. So before I reunited with your mother, Mycroft and I devised a plan to take over Sapori's identity, and my brother arranged all the forged documents. I asked for Violetta's permission. Of course, she was pleased to give it. She would have done anything for your mother. So, Irene Adler and Lucca Sapori were married in Milan. Our witnesses were Sophia and Robert Moon. That sham of a marriage, as you call it, solved many problems for us, not only as a family but especially for your mother. Nene used to get a lot of unwanted attention from men, ardent admirers, who would never have left her alone while they thought she was still single. Becoming Mrs Sapori eased things somewhat. More importantly, the underworld no longer associated Irene Adler with Sherlock Holmes."

"You know I'm amazed how you and Mother managed to keep it a secret all these years. Mother had Sophia, Violetta, and Ava, all privy to her secret, but did you have no one to confide in when you were in London?"

Father shook his head. "I wanted to tell Watson, but

decided I couldn't risk it. That would have been unfair and too dangerous to put him under such an imposition. Although I often wondered if he guessed. He remarked to me on several occasions how, over the years, my persona changed. Watson said I became warmer. I began to treat women with respect, express emotions, and even develop friendships. I was much more tolerant of people in general. Of course, all this was thanks to your mother. My only confidants in London were my brother and my housekeeper, Martha Hudson."

"Tell me, if you had to do it all again would you?" I stared at him curiously.

Father smiled. "There are several things I would change if I could go back, but no, that's not one of them. What a journey it's been."

"There is one thing I am curious about." I frowned. "When you went to mother's house in St. John's Wood to recover that photograph of her and Wilhelm Ormstein, why did you wait until the following day before you went back? You already knew where it was. Surely you wouldn't have done that if she had been anyone else. A man, for instance?" I stared at him incredulously. "You wanted her to get away with it, didn't you?"

My father chuckled, raising an eyebrow in surprise. "My dear Charlotte, I understand why you might think that, but unfortunately, I had a duty of care to my client, the King of Bohemia. It would be unprofessional of me to even discuss the matter, so I'm afraid I could not possibly comment."

We heard the sound of the carriage returning from the village. "Well, it sounds like they're back," said Father. "I'm feeling rather tired. I should return to the farmhouse. I need my rest." He stood, taking me in his arms, kissing me on the cheek.

"I don't have to return to Pennsylvania," I said. "I can defer my place and travel back to Sussex with you. I promised

Mother I would look after you."

Father held me by the shoulders. "I will not hear of it. I want you to promise me you'll go back and finish your placement and become the brilliant doctor we both know you can be." He paused for a moment. "Perhaps it might be wise not to mention we are related. Otherwise, your peers may consider you a genius, and they would be right, of course."

"Thank you, Father."

"For what?"

"For believing in me."

"My pleasure." Father sighed. "My dear girl, we both know you are going to qualify as a doctor. And when that happy day arrives, and if you still insist on coming to England, there are some excellent hospitals in and around London. In the meantime, we shall keep in touch by phone and letter. I need to keep an eye on your progress."

I nodded. "Yes, sir, I will do as you ask. What will you do in the meantime? Without mother by your side, are you going to be content with retirement?"

"We'll see. Mycroft and Watson will undoubtedly visit from time to time. Besides, I have my bees to keep me occupied, not to mention a horse to look after. And as for tomorrow, well, it's just another day, another adventure. I need to make the most of the time I have left. Sherlock Holmes is not ready to give the world his final farewell. Well, at least not yet."

"You will go on forever," I said.

Father smiled at me. "When we reach our declining years, death is our constant companion. My deathbed, when it comes, will be made all the easier from the thought of the deep joy and love bestowed upon me by my beloved family. That idea brings me comfort."

Father stared at me curiously. "Charlotte, why don't you stay up and have a drink with Francesco and your brother?

Are you aware that Francesco Espirito is in love with you?"

I stared at my father. "I'm aware that Francesco likes me. I like him too. I'm immensely fond of him, but I'm not sure about love. I've been holding out for a man who looks at me the way you looked at Mother."

"Then perhaps you need to look a little closer to home, Charlotte."

"No, nothing could ever come of it," I said, shaking my head. "Francesco and I live in different countries, thousands of miles apart. How on earth could that possibly work?"

"Ah, that old chestnut.," Father raised an eyebrow in mock humour. "When you look at Francesco Espirito you see only the boy from your childhood, you don't observe the fine young man he has become. But I'll leave it up to you to decide. I'm confident you will come to the correct conclusion."

He held my face in his hands and gazed into my eyes. "My dear girl, you're about to enter into a world where you can be anything, but I want you to promise me you will always remain curious. Tell me you will do that."

"Yes, sir, I promise I will," I said, tears welling in my eyes.

I sat and watched from the patio as my beloved father walked over to the farmhouse. He may have been world-weary, but he was still doggedly intent. There was nothing Sherlock Holmes couldn't do when he put his mind to it. This brilliant man defied all the rules, a genius of his time, this legend, my father. He stopped for a moment to speak briefly with Nicco, Ludo, and Francesco, before turning round to face me. He nodded and smiled at me. I had never thought higher of my father than I did at that precise moment. Then I realised how fortunate my parents had been to find each other.

The Irish poet Yeats's poem, "When You Are Old and Grey" came to mind. The lyrics always made me cry, never more so than when my father recited them at my mother's memorial service. The words he spoke would remain indelibly imprinted in my mind:

When you are old and grey and full of sleep,
And nodding by the fire, take down this book,
And slowly read, and dream of the soft look,
Your eyes had once and of their shadows deep,
How many loved your moments of glad grace,
And loved your beauty with love false or true,
But one man loved the pilgrim soul in you,
And loved the sorrows of your changing face,
And bending down beside the glowing bars,
Murmur, a little sadly, how love fled
And paced upon the mountains overhead
And hid his face amid a crowd of stars.

In earlier days, while sharing rooms with Doctor Watson, Sherlock Holmes had been known to mock the softer passions, but every Monday without fail, he sent my mother a single red rose in memory of the night they first met at La Scala. I watched as my father continued his walk with Ludo until they entered the farmhouse and disappeared from view.

Evening shadows were falling over the barn, the stars twinkling beautifully in the night sky as Nicco and Francesco appeared on the patio, laughing and joking together, clearly a little merry from their evening of intoxication at Ricardo's. Francesco greeted me with a smile.

"Well, Charley," he said. "As this is our last night together, Nicco and I agreed that we must come back early to have drinks. As your father has already retired for the evening, I'm afraid you're stuck with the two of us."

"Yes, of course, let's drink." I smiled at Francesco as I put my arms around his neck and kissed him on the cheek. Nicco discreetly disappeared into the drawing-room to decant the whisky.

"Francesco," I said. "Tomorrow I'll be travelling back to Pennsylvania to complete my studies. Then, after I qualify, I intend to move to England, to be close to my father. If you can wait, and please don't think for one moment that I expect you to, but if you can, then there may be hope for us. But first of all, you need to tell me one thing."

"What is that?" he asked.

"Do you think you could ever live without me?"

Francesco laughed out loud. "Never! I suppose I could probably *exist* without you, but why would I want to do that? I would follow you to the ends of the earth. Don't forget that I'm now a man of means and money, an eligible bachelor as you were so keen to point out to me. I would travel anywhere you are going to be, whether it's America, England, Italy, or even the moon, for that matter. Why I cannot believe it has taken so long for you to work it out, Miss Sapori, with all your cleverness. I have loved you from the very first time we played together in your mother's garden in Milan."

"If we are going to be together, Francesco, then it has to be on equal terms," I said. "I am my mother's daughter, after all." I smiled at him. "But occasionally, I do need a little reassurance."

Francesco took me in his arms and kissed me for the first time on the lips. My heart was racing, filled with an irresistible longing, as Francesco gently lifted my chin and looked into my eyes and said in his quiet way, "Whatever you want, I want."

Who could argue with that? At that moment, my thoughts erupted, and I felt an incredible sense of clarity. Thanks to my father, the concerns and anxieties that had previously saturated my brain had now become sated. I turned to Francesco, finally able to utter the words he had been waiting to hear because I felt them.

"I love you," I whispered.

My brother appeared on the patio carrying a tray with two tumblers of whisky and soda and a glass of red wine. Nicco picked up the wine glass and handed it to me. I stared at him, my brilliant brother, of whom I was so proud, who had kept my father's secret all these years to protect Mother and me. Nicco reminded me so much of my beloved father, who had sacrificed so much for us

"I propose a toast," I cried. "To the woman, the iconic opera singer, Nene Adler. She may no longer be with us, but her extraordinary spirit lives on." I smiled at Nicco, raising my glass. "And to our beloved father, the celebrated private detective, Sherlock Holmes."

My brother stared at me in utter amazement. I laughed. "Oh, Nicco, you're not the only one who can hold a secret. My dear brother, I have our parents' journals and you must read them. They have quite a story to tell."

My brother stared at me, a perplexed expression on his face. "Father told you?" he asked incredulously.

I nodded. My brother paused for a moment and smiled, raising his glass. Francesco and I joined Nicco in the toast.

"Per coloro chem, che amiamo, ovunque si trovano." To those we love, wherever they are.

The End

About the Author

KD Sherrinford was born and raised in Preston, Lancashire, and now resides on The Fylde Coast with her husband John, and their four children. An avid reader from an early age, KD was fascinated by the stories of Sir Arthur Conan Doyle and Agatha Christie, she read the entire Doyle Canon by the time she was 13. A talented pianist, KD played piano from age six, the music of some of her favourite composers, Beethoven, Schubert, Stephen Foster, and Richard Wagner, all strongly feature in her novel. KD had a varied early career, working with racehorses, show jumpers, and racing greyhounds, she and her husband won the Blackpool Greyhound Derby in 1987 with Scottie. Then to mix things up KD joined Countrywide, where she was employed for over 20 years and became a Fellow of The National Association of Estate Agents. Retirement finally gave KD the opportunity to follow her dreams and start work on her first novel. She gained inspiration to write" Song for Someone" from her daughter Katie, after a visit to the Sherlock Holmes museum on Baker Street in 2019. It had always been a passion to write about Irene Adler, she is such an iconic character, and KD wanted to give her a voice. KD recently completed her second book in the Sherlock Holmes and Irene Adler mystery series, "Christmas at The Saporis", and is currently working on the third.

KD can be found on her author page: https://www.facebook.com/profile.php?id=100078319333010
To find out the latest email: kdsherrinford@googlemail.com

Printed in Great Britain
by Amazon

24649565R00205